VANESSA - ALL HEAVEN BREAKS LOOSE

by

David L. Howells

VANESSA told the tale of how a personal life's goal for a man and his wife had become the Holy Grail for the newly created Fitzgalen Family, forged by the fires of ghostly battle fed by old Southern resentment.

VANESSA - FAMILY TREE pits the Family against both mortal and spirit forces, with results that not even the Family head could have foreseen. It will take more than the team that confronted Mad Annie to meet these new challenges with success, or survival. Their greatest challenge begins when the ground underneath cries murder.

Visit:

www.proteapublishing.com/familytree.htm

PROTEA PUBLISHING

Books by David L. Howells

Vanessa

Vanessa - Family Tree

Vanessa – All Heaven Breaks Loose

To my Mom and Dad, wife and children…

my own Family Tree

VANESSA

-

FAMILY TREE

DAVID L. HOWELLS

PROTEA PUBLISHING

Copyright 2001 David L. Howells. All rights reserved.

This is a work of fiction. Any resemblance to real person, places and events is merely coincidental.

Vanessa - Family Tree
David L. Howells

First Edition Worldwide

ISBN 1-931768-06-4 soft cover.

ISBN 1-931768-07-2 hardcover.

Library of Congress Control Number: 2002105275

Protea Publishing Company. USA

email: kaolink@msn.com

web site: www.proteapublishing.com

SYNOPSIS

Ryan David Fitzgalen was once an ordinary man in the extraordinary time of the Second World War. Naval experiments into high intensity magnetic fields not only greatly extended his lifespan, but also gave him the ability to see and hear spirits that remained to walk the earth.

Vanessa Mary Blankenship was a spirit that befriended Ryan and eventually fell in love with him. Going on instinct alone, she found a way to become his living partner and wife. Together, they began a quest to find lost souls and take whatever measures were necessary to guide them to the next step on their spiritual journeys.

Their greatest challenge of all had been to release over three score Civil War soldiers, held in thrall by the mind fractured spirit of Mrs. Anita Edwards, the murdered wife of a Confederate colonel and plantation owner. Despite the additional talents of lawyer Gustav Mendelssohn and his paralegal, Marianne Cabrini, only minimal success could be made in this miserable cycle of purgatory.

In the year 2047, into the picture entered two more players in the struggle: Ryan's great, great grandson, Allen Hawthorn and his widowed/remarried mother, Rachel Gladstone. It was the beginning of the Fitzgalen Family; a growing dynamic force that changed not only the course of their lives, but also those of a young woman, Melissa Banks and a southern cab driver, Ralph Kithcart.

The climactic battle on behalf of the soldiers had been fought and won, but not without casualties. Vanessa had lost her closest spirit friend, Annie. Gustav Mendelssohn was dead, but not forgotten. How could he be? Like Vanessa, Gustav remained on earth to give the Fitzgalen Family a second entity in their ranks.

'Vanessa', ended on a Saturday late afternoon on the porch of the Edwards Estate Main House in Milledgeville, Georgia. 'Family Tree' takes up where that story left off.

PROLOGUE

Dr. Jamsid Churdivera cleared his office desk at Northern Dutchess Hospital in Rhinebeck, NY. He had been on staff here for almost forty years, and served as one of the primary resources for the Dutchess County Coroner's Office for the last twelve of those years. That evening, he was scheduled to return to his beloved country of birth, Pakistan. There, he planned to live out his life in the company of his many relatives that lived there.

He was a meticulous man, but he was also an old and very tired man. Everything in his records seemed to be in order with one exception. It was normal for people of his age to have the occasional memory lapse, and he was known to misplace a record mini-disc (MiDi) or his keys from time to time. During his years of professional service, though, he had never been unable to recall performing an autopsy.

Yet the report was on the screen in front of him, dated only two days previous. He had literally stumbled on it on a final run through of his record keeping. He must have done it, but it was performed after that Chamber of Commerce meeting he had spoken at. He remembered the speech, but not much of what happened afterwards. Might he have eaten or drank something that was unhealthy, and might he have gone on to perform the analysis report on the young woman while, what, sleepwalking? Ill?

The report appeared complete, similar to all his reports. In the past, the 'hands-in' autopsy was the gold standard. No more. Computerized Axial Tomography had come a long way over the past half century. A full body scan was performed in twenty seconds or less and the information gleaned had eliminated so many errors of eyeball diagnosis. The structural images on the woman showed no evidence of trauma; no wounds, fractures, hemorrhage... nothing. The nude gray-scale image of the woman (with the odd item of complete lack of hair, which was not considered necessary by the software manufacturers to represent on the image) slowly rotated on the screen, demonstrating the three-dimensional capacities of the imaging package. The MD tapped a standard function switch and the skin dissolved instantly to reveal the fat and fascia beneath. Nothing. Another tap, and only muscles were demonstrated...absolutely nothing out of the ordinary. Textbook normal, like something out of his training manuals...almost exactly like that. Another tap, a skeleton did the slow rotational dance of its muscular sister. Nothing. GI, hepatic, pancreatic and renal systems, same answer. Lymphatic? Textbook healthy and normal. Cardiovascular...classic myocardial infarction involving extensive damage to the left ventricle of the heart. Everything else was so classically normal. It wasn't unheard of, but it was odd.

Chem-screen on a blood sample showed nothing on the standard toxin search. Well, whether he recalled being there or not, his faithful years of service had officially come to a close. The poor woman was dead and buried, as were all who had come under his post-mortem scrutiny.

The doctor turned off the screen, picked up the bag that contained his personal belongings (he never called them his 'effects'), and turned out the light. Before he left, he cast one last curious look at the now blank computer screen. Perhaps it was best that he was retiring today. Such lapses in awareness or memory could be disastrous in his line of work. That thought left him with a shiver up his spine. Dr. Churdivera closed the door on the past, and went on to live what was left of his future on the other side of the planet.

"Time." The young man looked up at the stars, for he could no longer see the trees from this last vantage point. It was so strange that things would come to this. The stars were eternal, or at least as eternal a thing as flimsy human beings could conceive of. They weren't, not really. It was just that the lifetimes of stars were long enough to surpass a human being's ability to conceptualize. God was supposed to be eternal, but trying to conceptualize His existence and qualities made the stars seem simple and grade school understandable by comparison. He took a breath, taking in the smells of the chilled and damp earth.

He had once said that his love for her was eternal. He told her that, more than once. There was a time when she had said the same thing to him. Time. That word kept coming up. Time was relative, according to the guy with the crazy gray hair. Even time was not eternal, if the Bible thumpers were right. God created time as the first item on His creation agenda. "In the beginning…" meant He created time before day or night, earth or sea, Adam or Eve. He looked at his watch. In a few hours, the sun would rise. Not that it meant anything to him. He would never see it. Nor would she, though he would be the first to go. Yet, he would soon be next to her, for all time.

One quick review before all thoughts ceased, not that it was necessary. He was a very thorough and clever man. His extensive knowledge of exotic botanical trivia had twice served his purposes, as he envisited that knowledge upon the woman who once loved him and then an old man; an Eve and an Adam, for in the ancient language, Eve and Adam indeed meant woman and man. Some used that information to say that God didn't create two single entities, but rather multiple individuals of two genders. Might that explain where Cain and Abel got their wives (whose names never found their way into the scriptures, but then, neither did the wives of the sons of Noah)? Others said that Cain and Abel were not individuals, but tribes, one leaning to the agricultural, one to producing livestock. Of course, that was idle speculation on things so long ago; they only mattered to those who didn't have a present-time life sufficient for their interests.

At any rate, that doctor was on a jet across the Atlantic by now, though he would soon find his own eternal rest just from natural old age. A college minor in programming had allowed the young man to pull off what might have been a stunt worthy of adulation among those brain dead frat boys at his alma mater, heralded with alcoholic belches and farts and toasted with slices of pizza. Well, those boys he had scarcely known were no longer in college. They were out in the real world, with their families. Damn it.

The man lay back, and took a last look at the stars. He closed his eyes, took in his last breath, covered his face, and whispered his last words: "I loved you." His watch, unaware that it no longer served any useful purpose, would die four years later. Until then, it kept perfect time.

I   INTERIM

The Georgia National Guard had arrived at the Edwards Historical Estate in coordinated forces with the Georgia State Police and the Milledgeville City Police at 6:56 PM. They found nothing to confront other than a handful of civilians on the porch of the Edwards Main House. That these people were dressed up as Southern Belles and Union soldiery was only worth a passing thought. The Guard was a fighting team, not one designed for investigation. So their second priority, after establishing the lack of someone to shoot it out with, was to establish a safe base of operations. The three tanks positioned themselves in areas for clear fields of fire, one of them at the cost of two prized peach trees. The Fitzgalen Family sat on the porch steps and chairs, chatting, pointing, and looking for all the world like a family watching a parade. Since none of them were visibly engaged in potentially offensive activities, they were (at first) ignored by the soldiers. Since the porch was the scene of primary reported disturbance, according to probably hysterical eyewitnesses, they weren't ignored for long. Major Kenneth McGuinness and Sergeant Nunzia D'Palermo, flanked by a squad of eight riflemen, walked up to the porch and identified themselves.

Allen Hawthorn was sitting on the top step. He established himself as the group spokesperson as he said: "Good evening Major, Sergeant. My name is Allen Hawthorn, CEO of Hawthorn Enterprises. The others with me are members of my organization. How can we be of service to you?"

The Major was not impressed. "(Polite little bastard.) Mr. Hawthorn, the State Militia has responded to a report of a significant disturbance to the peace. The focal point of said disturbance is, to the best of our intelligence and judging by your accent, supporting your Yankee rumps. Would you, or any member of your contingent, be so kind as to tell me what the HELL happened here?" That was his best shot at being polite in return.

The Major watched as the young man, to whom all the other porch occupants deferred to as their mouthpiece, looked slightly away. He couldn't see (or hear) that there was legal representation in the process.

"Major McGuinness, we will do our utmost to cooperate with you. However, the truth is that we have been trying to figure that out for ourselves. There was a lot of confusion with the mock battle and our party had gotten separated, only finding each other towards the end of the battle. Most of the ground damage you see is due to planted explosives used in the battle earlier. It's possible that it was those explosions that damaged this porch. I suggest you consult with the event planners and pyrotechnic people to find out more on that." Gustav was proud of Allen. There wasn't a single lie in that report, if you looked at it just right.

The Major wasn't in the best of moods. "MR. HAWTHORN! I have been summoned to respond to what appeared to be, well, a confrontation between two, things. I mean, um, did any of you see anything out of the ordinary here that looked like…for crying out loud, that looked like two female ghosts?"

Deadpan, Allen responded, "Major McGuinness, does the Georgia National Guard respond to hauntings?"

There was a snicker in the ranks of riflemen, which died a miserable death when the Major turned around to find who it was that found this situation so blasted funny. Unheard by any of the militia was the legal advice whispered into Allen's ear. *"Uh, Allen, please note that these are grumpy men and women with guns. Ixnay on the iseass-way."* Vanessa suggested to Gustav that his whispering was probably not necessary, now that he was deceased. The (ex) lawyer hit his forehead with his palm, noting afterwards that the action didn't have the old feelings of physical contact it once did, only an hour ago. This being dead was going to take some getting used to.

"Mr. Hawthorn, for your information, the Georgia National Guard responds when the Governor of this state requests intervention on behalf of the safety of this state. I don't know what happened here, but I am going to find out. You can cooperate and make this easy on everyone, or you can continue to be a wise ass. The City Police and State Troopers are here to investigate things. My job is to make sure that there is a safe environment for them to function in. Now, is there anything here that my men need to be concerned about?"

Good. A question Allen didn't need misdirection in answering. "Major McGuinness, you have my word of honor that, to our knowledge, there is nothing here to threaten life or limb other than a bunch of holes in the ground. Now, unless we are under arrest, we would like to return to our hotel suite at the Marriott. It's been a very long day."

The Major had the authority to arrest the lot of them, but on what charge? Whatever happened here, including his present actions, was going to be under intense scrutiny due to the sure to come sensationalism about the 'incident', whatever that 'incident' was. He had to be careful to keep the Guard clean on this one.

"Mr. Hawthorn, it is also my duty to protect civilian lives, and that includes yours. Until it is proven that this area is secure, I have to take prescribed steps, though they may inconvenience the civilian populace involved. We are also required to cooperate with the local enforcement agencies, and that includes making sure all potential eye witnesses will be made available to them in a timely manner. I will therefore require that your entire party…er…well, return to your rooms at the Marriott (how the blazes did they score those?) until later this evening when you may be asked to assist in the investigation. Does that suit you, Mr. Hawthorn?"

"Major, thank you for your clarity and professionalism. Of course, we will be happy to cooperate. Oh, there is an item we could use your assistance on."

Ken McGuinness already had a headache. This wasn't helping. "And that is?"

"Our lawyer, Mr. Gustav Mendelssohn, seems to have passed away. His body is over there in the hedges on the other side of the porch. Would you make arrangements to have it shipped to the Milledgeville Hospital morgue? We would be most appreciative."

The Sergeant and Major looked at each other while time skipped a few beats at this unexpected new situation. Being more action oriented, it was the Sergeant who ordered two riflemen to the far side of the porch. A rifleman cried out, "SIR, there is a body here in the bushes! He looks dead, Sir!" The sergeant screamed for a medic and ordered the body hauled out of the shrubbery. The men and women on the porch looked away as emergency medicine had to have its way on the remains of their beloved legal counselor. Gustav, on the other hand, was fascinated.

"*Ryan, they just ruined the uniform. There goes your deposit. Hmmm, standard CPR. Oh, here comes the emergency kick start team.*"

A smaller version of the current HUMVEE further tore up the front lawn and skidded to a stop as two men with a machine jumped out. It took less than fifteen seconds for them to set up the leads. "No breath, no pulse, no rhythm. OK, STAND CLEAR!"

The whine from the device rose and the prescribed series of three electrical discharges were released. Unlike many older shows of emergency aid, until truth-in-television took greater hold of the industry, there was no 'rag doll' bouncing of the body. Gustav had been concerned that he might be pulled back into his body, should these men and women be successful. He had heard about such things, and that such re-entries could be both upsetting and painful, but it had been too long. There was no life left in his former body to retain a hold on his spirit. Gustav looked over at his friends on the porch. They were obviously uncomfortable over the attempts to revive him, so he backed away from watching those who would save his life and walked over to those who would share it.

"*Dear friends. I regret that I cannot inform them of the futility of their efforts. Those fine young lads and lasses are attempting to start the heart of a lawyer. You can't start what isn't there.*"

Marianne looked up to her 'father figure'. "You old goat, it's bad enough that we can all hear Vanessa's stupid jokes, now. Do we still have to put up with yours, too?" Vanessa let that go without an ounce of indignation. Gustav wanted to sooth the aches, but wasn't too sure as how to go about it, other than making light of the situation.

"*Afraid so, dearest one. Bards of a feather, and all that. But take pity on this poor legal professional. I am now constrained to offer my legal advice as before, but cannot *issue a single bill for my services. How do you think I feel?"*

It was beginning to work. Gustav hadn't lost his touch. His continued presence combined with a lighthearted demeanor was contagious, as smiles began to replace the melancholy.

The sergeant walked up to the porch. She regretfully told them that there was nothing further that they could do for their legal counselor and that Major McGuinness would arrange transport for them back to their hotel, if they needed it. Mr. Mendelssohn would be brought to the Milledgeville Hospital morgue, as requested, where an autopsy would be required. When she walked away, Sergeant D'Palermo could only shake her head at how little sorrow those folks displayed, having just lost a friend. Yankees could be such a cold lot.

II   PIECES

"This is CNN at the top of the hour. Good evening. I'm Jim Dunnel and it is 9PM, Eastern Standard Time. A new conflict took place this afternoon at the Edwards Homestead Estate in Milledgeville, Georgia, an historic site from the American Civil War. Here with the story is Independent Correspondent, Dagmar Yaddow." As he was saying this, the anchorman's own image reduced and cut to the left, making room for another framed visage on the right. It was of a professional looking woman who was slightly nodding as the anchorman spoke, which was the sign and seal that the person about to speak was getting a clear signal from the anchorman.

"Hello, Jim. As you can see behind me in the floodlights, this is a war zone. I can see craters from explosions, blasted out windows, tank tread marks and bits of debris strewn in every direction. Yet, this is no third world post-battle setting. This is America's back yard, or rather, its front porch." Dagmar Yaddow had a way of speaking that commanded attention, yet she blended the personable in so that viewers felt like she was talking on their level. The screen now held only Dagmar's image.

"Two years ago, the City of Milledgeville began to ready itself for an event of epic proportions. The site of the Edwards Homestead represented a chapter in our nation's bloodiest internal conflict in its history, the Civil War. Through here passed elements under the command of General William Tecumseh Sherman. Here was once the home of one of General Robert E. Lee's most trusted Confederate officers, Col. Archibald Edwards. Here was written also a comparatively small but very sad footnote in that horrendous national epic. All this in an appropriate setting of what once was a plantation where slaves once toiled and tilled the earth. The City Council had, as a memorial, dedicated this site as a place to study and remember those times and those events. To further that goal, they had engineered a celebration of and at this site that pulled in tourists from all over the country, and all over the world. That extensive planning began to bear fruit when Civil War re-enactors were here yesterday by the thousands. Tourists by the tens of thousands."

Background footage began to run. Event sound was kept at quarter volume as Dagmar continued to narrate. "The celebration had all the ear markings of a successful endeavor capping off thousands of preparation hours. Consideration had already been voiced in the local halls of government to make this an annual event." Scenes rolled by, at no more than four seconds per clip, of crowds, men in uniforms, Southern Belles, square dancing, sheep shearing, children with ice cream cones, and an aerial view of full parking lots.

"Security was well planned, but even with the best of plans, getting this many people into one area is always an invitation for trouble. I'd like you to pay special attention to this next clip, for the three women that are featured will soon play another and much more bizarre role. Please note that the following sequence involves graphic violence and may not be suitable for some audiences." That set the stage so that not even a bathroom emergency would tear a viewer away from their home screen. The engineer initiated 18 seconds of footage showing how three women took on a large, hairy man. The man lost, painfully. Anchorman and correspondent images returned to split the screen, 50/50. Jim Dunnel's face had a definite hint of a grimace, while Dagmar continued her narration.

"Later that afternoon, something inexplicable happened. Jim, we are ready to run disc. Be aware that the temperature recorded in Milledgeville was seventy-nine degrees, Fahrenheit, at the time this was occurring."

The talking heads were boxed off to the right and left upper screen areas as a still picture took up the remaining screen. When that picture went into real time, both Jim Dunnel's and Dagmar Yaddow's images disappeared so as not to take away from what was to follow. One minute and nineteen seconds of uncut footage ran with no commentary, something that was almost unheard of in the history of televised news reporting. The scene took in the front porch of the Homestead Main House. Men in Civil War regalia were walking away from the house, the mist of their breath clearly visible, as were their expressions of confusion and fright of something that just couldn't be. Two of the soldiers appeared to be wounded, judging from the red stains down their shirts. Shortly afterwards, something exploded and several things all happened at once. It was too fast to take it all in. The action on the screen froze at the end of the disc and the images of both anchorman and correspondent returned to the upper corners of the screen.

"Jim, we're now going to run that last part again in one quarter time. Are we ready?" The main engineer nodded. "All right, let's roll it." Once again, the announcers took an invisible back seat.

The scene was now cropped for greater magnification of the porch. The glowing corona began about four or five feet off the ground on the left part of the porch. A figure could be made out to the left of the glow. It looked like a woman in a dress, but you could see through her to the house windows behind her. The glow leaped from her outstretched left hand and, in a blink (even at quarter speed), struck something a few feet to the right of her on the screen. The event brought to momentary view a second figure, also appearing as a female in a dress, as energy seemed to explode in every direction. That moment was frozen for three seconds as it clearly displayed both figures. Then, in slow motion, tiles on the porch roof could be seen to blow straight up and the windows of the Main House blow in. The picture shook as the shock wave reached the camera boom. The image froze at that point, just before the figures would have faded from sight again. The commentator reappeared on the screen's right upper corner.

"Jim, I emphasize that this was not part of the planned activities. No authority, civilian or military, has offered any explanation. No individual or organization has claimed responsibility. Yet, what followed this episode was even stranger. We are cued up and ready to continue." Dagmar's image was a bust shot. Hands, hidden to the world, asked a question of her engineer.

Not since Desert Storm or the September 11th tragedy did CNN have a greater market share of the viewing audience. The engineer muttered, "Damn right, we're ready." Back to real time, three more minutes rolled by, this time with commentary from the once again unseen hosts.

"As you can see, all security, staff, and guests have evacuated the area. The people you see around the porch have not been identified yet. The bolt of energy you saw before is now replaced by a lower intensity but constant glow that illuminates to more consistent visibility the two figures we saw before."

"Dagmar, it looks like they are wearing old style dresses and they definitely look female. There is a corona of, something, between the two of them. Are they trying to communicate with us?"

"(Look at their postures! Do they *look* chatty? Anchormen!) I don't think so, Jim. Their postures indicate hostile confrontation. Whatever energies they are using against each other, a side effect is to bring them to visibility. The glow keeps getting stronger and, here it comes. Right there! Two of the women watching from the right of the porch have stepped to the figure on the right and are supporting her. Now, look at the corona. It just got brighter, like adding batteries to a weak flashlight. Jim, it appears to me that those are the same two women that encountered that large male earlier."

"(Goddam know-it-all correspondents! Why wasn't I briefed better?) You could be right, Dagmar. The solo figure on the left seems to be able to handle the change. Look, there is a third woman, placing her hands on the others' shoulders. Is that the other woman in the earlier confrontation?"

"I only had a short time to review the sequences, but I'd say it's likely. That previous confrontation never gave a clear view of her face, but the hairstyle and dress is similar. Here's where a man steps up to the porch and puts his hands on the young woman's shoulders, followed by a rise in the glow. Now, two more men step up and do the same thing, another rise in the glow. You can now see rising interference with the camera reception. Now here the figure to the left drops her right arm from reaching behind her and is now bringing it forward, parallel to her left arm. Now, stop disc!"

Two billion, one hundred and seventy-six million people, around the world, watched as a blurry figure appeared from the left. It wasn't as distinct as the two figures on the porch, but it was definitely there. It looked like a man in a Civil War uniform, riding up to the porch on a horse. You could see right through both of them. "Now, run disc, tenth speed." The horse took two more very gradual steps and the screen turned to mush. At a signal from Dagmar, the engineer replaced the mush with the last clear shot of the porch, the players, and the horsed figure that had just appeared.

"Jim, that rider is wearing a Civil War soldier's uniform. One of the Edwards Estate staff historians, a Miss Nicole Redman, identifies it as that of a Union Private. She also identifies the woman to the left on the porch as wearing clothes dating to the Civil War. I had the opportunity to look inside the house earlier. The figure to the left bears a strong resemblance to the wife of the former plantation owner of this historic site: Mrs. Anita Edwards. Mrs. Edwards was once married to Colonel Archibald Edwards, a Rebel officer who died while under the command of General Hood. The woman on the right has on an outfit from a later time, we feel closer to the early to mid-1900's. In the short time we've had to run with this, your Eastern Seaboard Office has been working to get all the players in this disc identified. We should have more within the hour." The correspondent looked to her right, responding to someone trying to get her attention. She nodded and then turned back to the viewers. "Jim, news is happening. This is Dagmar Yaddow, Independent Correspondent, signing off."

"(Crap! She was supposed to stay and provide counterpoint.) If you are just tuning in, this is Jim Dunnel and we have, moments ago, witnessed an inexplicable confrontation in Milledgeville, Georgia. We have just heard from Independent Correspondent, Dagmar Yaddow. Let's turn to our Science Desk Editor, Janice Hardin. Janice?" Jim Dunnel now shared the screen with a professional looking middle-aged woman who had just a hint of a 'deer in the headlights' expression on her face.

"Thank you, Jim. (What the hell am I supposed to do with *this?*)" Janice Hardin had chaired the Science Desk for the past four years. She was a real pro. Not only was she an excellent researcher and a published scientist of note, she was also someone who could run with minimal data and pull rabbits out of her hat. But this was putting her punting talents to the test. "What we have witnessed has yet to be shown as a real event and not a hoax. The current technology in artificially generated images by holography exists to where these figures can be man-made. However, that equipment is bulky and I understand that no evidence has come to the surface so far that would indicate its presence. Also, holography would not explain the other, more physical manifestations I saw in the clips, including the thermal drop, the explosive initial event and the loss of the camera.

"IF this is on the level, there are possibilities that have to be ruled in or out. First, could this be a conflict between extra-terrestrials? Certainly there are forces unknown to us at work here. Yet, why choose such an odd place to 'duke it out', unless the place was only randomly selected.

"Second, is it possible that we have witnessed conflict between two spirits, ghosts, with a possible additional participation of a third? The location's history and the period clothes worn by those images support this approach, as does Dagmar's possible identification of a former owner of the property.

"Third, might we have had a glimpse into a parallel dimension? There has been speculation for a century that we share 'space' with alternate realities. Might the violence of the mock battle by the re-creationists have opened a portal?" One point five seconds of silence.

Jim Dunnel may not be fully appreciated by his co-workers, but he knew his business. The pause by his Science Desk triggered a response that would keep the flow going. "Janice, if I might interrupt"

"(Please, for God's sake, interrupt! I've shot my wad!) Yes, Jim?"

"How might the apparently real, normal people figure into this? I saw six people on that porch that you couldn't see through. Five of them participated in the conflict before the recording ended."

"Jim, in science, you can't assume anything. We have not proven that those five, or six, *were* normal people and we won't until either the authorities or our own resources are able to positively identify them. Rather than engage in baseless speculation, it is more prudent for us to wait on the results of investigations that the authorities are even now proceeding with."

"(What is this, pick on anchormen week?) Good point, Janice, and thank you for your in-depth analysis. More on this as it develops. It's ten after the hour and time to switch to our foreign correspondent in Malaysia, Vincent VanAiken, for an update on the civil unrest on that side of the globe. Vince?"

Zachary Lorriman turned off the screen. He had work to do, but this news item had caught his attention and his interest. He'd look again at it later, having recorded it. Usually news services only show the exciting stuff on reruns, so this might have been the only opportunity to record the whole unedited version. Besides the incredible footage, he also got a kick out of the blond 'Belle of the Ball' dropping that walking tree.

Zachary walked over to his work desk and called up the Poughkeepsie and the Wall Street Journals on his screen. His priorities were, in order, headlines, obits, comics, and business. All were speed read, except the business section and comics. His favorite strip featured a grown up Calvin whose son, Marvin, had inherited his old stuffed tiger, Hobbes. Then it was down to other business. He had a haunting by a murder victim to finish writing up and some business stats of his own to go over. It was odd, he thought, harking back to the news clip. In a preliminary report, there had been a death reported at the Georgia site. The disc footage of the ghosts must have taken priority, now that they had that bone partially analyzed and ready to throw to the public puppies. People die every day and everybody takes his or her turn. That's old news. What he had just seen was definitely something new. He'd check again in an hour. That should give the newsies some run time for hard info. Zachary Lorriman, businessman and paranormal investigator, wondered if one of those people on the porch had been the victim?

Allen Hawthorn thumbed the switch to turn off the screen in the common area of their suite, but continued to stare at the blank screen, lost in thought for a few minutes. He then looked around and saw his mother talking with Ralph Kithcart and Marianne Cabrini. They looked pretty involved with their conversation, so he went back to talk with Ryan Fitzgalen and Melissa Banks. Allen was getting a little concerned that their now doubled roster of entities hadn't shown up. "Not here, yet, I see."

Ryan closed his eyes and sensed for impending paranormal presence, but felt nothing. "No, son. It might take Gustav a bit to learn the transportation talent from Vanessa. Till he learns the ropes, they walk." They had tried to pick the entities up with Ralph's taxi, but Gustav just walked through it at first. His second attempt got him sitting in the Green Machine's back seat, but he landed on the ground when the car pulled away without him. The old German really let loose a string with that one, waxing long and loud that he had no trouble riding a dead horse, so why was there so much of an issue with a live car? Neither one of the men wanted to think what would happen if the hotel's elevator to the suite might leave Gustav behind in the elevator shaft. Allen had wanted to go downstairs and wait for Gustav and Vanessa by the elevator, but that would have been hard to explain to the Guard soldiers keeping them there under 'house protection'. Public protectors in general already looked upon the Hawthorn personnel with suspicion.

Melissa used Allen's intro to bring up something that was on her own mind. "Ryan? Allen tells me Gustav was your best friend since before I was born. He's dead, but…he's still here. No one seems overly upset about him dying. My best friend died back when I was a ski instructor. She hit a patch of ice and slammed into a tree. Everyone on the ski team was devastated and half of them went to therapy. This is so weird. I don't know whether to offer you my condolences or not. Should I?"

Ryan remembered thinking how shallow and thoughtless this lady was, back when Allen and he had first met only a short time ago. It just went to show you; no matter how old you get, you can still misjudge people. "Melissa, you are going to learn some new ways of looking at things. All of us here have been given advanced knowledge of what happens after we die. So far as we have been able to witness, it seems to be a good thing for those who pass on and cross over. For many years, I have dedicated myself to helping out those relatively rare few for whom the process gets jammed. It gets pretty hairy sometimes, but it's never been this bad. On the other hand, it's never been this good, either."

Allen smiled at the befuddled look on his lady's face. "Melissa, get used to the 'duh factor'. It's going to visit you a lot, just like it did me."

But, Ryan wasn't finished. He had a new audience. "Melissa, think about it. What is a ghost? Is it the entire soul, or is it another layer of our selves that encompasses our soul?" Marianne took Ralph's hand and hauled him over to Ryan's lecture. It was a good time for him to get to know more about what they did and why they did it. "A ghost, or entity, is cohesive and organized energy whose physical properties we have yet to describe fully. It's hard to do that, since most entities don't volunteer themselves to laboratory study. Yet, we've learned that they do have mass, for at least some of them do have the ability to react with matter. That indicates the presence of mass and energy in an entity. An entity is intelligent, as you have seen with Gustav, Annie and Vanessa. Many we've come across in the past didn't have the ability to chat your ear off, or if they did, didn't have the inclination to do so. Like people, each entity is different in capacities, personalities and desires.

"Since an entity comes from a person who dies, I've come to think that you, I, and everyone here are just ghosts anchored by the energy we call 'life' to biological machines called bodies. The three ghosts you've met all think, react, and emotionally feel. Melissa, what is it in you that's hearing me, or thinking, or initiating speaking? Is it your brain, or is it your ghost, or soul, if you would? Your brain has EEG detectable activity each time it's used, but what is actually interpreting that energy to enjoy a sunset or a symphony? Aren't these things 'food for the soul'?"

Ryan remained standing and speaking. The Fitzgalen Family sat around on the furniture, listening. Ralph thought it harkened back to Greek times, when Socrates would give learned discourse to his followers. "Think about what a ghost can sense. Vision and sound are the two things they primarily use to gather information. You and I utilize other senses, because they are important to the survival of the body: light and deep touch, vibration, pain, cold and heat. These things keep us from harming the body and help us maintain this machine until its planned obsolescence is completed. Ghosts don't require those things for their well being, so God apparently left those things out."

Melissa took it all in, then showed that she could be a teacher's prized pupil when she put her mind to it. She asked if she might inquire about a few things. Ryan magnanimously assented. After all, what could someone so young ask that someone as old and experienced as he was couldn't readily answer? "Ryan, each infant has a soul. Have you ever seen a ghost baby? When does the soul enter a body? In utero? At fertilization? Where did that soul come from? Was it implanted whole from God into the fertilized egg, or did it come in incomplete half-states from the sperm and egg, combining along with the chromosomes? And while you're at it, why do ghosts look like the person they inhabit at the time that person dies? Do the soul and the body grow and develop together? If what we sense in an entity is an outer layer to the soul within, is it the outer layer that became mind fractured with Annie while her soul remained intact, and is that outer layer an outgrowth of the soul or just another vehicle like the physical body? Annie and Vanessa both got tired at some point in the conflict…can souls or just their entity jackets get tired? When a ghost crosses over, do they leave that entity jacket behind? Another thing…if a ghost takes the form of the body they had, how come they have clothes on instead of walking around naked like when they were born? Are the clothes part of the entity or the soul?"

Socrates stood before his student, open mouthed and overwhelmed. He had stepped on an unexpected landmine of questions, ill prepared for the onslaught, and nearly clueless on the answers. Having an audience to lecture to suddenly lost its appeal, being caught so unawares like this. Vanessa popped into view. "Thank God!" thought Ryan.

"No one say a word, just clear your minds of anything except Gustav. Picture him here, happy to be here, in his three-piece. Now!"

The five who were used to sudden changes of pace and venue by now obeyed the request without changing heart rates (the newest member still had some acclimation to popping spirits to do). Seconds later, they were back to their magnificent seven, with an eighth for an apprentice. Exhausted from the day's ordeal or not, six mortals rose from their couches and went to greet their beloved lawyer. Gustav was happy now. This transport thing wasn't so hard with the 'feel good beacon'. Hopefully, the unassisted transit would be as easy to learn. He looked over at Vanessa and nodded. Gustav would do his best to repay the debt he just incurred by teaching her how to change her clothing appearance, hopefully without embarrassing Vanessa or himself.

Barbara Meissner was watching the screen with her new friend, Bill Williams, at the RPI campus pub. One of the slips of paper Melissa had left behind in her room had paid off. "JEEEESUS Bill! That's Melissa! Damn! Look at her. She's part of, wait. Isn't that Allen Hawthorn? IT IS! That other blond, the older one. That has to be Allen's mother. She was up to our suite once with him, visiting Melissa. It has to be her."

Bill could only look and think, "That's Melissa? That's the lady I had tried for earlier this week? Man, look at her in that dress. Whoa!" The lady was once a walking fashion magazine cover. Then she evolved into someone more approachable and down to earth. Now…wow! Aloud, he said, "Barb, they're saying no one knows who they are, yet. Should we tell someone?"

"Bill, Melissa is my friend. So are you, but if you rat on her, you won't be." She looked again at the screen. "What in God's name did Barbie get herself into?"

An hour to the south of the RPI campus, half eaten slices of pizza were getting cold on the plates sitting on the Gladstone TV tray tables. While the world viewing audience was fascinated with the report, few had the intimacy with a number of the players as the family in this particular home. Jerry turned to his father, while Janet could only stare at the woman who had tried for so long to be a mother to her. "Dad, is that Rachel? And isn't that Allen?"

Like his daughter, Frank Gladstone could also only stare at the screen. The unreality of the whole thing was almost palpable. Was that what Rachel was so all fired up about? That was why she left him and his kids behind? What was going ON here?

Milledgeville paramedic Kurt Mangela had just finished the paperwork on the second body he had brought in that day. He never liked bringing in a body and his long years of service guaranteed that a large percentage of the bodies that he brought in were once people he knew. He thought about this group from New York that had really put the whammy on the ER in the past week. Twice with that Allen Hawthorn kid, then a third time with all of the Edwards Estate burn victims. First time was when that Ryan guy hauled in Allen on the horse that ate all of the staff room donuts. He would have paid real money to have seen that one; the charge nurse still had laughing fits over it. Second time was when the living version of his most recent deceased passenger had told him all about that ghost at the Estate and how she had it in for Mr. Hawthorn by way of the most bizarre case of spontaneously remitting pneumonia he had ever seen. Now it was that group's lawyer/friend (an oxymoron?) that once again required Kurt's services, this time for a last ride. Gustav Mendelssohn had seemed like a right Joe to him. Kind of stuffy, but there was a good heart under that stuffiness. The meds list had showed that Gustav's good heart wasn't quite good enough to stand up to whatever happened when it hit the fan at the Estate. Kurt stopped at the waiting room. Staff and patients alike were crowded around the big screen. It was the first showing on CNN of what happened. Kurt couldn't help but walk over and check it out.

Ten minutes later, he got into the passenger seat of the ambulance. His partner, Jeannie Hafner, picked up the handset. "County, this is 696 back in service at 2115 hours."

Over the receiver came, "Copy, 696."

"So Kurt, what kept you so long in there? Kurt? Hellooo. KURT?"

Kurt turned to Jeannie. "Holy Mama Mary, Jeannie. Park the rig and grab your pager. We're going back to the waiting room. You have GOT to see this!"

Back in the suite, Ralph Kithcart was trying to tie things together with the help of Marianne and Rachel (while Ryan was trying to get some answers to Melissa's questions from the two ghost horses' mouths, and failing miserably). "The ghost soldiers are gone, Annie's children are gone. That I've got. Vanessa says that Annie is gone, too. Now, once you're gone, you're gone. So what's with this Natalie? She was gone, but she came back? Can they do that?"

Rachel shrugged. "Marianne, you're more experienced in this than I am. Can you handle that one?"

"Ralph, sweetie, first of all, you are one handsome hunk when you come racing in on a hay burner. I was proud of you, really. As for your questions, Natalie died the same time as Vanessa did, in the same place, side by side. Vanessa's spirit couldn't handle her failing to help the children she had come to love, so she went into the spiritual equivalent of a fugue state. That's where your mind blanks out on the past and you take off with I.D. unknown. Since she didn't know where she was or who she was, that may be why she wasn't bound to the site of her death. She was still connected to Natalie, though. Maybe that was because they died so close to each other and at the same time, maybe it was just because they loved each other. A duplicate, sort of, of the bracelet that Natalie had made for her when she was alive stayed on Vanessa's wrist, or was at least re-created, after the two of them died. That was how Vanessa knew even her first name all those years. It was the only baggage, besides the image of the clothes she died in, which Vanessa brought with her from life into death. I suspect that it was that link that allowed Natalie to come back and put her mind at ease and it was the same link that Natalie used to give Vanessa the tool she needed to defeat Annie. Also, Natalie was still only able to be at the church fire site, though it was now a playground. I guess that she may still have been bound to the site of death in order to make a visit from the other side."

All the conversations were brought to a halt by a knock on the suite common room door. The knock meant that it wasn't Family. Ralph went to the door and admitted Sergeant Nunzia D'Palermo of the Georgia National Guard, Mayor Linda LaRoche, the Mayor's Aide Elroy McBean, and Chief of Police Mark Hamm. The Mayor, who was the ranking public official, felt it was her duty to speak first. "First of all, I wish to extend my deepest condolences to you for the demise of your legal council, Mr. Mendelssohn."

Gustav could hardly believe his good fortune. This delegation wasn't unexpected, but questions that would infringe on Ryan's desire for a low profile wasn't on the Hawthorn Enterprises wish list. He had all of them right where he wanted them. Manufacturing an oversized hanky with a heart pattern, *"Oh God! He was such a good man. How will they EVER survive without his kind words and wise support? (Sniff, blow). Or was that wise words and kind support?"* This was going to be more than sweet.

Half the company gasped and two snorted. Marianne had the sense to quick-snatch a tissue to her face. The rest noticed and followed suit in desperation. The Fitzgalen Family knew they were in for 'Gustav's Revenge' and it wasn't going to be pretty. Allen grabbed another tissue, placed it in Melissa's hand with his right arm, and then pulled her close to him with his left. He put his own tissue up to his face to muffle what he was going to whisper into her ear. "Sweetheart, Gustav is going for major payback. Pretend you're weepy, if you can't keep a straight face."

The Mayor was touched, and the rest in her train felt bad about coming up here so soon after their tragic loss. She looked briefly (but hard) at the confused looking Guard sergeant who had commented to her about this group's lack of grief concerning the dead lawyer, and then continued.

"The body of Mr. Mendelssohn was brought to the hospital by someone I believe you are familiar with, Mr. Kurt Mangela. I assure you that everything was done on Mr. Mendelssohn's behalf that could have been done."

Frantically patting his chest and pants pockets, *"My wallet! That thief Kurt took my wallet!"*

Ralph held Rachel and Marianne closer and bowed his head, letting their hair hide his own expression. Marianne and Rachel were holding tissues to their own faces. Allen had Melissa to affect similar camouflage, but Ryan was flying solo. Gustav (that bastard!) had known him too long. He knew right where all of Ryan's Achilles heels were hidden. Fortunately, the Mayor and her party (thank God!) apparently were buying the desperately offered grieving image at face value without too much scrutiny.

Mayor LaRoche felt worse by the minute, but she had gone through more than a little effort to get this investigatory visit arranged. "I can tell that this is not the best time to talk to you about what happened back there, but you can hopefully appreciate that, as Mayor of this city, it is my responsibility to find out if there is a risk to the community."

Gustav calculated. The time was now. The guests were off balance and embarrassed at being there so soon after his death. What he was about to do would give his friends a breather from official inquiry and afford him the vengeance of a 'life' time. Why, wasn't it just last week that a member of his fine group of friends said something about him living and dying in his three piece? Didn't two other 'friends' (names not mentioned but with initials of RG and MC) say that his legs had never seen the light of day? Hadn't he taken enough badinage about him being a stuffy old kraut? Well, here he was, seen by only those same friends who were trapped in a delightfully awkward circumstance. Opportunities like this only come once in a millennia. He had been practicing his 'talent' during his walk with Vanessa earlier. Vanessa saw the mental 'gearing up'. "*Gustav? What are you up to?*"

"*My dear Vanessa, remember that catalog we took a moment to peek at? I promised to teach you how to alter your arraignments. Here is lesson number one for the Fall Catalog, page 23, and comes in white, red and black.*"

"*Gustav! No! (snort) You wouldn't!*" He did.

The Mayor was taken completely aback at the suddenly increased outpouring of emotion from the six bereaved individuals in front of her. The youngest lady, very pretty, was the first snowball of the avalanche. She suddenly leaned back with a wide-eyed shocked look, then brought both hands over her mouth and screamed. Whatever residual composure these poor people had left to them was shattered. As one, they all leaned back and gave utterance to their…grief? The sheer emotion in those voices! The heck with the investigation. She was human and that included being humane. Nothing was going to happen, hopefully, until tomorrow. The Mayor and company had at least made their perfunctory personal appearance. Paperwork could wait. It was time to go. Now. Quickly!

"Ladies and gentlemen, let us adjourn this meeting until tomorrow. I will give you the time you need to grieve. We found that Mr. Mendelssohn had made pre-arrangements for his burial back up in Rhinebeck, N.Y. We will ship his remains to the funeral home he had chosen in Kingston tomorrow, after we finish up the paperwork here. You may accompany him, if I can arrange it with the other authorities involved in this. Until tomorrow, then." The Mayor, the Chief of Police, her Aide and Sergeant D'Palermo turned around to beat a hasty retreat out the door, walking straight through the apparition they could not see or feel: a lawyer, hands in prayerful position in front of his chest, looking angelically up to the ceiling, wearing a Fredericks bridal-white, ultra-sheer, super-lacey teddy, with garters and fishnet stockings.

Most of the company, after the door was shut, fell slowly and helplessly to the floor. Ryan was the only one still on a chair, barely, mouthing 'You bastard' over and over again. He couldn't actually say the words. To do that, Ryan would have to have been able to take a breath.

From behind the coffee *(tea!)* table, Allen waved a tissue back and forth. He managed to get a breath in and yell out, "NO MORE, PLEASE!" He didn't dare look. Ryan leaned over and saw his descendent and earlier nemesis waving the surrender flag, just like he himself had done back on the plane down to Milledgeville. His tenuous hold on the chair lost, Ryan joined the rest of his Family on the floor, with a thud.

III MORNING AFTER

Gustav and Vanessa were watching the sunrise from the front of the Edwards Homestead porch, this time without Annie. For Vanessa, the porch seemed both dear and desolate, now that it no longer held her closest friend, next to Ryan. The rest of the Fitzgalen Family slept in, having been exhausted by their ordeals both at the Estate and from the rib stitches due to Gustav's short lived modeling career. They had also slept in because the goal for which they had striven so hard to attain had been won. In a single day, fifty men, fifty horses, one woman and two children no longer wandered as spirits on the earth, but had moved on to whatever the Creator had in mind for them. So, for the moment, there was no driving incentive to crack the whip. New goals were there for the taking but, for now, it was time to both savor success and lick wounds.

Sgt. Paul Wasserman, Milledgeville Police, never needed an alarm clock in his life. If he chose to open his eyes at 04:17:22 in the morning, you could set your watch by it. He wakened himself at 5AM on the dot because it seemed more orderly to do so. His wife, on the other hand, was bereft of any sense of rhythm, be it regarding a timepiece or a dance step. It was a source of subdued annoyance that her husband not only awoke at the time he chose on the dot, but didn't need any 'wake up' buffer time. She required about twenty minutes of easy listening turn of the millennia music, as her mind and body got up to speed. By the time her feet hit the slippers, Paul had done his stretching routine, showered, and was starting to rattle the pots and pans for breakfast. Her part of the bargain was to get the kids up, showered and dressed. He might have taken over that task as well, but she felt almost shamed into at least claiming that responsibility for herself. Paul was a loving man who would have given his life to save any member of his family, which sounded pretty nice until you also found out that he would do the same for a complete stranger and had come close to it, more than once, in the course of his police duties. Despite his 'regimentedness', there was a comfort level that she valued. Paul loved her, no matter how she looked in the morning. 'Opposites attract' was the only way she was able to explain their apparent 'mismatchedness' to her friends, and to herself.

Sgt. Wasserman had the oatmeal cooking, the grapefruit cut and sectioned, the coffee perked, the two choices of juice on the table and the toast and extra-lean turkey-bacon ready to make the scene on cue. He had heard more than once that he would have made quite a chef. Perhaps, but he wouldn't be happy doing it. He served a healthy meal for healthy minds and bodies. If you asked him, the stuff that came out of fancy restaurants was recipe for myocardial infarction. His morning duties occupied as little of his conscious thought as the average person's brain space would be devoted to tying their shoes. Paul's mental space was occupied with the task he had received from Chief of Police Hamm. His assignment to the independent correspondent regarding this ghost chase was definitely not his 'cup of Joe'. Balancing that tidbit out was the good news from the Chief, relayed late last night, that he would be sharing the assignment with Nunzia. He'd met her, long ago, back when he was with the Guard. That was before he got married five years ago. He had once had his eye on her, but they were of different cuts of cloth. Sgt. Wasserman laughed at that. As if he and Betty were peas in a pod.

A little later that morning, Paul Wasserman was impressed to discover that Dagmar Yaddow had been up half the night scrambling on the fact exchange. Police and news resources had come to grips long ago that they were symbiotes, entities that could thrive if they could learn to be mutually beneficial. Police authorities had discovered back in the 90's how helpful national exposure could be in finding felons who thought they could melt into the landscape. The program 'America's Most Wanted' started a trend of information sharing that made for a formidable enforcement and media team, with public participation as a third leg for the stool. Police and newsies didn't always get along very well and, at times, were at each other's professional throats. But they knew they needed each other and always buried the hatchet in the end, and in other interesting places.

The Independent Correspondent had a number of potential stories on her priority menu. All but the topic of the Edwards Incident, as it was coming to be called, were put on the back burner. Dagmar learned that Milledgeville Chief of Police Mark Hamm had assigned to her a Special Investigator, one Sergeant Paul Wasserman. Half an hour after they met that morning, she had decided that this man was plodding, thorough, with little imagination. He did, however, have an excellent working knowledge of local history, local people, and resources available to enforcement officials. Identification of the caught-on-disc participants was a relative breeze. They had files filling out nicely on Allen Hawthorn, Rachel Gladstone, Melissa Banks, Ralph Kithcart, Gustav Mendelssohn (deceased), and Marianne Cabrini. So far, though, the older man with the group had remained an enigma. That was one of the two headaches for Sgt. Wasserman, who despised loose ends. The other was that whole idea of hobgoblins was completely bogus to him, so keeping an open mind on the subject was next to asking for a miracle. He did, though, know of someone for whom this sort of stuff was bread and butter.

"Ms. Yaddow, I know a gentleman we would do well to hook up with. I'll talk to Chief Hamm about getting him down here." Dagmar had 'been around the Horn' and recalled that there was a heavy hitter on paranormal happenings the police used from time to time. He lived up north, somewhere.

A little later that morning, Zachary Lorriman was just finishing his breakfast. His Chihuahua, Atlas, was happily picking up the pieces of bacon and egg that had accidentally found their way off his plate and landed on the floor, as they did every morning. The phone chirped, as he knew it would. His 4AM wake up call on his clock that morning was intended to give him the time he required to finish up his latest ghost investigation report and clear his desk. It came as no surprise that he was going to be flying south for the winter, well, for the autumn, anyway. His travel agent was a nice older lady (semi-retired) who was used to his spur-of-the-moment flight needs. That included making provisions, in her opinion, for a rat with delusions of being a dog. Mr. Lorriman would not be separated from his precious pup, saying that it was the son he could never have. Getting it onto the flight was no problem. Getting it into the main passenger area was the problem and required creativity to clear that hurdle. He had once suggested to her to pass Atlas off as a Seeing Eye dog. She still got a chuckle out of that one. Her counter-suggestion of it being billed as one of those dogs that protected people with seizures was a better tack. Those fine animals were trained to keep others from initiating well intentioned but dangerous intervention on behalf of a seizure victim, when what was mainly needed was to let the dysfunction just run its course. Again, the size of the canine belied it's utility. In the end, the man had the resources to declare it an invaluable adjunct to his unique skills. An irreplaceable tool, so to speak, that couldn't be made to risk its function from depression anxiety due to being separated from its master. Only the man's (actually, his dog's) notoriety allowed them to pull that one off. By ten that morning, Zachary and Atlas were comfortably winging their way down south. A young couple from Macon was especially grateful to the man/dog team that shared the flight with them. Atlas was great with children and their little Wayne Allen was grumpier than usual. Zachary studied, Atlas was being petted, Wayne Allen was quiet and Wayne's parents snoozed. "Everyone a winner," thought the stewardess.

While Zachary Lorriman studied his download regarding the Edwards Homestead from the time it was first trod upon by deported English miscreants (who missed the boat to the Australian colonies) to the present, Sgt. D'Palermo received a call from her Commanding Officer.

"Sgt. D'Palermo, this is Major McGuinness."
"Yes, Sir, Major."
"The Governor has decided that military intervention is no longer required by the Guard. From this point forward, authority will reside completely with the local and state police forces. I will be leaving at O-nine

hundred hours. I am assigning you the task of closing down our participation smoothly. Do you understand your orders?"

It wasn't completely unexpected, but it was still disappointing. Sgt. D'Palermo would continue to follow the story closely, but from a distance, it would seem. "I understand, Sir. Will you need anything else from me?"

The Major had worked with D'Palermo before. She was a good soldier that commanded respect in what was still, for the most part, a man's occupation. He could hear a professional response, but could also hear the trace of let down in her voice by the timing of the response more than the tone of her voice. Good thing she couldn't see his paternal smile. A reputation, or even so much as a rumor, for being an old softie was the last thing he needed. "Sgt. D'Palermo, you will continue to participate in this investigation as my personal representative. The locals will need your expert eyewitness reports. That you grew up in this area is another plus. The Guard may be needed again and I want early warning and an assessment from a soldier's perspective, should that come to pass. You are to coordinate and assist a local sergeant we both know, name of Wasserman. He's been assigned as police liaison to the correspondent, Yaddow, we saw on the screen."

Now that was something else all together! YES!! "I understand, Major. You can expect the Guard on route home within the next two hours. Will that be all?"

"Yes, Sergeant, that will…oh, wait. One more bit of information. I was informed a short time ago that there will be a forth involved, some spook chaser from up north, name of Lorriman. That will be all, Sergeant, good hunting."

Nunzia D'Palermo set the receiver back on its cradle. "Isn't he that wacko with the mini-mutt?" Well, at least she'd get to see her friend Paul Wasserman again.

Zachary landed in Savannah at 9:15am. He had already given Wayne Allen a paw printed (signed) publicity photo of Atlas, along with an application for the Atlas Fan Club. Atlas had his own web site and had been featured on Animal Planet twice during previous cases. Animals have long been accredited with the ability to sense things that are beyond people's abilities. Besides acute sense of smell and hearing, dogs have given owners goose bumps for centuries by growling at empty rooms and closed closet doors. Smaller dogs often seemed to have been gifted with more acute senses, and Atlas was particularly blessed in this arena. Best of all, he was portable. Nothing pleased Atlas so much as letting his partner carry him out for sightseeing in his custom designed 'Atlas Pup-Sling'.

"Mr. Lorriman?" asked a uniformed policeman waiting at the gate.

"Yes?"

"I'm Sgt. Paul Wasserman." They shook hands. "Welcome to

Georgia. I'll be your liaison with Milledgeville law enforcement. We'll be meeting with Ms. Yaddow for lunch there. So, this is the famous Atlas?"

"Please, call me Zachary. Sniff, Atlas. Friend. No kill."

Sgt. Wasserman laughed. "That works for me. Call me Paul. My son, Eddie, is a member of the fan club. When he heard you were coming, he asked me to give him something." He reached into his pocket. "May I?" Zachary wondered how Atlas kept so slim. This sort of thing happened a lot more often than Atlas's vet would have advised as healthy. Despite that, one more man/dog friendship was cemented as Atlas munched merrily on a 'CHIWOWOW' doggie treat. Royalties from his dog's endorsements was the main income stream that allowed Zachary the freedom to pursue his fascinating but insufficiently lucrative hobby full time. Paul continued as they walked down the concourse to the baggage claim. "This is a pretty weird one. I assume you know some of the details, so if I get too redundant, let me know. We have six eyewitnesses to the craziest calamity ever to be live recorded still at the Milledgeville Marriott under 'protective custody'. As far as we can tell, they've committed no crime, so we can't actually hold them against their wills. So far, they've been quite cooperative, but not very informative. We've identified all but one of them, the oldest in the lot, and he doesn't seem to want to assist in this effort beyond giving his first name: 'Ryan'. We've no justification to force the issue at this point. Using the 'no visible means of support' (vagrancy) approach wouldn't really buy us anything, as the new CEO of Hawthorn Enterprises, who happens to be 21 years old and still registered in a tech-college in New York, has vouchsafed him financially. The previous 'acting CEO', Gustav Mendelssohn, was the one who died of a heart attack during the 'event' that was recorded. Absolutely no evidence of foul play was found during autopsy. We also found that the previous CEO of that company was Allen Hawthorn's father, Carl Hawthorn, who was killed in an auto accident when Allen was four. Back then, the company went by another name: 'Custom Properties, Inc.'"

Zachary pulled one of his two bags from the luggage carousel. The policeman continued. "The whole group is scheduled to take the train back up to New York this afternoon, taking the body of the victim with them. They seem to be a pretty tight group. One of them is the CEO's mother, another his college girlfriend. There's a recently recruited local taxicab driver and the dead lawyer's personal secretary who, by the way, turns out to be a black belt."

Zachary pulled up his other bag from the baggage return conveyer belt. "Paul, I'm impressed. How did you come across that last bit of information?" That sort of thing wasn't typical in bio's available in the average police initial search report.

"A friend of mine in the force was witness to a barroom brawl a day or so before the 'event'. She positively identified the secretary as someone who whipped a huge biker's butt. No charges were filed, by the way. She just mashed his face into the floor, then catapulted him over the bar counter. Witnesses have confirmed that it was pure self-defense and we didn't pursue the matter with her. Just with him. He's in the county lock-up at the moment. The two officers at that particular fracas weren't able to assist the lady in time and no one wanted the bad publicity of quote, lack of police protection, unquote, during the festivities. So we couldn't keep them here on the angle of 'presence being needed to prosecute', either. Besides, even if we did go that way, that would only buy us two of the group that we already have dossiers on." Atlas knew things were going to get interesting. While Paul carried Zachary's two bags as they walked out of the terminal (saving Paul the tip money to have someone else carry the bags and living up to the rep for southern hospitality), Zachary was stroking him in that special way he did when his mind was in 'full absorb/full interest' mode.

The bags weren't all that heavy, so Paul's continued data dump held no hint of strain. "There's more. The lawyer appears to have been close to everyone, especially the secretary. No one among his co-workers and friends seemed especially upset at Mr. Mendelssohn passing away at the Estate shortly before the Guard arrived. Posttraumatic psychologic shock, some supposed, but it didn't seem that way to a Guard Sergeant I know that was there. Later when the Mayor, her Aide, that same Guard Sergeant and the Chief of Police made a call on the group, said group fell apart in near hysteria. Maybe that was normal. I've seen delayed grief before, but I know the Guard sergeant that was there. She swore that they were more like, well, laughing their butts off and trying to disguise it. Sgt. D'Palermo is sharp and I would go with her instincts more than the Mayor's. They're all refusing an interview by Ms. Yaddow, the correspondent, by the way."

Paul clicked the remote attached to his belt with his wrist. The trunk and doors unlocked, the car started. He gently placed the bags inside the trunk. Zachary stopped Paul from closing the trunk lid. "Wait a minute, I need something in one of the bags." Zachary unzipped the larger suitcase and pulled out a funny looking contraption. A folding chair? This, he gave a deft yank, and it popped miraculously into a well made modified safety seat, which Zachary buckled into the middle front seat restraint. Paul had to pull out the wallet camera-card he always carried (hey, you never know) and snapped a picture. Atlas had his own protective dog restraint seat, complete with a four-point belt system. It was another item available for public purchase under the umbrella of Atlas's many endorsements. That gave Zachary a top of the line protection for his best friend and another royalty.

Paul pulled out of the airport and headed for the highway. Zachary was content to listen to Paul for the moment. His questions would come later. "That biker at The Inn was the same one that you might have seen on the CNN coverage."

That ended Zachary's passive mode. "Jesus! That guy looked huge! But, it wasn't the secretary who nailed him the second time, was it?"

"Nope, it was the CEO's girlfriend."

"Holy rat shit! What's with the kung fu kittens? Are the women there to protect the CEO, or Ryan? Are they bodyguards? Wait. There was another lady in that scene. I remember a blond that shoved a parasol into the bikers face and crammed some ice cream down his pants. Who…?"

"That was the CEO's mother."

Atlas was pleased that his pet's stroking had redoubled. Zachary's mind was in high gear. Who WERE these people? He was starting to think that this group was being allowed to return to New York not so much from legal technicalities, but out of civil self-defense. Paul pulled from a slot in the dash a portable PC and handed it to Zachary. Out of his uniform shirt pocket, he fished out a mini-disc (MiDi). Zachary dropped the disc into the MiDi slot, which auto-booted the screen. On the screen menu were seven thumbnail pictures. Six had complete names under them; one of them only had a first name. One picture was edged in black, indicating 'deceased'. Using the finger mouse-pad to expand each picture/data log, Zachary began to read about each subject with growing interest.

The Fitzgalen Family was finishing up their packing. Since the trip was by mag-lev train, it would only take five hours travel time to get back home. The weather up north was still chilly, so the clothes purchased for Peach State weather were mostly boxed up to be shipped. Allen saw Ralph come back from the phone with a satisfied look on his face, and asked, "What are you so happy about?"

"I thought of maybe finding a home for my Green Machine, but it's been my friend and business partner for too many years. AmeriTrak will be on-loading it for our trip up. Ryan might be limo-happy, but I prefer to drive."

"Smooth! Things are pretty cold up there. Hope your windows don't fail again." Allen remembered the nasty trick Ralph had played on the group. Ralph had accidentally 'stepped in it' and the trip from the Estate to the hotel afterwards was awful, especially since Ralph had pretended his power windows were fritzed shut. It was only of minor satisfaction to Allen that Ralph had to suffer with the rest of them on the trip to the hotel and told him so.

"Oh, yeah. That. Forgot to show you. Ever see these?" Ralph pulled out of a small bag that held items like his shaving kit, toothbrush, and a bag half filled with small, well, things.

"What are those?"

"Nose filter plugs. The local coroner gave me a few dozen. You never know what a fare might do in your cab." Ralph had been proud of his subterfuge, but the look on the young CEO's face gave him pause. Did he just make a mistake?

Allen's response answered that question. "HOLD ON! Everyone, get over here!" The others gathered around. Ralph realized that, once more, he had opened his mouth one too many times. "Our friend here was breathing fresh filtered air through THESE," Allen brandished the small plastic bag that held the evidence, "...while the rest of us overdosed on the manure he stepped on. How much you want to bet that Ralphie nailed that pile on purpose?"

Ralph was cornered. The villagers couldn't find any torches and pitchforks, so throw pillows and cushions would have to do. Vanessa and Gustav watched from a comfortable distance. She asked, *"Should we give Ralph a hand?"*

Gustav thought of that day with the twenty minutes of misery he had spent in Ralph's cab, and smiled broadly. *"No."*

Sgt. Nunzia D'Palermo had completed all the arrangements for the Georgia National Guard components to return to their respective bases. Their job had been mostly to stabilize a situation, not to investigate one. Now that the site was secured, it was time for others to do their jobs. Clean up operations at the Edwards Estate that didn't conflict with the forensic folk were underway. Light bulbs and glass panes had been replaced already and the front window frames were being repaired. The porch roof was 'slated' for that afternoon, once the window people were finished. The greatest irreplaceable loss was the antique glassware inside the house, now in shards, but that wasn't Nunzia's concern. She had a lunch appointment with the news correspondent wimp and her old friend Paul. She wondered about the forth person joining them and whether he was going to bring that famous dog with him. Restaurants usually didn't allow pooches unless they were Seeing Eye dogs, so maybe she'd get to see the mutt later.

The electronic paperwork (at least the Guard had made that giant leap with their accounting) on the bug-out had been sent out, so she had an hour or two to kill. Sgt. D'Palermo decided her time might be best spent on a diplomatic visit to the Hawthorn group, just to wish them a good trip. Paul had already dropped off the required incident statement forms to the Hawthorn group by PC transfer. If more input from this odd group was needed later, then video depositions would have to do. Maybe she might pick up something this time around. On her last visit, she could swear they were splitting ribs rather than bemoaning their lost lawyer. That went beyond bad taste. "Even to someone with my backlog of lawyer jokes," she thought on her way up the Marriott elevator. Walking down the hall, she could hear some kind of disturbance. It sounded like a mini-war! "What the hell?" She trotted down the hall to the door of the Hawthorn suite and, sure enough, that's where the sound was coming from. Someone was being attacked and was pleading for help! Her last two interactions with this screwy gathering of Yankees were both hallmarked with the completely unexpected. What ever happened to 'third time's the charm'? She quickly and quietly turned the knob, unholstered her service piece and very carefully opened the door.

Three women and two men were bludgeoning a man (judging from the trousered legs on the floor protruding from couch cushions being used as shields) with a vengeance, with, pillows? She had come in loaded for bear to find, instead, a gaggle of silly geese.

Everyone else's attention was to the matter at hand. The victim's reaction was hysterical laughter rather than true repentance, which didn't buy him an ounce of reprieve. He might have at least pretended to be repentant. Allen had gotten his licks in first, as he was the one who had made the discovery. Once he had his full share, Allen backed off to let Ryan and the lady-folk have their full swing at the evil hack. That's when he heard Vanessa's voice behind him say, *"Oh Allennnnn, look behiiiiind youuuuu."* The rest were too busy and too noisy to hear.

He turned towards the door and locked eyes on a feminine figure of military bearing, standing a few feet away in standard shooting crouch. Her hardware was in both hands, but at least it was aimed at the ceiling for the time being. Sgt. D'Palermo looked at Allen and asked, "Mr. Hawthorn, does that man need assistance?" It sounded not even good enough to be lame, but she didn't know what else to say. She felt stupid enough to still be holding her piece.

"At ease, Sergeant. Just some innocent revenge." Sgt. D'Palermo safed and holstered the pistol. By this time, fatigue was taking hold of Ryan and the women, and they had quieted down enough to recognize an unfamiliar voice in the room. They turned in time to see the Guardswoman return her weapon to her holster. They would have been simply stunned into sobriety, had not the ghostly members of their contingent been snickering at the whole ordeal. That was enough to be contagious and, once again, Sgt. D'Palermo was exposed to this group's strange predilection towards inappropriate outbursts of hilarity. She wondered, not for the first time, if they were all nuts.

When the dust was finally settled, Rachel walked up to welcome the visitor. That slightly annoyed Marianne, as introductory protocol was traditionally her job. Still, this wasn't the office. Still…

"I remember you from last night. You're the National Guard person. I'm Rachel and you have already met my son, Allen." She continued the introductions, secretly proud of herself for having the foresight to use first names only, pointing at each person as they were named. This would avoid having Ryan's 'first name basis only' stand out. "That's Ralph on the floor. That's Ryan, this is Marianne, Melissa and there's Gustav."

It was an understandable error, but one that caused a collective 'Oh, No!' Nunzia saw this on their faces. Rachel still saw Gustav and hadn't fully come to grips with the fact that he was dead. Gustav was still among them, almost as stuffy as ever. With Vanessa, Rachel was used to not advertising her presence. Rachel stood frozen in the face of her faux pas, not knowing how to recoup. Thankfully, the Guardswoman saw the look on Rachel's face and mistook its meaning. "Mrs. Gladstone, please, I understand. My name is Sgt. Nunzia D'Palermo. I've lost people very close to me, too. It's never easy. I only wanted to stop in and pass on my condolences and wish you all a safe trip. I will be part of the team investigating this sad affair, so you may be hearing from me again. Sorry about the intrusion. I thought someone was in trouble here and my training took over." She kept her mental video cam going all this time for review later.

    Ralph, the group dynamic expert, saw that it was time for him to bring things to closure before another slip could be made. Climbing out from under the pile of cushions he had tried to use as shields, "Sergeant, thank you so very much for stopping in." He shook her hand, but didn't release it. "We would welcome a visit from you, should you ever be up our way." He changed his grip on her right hand and then placed his own left hand on her shoulder. "Now, we have a lot to do to prepare for our trip home." With the deftness of a ballroom dancer, he combined his own motion towards the door with a graceful 'encouragement' that she naturally followed. "Would you please be so kind as to excuse us?" He opened the door. "Thank you very much." He nudged her out into the hall. "You have a great day, you hear?" Ralph began to close the door, smiling, nodding, and iced the cake with a friendly wave. He had learned from Rachel about keeping his head nodding while he talked, which encouraged agreement and cooperation from his target. Ralph made a mental note to pick Rachel's brain more often. Marianne was another wonderful resource on people management for him, but chatting with her would be reserved for less crowded times. The latch clicked, he turned, leaned against the door, and blew out a long breath from pursed lips and puffed cheeks.

    Everyone else converged on Rachel, who was apologizing over and over again. "I'm sorry, I'm sorry, oh God, I almost blew it! Gustav, I'm so stupid! Damn it!" At least she had the presence of mind to whisper her recriminations, lest the Guardswoman be listening in just outside the door.

    Each member of the family almost leaped in to stop the self-flagellation, but one 'ahem' from Ryan still had the power to hold them from taking further action. He motioned for Ralph to check the hallway, which was soon pronounced clear. Ryan stepped up to Rachel, took her arm and escorted her to one of the couches. The others followed. He sat her down and took his place next to her. Taking both of her hands in his, "Rachel, your son once had the insight to point out to me that I wasn't Superman. Let me return that favor. You are not Superwoman, though I believe you to be a super woman. I would not have made the mistake you just made, but that's only because I've been dealing with the dead for a lot longer than you have been alive. It takes time, dearest Rachel. You've actually done something positive, I believe."

    "Oh (sniff)? What?"

Ryan looked into Rachel's eyes. "That Guardswoman Sergeant strikes me as exceptionally perceptive. Ralph, not to worry. You will always remain our resident people-reading warlock." That made Rachel smile, remembering what an immense help Ralph was to her when she was devastated by Allen's hospitalization. "When that Sergeant was here last night with the other officials, I was too busy trying to keep my ribs intact to notice much else." He eyed Gustav, who just smiled and shrugged. "Fortunately, Vanessa had her head on straighter than the rest of us. She told me that, of all of our visitors, Sgt. D'Palermo was the one that didn't fully buy our falsified grief shtick. Your show of honestly upset emotions at your mention of Gustav's name probably calmed most of the suspicions on the Sergeant's mind. So, if you really want to learn how to put everyone else on this team in jeopardy, I refer you to our dearly departed shark."

"Well, excuse me. Were the garters too much? I thought they added a nice touch to my legs that 'never saw the light of day'."

That was the final healing touch that eased Rachel's mind. She also wanted to thank Vanessa for being so observant, but…"Where's Vanessa?"

Ryan looked around, thought for a moment, and smiled. "Spying on the enemy would be my best guess. Every household really should have its own ghost. OK, Family, let's break camp. Whoever hasn't filled out their depositions on 'the Edwards Incident', finish them up. Ralph, call the limo. Marianne, score lunch reservations at the Railport. Rachel, go wash your face. Allen and Melissa, I want you two to learn more from Gustav about running Hawthorn Enterprises. I've got some arrangements to finish up with Keyser Funeral Home." Everyone had his or her marching orders. So, they marched.

IV GANG OF FOUR

Sgt. D'Palermo rode the elevator down from the top floor, running over everything in her mind. Ignoring hotel guests as they got on and off, she started with the pillow fight and ended with the adroit expulsion at the hands of the group's cab driver. Her first impressions said that this was no loose conglomeration of individuals, but a team almost as meshed as one of her Guard 'special task' squads. The Hawthorn people were clubbing the cabbie, obviously just in fun. That told her that these were friends as well as a team. That hinted that the rules of the group were defined enough for efficient function, but loose enough for play. They were a machine, if not a military one.

    That young man, Allen, was the first to see her and take action. He seemed surprisingly calm in the presence of a military woman with a drawn weapon. Either he was one cool cookie, or he had been numbed by the previous day's activities. Maybe both?

    Allen's mother was the first to officially greet her. Nunzia stopped that frame in her mind, and looked around. The two other women were dabbing their eyes from snicker fits, but one of the women didn't look too happy. She looked almost indignant. It felt like the group didn't fully mesh on all issues, then. The mother, Rachel, introduced everyone. She used first names on all of her introductions. Didn't take an Einstein to figure out why she did that.

    She ran the mental tape again until she got to the look on the mother's face upon including Gustav's name on the intros. That look seemed more fitting to the occasion, more honest, but it still wasn't right. "Freeze that," she thought. "The other faces, they were also surprised, worried. Why? That didn't seem so much like grief as a major foot-in-mouth witnessed." Nunzia shook her head. The pieces were fitting together like a jigsaw, but the resulting picture patterns didn't match. At the sound of the tone from the elevator speaker, she stopped the first review at her gentle expulsion from the room and then put it on the shelf in a manner very similar to what Marianne had taught Rachel to do, earlier that week. Sgt. D'Palermo exited the elevator and stepped out into the hotel lobby. She would have to make some time to get to the meeting at the restaurant.

Paul Wasserman signaled the correspondent over to the table. When she got there, "Dagmar Yaddow, may I introduce Zachary Lorriman and Atlas, 'the wonder dog'." As usual, the notoriety of the famous canine encouraged yet another restaurant manager/owner to make yet another exception on this one occasion. The owner's second cousin was the health inspector, so there wasn't too much to worry about on that issue. The owner had wasted no time in getting a paw-print-signed picture to frame and hang on his establishment's wall, amongst the other celebrities who had sampled their wares. 'Capital Cuisine' was a three star on most tourist guides. The place was huge and served over three dozen conventions a year. The name of the establishment reflected not only on the excellent fare they offered, but also alluded to the fact that Milledgeville had been the Peach State's 4th capital.

"Hello, Mr. Lorriman. Hello, Atlas. Is there a danger of biting?"

"I only nibble, Ms. Yaddow."

That got a laugh from the correspondent and the policeman. Paul fished out another CHIWOWOW dog treat and handed it to Dagmar. She got the idea and gently handed it over to Atlas. While the happy canine munched, Paul took the lead on breaking the ice. "We should be joined at any moment from another resource, Sgt. D'Palermo. I've worked with her before, back in my National Guard days, and she's sharp as a razor. She'll insist on being called Nunzia, if I know her. Hey, Dagmar, you should see my cruiser. Atlas has his own special safety seat with a four point harness that looks like a miniature of the one in the State helicopters."

Dagmar had done a little research on Mr. Lorriman. She knew about the multitude of products aimed at height challenged pooches that, more often than not, belonged to fairly well to do people. She never understood that. It seemed like the more money you had, the more you could afford to feed a bigger dog. Richer people didn't go for smaller houses or yachts, did they? Big dogs on the lower end of the economic spectrum also made more sense, as they were used for personal protection in neighborhoods where you didn't like to use less than four door locks per door. What was it about glorified rats that wealthy people gravitated to, other than being able to use a teaspoon for droppings cleanup instead of a shovel? Petting them was bad for your back, for you either had to bend way down, or pick them up. Worst of all, their high-pitched yaps made your eardrums pucker. "Yes, I've read about some of the things for which Atlas is the poster-dog. The car seat, that's a fairly new one. There are dog treats, dog food, dog sweaters and raincoats with matching styles for their owners, dog shampoo and conditioner (conditioner?), Atlas mini-pooper-scoopers and doggie breath mints. And that's just for openers. I believe, Zachary Lorriman, that your dog could buy and sell the three of us."

Zachary chuckled, but he was thinking that this lady was pretty sharp herself. "Dagmar, your research is impeccable, as always. Atlas is not my pet, but my partner as well as benefactor and friend. He assists me in my calling and has allowed me the financial freedom to pursue it full time. You wouldn't believe what I get for his stud fee."

Paul was taking a drink of water while looking at the menu. That last sentence caught him mid-swallow and caused him to mist the exposed pages. Zachary and Dagmar were busy patting his back and asking him if he was all right when Atlas began to growl. From years of experience, Zachary stopped what he was doing; Dagmar could look after Paul. He searched the area where Atlas (sitting in his specially made restaurant high chair, available for public purchase starting this Christmas season) was focused on. About fifteen feet away, there was a woman in military uniform who had stopped cold in her tracks. It might have been amusing to see a soldier whose progress was arrested by a Chihuahua, had not Zachary been so adept at knowing what each sound Atlas made signified. But, this was a live person, and an attractive one at that. Guns were not known to make Atlas mad, at least not ones that were holstered. Atlas had definitely given one of his ghost growls. Zachary was sure of it. So what was going on?

The disturbance of Paul's aborted swallow reaction, the presence of a woman statue in military uniform and the growling of a bristling Chihuahua had brought two waitresses, a busboy and the maitre d' to the table. All three sitting, four standing and, gradually, most of the neighboring table occupants, were now staring at either Sgt. D'Palermo or Atlas. Like a smothering wave, the silence rolled outwards like a moving fire until the whole restaurant was still. The only sound left was the rattle of pots and the clink of plates from the kitchen, the whir of overhead fans, and the growl of Atlas.

On a wild hair, Vanessa decided to accompany the Guardswoman for a while. She studied the face of this soldier in the elevator, wondering why such an attractive woman would seek to spend her life in the military, other than the obviously favorable male to female ratio. She felt it unladylike to share mud and grub with men who trained themselves to shoot other men under the orders of yet more men with pretty metal things on their collars. The world had changed so much since she was alive, both times. Yet there were ways it always stayed the same.

"*Sgt. Nunzia D'Palermo, nice Italian name.*" It named an attractive face, thoughtfulness showing through the passivity of features. It was always the eyes that gave away intelligence. The elevator door opened and the stride of the soldier hinted at a well-trained body. "*Hey Sarge, mind if I borrow your bod? There's this Frederick's outfit, you see...*"

On leaving the hotel, the bright southern sunshine showed another clue as to this strange woman she was following. There was no attempt to slap on a pair of sunglasses, and so the woman's remarkable ability to adapt to the sudden change of indoor to outdoor lighting manifested itself. There was hardly even a squint to be seen. This was a woman in control of herself. Physically, anyway.

Nunzia opened her sedan door in the parking lot, got in, started the car, but just sat there. Vanessa had thought to go back to the suite, but why wasn't the soldier lady moving? Vanessa slipped through the door and sat on the seat. That feat had really confused Gustav after he died. Gustav was fine at going through a car door, or any door for that matter, and had mastered sitting on the car seat. But he would only wind up on the ground as soon as the car pulled away. Gustav had problems translating belief in still things over to moving things.

Just like finding Ryan, no matter where he was, the trick was to clearly image exactly what it is that you wanted and completely believe that this was what was true. What the Bible said was right on the money: 'what you believe, so shall you perceive'. Vanessa now stared at that staring face and wondered what was being perceived. Nunzia's eyes were scanning, almost like she was studying pictures, which was exactly what she was doing. "Shazzam, Sarge! What are you thinking about? You don't mind if I tag along, do you? I didn't think so. Thank you ever so much. Now I hope you don't take this wrong, by the way, you could use some serious make-up tips. And your hair, really! Much too severe. Let's take a quick stop at the local parlor and see what they can do for you."

Nunzia put the government sedan into reverse. There was no noise, as regulations required her to use full battery as much as possible. The solar cells had topped up the power levels, so it was run silent and accelerate at a modest pace. The earlier starting of the gas engine was mainly standard procedure to make sure it was functioning and to initially cool off the inside without draining the batteries too much. Vanessa saw that the soldier's face had lost its stoniness just before the car was put into gear. *"So you can set things aside when you want to. You know, it's really a shame you can't hear me. We could have such a lovely talk. My best friend had to move away and now I'm stuck nights with an insomniac dead lawyer. You have no idea what you're missing."*

The drive to the 'Capital Cuisine' was only ten minutes. Vanessa watched her driver park the car, get out and lock up. She followed the Guardswoman, envying the firm and shapely backside of her quarry. No amount of aerobics could change what Vanessa had, since she didn't breathe anyway. *"Look, can I just rent your body for a couple of years? I promise I'll give it back after only a few hundred boxes of chocolates. Really, I guarantee you'll get back what you have now and more!"*

It was getting on to noon when they entered the restaurant. Nunzia asked the headwaiter where the table reserved to Paul Wasserman was. He pointed her in the right direction and she walked straight to her objective. That's when a scrawny excuse for a canine got up on all fours on some kind of silly seat and growled at her. When confronted with yet another unexpected situation (and she had had more than her share of those in the past twenty-four hours) Nunzia naturally went into question mode. "What the hell is a dog doing in a restaurant, anyway? Why is that man staring at me? Why is the whole place staring at me?"

Vanessa froze as well. She, too, wondered what the dog had against this female grunt. She wanted to get a better look at the people Sgt. D'Palermo was supposed to be meeting with, so she sidestepped the sergeant to the left. The rat dog kept his eyes right on her and continued to growl. *"Uh oh. Nice doggie. Pretty doggie. Eat your dinner. Stop growling, please-pretty-*

please?" She tried to move in the other direction, but Atlas followed her with his eyes, still bristling and growling. One of the patrons turned around to see what the rest of the diners were looking at and knocked over his glass. That crash distracted Atlas for a moment and Vanessa quick-transported behind a half-wall that separated Paul's table from the one behind him. Atlas looked back to where he had seen a target, only to find it gone.

Paul looked at Zachary. "What was that all about? What was Atlas staring at? I've got a major case of the willies."

Zachary said, "I'm not sure. Thought it was GI Jane at first, but that didn't make sense." He turned his eyes to the still startled looking Guardswoman. "Atlas saw something, something that came in behind or in front of Sgt. D'Palermo, which I assume is who you are, then moved first one way and then the other. Ladies and gentlemen, I believe we had a visitor."

Nunzia felt the hairs on her neck rising and a prickle up her back. Something followed her in? From where and, for that matter, for how long? "Excuse me, but you must be Mr. Lorriman. Is whatever you are referring to…still here?"

Zachary looked at Atlas, who was now looking back and forth trying to lock on to what he had seen earlier. Paul Wassermann noticed that the dog didn't sniff for clues. It kind of figured, as Atlas's quarry never carried a scent. Zachary observed, "Whatever, or whoever it was, Atlas can't seem to locate it now. That glass falling must have startled whatever it was. Some people say that the sound of breaking glass can startle a spirit. Perhaps the noise frightened it away."

The maitre d' couldn't hold it in anymore. "Are you saying my restaurant is HAUNTED?" That was a mistake. Any patron within earshot, and that was quite a few given the continued stone silence from before, was now considering their course of action given a possible ghost within their presence. Five tables, as one, got up and hurried out the front door. Two of them had someone with enough presence of mind to throw a few bills on the table before they left. That was the snowball on the mountain. Nine other tables, which were wondering whether what they thought they heard was really what they had heard, saw the first five tables confirm their suspicions and followed suit. That made it fourteen tables gone within a space of forty-five seconds. The progression was exponential as every table, except one, rose and hurriedly left via the closest exit, including the emergency exits. They hadn't exactly heard what was going on, but why argue with fourteen tables? With them went eight waiters and waitresses, two bartenders and four busboys. The maitre d' (and owner) could only look in horror as his busy establishment turned into something out of an old Steven King flick, then, realizing the subject matter at hand (coupled with his concurrent loss of income), decided to take a mental holiday and fainted.

Freddie Murdoch was earning money for college by waitering. He had an order for three on his tray and straight-armed the OUT door. Immediately, he noticed something was different. The difference was so radical, it took a while for him to register that the previously packed establishment was now nearly deserted. Yet, there were his customers, so, for the lack of something better to do, he delivered the meals, taking care to step around the inert maitre d'. He asked the lady soldier, "Can I get something for you, ma'am?"

"I'll take anything on tap and some chips."

"Yes, ma'am." It took him two minutes to fill the order and nothing much changed in that time. The four people were all sitting, now; the dog was still standing in search mode. Freddie gave the soldier lady her beer and a bar basket of chips and pretzels, then excused himself as he was going to leave the building and run screaming down the road, thank you very much. Before he left, Paul handed him a five.

Vanessa was still hiding behind the half-wall. What was with the stupid dog? What did that Sgt. D'Palermo want with this group of people and said stupid dog? Slowly, she rose from her stooped position and peeked through the plants that sat on top of the partition.

Atlas had been frustrated with the lack of visual on the odd intruder. With that input denied, he began to utilize other avenues of spirit detection. Something in a more primitive part of his brain sensed something from a different quarter. So he did an instant 180 degrees, leaped up onto the partition wall, stuck his head through the ferns planted on top of the partition, and barked his head off. Vanessa leaped back and winked out mid-scream.

Atlas stopped his yapping almost as quickly as he had begun. Seeing and sensing that there was nothing left to protect his partner against, he returned from the partition to his specially made chair in peace. The news correspondent, both Sergeants and the ghost tracker (and dog) sat back down together and tried to make sense of yet another episode of Milledgeville Mystery Theater. Dagmar was the first to start the ball rolling. "Zachary, am I to understand that we have just had a visitation, or is your dog having PMS attacks?"

Zachary was rewarding Atlas by scratching him behind his ears. "First of all, Atlas is male. PMS is the purview of your gender, not mine. My buddy here is completely at ease with almost anyone but the vilest of our species, as long as they have a pulse. Spiritual entities, however, have always put him into a tizzy, as you have just witnessed. I have no doubt whatsoever that a spirit has paid us a visit. Sgt. D'Palermo…"

"Please, call me Nunzia."

Paul looked at Zachary and gave a hidden wink. Zachary continued with a trace of a smile, "…where did you come from, I mean, where were you just before coming to this beanery?"

"I was paying a visit to the Hawthorn people. Thought I might put in a diplomatic visit and maybe pick up on something that could help us."

Dagmar said, "Sounds like a smart thing to do. You might make a good correspondent if you decide to change occupations. Maybe you picked up more than you thought, though. Can you tell us what happened there?" Nunzia noticed that Dagmar was still eating. In fact, so were the rest at the table. One might think that people who had a brush with a floating dead person might have less of an appetite. Perhaps not, though, now that she thought about it. Zachary had extensive previous experiences with ghosts, supposedly. He was probably used to this sort of thing. Dagmar was a correspondent. Those people often got themselves into all kinds of stressful situations where you either ate while terrified or starved on the job. Paul was just too stolid and solid to be fazed. He had also seen some pretty nasty things in his career, one thing in particular when they were in the Guard together. Nunzia D'Palermo sighed, then turned her mental recorder into reverse and stopped it on that walk down the Marriott hall.

"When I walked from the elevator to their suite, I could hear sounds like someone was in trouble." She omitted the part where her gun was in hand. "I went in to investigate and saw five people clubbing a man on the floor, using couch pillows, while he protected himself with the cushions. Allen Hawthorn noticed me first and approached me, telling me that things were OK. His mother, Rachel Gladstone, then came up to me and introduced everyone. She used only first names. I can see her pointing to each person as she named him or her. Then something even weirder than the pillow fight happened. The last person she introduced was that lawyer, Gustav…and…she pointed to empty air…I think it was empty…holy cow. Could it be?" Everyone else was quiet, letting Nunzia get it out. "Rachel looked horrified when she did that and so did everyone else. Rachel I can understand, but why everyone else? Sympathetic, I could understand. Grief, OK. They looked like someone let 'a major cat out of the bag'. My God. Do you know where this is leading? At first, I thought that she had just had a grief caused brain fart, but it wasn't that, was it? The cab driver, Ralph, then jumped in and I have never had my ass so politely booted out of a room in my life. Hey, you know, all along I've wondered about this group's lack of grief over a close friend dying. I remember a couple of times when they were practically jolly right after we arrived at the Estate. I'm heart sure that last night, when I was there with the Mayor, it wasn't grief but hilarity they were displaying, poorly disguised behind tissues. Wait! I can see it now. None of those tissues were wet. They were all dry. No one tossed a used one for another. No one blew their nose. Son of a bitch, I was scammed!"

The three turned to look at Zachary and Atlas. The former leaned back and smiled. "So, we had a German spy, did we? No, it's not right that we jump to conclusions on the I.D., but it is a strong suspicion. Lets push this line of thought a little further. This is the group that was involved with a battle of what appeared to be the spirit of Mrs. Anita Edwards and another female spirit, yet to be identified. Those two have been documented by mass media, so we can pretty well assume that the Hawthorn group has a friendly and/or adversarial relationship with them. A spirit of a recently deceased lawyer hanging around them is likely, but perhaps not. For arguments sake, let's go with the positive. A group of six mortal people, one of whom refuses to be identified, seems to have a collection of ass-kicking females, a ghost lawyer, and connections to two spirits who have issues with each other. One of those spirits seems to have arrived with Nunzia, who had just come from their suite. Did that spirit come of its own accord, or did this group send it? Why? Might they suspect that Nunzia saw through their deception and wanted to scout the enemy camp? Ladies and gentlemen, these are only the questions that come to mind off the top of my head. It would seem that we have our work cut out for us, if we really want to unravel this mystery. Now, if I may, what level of participation and resources does this group represent?"

Nunzia was the first to answer. "I am tasked to offer my full time cooperation on this matter. I have a reasonable budget provided by the State to assist this team, but anything extravagant would have to be justified to my Commanding Officer. The Governor wants to find out what the hell happened in his home state's back yard."

Paul stated that he was on loan from the Milledgeville City Police Force, also full time, for up to the next month. He continued to draw a salary and could draw for reasonable expense account, though a city's funding wasn't quite what Nunzia had available from the State. The Mayor was very serious on keeping a handle on what had happened at the Edwards Estate and wanted to make sure it wouldn't ever happen again. He also suspected that she wanted to get in a little tit for tat, if possible. The 'Event' had thrown a major monkey wrench on a long planned city festivity. This mayor was not known for a 'forgive and forget' attitude.

Dagmar was, in a way, a free agent. Her income came from her work being utilized by the major news networks. Getting a news report took a lot of running around, planning, research, and the luck of the Irish. The hotter the item, the more seed dollars she could command from those who used her services. There were a couple of other stories she was working on, but this one was on the hot sheet and leading the pack for income potential. Besides that, it was damned interesting. "I'm in for at least one week. If nothing pans out by then that at least looks promising, I will be forced to go back to other stories I'm working on. I'm on board, if you can accept that potential limitation. My funding comes partially from a personal account I maintain for this sort of thing. Media moguls don't always fund me on spec, but this case is different. CNN is giving me a healthy draw account."

That seemed fair enough to everyone, so a list of priorities was drawn up. By this time, owner Alphonse Capuano, a.k.a. the maitre d', was finally waking up. Two of the hardier waiters were peeking through the front door windows, from a healthy distance.

First, each member of the Hawthorn group needed more in-depth research.

Second, this Ryan character especially needed nailing down. His secrecy could be hiding some big truths in the matter.

Third, identify that second female spirit and find out whatever they could on her background that might give a clue as to why she (it?) made such a dynamic appearance. Her clothes were of later vintage between the two female whatevers; was she a local girl from a later period?

Forth, research Mrs. Anita Edwards. How did she die? Were there previous experiences regarding her in the past with the Estate?

Fifth, research Hawthorn Enterprises, formerly doing business as Custom Properties, Inc. What do they do, how do they earn their money, is it a front, and how old is it?

Sixth, who was originally behind putting this Civil War recreation shindig together? Might it have been a front for something else and, if so, what the hell was it?

Seventh, who was that soldier that showed up in the last part of the video? That would be hard to identify, as only the back of his head, his right ear and back was seen.

Eighth, get a better handle on the forces involved with the Edwards Estate destruction using both film analysis and scene forensics.

The owner/maitre d' was fully awake now, still sitting on the floor and bemoaning the loss of his day's income. Two village policemen (who happened to be the same two that had been at The Inn where Marianne and Rachel had first met up with Hammer) came trotting into the restaurant. The alarms set off by three different emergency exit doors opening combined with the lack of the owner's response to inquiries called in by County Dispatch had prompted a visit by the City Police Rapid Response team while the firehouse was put on stand-by. Both officers were amazed to see the most popular eating location in Milledgeville deserted except for one table, the one where Alphonse was wringing his hands and moaning. They approached and saw a familiar fellow officer. "Hey Paul, what's the story?"

Paul answered, "Alphonse said something about a haunting in a loud voice and the place got spooked. Weirdest thing. Kind of like 'saying fire in a crowded theater'." Paul gave a subtle amplification of that last phrase.

That was enough for the two constables. Both took an arm of the restaurant owner and, gently suggesting that he accompany them to the station, escorted him out the door. The poor fellow was too shell shocked to argue and went along peacefully. Later, when he had had time to gather his wits, he raised quite a stink.

Dagmar asked, "What did you do that for, Paul? He wasn't a bad fellow."

His answer gave Dagmar pause to re-evaluate her earlier assessment of this man's lack of imagination. "I've known Alphonse since he started his first diner. The man is a smooth operator, inveterate opportunist, and one of the best exaggerator of tall tales you'd ever care to meet. He treats my family pretty nice when we're here, so I thought I'd do the guy a favor. You wait and see. He'll turn this little story around to his advantage, including the icing on the story's cake I just gave him. Uh…minor detail. Who are we supposed to pay our bill to? Them?" Paul pointed to the kitchen swinging doors. Four faces, topped with white chef hats, were peering around at the dining hall with looks of confusion and fear in their faces.

Everyone dug into their cash reserves, as no one was around to process any Debi-Cred cards, and dropped what seemed to be about the right denominations onto the table, plus tip.

It was getting on to noon and the Fitzgalen Family was gathering the last bits of packing together. Room service had delivered a light snack before the trip to Savannah Railport. Rachel, Melissa and Marianne were by the coffee urn, discussing group and business logistics once they returned. Of the three, Rachel's face appeared the most unhappy.

"I'll have to deal with Frank and the kids, but that's tomorrow. I just don't feel ready to face that today. Tonight, I need to get some place for Allen and me to sleep, and Melissa…um…hmm." This was a delicate topic to broach for a mother and one she should have thought of before. Should she arrange for her son to sleep with a girl he's not married to? Even though there was no doubt in her mind that it wouldn't be the first time the two of them were…together…she still felt funny about it. Rachel's mental protagonists, 'Cat' and 'Angel', were just gearing up for another debate mini-series when Melissa tried to defuse the situation.

"Rachel, I'm going to have to get back to RPI tomorrow morning for classes. I've got a big test. I'd be happy with a sleeping bag on your floor, Marianne, if you don't mind." Rachel's Cat and Angel started to sit back down, disappointed at a most promising battle being put on hold, when propriety took a holiday.

Marianne eyed her two companions and, with classic Sicilian tact, said, "If you two are through dancing around each other's delicate feelings, let's get down to some realities of life. Melissa, you and Allen love each other and it won't be the first time you two slept together. Rachel, we widows should know that life is too short, too unpredictable, and we've all been through too much together to behave like Victorian Bible Bangers. Am I right?" Wrecking ball diplomacy was messy, but it got rid of walls in a consummate hurry. Rachel's Cat and Angel sat hand in paw, stunned.

Rachel looked at Marianne, then at Melissa, and smiled. "Honey, as far as I'm concerned, you're Family, now. You and Allen decide together what to do on sleeping arrangements. It will be OK with me. I guess if Allen, as a child, accepted my sharing my bed with someone other than his biologic father, I can take a lesson and accept that he is a grown man." The three of them gave a group one-arm hug (due to the coffee cups). Unfortunately, the three cups had just been freshened up.

Allen, Ryan, Ralph and Gustav were on the couches, making funeral arrangements for one of their party. It seemed odd to ask the deceased what it was that he wanted on his tombstone, but Gustav was touched by the gesture, until he heard some of the suggestions.

  Ryan: "How about 'I'm off to sue the Devil…for unfair competition.'"

  Ralph: "Or 'Organs to highest bidder, heart in great shape, hardly used.'"

  Allen: "Hey Gustav, how's about 'I'm a lawyer, down below, lot's down here like me, you know!' At least it rhymes."

  "Funny, very funny. Now, if we are done poking fun at my former profession…"

  Ryan spoke up. "What do you mean, former? I haven't released you from service, yet. You'll find your contract is quite clear on this. Your salary check will be on your desk every two weeks, as always. If you choose not to cash it, that's your business."

  "Why, you sneaky, underhanded, conniving, back stabbing, Navy puke!"

  Ralph thought about that. "You know, he's got a point, Ryan. With talents like that, maybe we don't need another lawyer after all."

  "I thought it was poor taste to speak disrespectfully of the dead."

  Ryan fired back in mock admonition, "That refers to the dead that stay dead and quiet, not ones that prance around in filmy racy lacies while his best friends are busting guts trying to look properly grief stricken!"

  At that, the four best friends began to laugh when the trailing half of Vanessa's reaction to Atlas shattered their fraternity with an "…*EEEEEEEEEECH!!!!!!*"

  Ryan's Navy training kicked in. WWII war-boat people had a philosophy about unexpected loud noises…duck for cover. He dove behind the couch.

  Ralph's service experience wasn't quite so defensive oriented, despite his former Guard rotation. His career experience was more to observe and evaluate. But the sudden appearance of a very upset screeching ghost was more than he was prepared for. He observed Ryan diving for cover, evaluated his role as Ryan's major domo, and then responded in kind by ducking behind the recliner.

  Allen simply froze in the chair, his hands gripping tight, one with half a ham sandwich in it. Fifteen feet away, three hot cups of coffee were launched into the air. Fortunately, most of it hit fabric rather than skin. The hot coffee and the sympathy women have for others of their gender in distress added three more feminine screams to the mix. Later, during the ride home on the train, Ryan suggested that groups of prehistoric females could drive off hunger crazed saber tooth tigers with just their vocal cords.

Gustav was Army. The sudden scream and his comrades diving for cover knee-jerked him into his own basic training. There was a nobility in Gustav that had once demonstrated itself on a field of fire where he had stood firm before the enemy to protect his retreating troops. That protectiveness once again rose to the occasion. However, his mindset coupled to his spirit state had an odd side effect, for he was suddenly in uniform, complete with helmet, a rifle and sergeant's stripes. Army conditioning gave Gustav the most presence of mind to recognize hysteria, and he made the snap decision to end it. He also forgot that he was no longer in the Army, or alive for that matter. He took his military hardware, pointed it up to the ceiling and pulled the trigger. The report from the firearm did the trick, and them some.

Four women and three men were completely silent, staring at him. For his part, Gustav held the firearm in front of him, eyes glued to the front of the barrel. *"How the hell did I do that?"* With that question, the firearm simply vanished from his hands.

This new turn of events had distracted Vanessa from her upsetting experience. *"Gustav, Honey, it's bad enough that I can barely change the hem length on my skirt while you could model for 'Clothes Horse Anonymous', but you can actually whip up and fire off your own bazooka?"*

Gustav wasn't answering. His eyes now slowly rose to the ceiling. As they did, seven other sets of eyes did likewise, wondering... *"Well, no hole in the ceiling."*

Ryan nodded his head. "That would have been fun trying to explain. Gustav, there are a half dozen questions this poses, but let's put that on hold for the time being. Vanessa, you just puckered every petutie present. Sweetheart, what in Heaven's name happened to make you scream like that?"

"That Chihuahua barked at me!" She made that reply in her frightened, little girl voice. Again, there was dead silence for a few moments, then... *"It's not funny! Stop laughing! This is serious! Really, I mean it!"* Vanessa had her arms folded and was doing her best to keep on a serious face, but she then took a moment to listen to herself. Her frown quivered and then broke down altogether. Her news could wait until they got to the AmeriTrak Railport. The other ladies were going to have to hustle to change out of their caffeinated clothes.

V   DIVISION OF LABOR

The investigative group, working under the loose title 'Task Team', decided to divide up the duties and meet again tomorrow, but at a different restaurant. It was a foregone conclusion that they wouldn't be welcome at the 'Capital Cuisine' in the near future.   Fortunately, a majority of that restaurant's business was tourist and there were always new tourists to replace the old ones. Alphonse's main headache would be to find new staff. The old staff was not about to set foot in the place without an exorcist priest running interference.

All four Task Team members agreed upon a preliminary group trip to the Edwards Estate before dividing up to pursue their separate tasks. On their arrival, they could see that clean up, repair and forensic efforts were still underway. Half a dozen recycling-center trucks were hauling off dumpsters of the normal man-made messes. Holes in the ground from pyrotechnic charges and tank treads had been filled in and reseeded. Finishing touches were being put on the windows and roof. The tiles that had blown off the porch roof were stacked on a tarp and an FBI lab team was examining those and bits of glass from all but the front windows (the front window glass was mostly in dust form), as well as the shattered figurines from within the Homestead Main House.   Another team was dissecting the two cameras, fritzed during the 'Event', under a sun tarp not far from the porch.   An unseen third team was at Milledgeville General, studying and categorizing the random burns on the camera crews, Edwards Estate staff and re-enactors, caused by that first burst of energy shown in the video, the one that knocked out the roof camera. Most of the examining personnel had shirts on that featured 'FBI' on the fronts and backs. More than a few rolled their eyes when they caught sight of Zachary and Atlas, but there were almost as many whose minds were more open to alternative approaches that looked at the pair with honest interest.   One of them, from the table investigating the cameras, approached the four.

"Hello! You must be the investigation group we were told of. I'm Special Agent Russell Anderson, FBI, Forensics Division." The others shook the man's hand and introduced themselves. "So this is the famous Atlas, and you are his owner and trainer. I'm honored to meet you both. My wife, Agnes, has a scrapbook of articles about you guys. I'm a fan, too, along with my son, Richard. Look, it would mean a lot to them if…"   Five minutes later, Special Agent Anderson had a picture of himself holding Atlas, signed by Zachary and rubber paw-stamped by Atlas. Russell knew his colleagues would rib him about it later. He also knew that they would be easily silenced when they were told how much he could receive on NatNetBid for it. Not that he would have any thought of selling it. This was a collector's item and he could hardly wait to see Agnes's and his son Richard's faces when they saw the picture. Shame he couldn't have brought them down from Pittsburgh with him. School came first and Agnes was a top-notch veterinarian whose talents were in demand. Her waiting room would be the final resting place for the signed original. Copies would probably find their way to her next 'research advances convention' as well as to Richard's next show and tell at school. Russell was a good family man.

Dagmar felt it was time to start earning some coin. "So, Special Agent Anderson…"

"Please, Ms. Yaddow, if you would do me the honor of calling me Russ, I would be very pleased if I could call you Dagmar. I really enjoy your reports on CNN."

Nothing melted a correspondent's demeanor like an appreciative audience. "Well, Russ, like I was saying, we'd appreciate it if you could bring us up to speed on what your teams have been able to find so far. We'll be taking off on our own research later today, but anything you could tell us might save a lot of time by aiming us in the right directions. We've got a *lot* of ground to cover!"

"Sure thing, Dagmar. Paul, Zachary, Sergeant, you too, Atlas, let's start at the tables I'm assigned to." As they walked over to the two defunct camera dissections, Zachary was keeping a weather eye and ear on Atlas. As always, the little fellow was fascinated by activity around him, but nothing upsetting seemed to be in the area. There wasn't even a hint of a growl. Was the nest empty? Zachary wondered. There were one male soldier, one horse and two ladybird spooky things on that video. Might there have been more that were missed by the camera?

Nunzia was taking in all the details, again. This was her second time here and she wanted to see if anything was now visible that she had missed on the last go round. So far, zip. She replayed her mental recall of the video clip with the spook battle, picturing the players on the now empty stage. How odd that the televised video documentation was 'act one', but she had seen it only after personally witnessing 'act two', live, where the cast of characters were all sitting on the porch the previous evening. Oh, to have been a fly on that porch wall, she thought. What wonders might she have witnessed? Then again, would a fly have survived that blast?

Paul was ticking off his mental checklist of questions to be asked. He didn't always go by the book, but it was a good foundation to start an investigation from, even one as insane as this one was turning out to be. You had to start somewhere. His thoughts were interrupted when Special Agent Anderson called out to an older agent working at the camera table.

"Hey Charlie, need to show these people the cameras. Take five, will you?" A decidedly grumpy looking older man 'humphed' and strolled off to the food tent. Someone had suggested using the barn for refreshment purposes, but even that building was being examined for clues. "The first thing we noted on the roof camera was that the lens was shattered. Guess it was fortunate that no one at ground zero was wearing a glass eye." Dagmar shuddered at the thought. "Ditto the little screen they use to monitor what the camera is recording. Most of the rest of the device appears intact. Whatever that force was, it didn't disrupt the metal, plastic, or other structural components. Over here are the internal boards. This is the primary chip that digitizes the video and audio inputs, adds the time, date, location and company signatures to the signal, and passes it on to the broadcast jack." What should have been a one inch square of black plastic with seven metal legs on each side looked like an alien bug that flew too close to a laser. Other boards and components looked fairly untouched.

"We compared it to the damage of the boom camera. From what we can find and deduce from the video of the event, two damaging forces hit this camera. The first one was a chance strike of one of the focused energy reflections that caused random, second-degree burns on bystanders. It was also the one that popped off all of those roof tiles. There's an actual entry/exit disruption on the plastic casing of the camera body, and this chip was in a direct line between them. From what I've heard, the heat pellets dissipated with distance. One of the guys on the roof crew had a pretty serious third degree burn that went deep. Everyone else was further away and suffered only first and second-degree burns. Kinda makes you wonder why none of the people seen on the video you showed, Dagmar, had any burns at all. I mean, they were at point blank.

"The glass inside the house was shattered by a non-discrete power radiation of some kind. There was no directional bias; it just went everywhere. That was the force that eventually benched the boom camera. It took longer for that force to build high enough to reach that far, something like seventy-two feet away, but it was effective. The boom camera is actually still functional, once you replace the glass components. This force wasn't EMP (electromagnetic pulse), but rather it was destructive by being ultra high frequency vibratory. The glass in the house and in the cameras was shattered by high-pitched vibrations that fractured anything with a crystalline structure. Come inside; there's a table I want you to see. HEY CHARLIE, BREAK'S OVER!" From over at the food tent, they could hear another 'humph'.

The five people and one dog entered the almost restored Edwards Main House. All the glass shards and dust had been collected and cleaned up, being health hazards. There were tables set up inside. One had books; another had mechanical devices such as clocks, toilet paper dispensers and even a couple of Civil War era pistols. Russell went straight to a smaller table where jewelry was laid out in a shallow box. A ring was attached to the base of a magnifying viewing device. "Take a look."

Zachary was closest, so he bent over. "Whoa! Is… Was, that a…"

"Yep, diamonds. Two-karat center stone with two one-karat stones on either side. It was supposed to represent the loving couple with two children at their sides. It was an anniversary present from the Colonel to Mrs. Edwards. Even at that time, it was a valuable heirloom. Turns out that the Colonel's grandfather originally purchased the ring. All the stones are fractured. Since diamond is sterner stuff than glass and the stones were held together with the settings, they're still somewhat together, minus a facet or two. But one good flick with a finger would shatter them all."

Paul's police training was spinning its wheels. Lots of clues, but he had no gut feel as to where it was all leading. Paul Wasserman was an excellent investigator, when it came to the everyday variety of criminal insanity. This was something else. "Was anything else affected, besides the glass?"

Russell answered, "Well, there are the tiles, but that won't tell you any more than the burns on the bystanders. Discrete reflected packets of force that had a temperature component sufficient to scorch things."

Dagmar asked, "Russ, what about the cold that was reported. Did that leave any traces?"

"No, ma'am, but I suspect that it made the front windows implode more impressively. No shards there, just glass dust. It was like whatever it was that fired the energy pulse drew thermal energy from its surrounding environment, encapsulated it and let it loose in a cohesive force that might remind you of ball lightening. But lightening is electrical. These forces were thermal and vibratory. At least what we've been able to deduce with confidence so far."

Dagmar was used to interviewing, listening to nuances. "There's more to it than that. What do you suspect, or mean?"

"Well, I studied the tapes pretty close, trying to get a better idea as to what to look for. Whatever that energy was, it made the invisible visible. Heat and vibratory environments have never been known to be so, well, revealing. That's one question I've got.

"We're not supposed to over-speculate, but the living people on the porch looked to me to be familiar with the lady critter on the right of the screen, friends even. Both ghost critters looked and moved too much like humans for me to think they were extra-terrestrials. Their clothes date both of them back to before we were born. Unless that's some kind of front, it indicates that those two have been around for a long time among us and we didn't know it. You know, if you actually start believing in ghosts, you might just get real paranoid about who's watching you when you don't know it." Special Agent Anderson saw three of his 'guests' turn and look at Sergeant D'Palermo, whose face had turned a shade lighter. Agent Anderson's mind went into a higher gear, analyzing the composition of the team he was escorting, their questions and the current expressions on their faces. He had hit some kind of a sore nerve. Might he be able to get some guidance from these people? Time for Russ Anderson to make an educated guess.

"I see you've had dealings with at least one of the critters." All four heads snapped towards the FBI man. "Look, we're all on the same project. How about we help each other? I'll keep you informed of what we find if you tell me what you have picked up so far. Deal?"

The group was too young to have formed a clear leadership, and it might never do so, given the strengths of each personality. The confirmation of their suspicions of having a visitor at the restaurant was sufficient to tell team members that any assistance would be a good thing. They all consented as they passed Charlie on their way to the food tent.

"Humph."

Six tickets were presented at the station, eight boarded the train. The 'Green Machine' had been loaded and secured under the watchful eye of its owner. The transport casket for Gustav was likewise carefully installed in a luggage car. A prettier box had been ordered and was awaiting its destiny in Kingston at Keyser's Funeral Home. Across the Hudson River from there, a young man with a backhoe was digging up six feet of earth in Rhinebeck, N.Y. Gustav's parents and his son had been interred there in a family plot, and he felt it was a pleasant spot for his own final resting place (rest, indeed!). Gustav had made the arrangements years ago, when his heart condition had been first diagnosed. He hadn't told anyone back then. It seemed to be a manageable condition and his best friend might not let him play with the team as much if the truth were to be revealed.

Major Kenneth McGuinness was writing up his National Guard contact reports. Why was it, he groused, that activities involving keeping the peace always made for twice the paperwork as actual war? Wasn't it enough that men and women laid their lives on the line for their state and nation? He wondered if the Governor actually read his Manpower Report 4AA, Expense Report QR-99-1 and Post-Contact Synopsis parts A through R which included commentary from every soldier that came within visual contact distance of the Estate, equipment failure analysis and how many Band-Aids were used. He sat back and rubbed his eyes. His mind wasn't on the keyboard entries, but on the subordinate that he looked upon almost as a daughter. She was with that nitwit Wasserman, who didn't know what a good thing he had when she was with him. The twit. Wasserman left the Guard in favor of police enforcement. Well, that wasn't quite as bad as it might have been, but it still indicated questionable judgment, at least in the Major's opinion. Nunzia was scheduled to call him tonight with an update. He wondered what she might have found out so far. Probably not much, yet.

Milledgeville Mayor Linda LaRoche had finished meeting with her damage control people. They had discussed spooks, National Guard, Atlas the ghost hunting Chihuahua (she couldn't help but think that it sounded much too 'Disney'), hospital reports, lawsuits and repair bills, to name a few. The costs for damage and medical bills were the worry of the insurance companies, for the most part. Litigation for emotional trauma would, no doubt, be instituted by hundreds of mothers of traumatized rug rats. That would be the purview of their legal beagles, armed with all those waivers insisted upon by that poor lawyer who had the heart attack. She had a sad smile at that. The fellow was stuffy, but he knew his business. Her city was on national, no, international broadcasts. Ghost stories would drive many tourists away in droves, but would attract an equal, if not greater, number of curious folk to her city. The report she just had from the hysterical owner of Capital Cuisine made her smile. The man wasn't fooling her. Alphonse probably knew what a gold mine that this whole ordeal would mean to him, assuming he could get staff that would not be susceptible to the heebie jeebies. Properly spun, which the full coffers from the Edwards event would be more than able to finance, this whole haunting thing would be an ongoing cash cow that would keep her popularity high, keep her in office for at least another term and finance a dozen city improvement projects she had been lustily eyeing. A sports stadium for one. The Mayor wondered if the 'Milledgeville Ghost Riders' would be too tacky a name for an NFL football team. Her aide, Elroy McBean, was already out getting preliminary bids on that project.

CNN Anchorman Jim Dunnel was frantic. Here he was with a 'King Midas' wealth' of interest across the globe on the ghost story of the decade and barely squat to report on. His grandfather might have sympathized, had he still been around, from his own efforts on covering the early space launches. Truly those people were the ultimate experts of covering hours of airtime with zippo information. At least he had a lineup of experts on a dozen linked topics he could use for fill time, though half of them were fruitcakes as far as he was concerned. The sci-fi kooks were having a field day with this one, as were those who were thumping Bibles and hollering 'Armageddon', as well as the organizations promulgating anything from psychic healing to tarot card readings; all for a fee, of course. He had to laugh at that one. Nineteen years ago, a coalition of psychic groups loosely organized into something akin to a union. They claimed to have weeded out the fakes and scam artists from their ranks, having as members only those who had been proven to have an honest psychic ability. Jim had an interview lined up that evening with the acting President of ESPER International. At least their title didn't come out to be one of those silly anagrams, but rather referred to the common term indicating someone with extra sensory perception. The previous president of that bunch of screwballs had run off last spring to South America with a couple million of embezzled funds. The anchorman had every intention of asking the interim president why no one foresaw that happening.

The Task Team divided up into pairs. Dagmar and Zachary drew up a list of people to seek out and interview. Paul and Nunzia would spend their time on the research end of things. Russell would continue with collating FBI information and comparing notes with the Task Team on a daily basis.

The initial prospective interview list was compiled from police records to date, which included the entire Hawthorn group, Barney aka Hammer Jenkins (biker), Nicole Redman (tour guide), Kurt Mangela (paramedic), Peter Steinbaum and Percy Stains (boom camera operators), Robert Fellatini (Marriott concierge), Dr. Marc Benoit (Milledgeville ER medical resource and general practitioner), Frank Gladstone (husband to Rachel Gladstone and step-father to Allen Hawthorn), Martha Scholldorf Mendelssohn and Valerie Knudson Mendelssohn (former wives to the deceased lawyer, if they were available), Patricia Kupfner (owner/operator of Milledgeville Stables) and a blank check of RPI teachers/ administrators/ fellow students (regarding Allen Hawthorn and Melissa Banks).

The initial research docket included police and public information downloads regarding all members of the Hawthorn group, past and present (in particular this Ryan fellow), the Confederate Colonel Archibald and Mrs. Anita Edwards, any information about the Edwards Estate that might be relevant, especially regarding the presence of that mounted Union soldier, Hawthorn Enterprises slash Custom Properties, and any hard data that they could come up with regarding the mystery spook that fought the other one that looked like Mrs. Edwards. For that broad a spectrum to research, their best resource was the public library down the road from the Milledgeville City Hall. They would have not only paper and archival records that were biased towards including minutia regarding local history, but also high-density Internet connections they could plug their PC's into and a section where they actually vended drinks and snacks. Somewhere along the line, the public library systems decided to emulate some of the successful book/disc megastores, like Narnia, who had bought out Barnes and Noble, Wellspring, Brothers, and a host of others. It was an interesting evolution that included librarians having to do double duty as information resources regarding spiced coffees and herbal teas.

While the Task Team began their efforts, the objects of their interest were riding the mag-lev north. Like libraries and air-travel services, AmeriTrak had taken some hard financial survival lessons. As a result, the rail service had enjoyed a resurgence of popularity with their ability to carry far more luggage and even cars, make better time with their prime track routes (high speed magnetic train/track systems called mag-levs, with more track being laid all the time), larger executive compartments than the air-travel companies could offer (cars divided into four compartments, connected with an aisle along one wall of the car), better cuisine and reduced fare plans. Many people preferred the closer proximity of the scenery, too. Of a minor advantage was the traveling demographic that suffered from a fear of heights. What had come to pass was a dream come true for the rail systems, though it had taken the nightmare of the turn of the millennia terrorism involving the airlines and a few subsequent government bailouts to spark the funds needed to get the ball rolling from additional passenger loads.

It was time for the Fitzgalen Family to debrief in the gently rocking privacy. One thing they discussed was how the 'tuning in' at the Edwards event did affect some changes. The ability for Vanessa to touch solid objects and Gustav was…touched. Vanessa and Gustav could now experience something akin to touch with each other. There wasn't so much sensation upon contact as the realization that part of the one couldn't go any further in space occupied by the other. Vanessa could also now more easily make herself felt by living people, though it was still a task. Both were more able to manipulate inanimate objects for longer periods of time, with less 'rest up' time after each attempt.

Vanessa was still working on learning Gustav's talent for altering what kind of garb they might appear in to those who could see them. Gustav was making grudging progress with teleportation to places he had visited. It was so much easier when Vanessa and the family were waiting for him at the end of the transport line, guiding him in with their wishes for his presence.

The eight Family members were relaxing in their executive compartment. Hot cocoa was the drink of choice, along with crackers and (low fat) cheese to nibble on. Ryan was still the paternal mentor, and so, led off. "Now, Vanessa, would you be so kind as to tell everyone about your adventure with a National Guard Sergeant and Hell's Chihuahua?"

"Be nicer to me, Sweetie. Don't forget that you sleep and I don't. Now, don't underestimate that woman. She's sharp as nails and doesn't miss much. She was the one person who didn't seem to buy your fake grief last night and she didn't seem impressed with everyone's bereavement attitudes at the Estate the day before. The lady spent five minutes in the hotel parking lot just thinking. I could see it in her face. Then, she had the discipline to stow it all and concentrate completely on her driving." Ryan didn't look too happy about that. *"She went to a fancy chow house called 'Capital Cuisine', apparently to meet with some people. She made a beeline for a table where there was a woman and two men. One of those men had a rat dog sitting at the table on some kind of kid high chair. That dog could see me and let everyone know it."*

Rachel asked, "Vanessa, animals are often sensitive to things we can't see, but are you sure it actually saw you?"

"Sergeant D'Palermo froze and I walked to the right and left of her. The dog's eyes never left me. Someone broke a glass and distracted the mutt, so I zapped myself behind the half-wall behind the people at the booth. The dog didn't sense me anymore, so my money is on sight sense only or, at least, mostly."

Something clicked in Allen's mind. "That guy the little dog was with, late 30's, average build, just starting to go bald, dark hair, thin goatee?" All eyes were on the first mate of their ship. Vanessa nodded. "Well I'll be damned. It's him! I forget his name, but that Chihuahua's name is Atlas."

There were several snorts at that one. Marianne said, "You've got to be joking. Atlas? So, how come you know about this guy's dog? Is he famous or something?"

Gustav decided the conversation had been long enough without any contribution from him. Contribute he would, whether it would add to the conversation or not. *"My dear lady, history is resplendent with famous canines, factual and fictional, though of late there has been a 'pawcity' of them. Lassie, Rin-Tin-Tin, Cleo, Bullet, Apsa, Checkers, Scooby Doo, Astro, Augie Doggie and Doggie Daddy, Spuds McKenzie, Petey, Old Yeller, Perdita and Pongo…"*

Ryan had to interrupt. "ALL RIGHT, all ready! Jeeze, Gustav, it takes more than death to shut up a lawyer. Allen, I'm not surprised any more at your command of trivia, so please enlighten the rest of us. Who's Atlas?"

"Lorriman! That was the guy's name. Last name, anyway. No clue on the first. There's a fan club of the pair at RPI. I've even seen T-shirts with Atlas on them."

Rachel's light turned on next. "Atlas? Yes! I've heard of him, too. Some of my friends back home, the well to do ones, have little dogs they pamper a lot. The dog has something to do with a whole line of doggie whimsicals, like clothes, special food, treats, car seats and God knows what else. Allen, is that the same mutt?"

"I think so, Mom, probably is. I hope his rep is just hype."

Ralph Kithcart had been leaning back, his head against the wall, eyes closed. "Folks, I'm a cabbie and I'm used to hearing circular babble, but take pity on the new kid on the block. Would someone please tell me what all this trivia has to do with us?"

Allen searched for the right words. "Atlas and his owner are ghost hunters." It would have sounded hilarious to any other group. Not for this one with two ghosts in their company, one of who had had the screaming meemees due to said Atlas.

Ryan took out his pen, tapped it three times on the arm of his chair, and then held it up in the air like a maestro's baton. "OK, folks. You should know the chorus by now. 'It's…"

In unison, the seven in the chorus completed the sequence. "…a whole new ballgame!"

VI. INTERVIEWS

"Hello, Miss Redman. I'm Dagmar Yaddow and this is Zachary Lorriman. We know you've been through a lot already from your experience and from your first interview with the State Police. We're not investigating any crime; so don't be concerned about getting anyone in trouble. We're just trying to piece together what happened last Saturday. Do you have any objections if we record this conversation?" They were sitting in the main office at the Edwards Estate Tourist Information Center.

"No, ma'am, as long as when we're done I can get your autograph. You, too, Mr. Lorriman." Both interviewers glanced at each other with a mild mixture of being pleased with the compliment and jealousy of the other sharing in it. Both were professional enough to push those feelings to the side, for now. It was agreed that each would take turns interviewing, lest the interviewee feel pressured in crossfire.

"We would be honored, Nicole. Now, tell us, in your own words, what happened on Saturday afternoon. Make sure to include as many details as you can about the people you see in these pictures." Dagmar handed Nicole a short stack of digital prints. Each had a name inscribed in whichever corner had the lightest colors.

"Well, I first talked to Melissa Banks, that's this picture here, during the battle enactment." The image was the same one picked out by Rachel Gladstone on the day of the 'Event', according to the Chief of Security (who had been contacted earlier). "I think I saw her before, but it's hard to say. There were so many people there. I was preoccupied earlier with my tour groups and later with the battle. She had come out to the porch where I was standing, looking upset and confused. Her eyes were all red, like she had an allergy or something. We only had a few words together, mainly about staying on the porch for safety, then I turned back to watch. The next time I turned around, she was gone. I didn't hear her leave, but there was an awful lot of noise then. It would have been like hearing a whisper during a July 4th fireworks finale. I continued to watch for a while, when it started getting cold. It was so spooky. Kind of like when you go into a cave in the middle of summer. It's so striking how fast the temperature changed. I could see my breath. That scared me, a lot. Guess it shook up the actors nearest to the porch too, for they stopped what they were doing. Even the 'dead guys' got up. When they did, I felt it get even colder, so I got off the porch and moved away. It stayed cold until I got far enough away, maybe twenty or thirty feet. There was an immediate change to the normal warmth and that was just as crazy. I turned around at that point to look back at the porch and that's when something blew up. I saw a glow that lasted for a second, which seemed to explode in all directions. On either side of the glow I could see two figures in dresses, but I was too far away to make out much. To tell the truth, I was just too scared. When the thing blew up, I could see the tiles blow off the porch and felt a sting on my hip."

At that point, Nicole undid her jeans, turned to the side, and lowered the pants ten inches. This move was not expected by either interviewer and both did their best to remain professional and passive…one had more difficulty in doing so. Nicole then peeled back a gauze pad to show a burn mark on her hip. It looked like she had burned herself with an iron. "From what I could see at the ER, most of the others there had burns like this. Luckily, no one got it in the eyes. That's about all I can recall, because I ran out of there as fast as I could, along with everybody else. I did stop a couple of times to help women who tripped over their costume skirts, though." The pants went back up and Zachary successfully stifled a sigh.

"Thank you, Nicole. Zachary, do you have any questions?"

Actually, he had several, but this was not the time to ask for a phone number. "Yes. Nicole, wasn't there another member of that group of people we told you about that you saw?" He had read the original interview transcript from the police files. Dagmar was a little annoyed that she had missed that one. This guy was good.

Nicole picked out the side shot from the boom camera, taken unawares when Marianne was caught talking to ghost children. "Oh, yeah. That security lady. She had been hanging around the northwest fence most of the previous day, watching the house. She didn't do much else that I noticed, but I was not always there during the day. She seemed really nice, and said 'Hi' to me a couple of times that weekend. I hadn't seen her before Friday, that I can recall. No, wait a minute." Nicole Redman looked more closely and then scanned a couple of other pictures featuring Marianne. Now that her mind wasn't preoccupied with managing tour groups, it was easier for her to check her mental files from the past. "She looks kind of familiar, like I've seen her before. I don't know, maybe she was in a tour group a long time ago. I've got a good memory for faces, but I don't have total recall."

Zachary found that answer interesting. If that Marianne Cabrini had been to the Estate more than once, and those times were long enough ago that Nicole's memory of her were sketchy, it indicated that the Hawthorn group had been planning things for at least that long…possibly. "One other question. Did any of the strange occurrences Saturday show up any other time in the past?"

"Mr. Lorriman, there've been a couple of odd things that we're told not to make too much of. One was the family Bible inside the Main House. A lot of people have reported the pages turning of their own accord. Another thing is that a temperature drop, nowhere nears as bad as the one Saturday, occurs every day at around five o'clock in the afternoon. It lasts for a couple of minutes and then suddenly goes away. We're told to tell people who ask that it's a draft from a hidden cave somewhere that we call 'Old Faithful', because it's so punctual, you know?"

With that, the interviewers had run out of 'Event' related questions. Nicole left with two autographed 8x10's. She wondered if she would hear anything more about it, other than what might show up on the news. Zachary and Dagmar spoke for a few minutes, and then asked for the next two interviewees. The cameramen who were at the blow-up had been brought there at the Task Team's request. Neither man seemed overly happy about returning to the scene of the, what, crime? Other than initials and occupations, Percival Stains and Peter Steinbaum didn't seem to have much in common. Peter was twenty-three, tall and lanky, single and short haired. Percival was thirty-two, short and muscular, divorced and pig-tailed. Zachary thought they were the 21st century's answer to Abbott and Costello and got a chuckle that even their ages had the numbers in opposite order.

"You have already been introduced to my partner, Dagmar Yaddow. You may also know my other partner here, Atlas." Dagmar was definitely not pleased with sharing the 'partner' title with a scrawny producer of annoying sounds. "No one is in trouble here. This is purely a fact-finding effort to understand something extraordinary. I assume neither of you mind being recorded, given your occupations?" Both men nodded in unison, but said nothing so far. Zachary thought, "Alike, yet not alike. I wonder who'll answer first?"

Aloud, he continued. "Our M.O. is to have you speak freely of your experiences without us interrupting. When you are finished, we may have a couple of questions for you on specific points. Please, proceed at your leisure and try to give as many details of the people we've highlighted for you as having special interest to us."

Age before beauty seemed to win out here. Percival began first, while Peter leaned back and waited. "Pete and I were on the boom crew on Friday and Saturday. The boom allows us to shoot from ground level up to twenty feet above ground. Friday was pretty much cake, which we figured would be the case. As usual, we take about five total hours of stock footage, of which about three minutes total might be used for eventual airtime, if we're lucky. We get a bonus for every thirty seconds over one minute per shoot event that's used. That includes all the networks and their affiliates, plus we get a per-pic fee for stills used by the print media. One of those ladies you were interested in was there most of the day leaning against the fence near the Main House. Hey, she was a framer. Couldn't help but notice." Zachary hadn't heard of that term for an attractive woman. Dagmar had, since she had dealt a lot with camera people in her life. "She didn't do much but stand and watch the porch, like something was going to happen there that day, but nothing did. Saturday was a lot more interesting."

Percy's partner chimed in. "Hey Percy, tell 'em what she did, that talking thing."

"Oh, yeah. Guess she got bored or something. God knows we were. I was panning the crowd and zoomed in on her as an end-shot. She started talking, out of the blue. I looked from the viewfinder and could see that there was no one there for her to be talking to. Kind of weird, you know? Kept the camera rolling for half a minute, then she stopped." The still he picked up from the table showed Marianne with her mouth open. Someone versed in lip reading would have noted the classic signs of forming the letter 'R'.

The phrase 'no one there for her to be talking to' sent chills up Dagmar's spine. She exercised her right to jump in if she felt something was important. "Mr. Stains. Is there any possibility you could get us a copy of that clip? We already have permission from your chief, but could you expedite the process?"

Percival Stains nodded to his partner, who took out his own SatCom. This one looked modified from the ones Dagmar and Zachary were used to seeing. "Hey Choco, Pete here. Need a download from the Edwards C.F. That sequence with the security babe yakkin with the air. Yeah, Friday, that's the one. I'll be waiting." Pete looked at Percival, then thumbed the disconnect. Pete said, "Twenty-five." Percival, at the same time, said, "Thirty-five." Both watched the SatCom display while Dagmar leaned over to Zachary.

It was Dagmar's turn to be caught clueless on the lingo. She leaned over to Zachary and whispered, "Did I miss something? What did he mean by the 'Edwards C.F.?"

"Watch." Zachary had no intention on interpreting the initials. He was at least that much a gentleman. Moments later, the modified SatCom made a brief 'zip' sound.

"Twenty-nine, awright!"

"Gawdammit!" Percival fished out a ten and handed it over to Pete. "Two lousy seconds. You lucked out, string bean."

Pete pushed a release button and a MiDi popped out of the SatCom. He handed it over to Dagmar, who promptly filed it under P, for purse. Percival, still grumbling over the lost bet, went on. "Anyway, we got a pretty good sequence of the women and the biker. The older blond lady was pretty spunky, the way she went for him with her frilly umbrella. Really took the biker and the other lady by surprise. She backed off quick when he hollered and fell on her butt. The other tried to nail him with a kick, but she got caught and flipped. I saw the young blond drop the guy. Cringed myself when she connected. She didn't seem to want the credit for the deed; just slipped in, drop kicked, then slipped back out. I lost her in the crowd. That lawyer guy that died later, he showed up soon after and the three of them insisted on reviewing the shots we got. The older blond was giving the orders, seemed to know what she was about. The other two just stood by.

She had us get a face shot of the young blond, ran a copy, then took off. Didn't see them again until the fit hit the shan on the porch."

Zachary got more entertainment than information from Friday's report. Not true with Dagmar. Her 'partner' was used to being focused on researching and pursuing a lone target, and a dead one at that. Group dynamics was not his forte. She was listening very carefully and taking precise notes on anything that happened on Friday. If this whole ghost thing was engineered, then Friday was the day where you should be able to see evidence of preparations. The Saturday report would do more to flesh out how the whole Hawthorn group interacted, on top of giving hints as to how said Hawthorn engineering bore its fruit. She felt that was the key to get into their heads and discover what it was that they were hiding. She was certain they were hiding something. She could smell it.

"Pete and me saw that flash on the porch. We happened to be aimed there because of the action happening with the soldiers. Jeeze, fake blood and everything. We never filmed a real war, and I hope we never do. They really went to town on it. Anyway, I saw three ladies and that lawyer come out the front porch and the three men come up from the front yard. Those guys just stood back from the stairs and the lawyer hung back, too. The ghost on the right began to fall back, I guess she was a ghost, when the two older women came up from behind and caught her from falling. Hey, you can't touch a ghost, can you?" Zachary nonchalantly shrugged and asked Percival to go on, but inside his thoughts were racing along those same lines. "OK, well, they just stood there. There was that glow between the two ghosts and it got brighter when the two ladies touched that one ghost on the right. They were talking, but we weren't set up with the parabolic mike 'cause one of those musket shots would have buggered the rig if it was aimed right, so we couldn't pick up well on the conversation. All we had for sound was the wide-angle mike with spike sound suppression. The young chick came up and put her hands on both the ladies' shoulders, and the glow got brighter again. The ghost on the left looked pretty peeved, but she kept up the juice."

Percival separated out one of the pictures on the table. "There, that guy. He came up to the porch first and the two other guys (he pointed to two other images) stood to either side of him, like he was the boss. He jumped up the steps and put his hands on the young blond, up went the glow again. Then the other two did the same thing the older ladies did and, each time, the glow amped up. That's when I heard something in the camera make a real funny noise and the video went to hell. Before it did, it showed something coming up to the porch. I only caught a piece of it on the screen before it died. I looked up and saw what looked like a man getting off a horse. I could see through him and his horse, too. Not sure, but I think the horse and rider was more solid on the video screen than they were in real life, 'cause I could just barely see it, him, whatever, with just my eyes. I could see that there was conversation involved with each change, but before we left, I could see that the lawyer came up and put his hands on the other men's shoulders when no one was talking. Like, it was his idea and no one else's. It all got too much for me and Pete, so we dropped the bucket and took off. Didn't see much of anything else after that."

Dagmar and Zachary were both taking notes for a couple of minutes after Percival stopped speaking. Zachary looked up and said, "I've got no questions. Dagmar, anything you want to ask?"

"Percival, Pete, you two have been cameramen for a long time. You have a known talent for aiming where you sense the action will happen. Tell us, who on the porch was running the show?"

Pete spoke up. "At first, it was that lady ghost on the right. She moved her mouth, the live ladies jumped like they could all hear her. I think I heard her, too, but it was so faint I can't be sure. That Ryan guy was second to take command. She spoke, he listened. He spoke, the other guys jumped." He thought about it for a second. "Guess ghosts say more than just 'boo', huh? Were they actually ghosts?"

"We don't know, yet. Pete, you're pretty observant. Tell Zachary and me if there was anything your partner left out."

"Not sure if it's important, but it was that ghost on the left. She seemed to get distracted. A couple of times, it looked like she was having a seizure or something. Other times, she would look behind her, with kind of a worried expression. For a while, she kept one of her arms reaching out in that direction. I couldn't see anything in that direction, myself. The way I figure it, those two ghosts were dukin' it out. All the ghost on the right was focused on was the other, you know? Nothing else live seemed to matter to her. So, what was that lady ghost on the left worried about behind her? Maybe, she had a thing for that ghost soldier, or maybe the two ghost ladies and that ghost soldier weren't the only spooks on site?" Pete and Percival were thanked and excused. Dagmar and Zachary were thinking rapidly along completely different paths that would lead, eventually, to the same location. '…weren't the only spooks on site?'

Paul and Nunzia were at the library. She was pulling information in about the Estate. He was plugged in with his PC and studying the videos of the event and stock footage about the Estate and the surrounding area, running back to as close to the Civil War as he could find. After two hours of work, they compared notes. Nunzia started off.

"Judging from soldiers' diary entries and newspaper clippings, Mrs. Anita Brady Edwards was murdered by Private Jedediah Patterson who was part of a foraging party under the command of Major Benjamin Covington from the Union's XX Corps, which was under the command of General Sherman. This was during that 'March to the Sea' campaign we studied during our Guard training. The lady was married to a Colonel Edwards and he was serving in the Georgia Militia under the command of General Hood. Col. Edwards' group was attempting a flanking move when they stumbled across a Northern Army division. No one survived of Edwards' command. Anita Edwards was left with two children and was managing the farm, practically single-handed because her slaves had all run off. Then that foraging party came by. The two kids were accidentally trampled under the cavalry horses and Mrs. Edwards and Pvt. Patterson managed to kill each other when he tried to rape her.

"Paul, I've heard that ghosts can hang around when they die in violent or other mentally stressful circumstances. This seems to fill that bill. I mean, Jesus, it said that she had just heard about her husband's death, it was the tail end of the war when the North was slicing the state in half, she saw her children die, then she gets raped and murdered. Wouldn't that just push the average Jane over the edge?

"Now, on the Hawthorn group. Rachel Gladstone was married to Carl Hawthorn, who was the CEO of Custom Properties, now Hawthorn Enterprises. He was killed in an auto accident when his son, Allen, was four. His mother continued to raise Allen while the lawyer, Mendelssohn, stood in as acting CEO. He and that Cabrini woman pretty well managed the business. For some reason, the business didn't go to the widow. She did derive a substantial endowment from Custom Properties and she didn't do too badly on the life insurance policy. Rachel married Frank Gladstone, who had two kids from a previous marriage. He doesn't seem to have much to do with the business, from what I can gather. Allen had turned 21 a week ago and now he's billed as the new CEO, kind of a 'coming of age' thing, I guess. The kid was going to RPI, a tech college in Troy, NY, but is currently taking a hiatus for a semester, according to the RPI registrar. From what I can gather, the decision to take a break from college wasn't a planned one by the kid. Turns out that the lawyer arranged things just before the CEO's birthday, then finalized the break the day after the birthday.

"The mother is heavy into the volunteer thing and has done a lot in a small town in upstate NY called Hurley. I looked it up. Not much to speak of, other than a lot of colonial vintage stone houses and it was the capital of NY for all of a couple of days when the British burned Kingston. His girlfriend is still listed as a student at RPI as a sophomore. He was, or rather is, a junior. Other than that, there's nothing too odd about their records. No one has a police record of anything greater than a speeding ticket for Miss Banks. I can't find squat on the Ryan fellow. The lawyer was married and divorced twice. He had his only kid die as a child, but I didn't get a handle on what it was from. Mr. Kithcart was a long time cab driver in Milledgeville. Did a hitch as a mechanic in the Guard's Air Force. Divorced once, no kids. Seems to be a consistent worker with nothing unusual to report."

Paul was impressed, though not for the first time. "Thorough, as usual, Nunzia. You would have made an excellent detective. No, cancel that.

You ARE an excellent detective." Nunzia lowered her eyes slightly and smiled. "I don't have a feel on what you came up with, yet. Everything seems odd enough to be normal. No one was laying low to be inconspicuous. Sleeper agents in history went out of their way to be bland and un-memorable. Most people aren't like that, so a lack of something defining or unusual makes them stick out. Say, did Carl Hawthorn start Custom Properties?"

Nunzia tapped on the finger pad and pulled up another research section. "That was kind of strange. He was hired by another business, Obediah Properties, which changed its DBA to Custom Properties, Inc. shortly afterwards. Someone decided to keep the details of that company confidential. The first business had specialized in a unique living set-up for singles. After it became Custom, the business began to expand to similar situations, but for other interests such as jocks, musicians and animal owners. Here's a web prospectus on the company."

Paul looked and whistled. "Wow. I'm in the wrong business."

Something inside the Guardswoman's heart wanted to verbally agree with that last statement. Instead, "So, what did you come up with?"

Paul didn't have the long litany Nunzia did, but it was still interesting. "I loaded the pic's of the Hawthorn group into the Inter-Pol records. Zip on the legal issue, which agrees with your own findings. The program gave me the physical characteristics of each person, down to their exact heights. I found the dimensions of the porch components and used that as a ruler to gauge and confirm each individual's dimensions. There are genealogy programs that can use those measurements and offer another avenue of identification. I've used it before, though they sometimes can be iffy on the results. The only pic's recorded that match the college kids are their high school senior yearbook pictures. Mrs. Gladstone has been in the papers from time to time for her volunteer work. Mr. Mendelssohn shows up in a couple of business reports, early legal career advertisements and small news items in the local paper, college graduation and high school graduation. I didn't have a last name to cross-reference on Ryan and, so far, nothing is coming up on him. Could he be in a witness protection program?"

The Guardswoman thought about that. "Worth asking some higher ups. May not get the previous identity, but at least we can answer why he's a non-entity." Nunzia rubbed her lower lip a couple of times, an action that Paul had known to indicate a new line of thought. "Say, Zachary and Dagmar have been doing people research for a while. She does mostly recent and he knows more of researching the past. Let's see if they have something to add." Nunzia pulled out her military issue SatCom and speed connected to the other half of the team (she didn't think of Anderson as a full member, yet). "Hi, Zachary? Nunzia. We're making some progress, but wanted to bounce something off you. Paul's using the vid's to picture ID the Hawthorn group. We've managed to pull up some trivial stuff on everyone except that

Ryan guy. You two have been doing people research as part of your careers. Any suggestions?" Paul saw her listen for a while, noting her eyebrows rising a couple of times in that way he had come to know as her 'oh really' look. She closed the conversation with a 'thank-you' and broke the connect. Nunzia D'Palermo set the SatCom down on the table, turned to her partner, smiled and asked, "Paul, what do you know about the Mormons?"

The mag-lev train had pulled into the Rhinecliff, N.Y. station; the limo, the Green Machine and the hearse later pulled out. It was nice to be back, sort of, for everyone. The temperature was twenty degrees cooler, very few branches retained their leaves and, although their mission had been an amazing success with the additional blessing of getting both Allen/Melissa and Ralph/Marianne together, there remained duties tinged to the sad by being both uncomfortable and unavoidable.

Funeral arrangements were in process, including the notification of Gustav's former wives. He wasn't thrilled with the idea of seeing them again, especially both at once should they show up at the funeral. At first he thought he'd be lucky and they'd just send cards and flowers, until he recalled that there was a will to be read.

Rachel still had to personally face Frank. Worse yet, Jerry and Janet (sixteen and fourteen, respectively). What a pariah she had turned out to be in their eyes, she thought. Rachel's mental Angel had seen fit to bring out the home movies, much to her Cat's discomfiture. Every time Cat opened her eyes and took her paws out of her ears, there was the replay of the Family Medallion Ceremony on Rachel's mental view screen. Since melded families had become so common, it was natural to develop traditions to include all members of families as they went through the sometimes-difficult evolutions of family structure. Rachel and Frank, during their wedding ceremony, had placed gold necklaces around the necks of his children and one around Allen's neck. It looked like an inverted Olympic symbol, with two interlocked circles on top similarly linked to three circles below to represent all members of the newly bonded family. As if that wasn't bad enough, bemoaned Cat, Angel kept humming the tune to 'Will The Circle Be Unbroken'.

Adding to it all, there was the unknown of those investigative people they had left behind. None of them had any doubt but that they would see them again. Vanessa promised to try another snoop, but how would she really do that? She could show up at a number of places in Milledgeville because she had them logged in her mind and could instantly visit any of those places. But, were any of the investigators still there? And what about that dratted Atlas?

Crossing over the Kingston-Rhinecliff Bridge, Ryan signaled the driver for privacy. The dividing window went up. He looked at the crowded compartment (more so by two than the driver had thought). "Ahem." Six heads turned, as Ralph was following in his Green Machine, listening in to the conversation sent by Allen's SatCom. "People, we are a Family that has proven itself resourceful as well as resilient. After what we just went through, I've no doubt that there isn't anything the eight of us can't handle. Now, cheer yourselves up. I've taken the liberty of calling ahead for a dinner at Pavelli's. Roscoe isn't normally on tonight but, when he heard we were coming, he volunteered to come in."

Ryan was sure his news would perk up his tired family. It was almost successful. Gustav had loved Pavelli's cuisine and dropped the mood with a flat-toned, *"Oh, goody. A fine time for me to go on a no-calorie diet."* He then chopped the other leg out from under Ryan by asking, *"Tell me, does Roscoe know I've shuffled off my mortal coil?"* The look on Ryan's face told them he hadn't passed that bit of information on. Marianne saw Ryan's downcast expression, causing Sicily to square off with Germany.

"Why you stuffy, self-centered old Grinch. Is that how you treat your best friend who is just as frazzled as any of us, if not more so, but had taken the time and effort to cheer us up? Do you think that, just because you're dead, we should feel sorry for you? Vanessa kicked the bucket long before you did, buster, and she did it twice!" Marianne was seconds from bursting into tears and her outburst had caught everyone by surprise, even Marianne. "What's happened to you, Gustav? Did you leave your paternal instincts behind in your body?" Gustav, from natural reflexes, reached forward in a fatherly desire to hold the woman that had become a daughter to him, only to see his arms pass through their intended target. Now it was his turn to show a downcast expression, and his frustration came to the surface in full. Ralph, following in his Green Machine, wondered at first why Marianne was biting Ryan's head off. By her second sentence, he realized who the true target was and came fairly close to guessing what Gustav must have said to provoke Marianne like that.

That was a pointed moment for Gustav Mendelssohn. He had been feeling sorry for himself since he died, but realized that Marianne was right. This wasn't like him. He was in danger of slipping into a self-pitying mindset, which was understandable. It hadn't been his choice to stay on earth, but here he was because he had no other place to go. Still, it was a place with purpose and friends, despite the denial of mortal pleasures he had become accustomed to and treasured. For that moment, he controlled the immediate destiny of the evening and, possibly, for much longer than that. Gustav looked into Marianne's eyes and made a very conscious decision.

He smiled, even chuckled a little, and shook his head. *"Thank you, dearest one. I'm all right, now. Bless you. Ryan, please forgive me, my old friend. It's time for me to look on my new capacities for the blessings that they really are. I can support the Family with my legal wizardry in ways I never dreamed of before. The aches in my joints are gone and my vision is now excellent. Vanessa will now have my company, though it may be a poor substitute for that of her best friend, Annie. My alimony payments are officially over and Marianne can no longer threaten me with her little dish of warm water in the middle of the night."*

Ralph smiled to hear the laughter from his SatCom clipped to his shoulder belt. He rightly guessed that the sour kraut just unsoured himself. When the two vehicles arrived at Pavelli's, Ralph saw the limo occupants disembark in a visibly much better mood.

At the County Jail Facility located in Milledgeville, the Corrections Officer met the Task Team representatives. "Yes, Ms. Yaddow, Mr. Lorriman. The Chief said you'd be coming. I'm Captain Robert Tibbets. The prisoner is being held in A3. I'll take you there now. He's scheduled for arraignment the day after tomorrow. He knows the arrangement."

The 'arrangement' was that his cooperation would lower the biker gang leader's charges to aggravated assault with public service time as his punishment. This didn't sit well with the judge, but the order came down from the top state office. It had to. Georgia judges weren't known to be affectionate to bikers.

"Yeah, so what do you want to know?" Bikers tended to be grumpy in jail, despite the free food and clean sheets. They were creatures of the open road and imposed restrictions never set well. Hammer didn't watch much news, unless there was some sort of juicy disaster, so he had seen the correspondent once or twice. The guy with the dog was news to him.

"Mr. Jenkins, we'll only take a few minutes of your time. Mr. Lorriman and I are mostly interested in two women you had a couple of run-ons with. What can you tell us?" The pictures were scattered on the table, but the prisoner wasn't looking at them.

Hammer tried to think of a way to parlay this into something more than he was offered. "You know, I got hit by that broad pretty hard. My memory's kind of fuzzy. Maybe I got brain damage or something."

Zachary wasn't used to dealing with this sort, but Dagmar was, and patience was not the path to success. "Well, Mr. Jenkins, we'll see if a nice long rest will recuperate your memory. See you in about two years." She quick gathered up the pictures, got up, and her partner had the presence of mind to follow suit without looking too surprised.

"WAIT, now hold on there, missy reporter. Don't go running off on ol' Hammer like that. That's no way to treat an American veteran, now is it?"

Dagmar didn't turn around, but she did stop. "Mr. Jenkins, you have never served in the American military, so let's drop the bullshit right now or say goodbye." Her hand grabbed the doorknob more for drama than reality, as the door was locked from the outside and could only be opened by the guard.

Barney 'Hammer' Jenkins sighed. "Look, lady, I'm just a part time accountant who likes to have some fun. How 'bout let's get this talk over with so all of us can get on with our lives, OK?" Both interviewers turned around and returned to their seats. Hammer didn't find it easy to admit he'd been trashed by the opposite sex. His machismo rep had already suffered serious setbacks with his road kin and here he was talking to someone who could tell the whole damned world of what happened to him. "The pack and I were at a bar having a few quiet drinks when I spotted the two birds. I walked up to them and said 'Hi'. That was pretty much it. The darker skinned one held my interest more, so I dismissed the other one. She didn't look too interested in fun, anyway. Besides, I saw she had a wedding ring on. Spic Chick told me to take my hands off her shoulders; honest, that's all I was touching, then she kicked me in the jewels and drove my face into the floor. Never saw it coming. I saw red and jumped for her, you can't really blame me for that, only she didn't stay put. Lady must have seen too many Jackie Chan Junior flicks, cause she kind of dropped down and stuck her foot in my gut. Next thing I know, I hit the bar bottles and the bartender was yelling at me to get off of him."

"That's better, Mr. Jenkins, or Hammer, if you like. We're also interested in a young woman that your fellow biker, uh, Barry Nicholson, told us of. He's the only one of your 'pack' we've been able to locate."

Hammer's lack of reaction confirmed to Dagmar that he never saw Melissa intercept his revenge at the Estate. Nor had he caught that vignette by watching the news. "That night, we took off for Savannah to crash in a hotel we had reservations for. Took off early the next morning to get out of paying the full tab, since there were about eight of us in each room, and that's when Barry scored big time picking up that babe at the bus stop. Barry's really OK, but he's got some mind challenges. I sort of watch out for him."

Dagmar handed her sheaf of photographs to Hammer. This time, Hammer carefully leafed through the photographs, then pulled out one of Melissa dressed normally from a news photographer shot the day after the Event. "Yeah, that's her. Guess even a blind squirrel gets an acorn sometimes. Barry's kind of weird." Then, seeing the looks on their faces, "Yeah, yeah, even for a biker. He has some kind of genius for numbers, you know? Not too bright when it comes to women, but you should see him handle a hog. The guy's a real pro with that. Numbers and biking are where he can shine, if you get me. He could work in a circus and make some decent green if he wanted to, but he likes to just ride free with me. That chick must have bailed on him, cause he lost her in the line going into the parking lots. Didn't see her after that." Hammer pointed at the pictures of Marianne and Rachel. "I saw those two buy a couple of ice creams at the event place. I went up to them to settle scores." Hammer knew this conversation wouldn't be held against him, so might as well tell the truth. He'd lie, but he had no clue as to what it was that these two really wanted to hear.

"Now, this is the truth. I didn't do anything bad before Blondie shoved her umbrella in my face, so I grabbed it. Self-defense, you know? Then she shoved her ice cream down my pants. Damn that was cold! I didn't ask for that, really, she's the one that assaulted me!" Zachary had a sudden urge to laugh, bringing back an old kid's rhyme where 'I scream for ice cream'. "She fell back on her ass, I didn't push her or anything, and her spic friend tried to do another kickball exercise. I was ready for her this time and flipped her, right on top of Blondie. Hey, those two probably enjoyed it. So far, it was all self-defense, but that's when I walked towards them and it wasn't for a goodbye kiss. I could have said it was to help them up, but I'd be lying. Look, I was mega-pissed off with the umbrella and the sundae, not to mention my busted nose from before…I had a right to be, you know? That's when some cowardly son of a bitch got me again, right where Spic Chick nailed me the day before. If I ever catch him…"

Dagmar began gathering her pictures, but paused. She couldn't resist the temptation and there was an order of protection against him even being in visual contact distance as those women, anyway. Zachary saw what was coming and, this time, fully agreed with his partner. He couldn't wait to see the look on the big guy's face.

"I'm afraid it is impossible for you to catch the man who did this to you, Mr. Jenkins. In fact, the combined efforts of the FBI, CIA and Interpol wouldn't be up to the task."

"Huh?" Mistaking the reporter's meaning, he had mixed feelings. So, the SOB kicked the bucket? What else could the lady mean? "Look, I'm sorry the guy bought a permanent mud bath, but I didn't have anything to do, uh, with…"

Dagmar was holding up Melissa's Southern Belle and blue jeaned pictures, waving them back and forth. She smiled when the man's lowering jaw indicated that he finally got the message. Returning the pictures back into the manila folder, Dagmar Yaddow put closure on the interview. "Mr. Jenkins, there are a lot of us that are fighting back against people like you. In the past few days, you've met with three of us, and we're the nicer ones. Some of us like to play with scissors. Please keep that in mind the next time you feel the desire to think with your tallywacker instead of your brain, won't you?" With that, she knocked on the door and the Captain appeared to open it. "We're through, Captain, thank you for your time." Zachary nodded as he, too, passed out of the interrogation room. His estimation of the professional he was working with had just gone up the scale a couple of steps. Dagmar's estimation of those women they were 'stalking' had also been growing, and she was beginning to have nagging feelings of guilt for her participation in this 'Task Team'.

Barney 'Hammer' Jenkins was left alone with his thoughts for a few minutes while the Captain escorted the Task Team members to the door. He thought hard about what that news lady had said. Normally, an authority figure preaching to him would have zero effect on his feelings or self-image, but pain is nature's best teacher (sitting down was still an exercise in delicacy for him). Besides, he wasn't as young as he used to be. Maybe it was time for a change. "If one more broad does the can-can, I'll be permanent 'can't-can't'." The thing the news lady said about scissors had really sent a chill up his spine.

Moments later, the door opened. Hammer walked down the hall astride the Captain, wanting to recover at least a small vestige of his tough guy image, scratching his head. "What's with the fuckin' dog?" The Captain only shrugged. It didn't fit the image of a police official to admit being part of Atlas's fan club, especially to a biker pack leader. His wife had a very spoiled Pomeranian.

The last scheduled stop for today on the interview route was Milledgeville ER. The Hospital Board of Directors had been contacted by the Mayor, who had been politely requested by the Governor of Georgia to pass on the recommendation that full cooperation of all medical personnel with the special Task Team would be greatly appreciated. In lay language, give these people what they want if you like your certification to operate the hospital. So it was that Dr. Marc Benoit and paramedic Kurt Mangela found themselves sitting in the very room where Ryan's horse, Maribelle, had her doughnut orgy. Dagmar and Zachary noticed that the interviewees were less than enthusiastic to be there, avoiding eye contact and fidgeting in their chairs. Dagmar had interviewed medical types before. Many of them truly believed in the sanctity of treater/treated privacy and both of these men had excellent reputations. Her experience was what had marked her as the lead in this dance, though it was Zachary's turn.

"Dr. Benoit, Mr. Mangela, you have our solemn word that what you disclose to us will not be made public. We mainly need to gather as many facts in this case as we can because, to tell you the truth, no one has a clue as to what really happened and we just don't know what fact will unlock some very important truths. Millions of dollars of damage has occurred and a man lost his life in the process. Thousands have suffered psychological trauma and almost two dozen people were treated in this hospital for second and first degree burns. Since the members of Hawthorn Enterprises played a major role in this craziness, intended or not, we feel that they are keys in this mystery. We can subpoena all the records, but I think we can get enough without all that mess and publicity right here. This way, we can best protect that code of privacy that you health professionals live by. Fair enough?"

Dr. Benoit and Kurt looked at each other, sighed and nodded assent. Dagmar was pretty good in the surgical use of the velvet-gloved iron fist and she added one more layer of velvet by saying, "This conversation will be recorded only for study, not for replay to the public or a court of law. The fact is, no law as far as we can tell, has been broken. No one is in trouble."

Kurt shrugged, bowing to inevitability, and so began. "Last Friday, we got the call for a respiratory emergency at the Marriott. Turned out to be that Allen Hawthorn guy and he looked serious bad. Blood pressure was beginning to drop, lungs were filling up with fluid, extremities and lips were turning blue." Dagmar and Zachary both thought, "What the hell?" at the very same time. This news was completely unexpected and the roller coaster had just begun.

"In the same suite were that lawyer and the kid's mother. Mr. Mendelssohn must have had some emergency experience, for the guy was big time cool under pressure. He already had the oxygen on full blast being delivered by a non-rebreather mask and had Allen's upper body elevated to reduce the lung filling. The mother was pretty together, too, given the circumstances that it was her kid's life at stake. She was going to tell us something, but I could see her eyeing Mendelssohn for permission, first. Mendelssohn took me to the side and told me a pretty hairy story on what the cause of the arrest was: ghost voodoo." Zachary's pencil point broke. Dagmar's elbow slipped off of the chair armrest.

"He said that there was a spook at the Edwards Estate, the ghost of Mrs. Anita Edwards, who had put the royal whammy on Allen. We had managed to get an advanced I.V. system hooked up that oxygenates the blood even with no lung support and it was a damn good thing we did. The kid stopped breathing, even with the mist we put in to drain the lungs. Really touch and go, there, but he stabilized and began to breathe again. Not sure if it was something we did, though. The timing of his stabilization wasn't quite on cue with what we were doing. Anyway, Mendelssohn said that I should do some research on a foraging troop that went through that area during the Civil War, when Sherman was stomping around the South, you know? We got the report from historical records. About sixty men were in the raiding party on the Edwards Estate where Mrs. Edwards lost her kids and her life. Every one of them, the soldiers that is, was dead half a year later, two thirds of them from a respiratory problem that resembled what Allen was going through. The rest were war casualties. We brought the kid and his mother in. The lawyer stayed behind, saying something about 'holding down the fort'. Rachel, the kid's mother, was made of pretty stern stuff. Most mothers would be either hysterical or comatose. This one kept her cool, but you could tell it wasn't easy. I turned over the kid's care to Dr. Benoit, 'cause he had grown up in Jamaica and had told me some pretty weird voodoo stories. Doc, it's your turn."

Dr. Benoit really didn't like this invasion into his privacy ethics, so the chance to blow the inquisitors out of their reality waters gave him some personal satisfaction. That what he was saying was all verifiable truth made it all the better. "Kurt filled me in and left to say goodbye to the mother. I went into the room where the young man was resting, reading the report on the Civil War soldiers on the way. I was pretty surprised when Allen was awake and alert, like nothing was wrong. Given the shape he was in when he was admitted, that kind of recovery was medically impossible. Shortly after, he was released. Oh, Kurt, remember that this wasn't the first time Allen was in."

Kurt was beginning to enjoy this, too. "Oh, yeah. I didn't bring him in, but on Thursday, that guy Ryan hauled Allen into the emergency room while riding a horse INTO the emergency room. The kid had fainted, or something. It looked like some kind of coma, the head nurse told me. The horse made history by getting herself into this room and eating all the doughnuts. The kid perked up again. No one got much on the how's and why's of that one. One of the interns though told me that Mr. Mendelssohn pulled a fast one and had the cab driver that brought them in committed to the psych ward just to keep him around when the group of them wanted to leave the hospital. A real card, that one."

It was a good thing that the recorder was going. Zachary had given up on writing anything. He and his partner could do little but stare open mouthed at the insanity being related to them by what, to all appearances, were two sane and professional individuals. Dagmar barely had the presence of mind to ask, "What, I mean, where might the horse have come from? Did it belong to Ryan or Allen?"

Kurt said, "No, I believe Ryan and Allen rented the nag from the Milledgeville Stables." The interview was officially ended and the two healers took their leave of two stunned interviewers who were too agog to think of something reasonable to ask. Atlas had been quiet all along, but hungrily eyed the doughnut crumbs.

"Zachary, did you ever…"

"No, never! Jesus H. Christ! There's stuff here I've never heard of, ever! Not even close!! I'll bet half my stock portfolio that you haven't either. What's worse, I've got the definite feeling that we've just scratched the surface. Come on. Maybe we can catch that stable before it closes. The reception desk probably knows where it is."

They just made it, half an hour later. Patricia Kupfner managed Milledgeville Stables, and asked Zachary not to bring the dog near the horses. "Chihuahuas in the past have wreaked havoc in the stables. Atlas may be well trained, but I can't afford to take a risk." It was all right with Dagmar and Zachary. They didn't really *have* to see the infamous Maribelle. "Yes, I remember Ryan and Allen. Nice people; shame Cumquat bolted on the boy like that. Thank God my horse came back safely and Mr. Hawthorn turned out OK. He thought it was funny that one of his sneakers was still in the stirrup."

Zachary and Dagmar looked at each other. 'Cumquat'?

"We never figured out what had happened. Horses may have been domesticated for millennia, but that doesn't mean we know all there is to know about them. I remember that Ryan came again the next day with another man, whose name escapes me. Then, the three of them came by and rented horses on Saturday. I remember that. All three of them were dressed up as Union soldiers. The horses scattered at that Edwards event when all those explosions happened, but all came home safely." There was little more gained in that interview, but neither Dagmar or Zachary felt they had been shortchanged.

Nunzia and Paul were sitting at the PC console. Paul had entered the physical dimensions and the picture samples from the video into the Mormon database. The quality of the pictures hadn't been the best, so it took a full minute for the search and nothing came up with any degree of confidence. Nunzia suggested that perhaps they should retro-alter the age factor in case the only comparison pictures in the database were when Ryan was younger. There was a side program for this, for a fee. Sometimes connections were made with high school yearbooks, old news clippings and even some campaign posters had been known to make positive ID's. The program took a 3D version of Ryan and retro-aged it to multiple images, each an estimated five years apart. The search resumed. Under each of the six computer-generated pictures was a red and a green dot. All were red dot highlighted, until the one that listed [age-est/25] was replaced by the green dot glowing its announcement of success. The [age-est/20] was next on the green light list. The rest remained red. The advantage of running this program was that the results were of a higher confidence if the multiple age-based hits identified the same person. In this case, it identified only one name, primarily from U.S. Navy records. The second resource was a high school yearbook of that same person. The results, however, had to be wrong. The dates were way too far in the past. They ran a print on the result, though. Perhaps the findings were of Ryan's father (grandfather?) and there was a very strong family resemblance. It was a start, anyway. Next on the line was the female spook on the right. That one took longer to search, but the result was very interesting, and very sad. But, what was the connection? Discussing this would have to wait, for it was time to get their information to their teammates.

Back in the Hudson Valley, Allen, Melissa and Rachel had taken Marianne up on her offer to sack out in her home, again. Melissa would miss one more day of school and attend the funeral. Gustav's ex-wives were to arrive the next morning and Ryan had said that both of them would attend the reading of the will. Ryan and Ralph opted to 'bach' it at Ryan's apartment. Vanessa and Gustav tagged along with them. Before they parted ways, Marianne had one more question to ask.

"How come the dog? That really has me puzzled. I've heard that animals can sense spirits, but there's something about this dog."

The Family's new trivia resource, Allen, spoke up. "Atlas, according to a buddy of mine in his fan club, can actually see ghosts. It's clairvoyant, if you will. It's owner, Lorriman, keeps it with him everywhere he goes. Lorriman is Atlas's 'home', so when something odd comes near Lorriman,

Atlas acts to protect his home. I've thought that if Atlas could get out and about by itself more often, it might not be so hot to trot with the passing entity. Rumor has it that the two even go to the bathroom together."

Vanessa was still a little upset over her encounter with Atlas. *"That kind of explains a few things. The mutt got testier the closer I got to his owner. Should we be worried? Even if Atlas sniffs me or Gustav out, what can or would they do?"*

Allen continued, since he was the one most familiar with the man/dog team. "Atlas and Lorriman are mainly detectors of spirits. As far as I know, they never did anything to actually get rid of them, or help them move on. I could be wrong. This wasn't a big interest of mine."

Melissa yawned as the limo pulled up to Marianne's home. "Well, his merchandise has found its way into some of my parents' friends' homes. If you have a small dog, their company somehow 'sniffs you out' and gets you on their contact list. Marianne, as to your original question, I guess that this group of people have a ghost sensitive dog along because they suspect maybe we have some ghosts around."

Vanessa was listening closely and thinking hard. How could she short-circuit that pooch? Something told her that this Atlas, despite its diminutive size, was about to shrug.

It was late, but 'Rosie and Lillith's' was an all night café on the western outskirts of Milledgeville. Four patrons had commandeered and joined three tables to accommodate meals, notes and a printer/PC combination. Gwendolyn had been the waitress for those tables and wasn't too happy about having half of her assigned income-producing area being hijacked by one group. They could have been squeezed into a booth, maybe with an extra chair. She had a Doberman, so Atlas and his owner didn't look familiar to her. Gwen whispered to Perry, the busboy, that these people seemed pretty fired up about something, but each time she went to fill their coffee cups, they clammed up. Perry had recognized the correspondent, as he had more time for the tube. He wasn't a single parent with two jobs, just a part time student with one full time job. He told Gwen that he thought they might have something to do with that fiasco at the Edwards Estate. That perked up her interest and gave her a possible wedge for a decent tip. She had heard a lot of comments about that place from her customers over the years (since spouse abandonment forced her into an extra job). With a regular coffee pot in hand (no one at that table had wanted de-caff for the past hour), she went up with the checks and a refill. As usual, the customers quieted when she topped off the cups, though they still seemed friendly enough.

"Say, folks, what do you think of all that whoop-de-do at the Edwards Estate?" All four sets of eyes snapped to attention. Bulls-eye! "Sure was a lot of craziness there and that's a fact. I've heard all kinds of stories about that place over the years. Did anyone tell you about the Bible that turns its own pages?" Five minutes later, Perry noticed that his buddy, Gwen, was sitting with the customers she had earlier groused about. He smiled. That was usually a sign that his friend would be getting a good tip. She could use it, being a single parent.

Everyone had fallen asleep in record time. Gustav and Vanessa listened to Ralph and Ryan making satisfied sleeping sounds.

"My dear lady, you have been looking pensive all afternoon. Might I inquire as to your thoughts?"

"Will you talk normal? Yes, I'm concerned. It's that pooch, Atlas. I'm not worried about myself, or you, for that matter. That group is out to hunt down the reasons for the Edwards blow-up. They're going to be dogging Ryan, pun intended, and everyone else as well. How can we keep up with our mission with that kind of scrutiny? The blasted Estate battle is going to be the war cry for every lunatic in the world who's fascinated with the occult. The footage went international. What do you want to bet that the airlines are getting booked up from every continent to either Georgia or here? It's bad enough that they're all fruitcakes. They're going to be fruitcakes with money to waste and time on their hands."

Gustav thought about it for a while, as Vanessa fumed. "Vanessa, I think you may have a point, there. I hadn't thought of that angle. Look, we've got some excellent resources of our own, both financial and manpower wise. If enough time goes by without any more fanfare, the thing will have to die down. Most of the passing interest will be on the Estate and that cupboard is bare, now. Atlas will have nothing to sniff out. As long as you and I make scarce, Quasimutto will strike out here as well. Ryan will lay low and everyone else will cover for him."

Vanessa sighed, bowing to the logic of the proposal and even grateful that her new 'soul-brother' was talking a little less like a perennial pedantic professor.

Barry Nicholson was lonely. The pack had pretty well disbanded for parts unknown. Hammer was in the slammer; the only friend he had. He knew that the group had put up with him mainly because Hammer had taken him under his wing. His talent for numbers had bought his friend and he a lot of extra time and money. It wasn't really work for Barry. He actually had fun doing all those income tax accounts and Hammer liked him. Barry felt certain of that. An inner child could sense between the lines and Barry's inner child wasn't as submerged as most. Everyone else was gone. No one volunteered to take him along. He had nowhere else to go, so, here he was in one of the recently jammed up motels that now had plenty of room. He'd go visit Hammer at the county lock-up tomorrow.

VII GRAVESITE

Ryan awoke. It was good to be back in his old room, again. Hotels were pleasant places where someone would come in and clean up after you, but nothing replaced home. It had been nice to wake to the smell of coffee and breakfast where you could stay in your house robe and slippers to eat. Well, it was time to rise and shine and hit a local diner. Most of the morning waitresses knew him well at the Texas, the Artemus, Michael's, the Colonial and Dietz's Stadium Diners. Ryan's brow furrowed. He could smell something. It smelled like…

Ryan's partially opened door opened the rest of the way. "Good morning, Boss! Ran out and picked up some grub makings. When was the last time you looked in your fridge? Things were growing in there, fella. Throw on your bunny slippers. I've got bacon, eggs, toast and coffee just about ready."

Ryan squinted at his clock, then at the doorway. There was Ralph, dressed, awake, chipper. Breakfast was ready? He'd get Gustav on the ball about getting Ralph and Marianne together, quickly. "Ralph, I thought you were one of us."

"I adapt to the situation, Boss. When you live on your own and by your wits, well, you learn to take care of yourself. If someone is willing to do that for you, fine. Until then, you do it yourself. Now get moving, we've got a will reading and a funeral to catch."

"Shit," thought Ryan. He'd almost forgotten (most likely on purpose, he admitted to himself). Speaking of which, where was the dearly departed, anyway?

Everyone at Marianne's was fed, up and about. Vanessa had told them she needed their help with training Gustav. Once again, they had all concentrated on imaging him there and happy and, even with the lesser in numbers than the first time they tried it, Gustav appeared from the office right on cue (they had synchronized clocks on the effort). That was a good sign. Vanessa would go back later, when the two 'R's' were up and about to see if only two homing beacons would work. She smiled upon remembering 'baby steps', and how they applied to Annie Edwards.

Rachel, Melissa and Allen were cleaning up dishes, putting the folding couch back together, brushing their teeth, and starting to make arrangements and plans for the day. Marianne had been talking to Vanessa about the funeral, but had to make a restroom visit. It seemed natural for women to take trips to the restroom together, so they both went off to continue the conversation. Melissa was talking to Gustav while she fluffed a few of the throw pillows. Allen spoke to his mother in the kitchen.

"Mom, what are you going to do about Frank? You have to call him sometime."

"I know, Allen. But I don't know what to tell him. Frank isn't a bad man. He's a very good man, he really is. This isn't fair to him at all and I feel lousy about it. But this work that Ryan is doing; it's the kind of thing I've dreamed of all my life. Some people were born to accomplish great things. I believe I was put on this earth to serve others in crisis. My heart says that this is the way being pointed out to me. But, I feel so badly about abandoning the kids and my husband."

For all those years, Allen had relied upon his mother to be his rock. Payback time. "Mom, you've told me that, when there is no good way at a crossroads, you are often better off to do nothing and wait for guidance. Besides, maybe there's room for family and Family. Something else to consider. We both have heard of some world famous people who turned their backs on family, friends and lifetime careers in order to do something they thought was of greater importance."

Rachel had been getting misty eyed, but that last sentence perked her attention. "Oh? Who might they be?"

Allen smiled, hugged his mother and said, "Disciples."

With Allen involved in a private conversation with his mother, Melissa took the opportunity to chat with the Family lawyer. "Gustav, what's it like, being dead?"

One of Gustav's goals in death was to talk more 'Joe Average', but it wasn't easy. *"Melissa, it's kind of like being aware, but numb. You walk, but you don't really feel the floor. You weep, but you can't shed tears. You speak, but you don't breath to do it. It's like a wakeful dream that doesn't end. It's frustrating, not being able to touch someone you care about. I am only now learning the scope of what Vanessa must have gone through. I really want to help the Family now, despite all this. The transport thing that Vanessa does is going to be very important to us. The homing beacon of the Family is a start, but that requires planning and coordination. I don't want to be more of a pain than a help."*

Melissa was young, but she was sharp. Her mind was looking at all she had learned so far and was in brainstorm mode. "OK, let's work on that, if you don' t mind me taking a stab at it." Gustav eagerly nodded encouragement. He was desperate. "Vanessa, from what I've heard, can zap to Ryan anytime, any place, because she's tuned into him. She got tuned into him at that Navy experiment. All of us are now 'tuned in' to each other, aren't we, thanks to the Estate thing? Shouldn't you be able to zip to where she, or any of us are, just by focusing on the person you want to be with? You appear in the clothes you think about by imaging yourself in them. Why not try the same approach by seeing yourself happy and standing in front of, say, Vanessa, with her being happy to see you as well. I picked her since you two are closest in states of being. Be a next step for you, since you've already made progress."

That sounded logical to Gustav. Vanessa had told him something similar, but didn't mention the part about both parties being happy. Maybe that was something she just assumed he would naturally know to do. He closed his eyes, sort of. If necessary, he could see with his eyes open or shut. His spirit interpreted this action as closing his awareness of the immediate surrounding area in order to focus elsewhere. Gustav pictured himself smiling and happy, standing in front of Vanessa, who was smiling back at him. He opened his eyes and, to his great joy, there was Vanessa looking right at him. But, his image didn't match the reality and that was the pebble that started the avalanche. She wasn't smiling. She looked...alarmed?

It was only then that Melissa realized where Vanessa had disappeared. At the same time she was saying, "Oh, no...", all hell was just breaking loose behind the bathroom door. "AAAAAAHHHHHHH! GUSTAV! GET OUT OF HERE!!!" Gustav heard the scream behind him. Marianne was still on the john and very upset about having a gentleman caller at this particular time. Gustav instinctively did a one-eighty to face the source of the turmoil and saw nothing at eye level. Peripheral vision showed a likely source lower down. Shifting his gaze in that direction made manifest his faux pas and gave him all the evidence he needed to know what room he had transported to. His turning around only made things worse. Now Vanessa added to the upsetting female reactions, once again from behind him, further adding to his turmoil and confusion.

"Gustav! What are you just standing there for? Get OUT of here, Godammit!" This was most upsetting for the poor man and he leaped for the door. Not thinking clearly, he realized that the door was closed and would crash into it. He tried to stop, forgetting that he would normally pass through the door in his new state of being. Gustav was halfway through the door when his efforts at braking proved successful. Unfortunately.

Melissa was looking at the bathroom door. She saw what happened and, though she didn't understand the gravity of the situation, realized that it was time to call for help. "ALLEN, RACHEL, GET IN HERE, QUICKLY!"

Ryan and Ralph had finished their breakfast, with Ryan fully decided that his dining partner for the morning had little of the charm of any of his waitress buddies. It could be worse, though. Ralph was good company, in a non-feminine sort of way, and was even scraping their dishes when the phone rang. "You mind, Boss? I'm closer."

He might as well get used to it. Ryan was going to have to make himself scarcer to the general public. He knew the main body of hounds would be coming before too long. Several had already tried and had been fended off, for the time being. "Go for it, Ralph."

Ralph picked up the phone; Ryan watched and listened. Very few people had his number, but not all of them were Family. All that work on the Edwards event had him in contact with a select group outside Hawthorn Enterprises. Ralph's face immediately caught Ryan's interest. Each change in expression only amplified that interest. A 'You're shitting me!' put it over the edge. "Ralph, what the hell's going on?"

Ralph hung up the phone with an incredulous look on his face. "Get dressed, right now. We have to get to Marianne's. Gustav is stuck in the bathroom door. Screw the limo, we'll take the Green Machine." Ralph stopped at the front door, his hand still on the handle, and turned. "Ryan, does this sort of thing happen often?"

The only answer he received was, "The bathroom door?"

It would take Ryan and Ralph about fifteen minutes to get there, even making the lights and avoiding creeping Cadillacs. During that time, Melissa, Rachel, Marianne, Vanessa and Allen were doing their best to be supportive, serious and not break out with the post-fright tension-release giggles. Gustav had his hands and arms free in front of the door (they had been brought forward to ward off impact with the door) and his left leg free behind the door. The mid-body and right leg were stuck *in* the door. Helpful suggestions were dying before they were finished. Gustav, arms folded, listened to 'What if we..., Suppose we try..., *How did you*..., Maybe if...' Not one thought could be completed. No one had a clue as to what to do, much less on how to do it

Even though Ryan had screwed his courage to the max, he was unequal to the task. On walking into Marianne's home, he took one look as Gustav folded his arms and executed a perfect Mr. Spock single eyebrow raise, and Ryan blasted out laughing. That spark ignited the fire as poor Gustav had to suffer the slings and arrows of one very outrageous fortune, which is what he fully expected and didn't really mind all that much. It was the Fitzgalen Family formula for stress release and it encouraged creative thought. At the moment, he was ready to sing Dixie in a tutu, if it meant getting out of that damned door.

Wiping his eyes, Ryan asked for a complete rundown of what happened. That done, to Marianne's complete embarrassment, Ryan sat down to think. The expected cup of black java appeared in his hand as he extended it. His eyes began to dart, his thumb and first finger of his free hand began to stroke his lower lip. "Gustav, you were pretty upset when this happened. Tell me exactly what you were feeling."

"How the hell do you think I was feeling? I embarrassed poor Marianne in the worst way, she was screaming at me, Vanessa started screaming at me, too, and all I wanted to do was get out. Even forgot I was dead and tried to stop myself from bashing into the door, and, and... Hmmm."

Ryan was nodding. "I think we may have the key here to what

happened, but it may not answer what to do about it. When Vanessa wants to pick up something, she has to focus hard on that task. Gustav was hard focused on the task of getting out of the bathroom. So far, in getting Gustav to appear somewhere the easiest way, we've been using the incentive of happy emotions as part of the homing beacon. In the past, energies released by Annie and Vanessa, had negative and positive emotional overtones to them, respectively, and the difference there made for differences in the aspects of the energies they commanded. On Annie's part, it was a combination of hatred, revenge and even a twisted form of love for her children that created an aggressive and destructive energy. Vanessa fought with love for the real Annie, for Jason and Rebecca and for all of us, creating an energy that was just as powerful, but purely defensive. Gustav's emotional state, and therefore his energy, was chaotic, disruptive and his task was prematurely aborted when he tried to stop smacking into the bathroom door. Now, whatever circuit you used to protect yourself from bashing into that door, even though you would have gone through it had you been in a calmer state of mind, is stuck in a loop. Loops are common with entities, but I've never seen one do this before. I'm not sure what to try."

Ralph scratched the stubble he didn't have time to get rid of that morning. "I wonder. If it was being upset that got him stuck him there, maybe the opposite will get him out of it. Opposites cancel, like fire and water. Look, how about we all go to the other end of the room and do what we did that first night he showed up at the Marriott. You know, 'happy, happy, joy, joy'?"

The others looked at each other, and agreed that it was worth a shot. Nothing else was happening in the suggestion box. The seven walked twenty feet to the other end of the room. Gustav did his best to clear his mind of any upsetting thought. Ryan said, "OK, everyone, on the count of three. One. Two. Three."

All eyes closed and Gustav could feel the warmth radiate from that corner of the room. He tuned into it, closing his own eyes. When everyone opened their eyes, there was Gustav among them...on one foot. Marianne looked back to where the problem had been. "Oh, crap! Look!" Everyone did, though to do it, Gustav had to hobble. Something wasn't right. He could see the reason why. Most of the bathroom door was there. Missing, as if someone took a laser cutter to the door, were perfect holes marking where Gustav had been merged with the wood. Marianne was almost in tears. "Oh, Gustav, I'm so sorry. I'm the one that got you into this mess!"

Melissa was already in tears. "No, it was ME who forgot where Vanessa had gone to when I told Gustav to go to her." There was an actual argument brewing between the two women as to who was more at fault. Everyone, including Gustav, tried to calm the self-recriminations, while trying to balance on one leg. Melissa was gradually reassured, but Marianne was gearing up, saying to herself, "...and I'm the one who's going to get you out of it, by God!"

Happy thoughts didn't get her surrogate daddy stuck in that door. It was his being upset over her being upset with him. Her Sicilian blood was boiling mad right now, mostly mad at herself and the predicament her actions had initiated. Fighting fire with water be damned! Fighting fire with fire was what she resolved to do. While Gustav stood there on his left foot, bent over where the door was bonded to his being and feeling like a lawn decoration, Marianne excused herself to the kitchen for a moment. The rest were left behind, as before, scratching various parts of their craniums and trying to come up with something practical to solve the conundrum. Rachel thought they might set fire to the door segments still bonded with Gustav and let it burn out of him, but Allen thought that it might harm Gustav because he was now bonded to the material and, besides, at best Gustav would be a walking streak of soot to anyone who might look his direction. Ralph was about to suggest they employ a few hundred out of work termites to tackle the giant splinter when Gustav and his beloved Family heard Marianne screech for the second time that morning. Once their ears stopped ringing…

"I can't STAND it any more! I'M responsible for this! I don't deserve to LIVE!" To the collective horror of the seven, Marianne stood at the entrance of the kitchen, red fluid dripping down from the wrist of the hand that held a knife poised over the other. There was a collective cry of anguish as all seven raced to their Marianne, who had obviously slipped a cog, big time. Vanessa and Gustav, though, were able to arrive there far faster than the rest. In an instant, both were at her side. Gustav struck at the horrid and hated knife with all his might, using the same roundhouse that had once decked a marine in one shot. The implement went flying and imbedded an inch and a half into the kitchen ceiling. In those few moments, the rest arrived. Ryan and Rachel each were able to grab her wrists, Ryan applying pressure to stop the hemorrhage. It was all so sudden, so nightmarish. Marianne simply stood there with a smug, self-satisfied smile on her face. Was she insane?

Not one of the newer members had heard Ryan curse before. Not one of the older members had heard it this intensely. He had never come this close to losing someone he loved so deeply so tragically, other than Allen, oh yes, and Gustav. But in the one case, he wasn't directly present at the time. In the other, he had just concluded his visit to Armageddon and Gustav was still there in spirit after his body flew over the Edwards' railing. This had the shock of immediacy, surprise, and presence. "Marianne, what the FUCK are you doing? GODAMMIT, bitch! For CHRIST's SAKE!"

Marianne loved them all and regretted the anguish that what she had to do had caused, even before she did it. It was a gamble, but… "My one and only Gustav, you came to my aid, without a beacon. It worked. Please, everyone, forgive me. It was the only way." Surreal took over again. What was Marianne babbling about?

Ralph, the people analyzer, the one who had fallen hook, line and fishing pole for the lady, was the first to catch on. He looked back and smiled. Ralph walked away from the incredulous others, Ryan still holding Marianne's wrist and getting ready to call for emergency medical assistance. Ralph bent over, then turned around and called out, "Marianne, you are a freaking *genius!*" The others turned around to see what looked to be two wooden cutouts of some kind. The light began to dawn. Ryan held up the wrist he had grasped and looked at it, then sniffed.

"Ketchup! You little witch!" Relief and admiration rushed in to replace the fear and turmoil in Ryan's heart as he embraced the other woman in his life. No one knew whether to laugh or cry, so they alternated between the two.

Gustav beamed. "Daughter figure, you got brass ones."

The Task Team had breakfast at the same diner where they had a late dinner the night before. One got on her SatCom and made reservations at the airport. Another used his device to call a cab company, who was accommodating despite the very recent loss of one of their best drivers. The airport call took a little longer, as the man tried unsuccessfully to explain their requirements in Chihuahua transport to a rule bound employee. Zachary's second call to the Governor's office took care of that problem. A final call to the Mayor's office was made, asking for a minor duplicity. The caller made note of the Mayor's unexpected delight in compliance.

The funeral service was held at the Hurley Reformed Church, just outside of Kingston. The structure dated back to colonial times (1801) and was a favorite of Gustav's. The eulogy was delivered to an almost full church; business associates, the Fitzgalen Family, a baker's dozen of waitresses, six diner and seven restaurant owners, a score of previous clients, close church members, the Kingston Limo CEO plus four of his full time drivers, Roscoe from Pavelli's, Mr. and Mrs. Pavelli and Gustav's former wives. The latter two had sat together (but not too close together), removed from the rest. You could sense the hard feelings from the one, but mixed feelings from the other. Most of the Family suspected that the two were mainly there for the reading of the will. The media and the general public that showed up were respectfully turned away at the door. It had been made clear that general admission was valid only at the viewing and the interment.

Reverend Hoppenfeld was personable, honest, and truly sad to have to say goodbye to his long time friend. "There is an old term found in Christian churches of all denominations: 'Kekkers'. It stands for so many whose participation with the church was limited to twice a year; it stands for 'Christmas and Easter Christians'. I've known Gustav Mendelssohn for nineteen years. Despite his personal obligations in many endeavors, he attended services far more Sundays than he missed. Yet, even when he didn't attend, he made sure to keep his weekly support of this church current. That says something about the man."

Ralph noticed the bitter woman lean over to the melancholy one. Whatever the one that leaned over had said, the other didn't seem very pleased to hear it. Moments later, he saw the second lady scoot a couple of inches further away from the first.

"Money has been a necessary evil, even when our Lord walked the earth. Yet, even He spoke of its positive use and symbolism when He told the tale of the poor woman who gave despite her great poverty as being far more to the Father's liking than the wealthy that gave a pittance of their surplus. Gustav gave generously; yet, financial support is not where it ends, my friends. God gave each of you talents to express yourselves, to earn a living for your family, to set yourself apart as a unique and gifted individual. Gustav Mendelssohn was a lawyer, and a good one. Whenever there was a legal issue this church had to face, my friend Gustav was there to donate his time and considerable energies on our behalf. When it involved a member of this church, he insisted on remaining anonymous, but still lent his expertise and never asked for recompense. That, too, says something about the man."

Marianne was sitting next to Ralph and noticed his attention drawn to the former wives. Another whisper, another displeased reaction, another scoot. She shared a look with Ralph and both shrugged. Ralph wondered what that one was saying to the other. The first one was the ex who had given birth to the son that had died. Was that why she was so sour?

"My friend Gustav and I have had many quiet chats. He had such unique and refreshing attitudes on what life was all about, and what death was all about. Through him, I came to accept that an honest and honorable death is not a punishment, but a reward. It is the next step we take on our journey to the Father who loves us, who guides us, who keeps for us a home in His Kingdom. There is joy in my heart that my very good friend has received a well-deserved rest and reward." Very few heard the 'humph' from the choir loft. "And so we bid goodbye to a good man who was full of years and whose years were full. Let us follow the example of a truly spiritual man who did much but said very little about it. That is the sign and seal of a true Christian, one who lives a life to shine as a candle in the dark valley. A candle in the dark makes no noise, but rather draws others to it by shining from within and sharing the warmth that the creator endowed it with. Now, if you would turn in your hymnals to page two hundred and sixty nine…"

Allen had been thumbing through the hymnal during the service, quietly. When the page was announced, he turned to the indicated final hymn. He looked at the left upper corner of the piece and noted the suspected year of hymn authorship being 1895. He smiled. Other than the occasional 'Negro spiritual', it was one of the newest works he had been able to find in the whole book. "Practically top 40," he thought. It was a good thing that Gustav and Melissa were up in the choir loft. That kept them out of direct sight of the sighted. God knew what sort of stunt the man might pull at his own funeral. It was bad enough when one of Gustav's less than beloved colleagues attended the wake, shmoozing up to Allen's whole group in an obvious attempt to worm his way into Gustav's old job. At the casket, said lawyer knelt in prayerful respect. Yeah, right. Gustav had waited for that moment, for he then reached across to his own dead hand (that had to be weird) and extended his right middle finger. The poor guy hollered himself hoarse. As Gustav quickly tucked the finger back, the colleague looked in terror at Gustav's dead face, only to see the corners of the mouth turn, slightly, up. Allen wondered if it was inappropriate to engage in funeral frivolity when it was your own shindig. He hoped not. Allen had every intention of pulling a few stunts of his own, God willing, when his time came.

When the final hymn had been sung and Reverend Hoppenfeld had delivered the benediction, the mourners began to file out. Martha Scholldorf Mendelssohn was the first to leave, practically strong-arming her way through the others. Valerie Knudson Mendelssohn filed out gently with the others, misty eyed, feeling as melancholy as she looked.

As the funeral procession proceeded across the Hudson River to the Rhinebeck Cemetery, the hearse led the long line of cars. The relative privacy of the church ceremony didn't deter other well-wishers or the morbidly curious from the final step in Gustav's public farewell. Ralph and Marianne drew the third slot in line and were in the Green Machine. Gustav, Vanessa, Allen, Ryan, Melissa and Rachel were lined up second behind the hearse in a stretch donated by Kingston Limo. Gustav had been one of their most cherished customers. Behind them was a line a quarter of a mile long.

"*You have to hand it to Marianne, Gustav. That stunt she pulled to get you 'unadoored' is one for the books. You raised one smart cookie.*"

"*I didn't need to raise her, dear lady. She came with all the raw ingredients. All I did was refine the mixture a bit. But I'm glad I never had to face her in court. She would have been formidable. Vanessa, that young lady means a lot to me. She's helped fill an emptiness in my life that's been there ever since my son passed away. I'm really happy she's found Ralph. He's a fine addition to the Family.*"

Ryan nodded. "We owe that pretty much to you, old friend. With Ralph, you spotted, scouted, baited and hooked him. You and Marianne are a complementing team. Marianne is headstrong, quick to take actions that are akin to swatting a fly with a Buick. You, however, were always more the subtle and circumspect one, like a patient spider. Both of you got the fly in the end in your own impressive ways. Now, Gustav, might we count on your continued circumspection with your behavior at the interment? I really don't feel like clowning around at this one. There are just too many locals we live among here that will be attending with us and all too many of them probably think we're Martians. Besides that, Mayor LaRoche said she would be sending a representative to the interment."

"Not a problem, Ryan. It never crossed my mind. I'm 'Gustav the Angelic', now, or haven't you noticed?" The company breathed a collective sigh of relief at that. "So, Ryan, who'd the old battle-ax send?"

"Not sure. Maybe that goofy aide of hers."

The procession had pulled into the cemetery entrance off Rt. 9, a quarter mile south of the corner where the Beekman Arms was located. Rachel had suggested the Arms as a quiet spot to gather after the funeral. She then asked if it was all right with Gustav, who wouldn't be able to partake as he did the last time. He was touched at her consideration and assured her that it would be fine. *"Besides, some things haven't changed. I can look at the waitresses and still not be able to do more than that."*

There was a soft group laugh, when Vanessa spoke up. *"Oh, no!"*

Ryan turned to see the expression on Vanessa's face. "Sweetheart, what is it? You look like you've seen a…wait, that can't be right."

Pointing to where there were people waiting near graveside, Vanessa stammered, *"It's HIM. I mean it's THEM, IT, I mean. LOOK!"*

Down the sweeping turn, with stones and sepulchers everywhere, they could see that a knot of people had already begun to gather ahead of the processional crowd. A little separated from the rest was a group of four people, two men, two women, and one, little, dog? Ryan took command by knee jerk. "Gustav, Vanessa, you two, bail. I'll wander back and check on you later. The guy might bring the mutt over to the limo, go NOW!" Vanessa and Gustav dove through the limo door. Ralph and Marianne were driving in the Green Machine right behind and were quite surprised to see the sudden exit. Why would Ryan and company boot the shades? Marianne spotted the reason, confirmed by the 'line of sight' SatCom transmission received a few moments later from Ryan.

Ralph parked behind the limo, looked at the enemy and said, "That's Atlas? That's the 'Hound from Hell' that had Vanessa in frenzy?" Ralph might have gone on for a few more lines, but he saw his lady's left eyebrow begin to lower as she took on a definite glower. "Oops."

"Mr. Kithcart, Vanessa is someone you don't put down if you want to be friends with me. I think this past weekend is proof enough of that woman's courage. Now, I still have that shallow dish of warm water and it won't work anymore on Gustav. You, however, still have a pulse and are fair game. Do I make myself clear?"

"Shutting up now, ma'am."

"Good. You can get something else straight. I love you. That doesn't mean I have to always like you, just most of the time. Don't get nervous, Ralph, that's just the way I am. You can make it up to me, later." The lowered brow changed into a wink and she got out of the Green Machine. Ralph said a one-line prayer to the patron saint of those who are in love with aliens and opened his own door. Halfway to the gathering point, Marianne's arm in his, he stopped.

"You love me?"

Sgt. Nunzia D'Palermo had been mixed on bringing the dog along. Like so many other military tactics, it was a two edged sword. Here was a clear signal to the incoming targets that advertised their presence from a distance, but it was also an early warning system for spirits who had already demonstrated to her an unparalleled capacity for camouflage. For that matter, she was a little mixed on arriving with the full Task Team to the funeral. The counterbalance was that she wanted everyone there to gather all the observations they could get their hands on. Ostensibly, they were there as the Mayor's personal representatives. Her Honor just, somehow, neglected to inform the Hawthorn group as to how many were in the contingent. It was tacky, but those who played strictly by the rules seldom won the war.

For her, the whole ghost thing's validity had been gradually gelling as 'more probable' with each passing discovery. The evidence had been piling up and standing here in this graveyard was putting the whole thing into a very real and present likelihood. Her senses were on full alert. "There they are. That hack must be pretty attached to his cab to bring it up here. Thought he would have sold it."

Sgt. Paul Wasserman hadn't slept well the night before. His was the visible world and this foray into the paranormal was not setting well with him. He also was out of his beloved South and walking among Yankees. People up here talked faster and funny. They talked like…tourists. "Hacks and their cabs become common law couples after three years. It's in their contract, I think." Moments later, Paul was at a loss to explain what seemed like an inappropriate time for the Hawthorn office manager and their cab driver to smooch. It didn't last long, but it sure didn't seem an embrace of funeral conciliation.

Dagmar Yaddow studied the scene with a practiced eye. The hearse had parked strategically to keep the carrying distance down to a minimum, with most of that distance being a mild downward slope. That minimized the odds of a stumble for pallbearers, not to mention the chances of a hernia or pulled shoulder. Caskets were not light, though new water and airtight lighter materials reduced visits by the departed's bereaved bearers to their respective chiropractors. She also recalled that it had been made clear that no photography of any kind would be allowed at gravesite. Why? It wasn't something people normally did, taking pictures at a burial, but some of the more morbid types might. A point was made not to have that happen here. Was Ryan paranoid of having pictures taken of him? A little late for that, given the stills she had from the Edwards Estate video. Maybe it was because they didn't want the magic of film to capture a shot of that wispy warrior woman and her legal beagle sidekick. Kind of late for that, too. There was the Reverend, talking to the Hawthorn group. She thought, "Wait a minute. There are six of them. Are they the pallbearers? Three are women, but they looked strong enough." Dagmar squinted. All the women were wearing flats. "Yep, they're going to be the bearers." That seemed so sweet, and it made it impossible for her to look at them as 'the targets' anymore. Aloud, "Looks like Hawthorn and company are going to be the bearers. Any sniff from Atlas?"

Zachary Lorriman didn't go in much for funerals, though he was about to open a line of Atlas, Inc. dog caskets built into the shape of doghouses. He had mixed feelings about getting involved with that aspect of canine care, given his feelings about Atlas, but the profit margin was incredible and the potential for repeat business due to the relatively shorter life spans of canines made the venture irresistible. He wondered about Hawthorn Enterprises and whether they might like to diversify by buying out his business interests, plus a generous stock option and consulting fees. He was spending too much time with the nuts and bolts of maintaining a hobby that mushroomed into a gold mine. He had learned the hard way that gold miners worked damn hard for their money. "Nothing nearby. He's got a passing interest in that older section of the cemetery over there. After the funeral, I might take a walk in that direction." He indicated a knoll where there were some very old looking stones and monuments. Even from this distance, you could tell that there was significant weathering on many of the granite stones.

Vanessa and Gustav kept behind two high, aged, granite monuments. It was a family plot for the Elmendorf's that represented four generations. Stuck there for safety from detection, there wasn't too much for them to do. Though Vanessa had known Gustav for decades, they had never been able to have an actual two-way conversation before last weekend. It felt good to be able to talk together and so they passed the time as the words of Reverend Hoppenfeld carried over the sound of the chill breeze.

"Well, old friend, looks like you were late for your own funeral."

"Funny lady. Do you have any idea the sort of fun I could be having down there now if it wasn't for that yap dog? Will you look at that crowd? Half of them hardly said 'boo' to me when I was alive. I could be down there right now and give them a 'boo' they'd not soon forget. Ah, well. I'm dead now. Maybe it's time I grew up." He looked around. *"Pretty old section, here."*

Vanessa was looking down to the open grave. Their friends were slowly walking the casket to the bier. It seemed sad, but she was so proud of them. An odd thought occurred to her. *"Hey, you know a lot of off beat things. Why are graves six feet deep?"*

"Is this another joke?" Vanessa assured him she was serious, for once. *"Hmmm. You know, I'm not exactly sure. People used to have head and footstones to symbolize the head and foot of a bed. It was easier for the bereaved to think of them as 'just asleep' that way. Over the ages, we dropped the footstone for some reason. We bury people out of respect for their bodies, not wanting them to be violated by carnivores. It's*

kind of dumb, when you think of it. Were it up to me, I'd rather a faithful Fido get a nibble of my shanks than to be infested with worms. Anyway, you need to get the body deep enough to avoid that happenstance."

"Gustav, when was the last time you heard of any animal digging anything up that was more than two feet under? I get the feeling that the 'six' figure has more meaning than that."

When Gustav had no direct answer, he went into trivia dump mode. He was often able to drop an info byte that someone else might be able to pick up and expand upon. "I recall that, before there was much by way of autopsies, people would sometimes be buried alive when they were, say, catatonic. That came to awareness, I suppose, when a disinterred body would be in a casket with nail scratches on the inside. It is my understanding that, long ago, graves got recycled after a certain amount of time had passed and the bones of the long dead were sent to 'the bone house' in order to free up ground space for the more newly departed. I read somewhere that about one out of thirty or so caskets had evidence of efforts to escape." Dead or not, that gave Vanessa the shivers. "In response, a bell would be set up over a new grave with a string that went down into the casket and be tied to the occupant's hand. If a person should waken, they need only move their hand and the bell would sound. People would listen for it during the night, as well as guard the cemetery from grave robbers. That's where we got the term 'graveyard shift'. If, after a funeral, you saw someone that was a doppelganger for the dearly departed, it just might be that person resurrected from the grave. He or she would be a 'dead ringer'. It used to present some pretty interesting arguments in courts, as said dearly departed tried to get back from heirs their inheritances."

It was all very interesting, but it never did answer the original question. Vanessa sighed a whispered, *"Well, that's Gustav."* The casket had been laid on the cradle and was fully lowered into the grave. It looked like the Rev had said his last rites, or whatever it was they said at times like this. People were filing by the grave, each dropping a handful (or, for the more fastidious, a trowel full) of dirt. You could hear the dull sound of dirt clods on wood with each contribution. There are sounds that have great sadness and thought provoking solitude to them, such as the sound a rope would make in the middle of the night as the wind slapped it against a flagpole, or the hum of a lone streetlight on a dark road, back when they hummed, that is. Yet, few had the power for sad contemplation offered by dirt falling six feet and striking a wood (laminate) coffin.

People started going back to their cars. The discretely placed backhoe was waiting for everyone to leave before finishing the job of interment, though with this many attendees, its job would entail less effort than usual. Gustav's mind wandered back to Vanessa's original question. *"You may have a point on the animals and how far they could dig, my dear. Perhaps the six-foot figure was more designed to foil the two-footed kind of beast. People were shorter back then, and…"*

Gustav tried to shift his position to look around the cemetery again, but couldn't move his left leg. That didn't make sense to him. He had been freed from the bathroom door. Why was he stuck again? He turned to say something to Vanessa, only to see her looking down with terror on her face. That wasn't right. What does a ghost have to be afraid of? He looked down to see for himself what it was that she was staring so intently at. Each of them was being held fast to the ground by, to all appearances, what seemed to be a pair of hands coming out of the ground. This was seriously pushing his envelope. Gustav shook his head. *"Vanessa, this just doesn't seem to be my day."*

The funeral crowd was disbursing while the Fitzgalen Family was gathered together in the chill wind. An elderly woman walked gently up to them and introduced herself. "Excuse me, I'm Valerie Mendelssohn. I wanted to thank you all for giving Gustav such a nice funeral. He really was a good man, wasn't he?"

Ryan was silently elected to respond for the group. "I'm glad to finally meet you, Ms. Mendelssohn. Gustav's the best friend I ever had and he is going to be sorely missed by more than just us." Allen thought about that last line and realized that it was a very kind yet elegant misdirection.

The elderly and kind faced woman asked, "Could you possibly tell me, please, how he passed away? I saw the television coverage of that horrid mess down in Georgia, but the screen didn't show what happened to Gustav…but you were there. If I'm intruding, then please just say so."

Marianne was back in her management mode. She could see the glance Ryan gave to the old section of the cemetery and she took a split second to see that the 'enemy' was starting to move towards the parked cars. No problem there, so far, yet. Her jumping in with both feet and taking Valerie's arm and talking like they were old friends surprised everyone except Ryan. He was used to Marianne being an invaluable mind reader. "Why, Ms. Mendelssohn, you and I just have to meet." She began gently peeling the woman away from the main group with smiles and animated conversation. "Gustav was like a father to me." There was only one line of cars on the single lane road, albeit a long one. One of them had to be her transportation. Probably one of the cabs. "Do you think you'll be here long enough…" Marianne's voice faded as the pair walked off.

The others caught on when Ryan smiled and said, "Just like Ralph did to that Guardswoman. I don't pay her enough. Shall we all take a stroll to the haunted section?"

The 'gang of four' had been keeping a weather eye on the targets. Duly noted was the elderly woman who paired off with the paralegal, followed by the rest of the target group taking a leisurely pace to the section that Atlas had given a passing interest to earlier. They continued to walk to the rental car and got in. It was chilly and the car offered warmth as well as a shielded vantage point to watch what might happen. Atlas was watching, too, with a soft growl and the fur on his back just starting to stand up. No one said a word and blinks were infrequent. The window tint was set at just dark enough so that those outside wouldn't be sure if the occupants of the car were watching them. The number of cars jockeying to leave the cemetery should buy them some protection from Hawthorn scrutiny for a while. It was perfect. Or so they thought.

Ryan and company could see Gustav and Vanessa looking back at them. They also could tell that something wasn't right. The two spirits looked more troubled than old Jacob Marley of Charles Dickens' fame; more upset than they should be with the ghost hunters now safely in their car. They were about fifteen feet away when Vanessa mouthed Ryan's name. No sound came to their ears. That struck Rachel as oddly similar to a cat she used to have that would issue the occasional silent meow. Gustav broke that silence by calmly saying, *"I regret to report that we have ascertained yet another complication to the day's activities."* Only the full return of his old style of speech pattern pointed to the fact that he, too, was shaken. Gustav pointed to the ground, now that the Family was gathered around and all eyes followed down. Ryan admonished himself to remain calm.

"Well, people, it looks like we'll be getting back to work earlier than anticipated. Thank you, Gustav and Vanessa, for digging up a new customer. Would you introduce us…oh, everyone? Can you see the two hands coming up from the grave and holding our two entities hostage?"

Allen said, "No problem, Boss, but Melissa fainted." Everyone looked at her limp form now being fully supported by Allen. "Is this some sort of Family initiation rite, having to pass out from terror?"

Rachel came to Allen's aid and helped keep Melissa upright. From a distance, it would look like the group was consoling each other in grief. All the better. "It would seem so, Honey. Ryan, I thought things would calm down after the weekend. Do we get overtime for this?"

It hadn't taken too long for the new members to learn that keeping a light conversation was essential in this sort of business. Hysteria was a very real danger, especially with the Fitzgalen Family's stock in trade. Vanessa was regrouping her wits, but Ralph's bladder needed attention real soon. Melissa moaned, opened her eyes, looked, groaned and went back to the comfort unconsciousness offered. Graves where hands could grab your ankles was just too much like a nightmare for her. Allen looked at Ralph. "He's the only one who's always stayed on his feet and conscious. Ralph, what's your secret for not fainting?"

"You wouldn't believe what I've seen as a cabbie, kid, though I'll admit that this is top ten on my 'weird' list. Ryan, what do we do now?"

"Have either of you tried to speak to the entity that has grabbed your attention by way of your ankles?" Both ghosts shook their heads, chagrined. "Well then, I'm going to pray." Ryan got down on his knees and it seemed to the haunter hunters that the group was offering an intercession. It was interesting to them that it was the man with no last name leading the effort. Ryan directed his comments to the hands and whoever owned them. "Hello, there. I'm Ryan Fitzgalen. Can you, who have reached up to us, hear me?"

From the cold ground came a muffled response. It was not because there was dirt between them and the speaker. Spirit speaking didn't work like that. It was more from the lack of practice on the part of the speaker of being addressed or responding. *"I, ammmm, whooo? Elmmmmennnndooorff..."*

The hands appeared rough and masculine. A worker's hands. Ryan glanced at the monuments. There were names of quite a few people of that family in the plot. The hands didn't appear too aged, so Ryan did some quick calculations on the birth/death spans on the male Elmendorf family members. Ah-hah. "I can hear you. Are you Bernhardt Elmendorf?"

Silence for half a minute, then, *"Yessss. Mmmyyy naaaame. Bernnnharrrdt. Yesss. Yess. Yes."* Allen thought that practice made perfect. Melissa had awakened and made a strong conscious effort not to look down. She heard the voice from the grave, then went back to sleep again. Rachel wasn't used to this sort of load. All the babes she had ever carried in the past wore diapers.

"Ralph, Melissa is getting a little heavy for me. My shoulder is a bit sore from helping with the casket. Would you mind lending a hand?"

The Hawthorn hunters in the car saw that the extremely bereaved and three sheets to the wind young woman had been shifted to the cabbie and CEO for support. The men thought it might be a fun group to be in. The women thought it was gallant.

Vanessa turned to Gustav. *"Another German. You know, you guys can be a real pain."*

"Oh, really? And I suppose 'Vanessa Blankenship' is a nice Jewish name?"

The last thing Ryan needed was to let the two magpies have free rein. "Can it, you two. Bernhardt, we're your friends. We'd like to help you out. What is it that you would like us to do for you?"

"I want...to see...sky and, birds, the sun, my family, my farm. I'm lonely. So long. Where is (ten second delay), *my family?"*

Marianne had walked up just then, having made an after dinner date with Valerie. "For Heaven's sake, don't we get a break once in a while? If you have to play with the ghosts, Ryan, couldn't we go find some down in the Bahamas? Whose hands are those?"

The newbies took due note, again, that the veteran members of the Family weren't fazed by much. Ryan glanced to the sky in his usual 'Why me' expression. "Later, kid. Bernhardt, you are going to have to listen to me very carefully if I am going to help you. All of your questions will be answered, if you will just be patient and cooperative. First of all, will you please let go of the two ankles you have grasped?"

"Nooooo. Youu might leave meee. Iii amm afraid."

"Alright, that's fine." Gustav and Vanessa shot a look at Ryan that clearly stated 'What do you mean, fine?' "When you can see the sun again, though, will you let go then?"

Moments passed. The Task Team members were beginning to wonder about the gathering. Perhaps they were reorganizing their business matters, or lives, or something. *"Yeessss."*

Ryan passed his hand through Bernhardt's hands. No touchee, no feelee. "Rats," he thought. "Bernhardt, we are going to try something. Relax as much as you can. Everyone, happy, happy, joy, joy aimed at the owner of those hands. Vanessa and Gustav, lift your legs together. Now." Some progress was made. They were able to lift about four inches. "Hmmm. OK, folks, softly now. I want to hear the first verse of Amazing Grace." It seemed that music did have powers and that particular ditty had been around for a long time. Surely the good Mr. Elmendorf had heard it during his lifetime. It bought them another few inches.

Nunzia could hear the song through the cracked open windows. Wasn't that touching, she thought? This group must have been very close to spend all this time and effort on behalf of their fallen comrade and she began to feel badly about how she had previously judged these people as being cold. It reminded her of Corporal Charlotte Riley. They had gone through training together. It was at a chopper deployment training exercise and Charlotte was the last one out. The pilot had absolutely no warning of the appendix that burst. The spasm of pain he went through twisted the chopper's collective and the blades tore through Nunzia's best friend. Nunzia had seen it first hand. So had Paul.

Charlotte had been a rock for everyone else. Nothing seemed to faze her and you could have brought any problem and placed it right on her shoulders. None of her training squad had ever forgotten that friend and comrade in arms. Yet, why was the Hawthorn group offering intercessions for their own fallen comrade so far away from his grave? The crowds had dispersed. There was no one at gravesite. Why was it that the pieces from Hawthorn puzzles never seemed to fit right?

Gustav and Vanessa couldn't go any further. It wasn't a question of leverage. The problem was resistance. Ryan wasn't surprised. "Bernhardt, you are making progress, though you may not be able to feel it yet. Hang on just like you've been doing. We won't leave you. Tell me, what is the last thing you remember?"

Melissa had awakened with the music and steeled herself. She felt humiliated at having set the 'Fitzgalen Family all-time-high' for passing out and wasn't about to set her sights on the Guinness Book of Records. *"Can't moove. Frozenn. Can hear, can't speak. Cryinggg. Family. Darknesss. Silence. Timmmme."*

Marianne had heard this sort of thing second-hand before. That had been bad enough. Hearing it from the horse's mouth notched it up a few levels. Her eyes were beginning to mist. She was just about to blame it on her 'Sicilian emotional gene' when she noticed that the others had passed that point already and were scrambling for tissues.

"Jeeze, I guess they were really close," said Zachary. "That Ryan must be doing a real tear jerker of a prayer. Maybe he used to be a preacher?"

Dagmar continued the thought. "Preachers hear a lot of confessions. Maybe he heard one that the confessor regretted letting out of the bag?"

Nunzia thought that it was a possibility, but the internal nagging continued. It was that same feeling she had back at the Marriott in Milledgeville in the Hawthorn suite. It looked right, what Zachary said had sounded right, but it didn't feel right. What were they missing? Why was Atlas still growling? What was Ryan really saying?

"Bernhardt, it's going to be hard for you to accept what I am about to say, but you have to if you are ever going to see the sky and birds again. You had a sickness and were paralyzed. Your family thought you were dead. They buried you. You woke up in your casket, but couldn't get out. Eventually, you died from suffocation. You can't see above the ground because you are six feet underground (Vanessa and Gustav snapped a quick glance at each other) and we are trying to pull your spirit up from your grave. What you have ahold of are ankles. You are reaching above your head and holding onto ankles of those above ground. Can you understand me? Can you let go of your past? You have friends up here that want to see you. It's time to let go of the earth, farmer. The sky awaits."

No sound came from out of the grave. Nothing changed for a full minute, then for two. It was slow, but there was a slight progress in the leg lift effort. Everyone balled their fists and unconsciously began a slight rocking motion, as if by will they might encourage a racer to greater effort. There were random whisperings of 'You can do it', 'Come on', 'Try harder', 'Keep going'. Seventy-five feet away, there were four facial expressions of 'What the heck?' The observed private memorial service had changed to something more resembling a track meet bleachers section.

The top of a head was spotted. This had to be the craziest birth any of the Family had ever attended. Rachel had unconsciously started her Lamaze breathing, until she caught an amused look from Marianne. Then, like a pealed grape, Bernhardt Elmendorf made the scene. The momentum, or momentum's spiritual equivalent, caused him to let go of the legs that pulled him from his cold grave. He looked around in wonder. The Family also looked in wonder at him, until their fog of joy was interrupted by the frantic high pitched barking of a dog that had decided that (despite the distance) three was a crowd. They looked in that direction to see that, besides the limo and the Green Machine, there was still one car at gravesite. Between the noise within and the scrutiny without, the occupants of said car decided that it was a good time to bug out. As the vehicle took off, Bernhardt looked at it with amazement.

"*Is that some sort of a monster?*" He looked about at the Family. "*Why are you all dressed so odd?*" Bernhardt thought about it for a moment and, before anyone could answer his questions, he asked one more. "*What year is this?*" If what this Ryan Fitzgalen fellow said was true and, so far, it seemed to be…

"Welcome to the surface, Mr. Bernhardt Elmendorf. It is the year 2047. You have been down there for one hundred and forty-five years." Ryan pointed to the monument. Bernhardt looked and began to read.

"*Oh, mein Gott. Agatha, Helga, Heinrich. My little brother, Karl? My whole family? Gone?*"

Gustav reached out and put a hand on Bernhardt's shoulder, as the spirit had already proven that they were contact compatible. Vanessa did the same and said, "*No, Bernhardt, not gone. They're just not here. Your family is waiting for you. All you have to do is walk away from this place.*"

"*To see my family, that's all I have to do? Which way? But wait. I must thank you, first. But…how?*"

Gustav smiled. "*You already have, my friend. This is our purpose, to help people like you. Listen to your heart, now. It will point the way.*"

Bernhardt looked at his benefactors, and then looked around. They saw him stop turning when he had faced the east. Now, wasn't that a coincidence? He began to walk in that direction, but stopped just as a soft glow had begun to envelope him. Bernhardt turned, but could not find words to express what was in his heart, other than to say, "*I can hear my children.*" He turned back east, took a step and was gone.

VIII   REFORGING

To the south, a savant biker sat across from his only friend in the world. Visiting hours at the county jail were spent at a six-paired-seat security counter with the same glass used by armored car windshields. That extra security measure was taken shortly after an incident where his disgruntled wife cut a repeat offender rapist's future career short. Reinforced Plexiglas was officially declared as an inadequate barrier to settling scores. The story of how the woman had brought a weapon of that high a caliber into a low security facility's visiting area was one for the books. It was the first actually videotaped murder by cleverly modified BK (below knee) prosthetic leg. The late night show comics had a field day with that one.

    Barry sensed that Hammer seemed different, now. It was a good difference, he decided. He would hang around for the hearing the next day. His friend promised him that they would stick together when he got out of jail. The savant didn't know that he was the man's only real friend, too. Hammer didn't realize that, either. Until now.

Earlier that morning, FBI Special Agent Russ Anderson called his supervisor to let him know that the Task Team had requested his presence in New York. The Task Team needed assistance from someone the Hawthorn group would not be familiar with. This contingency had already been planned on, so the call was a formality. The ticket was waiting for him at Savannah Airport and he was being let off at the front gate even as he was thumbing the disconnect on his SatCom. Trotting into the airport, he made a second call. This one was not a formality. It was to his wife, Agnes, informing her that he had to delay his return to his family for a business assignment, once again.

Major Kenneth McGuinness, of the Georgia National Guard, hit the disconnect on his SatCom while sitting in his golf cart. His party of four waited patiently, as they should. He outranked them all. The game soon continued, but his subordinates had to be extra creative in order to allow their Superior Officer to win.

CNN Science Desk Director Janice Hardin hung up the phone. The screen to her PC listed a number of things just discussed with Dagmar Yaddow, things that might focus some of the Task Team's efforts into a narrower bandwidth. There had been a plague of some sort that had struck a bunch of Civil War soldiers with universally lethal effect that Dagmar was interested in. Also requested: anything she could find on animal sensitivities to ghosts, anything that might detect the presence of a ghost, and anything that might be used against a ghost, including a list of reputable exorcists. While Dagmar Yaddow was not an employee of CNN, there were understandings of cooperation that kept the best free agent correspondents near their former mother hen. Any experienced mother will understand that the chick that leaves the nest will usually stay somewhat interdependent, if you arrange the apron strings just right.

Linda LaRoche, Mayor of Milledgeville, hung up the phone after speaking with her aide, Elroy McBean. He had been a busy little man and a productive one. In three months, the international convention of ESPER, a group of off-center but reasonably well to do people obsessed with the paranormal would be gracing their fair city. Shards of the Edwards Estate porch that had blown from 'whatever the hell it was' that exploded there was making a nice little glassed in display along with samples of imploded glass dust at the Edwards Main House. That display would set records on the item being most photographed during Estate tours. She was also pleased to have been informed that the Main House no longer experienced spontaneous Bible page turning or sudden drops in temperature on the porch.

    She had been busy, herself. The FBI forensics teams were finally packing up and leaving; their supervisor being convinced he had the psychic impression of the Mayor's foot on his rear end. Mayor LaRoche was a practical woman. There were times when science had to give way to economics. This was one of them.

Barbara Meissner, Melissa's best friend at RPI, hung up her dorm room phone. She had collected Melissa's scholastic requirements for Monday and Tuesday and loaded them into a MiDi. ALL the professors were cooperative, for word of where Barbie Babe had been had percolated up to the administrative levels. She stuck it into her PC and fired it off to Melissa's SatCom connect, along with her best wishes. Melissa would be back the day after tomorrow and Barbara couldn't wait to find out more about what had happened last weekend.

Frank Gladstone sat at the kitchen table. The kids were off to school and he was alone again. His wife (?) was not home, hadn't been home, and may never come home. What was worse, he had seen the video that included Rachel in what looked to be a dangerous situation. Not for the first time, Frank wondered what kind of a man he was. He had struck out giving himself a lifetime companion and giving his children a solid home a second time, or had he? He wasn't totally sure and that lack of surety was driving him to distraction. Why hadn't he called her, told her what he was feeling and how deeply he felt about her, other than his dread of what her response might be, that is? Things that once seemed important to him as fodder for argument in the past now seemed so petty and meaningless. What had he been thinking back then?

Frank Gladstone had just decided to make the call he had been dreading when his phone rang. The ID readout raised his heart into his throat. It was what he had prayed for and feared the most. Frank's hands were as wet as his throat was dry as he picked up the receiver.

Rachel and the rest of the Family had skipped going to the Beekman Arms for now. They were too wrung out to enjoy the ambience there. Perhaps tomorrow. The trip back from the Rhinebeck Cemetery had been completely silent, as each Family member was lost in private thoughts of what had just transpired. They made for Marianne's place, picking up Chinese along the way. No one felt much like putting a meal together. Once they arrived, Rachel excused herself, for she could no longer excuse herself. There was something she had to do and it was overdue. It was time.

"Hello, Frank? Yes, I'm all right, thank you. Allen's OK, too, and so is the rest of the group I work with. Yes, I'm working with them, now. How are the kids?" The answer was worded as nicely as he could arrange, but the underlying import stung Rachel's heart. This wasn't right. Even if she was going to cut it off completely, having this conversation by phone was just not right. Her inner voices she thought of as 'Cat' and 'Angel' were not just in accord on that matter, the two of them were screaming at 'Referee' in harmony. "Frank, I'm still working things out. I don't want to make a final decision with you over the phone. No, I'm not ready to come home, yet. Will you meet with me tomorrow? Yes, ten in the morning will do fine. Where? Tell you what, make it the noon hour and I'll treat you to Pavelli's. They have a wonderful lunch special. Fine. No, I'll meet you there, and Frank? Would you please tell Jerry and Janet that I love them both very much and how sorry I am, and, and, oh, Frank, I've got to go. I'm so sorry." Rachel hung up the receiver and stood there staring at it with stinging eyes. Lunch special, indeed! As if the knot in her stomach would allow even a potato chip.

On the other end, a man contemplated the communication device in his hand, wondering whether to gently place it back in its receptacle, or to throw it through a window. His British upbringing prevented the latter option, but it had been close.

Rachel returned to the living room and sat quietly. The others respected her desire to reside on the periphery for a while, but felt it was time to share amongst themselves. Ralph began with, "Ryan, if I die tomorrow, I sure would be disappointed, but I wouldn't feel cheated out of having lived a full life. Between the Estate and this, my emotions have been stretched out on the rack. Is it like this each time you help an entity?"

"It varies, Ralph. Sometimes it's just as if you helped a little old lady across the street. Other times will leave you with parts of your heart in puddles. You can see how addictive this sort of thing can be, despite the havoc it plays with your insides."

Melissa spoke up. "I'm very grateful for being part of the Family, but I feel I have to continue my education. Allen, you ought to finish up your own requirements, I think. Will you have time for it, though?"

Allen looked at Ryan. "Will I?"

"Shouldn't be too much of a problem. The business is pretty well self-running, as I've said. A lot of that was due to the efforts your father made, followed up on by Gustav and Marianne's magic powers of choosing the right people for the right managerial jobs. Checking up on it should be regular, but not constant. Management is mostly common sense and knowing what experts to ask the right questions of. The semester you're taking off should give you enough time to get a handle on how to manage things mostly from your PC and SatCom. Many CEO's do that nowadays. Rachel, your own time will also be more your own than you may have thought. I know you are considering how your life is going to pan out, so keep that fact in mind. If there is a shoulder to cry on or an ear to bend on your wish list, I'm your Santa Clause."

Rachel smiled, nodded her thanks, but remained silent. She didn't trust her mouth to do more than trigger an emotional outburst at the moment. Allen wanted to give his Mom a hug, but sensed her fragility and tenuous hold on decorum. Sometimes, it takes more love to stay away than it does to approach, and it takes the greatest love to know when to do which. Marianne excused herself to get to her date with Gustav's second wife. She had moved up the time, knowing that an early bedtime was going to be best for everyone tonight.

Since his lady was going bye-bye for the time being, Ralph recruited Allen to help him with a handyman's project. The Green Machine had quite a repair shop in the trunk. A cabbie never knew when he might have to repair anything from a suitcase to a child's toy. In Ralph's repair kit was the most amazing glue; it stuck to everything except skin and was completely non-toxic. Du-Pont made a real killing with this one, which saved it from a hostile take-over after it had been devastated from all the cancer suits from their 'in-a-can' chemical anti-stain carpet treatments they had marketed a decade ago. Twelve minutes later, Marianne's bathroom door was almost like new again, allowing her to take down the privacy sheet she had draped over it earlier.

Vanessa then strong-armed Gustav into passing through that door a couple of times. He knew the story about getting back on the horse after being bucked off, but still he couldn't screw up his courage enough to go through under his own power. The Family got into brainstorming ways he could take that first step to overcome his phobia. Suddenly, Vanessa got the giggles. She focused and turned the bathroom door handle, opened the door and verbally hauled Gustav inside. Ryan didn't know what Vanessa had in mind, but the expectant smile on his face told everyone that this was something not to be missed. They could hear muffled mumbling of a feminine voice behind the once again closed door, then silence. Then sounded the pair of them in synchrony, bravely speaking words that completely confused the two younger members of the Family.

"Fights a never ending battle for Truth, Justice and the American Way!" Seconds later, Gustav burst through the closed bathroom door, resplendent in his red, blue and yellow costume. Rachel, Ralph, and Ryan were roaring (Gustav would HAVE to do a repeat performance for Marianne!). Since the Man of Steel met his demise in the comic book industry three decades earlier, Melissa asked Allen, "What does the 'S' stand for?"

Gustav's formerly favorite diner's owner/manager, Dot, had no problem with Atlas. Her miniature poodle sported one of his sweaters (from the Ivy League Collection) back home. Her Jury Box Café had a large three-side-benched booth in the corner where four people and a famous canine currently sat. A fifth customer came in the door, as Mr. Lorriman had forewarned her. The man needed no directions and made for the group. They seemed like such nice people. Mostly Southern, from the sound of their accents. They usually appreciated hostess courtesy more than her fellow New Yorkers. Pity.

Russ Anderson pulled up a chair, not wanting to crowd those in the booth's bench seats. Hands were shaken all around. He filled in the others about the closure of the on-site forensics set-up. They had been winding things up, anyway. There wasn't much more to report than what he had already told them. The infrared scans, ultraviolet scans, and even the Bureau dog teams hadn't been able to sniff out a thing. The people with burns were healing nicely, the Homestead Main House was fully repaired and he expressed his amazement at what price the roof shards that weren't under display glass were going for on the world web auction blocks. The only other thing he had picked up was historically interesting, and maybe significant. Russ related the story of a Union Private having been buried in a slave cemetery not far from the Estate Main House. Who knows? Maybe that rider in the video was that same person…one Private Jedediah Patterson.

Dagmar took the horns and brought Russ up to speed, as the others polished off the remains of their late lunch. It took a while, for there was not only the funeral, but also all of the interviews and the research done to date. She did a very nice job of encapsulating the whole thing into as much a coherent package as could be done. That sort of thing was how she earned a living, after all. Russell Anderson got so caught up in it all that only when the group left the diner did he realize that he hadn't ordered anything to eat. Russ picked up a to-go cup and a Danish, then hurried out to rejoin the others.

The day had come to a close. It was Monday, October 2nd, 2047. Vanessa and Gustav watched over the Family as they slept. Ryan and Ralph had left for the bachelor quarters. Allen decided to stay with Melissa. That had slightly disappointed the other two bachelors, though, truth be told, both would have thought Allen nuts for doing otherwise. Gustav was getting the hang of the teleportation that Vanessa was so expert with. Being a guardian angel sounded good on the surface, but he soon got bored hovering about while everyone else snoozed. Getting Vanessa to learn his talent for changing raiment was not an easy task. She was able to make significant changes for a few moments (a completely new style) and minor changes (changing her dress color) for almost a minute. They had moved to the front porch of Marianne's home, so as not to disturb the mortals.

"*Look, it took practice for me to bop about like you do and, even then, you are still the reigning queen on that particular trick. When I was a young boy, I saw a juggler at the circus. I decided then and there that I would learn how, also. Do you have any idea how many oranges I bruised and still couldn't keep them in the air for more than ten or twelve cycles? Mom used to yell at me for both the wasted oranges (she juiced them later) and for running around the house.*"

"*How ironic that you grew up to juggle books, instead. Why were you running around the house?*"

"*Will your barbs ever cease? As for the running, beginning to juggle almost always has the person tossing the balls or fruit progressively further out in front of them for some reason and they wind up doing the 'novice's sprint'. I was banned from practicing in the house after the second lamp broke.*" Gustav shook his head and raised his eyes in mock pain, but his soul companion knew him better than that. Still, she knew that she often pushed things too far.

"*Forgive me, Gustav. I am really very grateful for the lessons and promise to practice. There's no hurry, though. I've come to realize that Ryan loves me for what I am now as well as for what I was before. Not every woman feels that in her heart like I do. I'm not even sure why I feel your, talent, is so important. Probably a woman's desire to change outfits once every century or two (giggle). Can you imagine the trouble I would have caused my dear husband had I died a nudist?*"

The deceased esquire cackled at that one. The more he thought about it, the more he laughed. Had he still had his body, his ribs would have been sore the next morning. Vanessa smiled that she had given her newest best (male) friend the gift of laughter, for Gustav wasn't known for jocular outbursts. She wondered if its current intensity was just a needed release from the experiences of the day or the post-mortem residual preference the male gender had for off-color humor. For that matter, she mused, why was anything dealing with matters sexual called 'off-color'? What was 'on-color' and what color were they talking about? Gustav had been winding down, so Vanessa told him the thoughts she was just entertaining, adding, "*You can curse a blue streak, see red in anger, turn yellow in cowardice, or white with fright, or green with envy."*

"Good Lord, Vanessa. Pedantics? I'm rubbing off on you. At least, you're no shrinking violet."

"Good Lord, Gustav. A pun? I'm rubbing off on you." With that, Vanessa focused her energies and, for a full thirteen seconds, managed to appear wearing a three-piece business suit, giving Gustav another case of the chuckles. He, in turn, managed enough sobriety to similarly cross dress into a fair approximation of Vanessa's outfit, leaving the pair in a helpless pile of snorting ectoplasm.

Neither paid heed to the rented Chevy Hurricane that cruised by for the third time that night. The occupant noted that the lights had finally gone out and the porch remained empty. Coming up empty handed on surveillance duty, he turned the block and headed back to his room at the Holiday Inn. Maybe this time, he'd negotiate that nutty traffic circle right and not wind up on the Interstate again.

Marianne nestled into her bed, her thoughts alternating between Ralph, Valerie Knudson Mendelssohn, and Bernhardt Elmendorf. "Life goes on with all of us, doesn't it?"

Bernhardt lived his life, died his death (tragically), and today was the day he went on with the next step in his spiritual life.

Valerie had once been Mrs. Mendelssohn. That marriage fell apart (tragically), but she went on. Yet, today, she reached back for a piece of her past and shared it with a stranger, now a friend. You could still move on to the future and keep the treasures of the past, as long as those treasures didn't turn into baggage.

And Ralph? Her thoughts of him weren't so much about his moving on, as it was her own new direction that included him in the picture. She had a life that was also altered by death (tragically). Since then and until recently, a Fitzgalen ghost rescue that she could only share in with second hand accounts from Ryan would be followed by nights of passing wishes that Mike could still be here to share such moments with her. It was time for Marianne Cabrini to move on, both with a greater level of participation in the Family and with her letting go of Mike Cabrini. After all, she had been holding onto him, not the other way around.

Mike, like Bernhardt, had lived a full, though shortened life. Marianne, like Valerie, had learned that you could treasure that past and get on with a new life and new directions. She had been blessed with a wonderful husband, got promoted in an already rewarding career by becoming clairvoyant, and now had been given a delightful taste of a new loving relationship. With a contented sigh and a softly muttered "Booboop bee doop," she fell gently and happily asleep.

IX TUESDAY

Allen had grown up with his mother waking him up for school. A gentle nudge was rocking him once more with a sweet voice telling him it was time to wake up. He smiled in anticipation of oatmeal, or French toast. Those were his favorites. When he opened his eyes, once again there was yellow hair to greet the colors of dawn. The face was different, but just as loving. Allen smiled again. "Another morning, another restaurant. Which one today?"

"Rachel said that Ryan called. He wants us to meet him at the Holiday Inn, something about a nice breakfast buffet. Allen, how long has it been since you had a home cooked meal?" Allen had to think about that. It hadn't been all that long since he had visited his mother from RPI, but the events of the past week (is that all it had been?) had expanded to encompass a seemingly much greater span of time. "I thought so. Baby, I'm going to learn to cook. Rachel said she'd teach me." Allen sat up and looked at the lady he had almost lost. All that and she cooks (someday), too? Thank you, God!

Marianne breezed through the living room. Activity was beginning in earnest in preparation for the day. "Get up, you two love birds. Train leaves Cabrini Station in half an hour and I only have one working shower until Ralph fixes the one upstairs." Allen and Melissa looked at each other and began to smile most wickedly. "Not in my house until you're married! Get it out of your minds. I have to draw the line, somewhere. One at a time! Now, get moving, you slugs! Rachel and I have already had our showers."

Allen let Melissa go first, while he folded the blankets and put the couch back together. She always needed more time after a shower to do whatever it was that women do than he did, especially when it came to hair. Allen snickered to think that, upon the expulsion from the Garden of Eden, God saw fit to further curse Adam and all of his descendents by giving Eve a brush and blow dryer. Melissa soon came out in a borrowed terry cloth robe and her hair up in a towel, using a hand towel to try and get some water out of her ear. Allen smiled at her on his way to the bathroom. "Hey, genie, what do I rub to get my three wishes?" He then made the mistake of turning his back.

Marianne and Rachel were in the kitchen. Vanessa had joined them, leaving Gustav musing on the porch and staying away from the general confusion. The three shared company, while two shared coffee, when they heard a *'crack'*, followed by a masculine screech, followed immediately by an indignant complaint that the towel had been wet. Then came the sound of four running bare feet. The three mother hens smiled at each other. "Kids!"

Ralph and Ryan were already at the Holiday Inn restaurant. The buffet was pretty good, as Ryan had said, and they had both gone for seconds. That would give the rest of the Family more elbowroom at the table when they arrived. Ryan may still have his legal beagle around in spirit, but breaking bread with a companion who eats had become a morning tradition for too many years. He was happy to have Ralph along on his journey. The man was definitely good company, sharp witted, and had insights into how people ticked that had already proven invaluable.

"Look, Ryan, those four people have got to be around here somewhere. We know who they are and they are on your turf, now. It shouldn't be too hard to locate and keep an eye on them. You have resources, here. Put a tail on them, quiet like. I'll volunteer for the first spy shift."

Their booth was the first to the left upon entering the dining hall. From there, Ryan and Ralph could command a view of the whole dining area and not be visible to every person that walked through the hallway that connected the hotel rooms to the main lobby and restaurant entrance. The hallway was frequently used because of that connection and that it was where the phone bank and rest rooms were located. That security cut two ways, though. It kept him from noticing Dagmar Yaddow, who had arrived first for the Task Team's morning planning session and was now standing in the hallway only about seven feet away. Dagmar had a phenomenal memory for voices and she immediately latched onto and identified Ralph's, whom she had overheard at Mr. Mendelssohn's funeral. Paul showed up at that moment and she put her finger to her lips. He froze, and then sharpened his hearing. They could now hear Ryan's voice.

"Keep it down, Sherlock. The walls have ears. There are too many unknowns wandering around hotels. We'll do some planning for the day, but save the essential details for the limo. So, there are four 'Mayoral ambassadors' we need to be on the look out for. I can't really blame LaRoche for wanting to get in a parting shot, after what we did to their weekend extravaganza. We know about Yaddow, the correspondent. She's a newsie, so that makes sense. You know the police sergeant, Wasserman? That confuses me. What is a Peach State local cop doing this far north? Is he LaRoche's mutt sent here for payback? Then there's Guard Sergeant D'Palermo. She's another southern peach weathering the northern climate. What gives with that? Does the Georgia Governor think we're a threat to his state? Finally, that questionable ghost hunter turned entrepreneur and his mutated weasel. I suppose his being here makes some sort of sense."

Zachary had arrived in time to hear that last comment. Atlas sensed his partner's outrage and was working up to a growl when the other two glared at him. Atlas stopped suddenly when Zachary's thumb and index

105

clamped his mouth shut. Ryan and Ralph had both thought they heard something, but politely saying nothing, each assuming it was the other man's digestive system sounding off. Russ and Nunzia arrived at the same time, which raised a hackle on Paul's neck, though his conscious mind refused to recognize it.

"Ryan, those four are obviously together and here for a reason. I've been thinking about it. You have a military type, a police investigative type, a news gathering type, and a ghost hunter type. Put those flowers together and what does the arrangement suggest to you?" Ryan liked the analogy and it brought insight.

"A cooperative effort, with the resources of each organization they represent. Those organizations represent a city, a state, and a worldwide news broadcasting interest that have collectively contracted a ghost hunting man-dog team. That's double-plus ungood. Look, the others will be here any second. Let's table this for a minute. I want to simmer on this."

Nunzia looked at the others. They just proved that Russ was an unknown to them. Good. Used to silent signals and to taking command, she pointed to Russ and then to the restaurant, cupping her ear with her hand to indicate his mission. He nodded his understanding. She pointed to the others and herself and then down the hall. The four made quick tracks. It wouldn't do to have their dark horse illuminated to the upcoming target arrivals by their presence. Russ took a moment after his teammates left, squared his shoulders, went in and chose a table not too close to, but not that far from, his targets.

During the limo ride to the Holiday Inn, Allen had a thought on another track. "Hey, getting buried alive. Do you think that sort of thing still happens? How common did it used to be?" Trivia alert. All eyes automatically turned to Gustav.

"What am I, the answer man? Well, it certainly doesn't happen that way anymore, at least, not in any civilized country. You actually have to pass a final exam to be declared dead and allowed to be interred. Used to be you were cut up and your organs removed for analysis. Now we mostly use Computerized Tomography, electrical field detectors and thermography. Still, a coroner has to be pretty careful and the definitions of death can be a little hazy. Remember the tale of Mary Safford? Brain death is still a foggy area, legally and in the lay public's mind. However, I'd be surprised if Bernhardt was one of a kind." Gustav looked at Allen, sensing his racing thoughts, and realized where this was leading. If Bernhardt was only a sample, then... *"Mein Gott!"*

Marianne's eyes widened. "Others? There are others like that poor man?"

Allen held up a hand. "Let's not get hasty. We don't know if being buried alive is a guaranteed ticket to being an eternal ground hog. Let's look at this thing closer and get an idea of what we are dealing with."

Rachel was also wide eyed. A century and a half of darkness and loneliness for that poor Bernhardt. Those Civil War soldiers had it pretty rough, but at least they had each other's company and changing scenery, not to mention a unifying goal to strive for and give them purpose. How many rooms did Hell have in it, anyway? "Vanessa, you said that Annie could sense the spirits in the ground. Is that something you can do? Gustav, could you do that?"

The two entities looked at each other. Ladies first. *"I'm having enough trouble just changing outfits. I don't know, Rachel. I left that for Annie, completely. I've no clue on how to even begin trying. It's kind of like learning another language and the only teacher I know of crossed over to the other side. Gustav, I suspect you're too new at this, but maybe not. You picked up on outfit changing right away and you are making faster strides on my shtick than I am on yours. Maybe you have more of a chance at learning the underground thing."*

"Maybe, possibly. I'm willing to try. At least Annie showed us that this is something that can be done. Hopefully, it will be like the four-minute mile." Blank stares. *"Oh, come on. What has happened to our educational system? It was a barrier in track events where it was generally accepted that no one could break it, until someone ignored the fact that it was impossible and did it. After that, others followed suit. The ability was always there, just not the belief. Underground ghost hunting? I believe it can be done because it has been done. The rest is just mechanics, I suppose."*

Melissa sighed. "It's a shame we can't steal that pooch that can sense ghosts. Maybe he'd be more sensitive on underground spirits than our people ghosts are. I mean, dogs can smell and hear a whole lot better than us, can't they? And don't their noses spend half the time on the ground? I'd just take him on a walking tour of all the old graveyards." Were it not for the noise of the road and traffic, you could have heard a pin drop. "Did I say something?"

Eyes were meeting eyes, breaking contact and meeting other eyes. Heads were turning, nodding. It was brilliant. Ideas began flying back and forth. They could get rid of a potential enemy by putting it to good use on their own behalf. That Lorriman was a businessperson; he was dollar oriented. If his dog couldn't be purchased, then perhaps he himself could be hired onto the Fitzgalen team. If the guy's life's goal truly was ghost hunting, what better group of people was there for Lorriman to hook up with? The man couldn't do anything with entities once he found them. He needed the Family to complete his half of a mission and, maybe, they needed him! The excitement began to grow, until Marianne invoked a new Fitzgalen tradition she just invented. "GROUP SMOOCH!"

The limo driver was used to the Hawthorn group, as they were now known by. The sudden limo-lurch from the activities of his charges wasn't the first for him. Rich people were eccentric. Had they been poor, they would probably be declared nuts. However, had they been poor, they wouldn't be riding in his limo. They're riding; therefore, they're eccentric. That was OK with him. Eccentric people often tipped well. He pulled into the let-off point, discharged his clients and drove off, not in the least disappointed. Shame about Mr. Mendelssohn, though.

The Family discovered their founder and his major domo sipping coffee at the restaurant. The place was full enough for a pleasant conversational background buzz, but not so full as to feel crowded. Knowing they were in for the initial lecture, all automatically went for the buffet. Once seated, they ate while Ryan talked and Ralph kept an eye on the crowd, looking for familiar faces or suspicious characters. If the enemy (as they had come to be known as) knew that they were identified (and how could they not, having been at the interment?), they just might be doing something underhanded and sneaky. Like he would do if the shoes were on the other feet. Ralph searched while Ryan talked.

"First of all, I admonish each of you to keep your comments innocuous. There are too many strangers in hotels with too many ears. This is to plan the day. We'll get into the details later."

Ralph half listened. He was scanning and thinking, "Let's see, two families with kids, five male groupings, eleven female groupings (there was a garden club meeting posted on the hallway event marquis, so half the female tables were on the far side of fifty years), and five single diners; three male, two female." He had already covered most of what Ryan was chatting about, so he felt OK about playing sleuth. The families and the ladies felt right. Two business groups were oriental. They were too busy with rapid fire chatting to observe or hear anything. One business table was headed by Mr. Ego. It looked like everyone there was paying rapt attention, but Ralph could see through that. Those guys were bored stiff. Each time one felt a yawn coming on, he used a glass of water or fork of food to hide it. Since they all used the same M.O., it had to be learned and shared behavior. That indicated a less than honest, but longstanding, relationship. Between that and the fact that Mr. Ego hadn't shut up since they arrived, even when his mouth was full, Ralph crossed that table off his list. Most of the others he had eliminated as having had been there when they had arrived. Ryan had purposely not made reservations.

"Rachel, I understand you have a meeting today. Allen, since you'll be with me today full time and your car is nearer, would you lend your mother your car? It's still in the office parking lot?" Allen answered with a nod. "Good. Melissa, you've got to get caught up on your studies, I hear. Would you feel comfortable doing that at the office, as we have excellent research and production facilities there? Fine."

Ralph's eyes narrowed. That left one single male, one single female and one double male group. None of them were making any kind of eye contact. If one of them were a bogey, he or she or they was/were a well trained one. If so, that's bad. How to flush out the Grinch? Ralph thought a second and then smiled. Ryan continued.

"Very well, I see we've taken on fuel. Marianne, you are needed to clean up backlog at the office. We need a new legal rubber stamper. We will, from time to time, need a name on a document." Ryan glanced up and to the left, acknowledging that he would still rely on Gustav for most of his legal advice needs. "You WILL have help with that search."

Ralph plotted. The level of dining hall conversation was a background mush, but when you hear your name or something of primary interest in such a mixture, your subconscious amplifies it to please the conscious (that's a good id, here's a biscuit). Ralph would have to start and stay on a level tone, if this was going to work. He took his unused napkin and drew a circle surrounded by eight smaller circles. He then drew three more circles, two had either 'male' or 'female' inscribed, one with the number 'two'. Then he wrote one word on the work, and covered it up with his hand so it didn't distract his friends from what fearless leader was speaking about. When Ryan paused for a moment...

"Ryan, there is something I need to attend to with the Green Machine, no emergency, but I've been meaning to get it taken care of for a long time and this seems like a good time to do it, so if you don't mind, while you finish up, I'll GO-STay with the car." It wasn't important that his friends looked at him like he was babbling, especially because the Green Machine was back at Marianne's. He saw a definite head twitch and a glance. It was only for a fraction of a second. That was enough. Interesting. He underlined the circle that was marked with 'male' and excused himself from the table. His second priority was now to peak around the halls and see if any of the Task Team members were about. The others at the table noticed the drawing/note. There were a bunch of circles, some with a number and/or 'male/female' in them, and the word 'BOGIE'. A circle with the number '1' and the word 'male' had been underlined. Vanessa caught on first and tip-toed over to the gentleman that the coded map indicated, jumped up and down, pointed and shouted, *"SPY, SPY, he's a spy! Nyah, Nyah, Mr. Spy, we're on to you now!"*

Russ Anderson, FBI, had been listening very carefully, following the craft he had been trained in for, years before he found his Bureau niche within the forensics field. He watched, using only the peripheral vision that had made him a formidable opponent on the FBI basketball team. His main target had been careful to reveal nothing incriminating. Crafty bird, this one. Nothing seemed too out of place, as far as he could tell. So, what the hell were they all suppressing laughter for? No one had cracked a joke. Did someone fart?

Vanessa was on a roll. She walked through the table and, to those with eyes to see, looked all the world like she was sitting on the man's breakfast plate. The Family took a collective breath, trying to maintain their composure and decorum, lest this investigative spy be given the ammo needed to have them all committed. No one dared to move. All aimed their faces in any direction but one and tried unsuccessfully to keep from looking in that one. Most thought they'd get out of this peacefully and have a nice chuckle about it, later. Ryan and Marianne knew better.

When the man reached with his fork and speared a sausage, Allen melted under the table like laser struck butter and Melissa had to run out of the door before the fellow could take a bite of it. She squeaked out, "Ladies room!" Rachel and Marianne were hot on her heels, grasping at the straw that 'all women go to the bathroom together' as their excuse. Gustav was thoroughly grossed out, but laughed anyway, enjoying his freedom to make all the noise he wanted to while his best friend hung onto decorum by his fingernails. Ryan could only squint, hold his hand over his mouth and make little raspberry sounds. He couldn't get away, for Allen was clinging to Ryan's leg, whispering (when he could breathe), "Ryan, make her stop, please, make her stop, I gotta go pee." So much for keeping a low profile, thought Ryan, but what was life for anyway if you couldn't get a good belly laugh out of it? Ralph was going to be royally pissed for having missed this one.

Russ got up to leave. This was getting ridiculous. These people were insane. Who was the 'her' the Hawthorn CEO was referring to? He left a tip, took his check and paid it at the register next to the entryway. The lady cashier asked how he had enjoyed his breakfast, then whispered, "Sorry about the silliness, there. You know how eccentric some business types can be."

Allen was crawling back out from under the table with a case of the hiccups. Ryan turned to face him, calming himself down and trying to sip some water to cool his irritated throat.

Russ replied, "Very good, thank you, and not to worry. Oh, would you please tell the chef that that was the best sausage I've ever had. Where did it come from?" He paused when he heard something that sounded, almost, like a trumpeting elephant.

The ladies had finally calmed down enough to make a reappearance. As they filed out of the restroom, they met Ryan and Allen coming the other way. Allen kept walking to the bathroom further down the hallway, hiccupping about once every third step. Melissa stopped Ryan before he could follow. "How did Allen get all wet?"

Ryan trembled out a reply, his voice half an octave higher than usual, and then had to make for his respective restroom door. The ladies did a one-eighty with a collective suppressed screech and put in another ten minutes recovery and primp time. Ralph had gotten tired of waiting and wondered what had happened. He wandered back and saw that his party had left the table, somewhat in a mess. He walked over and put another ten spot near where someone had been a bit careless with their water. Back out into the hall, he heard sounds coming from behind the two restroom doors. The women's door drew him near first. He could hear familiar sniffling and snorting. What had he missed? Vanessa poked her head through the door to check whether the coast was clear and wound up nose to nose with Ralph. Ralph yipped and jumped back as Vanessa popped back into the restroom. The hen cackling amped up a few notches. Ralph took a breath to recover from the surprise door trophy, went to the men's room door and peeked in. Allen had used up half the paper towel supply to dry off his hair, face, and shirt. "Jeeze, what happened?" Ryan refused to say anything more until they could get to the limo.

Zachary was in his room with the rest of the team. Russ had knocked on the door and was let in. "I tell you, those people have to be on drugs or something. The whole group dissolved into hysteria for no particular reason after the cab driver had left."

Nunzia had the most experience with the Hawthorn sense of humor. "They're like that. I thought they were just adolescent, but it doesn't fit with the rest of what they do. It's like their lives are filled with inside jokes that no one else can understand." She stopped, and furrowed her brow. "Or hear." She looked meaningfully at Zachary, who nodded knowingly. In an environment where she was off balanced from the lack of situation experience, Nunzia reverted to Sgt. D'Palermo. "Lady and gentlemen, I no longer doubt that we are truly dealing with the supernatural. When you have an enemy you can't see, you have to gather intelligence from the fruits of his labors in order to shoot for the best and prepare for the worst. The video from the Edwards Estate shows these Hawthorn people to be at least familiar with and supportive of one female appearing non-human that I will refer to, from this point on, as a ghost. I saw them right after the shit had hit the fan and they seemed curiously low on the grief scale despite the very recent passing of their legal representative, who was the interim head of their organization until Mr. Allen Hawthorn had entered the picture only days before. The visit we had to the Hawthorn group later that evening showed them to be unusually jolly, even cracking up, and trying their damnedest to hide it under the guise of grieving. The following morning, I walk in to their hotel suite and the CEO's mother slips and points to a place in the room where no one was visible and introduces me to the recently deceased lawyer. She was horrified. Why? Was it because she had broached a sad subject, or because she had let the cat out of the bag?

"The scene at the funeral had Atlas suspicious of a section of the graveyard, a section to which, after the ceremony, all but one of the Hawthorn group made a beeline for, later to be joined by that one person who had taken a detour with one of the mourners. And who was that mourner? Why, it just happened to be the widow of the man whose spirit had been introduced to me the day before. The group of them performed some kind of ceremony, acting rather out of the ordinary and, at the culmination of their little ritual, ghost sensitive Atlas started ricocheting off the walls in the car and yapping his head off. Now, this morning, for no particular reason, these people begin once again to enact inappropriate bursts of laughter at something not visible to a trained FBI agent. I sincerely hope I'm not the only one to be able to put the pieces of this puzzle together. This group of people, led NOT by the young CEO but rather by the man with no last name whose only traces on a people search date back to World War Two, are in connection and communication with members of a world not our own. People, I have a strong suspicion that these people are in league with Satan." The maid down the hall looked up from her sheet cart when she heard the combined "WHAT?!" through the closed door of 104. She shrugged, then went back to her work

"Look, people, I've been doing a lot of thinking and research. Think about it. OK, maybe the satanic conclusion is premature, but keep an open mind, will you? Ryan has a twin that lived back in the 1940's, at least, that's the last reference to someone who just happens to fit this man's description with an age regression to the mid-twenties. That man was in the Navy, stationed in Hawaii just after the Japanese attacked Pearl Harbor. I had my Major look into that person. The research the Navy had been doing at the time has only been declassified for the past thirty years. That man just happened to have the name RYAN David Fitzgalen. Another coincidence? He was released on medical discharge. The report was pretty detailed and it said that this Ryan had been involved with some failed experiments in using super-magnets to enable boats to avoid radar detection, had been injured in the performance of those duties, returned to duty in R and D (research and development), then later released after, among other things, he had been reported as claiming to have talked to a doctor who had already died during the original Japanese attack. The records search shows him later to have a significant lifestyle change for the richer, but with no obvious occupation to support it, and then he seemed to drop from sight altogether. Where did that money come from? Before he vanished, he had married one Vanessa Fitzgalen (her maiden name couldn't be located), but we couldn't find much about her background. Zachary, that Mormon search engine came in handy. Major McGuinness made use of it and came up with some interesting results. The woman he married was curiously close in description to someone who died just before their marriage in St. Louis, someone who happened to live, where else, in St. Louis. There is no body to disprove a relationship between the two women, as the one who died was reported as having been cremated. How many oddities does this trail turn up? Any of these out of the ordinary things could be chalked up as coincidences, but there are just too *damned many of them!* And whom does this current Ryan fellow associate himself with? With three women possessing formidable martial arts skills. He has, or had, a lawyer running a business, but who is the true recipient of the profits of that business? The former CEO's kid or his widow? They lived well, but not that well. From what I've been able to gather from a phone interview with the

Kingston Limo Company, this guy Ryan is chauffeured everywhere and eats at restaurants almost every meal.

"All of the others have fairly normal backgrounds. It just happens that we are able to easily get from those people their full names. Only Ryan keeps silent. Why? Could this man truly be over one hundred years old while looking mid-fortyish? Now, try this one on for size.

"Over the past seventy out of our nation's two hundred and seventy one years, our country has suffered over half of its reported and recorded natural disasters, such as floods, quakes, fires, tornados, hurricanes, and even a volcano. Recently, the world has been watching *wars*, specifically the conflict in Malaysia, and *rumors of wars*, namely the falsification of the Civil War re-enactment. Sounding familiar?

"The dead would indeed appear to be walking the earth. Would any care to dispute the unnerving resemblance in this diorama to the last book of the Bible?" There were no takers. The other four had thought their Guard representative had slipped a notch in her Bible belt at first, but now, they weren't so sure.

"From what we have been able to gather from the owners of the Milledgeville Stable, three *horsemen* from the Hawthorn group rented horses on that day and rode to the Edwards Estate; their arrival concurrent with the beginnings of destruction and conflict seen around the world that went far beyond what the planners had intended for entertainment."

Dagmar had covered religious fanaticism before, but this was getting too close to believable. It wouldn't take too much more for her to tip in a direction she had taken an oath long ago to avoid. Paul was a man solid with his Christianity, his life, and his career. On this path he sensed danger, but Nunzia was making too much sense. He was hypnotized and it didn't help that he still had deep affection for the speaker. Zachary had seen too much by way of the spirit world to be afraid of shades, but this had a level of scariness that he had never felt before and it was thrilling him. He was actually salivating. Russ was a fish out of water. His opponents always had heartbeats, were mortal, and were stoppable. But this? He had to stop the train before it took them all to a place they didn't want to go.

"Sgt. D'Palermo, you say that three men rode their horses into the Edwards Estate and you speak of The Book of Revelations from the New Testament. I admit that there are some unsettling resemblances between the two, but there were also outrageous coincidences between the assassinations of Kennedy and Lincoln. I saw a list of them that would have choked a horse, so to speak. Sergeant, didn't the Apocalypse have four horsemen?" That last question-observation was meant to derail this runaway locomotive they were riding. It backfired.

Sgt. Nunzia D'Palermo reached into her military issue attaché and pulled out a still photograph taken from the video just before the boom camera burned out. It showed a man of military bearing in the lower left corner riding towards the other horsemen previously listed, all waiting at the porch where destruction had just taken place and where a man was soon to die, a man who would not be mourned by his comrades. Russ couldn't take his eyes away from the picture. None of them could. It chilled them to the bone and beyond, when they saw Nunzia's finger point to the image in the left low corner, and heard Nunzia's dead flat voice say, in slow, measured, syllables, "And the forth horseman rode a pale horse, and his name was...Death."

The room was a still life portrait, until someone decided to breathe again. Sgt. Paul Wasserman, Southern Baptist, looked up with the color drained from his cheeks. "This man, Ryan, is the God damned anti-Christ?" Nunzia knew Paul. He was a Southern Baptist for who 'darn' was an expletive to be used with discretion. She had at least one convert.

Major McGuinness hung up the phone. Seemed he was doing a lot of time on that thing, lately. This time it was to the supervisor of that FBI Special Agent Anderson. The G-man had asked his Bureau department to research the identity of the female ghost figure on the right in that video. They did just that and, no matter how far they went back, no local lady could be found to answer that description. It amazed the Major how such a big and powerful organization as the FBI could have such big and powerful blinders on. Who ever said the ghost was local?

He went over to his PC and inserted the MiDi with the isolated and enhanced (by military grade software) still pictures on it, then made the contact to that fascinating Mormon site. The information was requested and the Major tapped it in, which mainly consisted of a multiple pose download from which the Mormon programs could work. He also tapped in the dimensions of the porch posts to use as a reference ruler. Once running, it would take anywhere from a few minutes to half an hour for the program to spit out a result (the variance due to where he was in line with others interested in the past). He went for a cup from his carafe and then returned to the chair. The Mormon program was diminished to the corner of the screen as he inserted the next MiDi into the 'sister-slot' (there were three in all with the military issue models), the one with the results already obtained from the Mormons; the one on Ryan. The improved response that didn't need the retrograde aging angle was due to the better quality of data that had been submitted. The Major figured that the result had to be a grandfather with particularly potent genes. He smiled. This possible ancestor to the modern day Ryan was a Navy man. He laughed out loud, connecting the Navy to persistent genetics. Wasn't the Navy always boasting of how strong their 'sea-men' were? Maybe the current Ryan was a clone project. After all, Ryan Fitzgalen had been involved with another black project in Hawaii. Maybe they cloned him. Hey, it might have happened, but did they have the technology back then?

Probably not. That scientific expertise mainly arose about four decades ago and had since been banned worldwide. Two hundred women had undergone clone technology pregnancies. It had been performed in international waters on a chartered ocean liner, more to avoid interference with demonstrators than skirting legal officialdom. About a third of those pregnancies were either spontaneous abortions or stillbirths and almost half suffered birth defects that ranged from the mild to the severe. That left about two score couples that were spotlighted by pro-cloning factions as being the miracles of the century, which fueled the fires to improve the technology to reduce the 80% 'poor result' rate. The second round of two hundred desperate women who opted for the upgraded process made news of such international repugnance, the Major recalled, that the ban on the process was almost unnecessary. No one dared to either perform the procedure or have it performed upon themselves after that bioethics terrorist group had managed to covertly substitute the maternal or paternal DNA being used for the mothers to carry to term with that of chimpanzees. Normally, that item would have been caught a lot earlier along the pregnancies, but that group of women had been slated to stay on that boat and away from demonstrators for the full nine months. The discovery that something was terribly wrong didn't occur until the early third trimester's planned first ultrasound imaging for those poor women. One could only imagine the look on the ultrasound tech's face when she finally realized why that first imaged infant didn't look right. It was too late for abortions and not one had the inhumanity to put the baby chimps that they were still carrying into a high-risk preemie birth, and so they carried to term...except for the three whose minds snapped and dove overboard. None of the others ever fully recovered their sanity, either. Not one.

The Major sighed. Terrorism. It was one of the many things his organization was tasked to fight, and yet, there were times when it had proven effective in changing the course of world opinion. Hadn't the Boston Tea Party been a mild form of terrorism? And what of all the CIA sponsored 'surgical covert strikes'? Wasn't that a nice way of saying 'assassination'? When the results of a 'terrorist act' were considered beneficial to society, it changed how people looked at said act. To the Spanish, Sir Francis Drake was a pirate, which was sort of a terrorist, but the English looked upon him as a dashing privateer who was loyal to the Crown. Even today, there were elements of French and English culture that looked upon Joan of Arc as a Saint and witch, respectively. Then there was terrorism that was clearly evil, but had unintentional results for the better. Certainly the Osama bin Laden attack on America would be the shining example of that one. That series of cowardly acts created a far stronger, devoted and focused nation for the US, and brought together scores of bickering nations into a unity formerly unknown.

This Edward's thing...could that be construed as a terrorism event?

Certainly there was a worldwide exposure to a violent confrontation, thanks to the media, and there was a resulting alteration of world consciousness, regarding just about anything that had a religious meta-tag to it. Was this whole thing an engineered event of destruction and minor physical assaults by way of second degree burns in order to affect the way the planet thought? Were the Hawthorns terrorists?

As he mused, his surrogate military daughter's requested task was underway. Major McGuinness looked in amusement at the entry screen for the Albany Heraldry Corporation. Now, wasn't that pretty? A tree logo that changed its leaves according to the seasons.

Not far from where that tree image entertained the Major, a City Court Judge had just heard the legally worded list of what this bad boy had been up to. "Barnabus Jonah Jenkins, you have heard the charges brought against you by the City of Milledgeville in the State of Georgia. How do you plead?"

Hammer stood before the Judge, three fourth's of his facial and head hair now of historical interest, only. Barry had not only picked up Hammer's best shirt and pants, but had taken them to the Luckee Laundromat drop-off in town that specialized in stain removal and button sewing. Barry paid cash, as most inveterate bikers tried to do as often as possible. The ubiquitous Debi-Cred cards, they were sure, were ways that Big Brother kept track of everything you did and where you did it. There were the gold and silver versions, which had certain purchase amount limits and utilized the fingerprint match. Higher amounts required the platinum card, which involved the retina scan match. Employers liked the cards, for it allowed them to pay their employees by dropping their cards into the Cred/Pay and tapping in the earned amount (minus with-holding) and minimized the amount of cash on hand that could be stolen by outsiders or pilfered by insiders. Pin numbers, fingerprint and retinal scan security measures kept electronic thievery down to a reasonable level. Those that were clever enough to illegally circumvent the system, but got caught anyway, were usually quickly convicted and sent to a specialized incarceration facility where they did work for the government, who had learned long ago that it truly does take a thief to catch one. Said institution of reformation's 'cells' looked suspiciously like efficiency apartments, and their menu selections contained an unusual amount of 'junk food' items. Unfortunately, that still left those most clever individuals who never got caught. Well, no system was perfect.

"Guilty, your Honor."

"Barnabus Jenkins, the State of Georgia accepts your plea of guilty and sentences you to three months of public service work. You will work from 9 PM to 1 AM at the establishment where you first made acquaintance with our local police force in recompense for damages incurred from your previous behavior. Part of your duties there will be to maintain orderly behavior from the patrons." Georgia judges did appreciate sentences with 'cruel ironies'. "From 1:30 AM to 6 AM, you will then pull a half-day work shift at Milledgeville Hospital in the ER department as an orderly, where you will see first hand examples of unnecessary tragedy due to stupidity and arrogance. A meal will be provided for you, if you wish, by the hospital or you may purchase sustenance from your own resources. Wages you earn at the ER will be donated to the Milledgeville Community Fund, earmarked for distribution to assist families of drunk driving victims. Tips at The Inn are yours to spend as you wish." In other words, if this man wanted more than one meal a day, he'd better learn the meaning of honest work and civil behavior. "There is a bed for your use at The Inn that will be provided at a very nominal cost." The Judge thought that, between that expense and additional food cost, the creep might just lose some of that beer gut.

"Your behavior in our community is expected to be exemplary, which means that if any officer has to look twice at what you are doing, you are not fulfilling the requirements. One transgression will mean a reprimand. A second will land your can back in jail to serve out a two-year incarceration. Do you understand the terms of your sentence?"

"Yes, your Honor, I do." Barry liked the change in Hammer. Normally there would be harsh words and bravado, but this new way was much more peaceful. Barry liked his world orderly, like a fine, long, column of numbers.

While a Georgia Judge sat on his bench, wondering why this leader of an outlaw biker gang was being so respectful and cooperative, an even more confused Rachel sat in Allen's car. Why did young people prefer vehicles with so many buttons, gauges, dials, knobs and things for which she didn't have a ready explanation? She had the key in her right hand. Every car she had ever been in had a key slot accessed by the right hand. There had to be a place to put it. Allen had given it to her, so it had to start the car. He was probably looking out of the office window right now, snickering at his gadget challenged mother. Rachel tried using the key as a slot divining rod, aiming it at various places to see if it would somehow know the way to go from previous experience. For all she knew of current automotive technology, the stupid car might be equipped with a key tractor beam.

"I believe it goes right there."

Rachel's head hit the low roof. "Gustav! Would you please give a lady some warning before popping into her car? No wonder Ryan fled from Vanessa in Hawaii. Thanks, anyway, for the directions." She rubbed her head. There was the slot, right where Gustav had pointed to. It was between a bank of mysterious rocker switches and some indicator lights that might either announce incoming missiles, or warn the driver that his fly was down.

"Mind if I ride along for a while? I'd drive, but my license expired when I did." The car started nicely and at least the gear lever was not difficult to understand. *"I think you may need a little Mendelssohn mental magic".* The sporty

GM Mastiff pulled out of the parking lot. Rachel had left early to take a slow drive and get her thoughts together before meeting with Frank. *"People are always seeking wisdom by contacting the dead. I work cheap by having removed the middleman. Besides, money keeps falling out of my pockets."*

"I suppose. Gustav, I'm not sure at all what I'm going to say to Frank. I don't know if I love him, or if I ever really did love him. Carl keeps popping into mind, Frank doesn't. Frank does things that get my goat. Carl didn't, well, not as often. I want to be with the Family, but I swore that Frank and his children would be my family. You aren't supposed to keep secrets from your husband, but with my new vocation, I'd have to keep many. You are supposed to be there for children, but who knows what my schedule would be, doing what I'm doing? My leaving hurt our…his children, I'm sure of it and I'm very ashamed of it. Oh, Gustav, I'm in such a pickle."

"We should have talked long before this, dear one, but I'll do what I can. Let's get to the basics and see where it goes from there. Rachel, why did God put you on this planet?"

Why was it that the simplest questions were the most complicated ones to answer? Rachel looked at what had made her Rachel over her lifetime. All those volunteer clubs. Being a wife and a mother. Even going back to girl scouts and the groups she had gravitated naturally to in school. "To help others, I think."

"I agree. You are a natural nurturer, a facilitator and, to better accomplish that, you are an organizer. Your natural gift of giving gives you, in return, sustenance to your soul. You are also a moral person. It is part of the foundation that you use to give from. You give because you feel it is the best thing to do, that it is right to do. Morals, though, are all encompassing; they overflow into other areas of our lives. Since your morals are based upon your biblical upbringing, you have aligned with the codes outlined in your religion. That includes fidelity to your family. You have two families to divide your fidelity between and therein resides your cognitive dissonance. Your 'pickle', that is.

"The one family is the one you swore, before a representative of the religion that you base your life on, that you would honor and attend. To deny them would be to deny yourself. The other family is the one that you have discovered to be the best opportunity to fulfill the purpose that God has put you on this earth for. To deny them would be to deny yourself. You have constructed a situation where trying to do both would deny your ability to do either. You can't fish. You can't cut bait. You can't just sit in the boat. Is suicide out of the question?"

"I assume you are joking. Even if you weren't, where would that get me? I'd still be here, wouldn't I?"

"Yes, but Frank and the children would then accept your departure and you would have fulfilled your wedding vows. Most contracts have an escape clause. With marriage, it's 'until death do us part'."

Incredulous, Rachel pulled off the road, put the car in park and turned to face this very strange man. "Are you actually suggesting that I do away with myself? Gustav, that goes against everything I believe in, even more than any of the other choices."

"Good, now that we've got that behind us, I won't worry about you making a decision of desperation and driving off a cliff. Most suicides are committed by sane people in a moment of panic. That was something I wanted to get off your list of options, but you yourself had to take it off." Marianne was right, Rachel thought. Never underestimate Gustav. She wondered why Valerie and he didn't get along. "There is no way out of the prison you have constructed for yourself. You believe that and so, it is so, as long as you continue to believe it. The answer is to change your beliefs. A belief is a choice. Choose a different belief. It's not as hard as all that. Most people need a person of significant authority to accomplish it, but I feel you are beyond the need of a 'rite of passage'. You are your own mother/father/teacher/preacher. Now, look at the situation with your new chosen eyes and find the way."

Gustav leaned back to watch his pupil fail. Failure was the only you learned. It would probably take several falls before she would get it. Perhaps as many as five, as few as two. Rachel put the car back in gear and started back on the road. Driving was mind-time for her, as it was for Melissa.

"OK, I'll give it a go. Let's start by believing that I can do it all and see if the means will appear by being needed to fulfill the goals. I love Carl. No." Fifteen seconds of silence passed as the new frame changed the picture. "I love the *memories* of Carl; for that is the only place he exists on this world. Memories are precious blessings, but they become a curse if they prevent me from going forward. If the shoes were on the other feet and I saw that Carl was holding the torch for me and forsaking the living people who loved him, I'd boot him one. Let's put Carl into one of my boxes on the shelf and pull it down when I need a smile."

Gustav was somewhere between irritated at possibly being wrong and impressed with Rachel's acumen, thinking, *'How on earth did she get all of that down so fast?"*

"I love Frank. I wouldn't have married him if I didn't, but somehow my heart misplaced that feeling. Love doesn't die. Once it's there, it remains, whether we're aware of it or not. I loved, so therefore, I love. You know, I think I can feel it now, at least a part of it. Remind me to put some flowers on your grave today." Gustav heard Rachel's voice gradually and steadily lose the whimper tremble and gain strength. So much for multiple failures before she succeeds.

"I love what I'm doing now and can work it out so that I can be of help with both my family and the Family. I'm Rachel Hawthorn Gladstone, the best organizer you have ever laid eyes on. His children may not have the full time mother in me that they had wanted from their biological mother, but they will receive from me the best I can give them. They will have to work out their own bugs with that in their own time and ways. I can't run their lives for them, only offer my experiences and support. Gustav, what had I been so upset about before?"

"*About things that don't exist.*"

She pulled into the restaurant parking lot, surprised. "How did we get here already?"

"*By being ready for it, dear Rachel.*"

"I wish I could hug you."

"*I'll take a rain check on that. Meantime, I believe that my surrogate hug representative is waiting for you on the porch over there. Is that Frank?*"

Rachel looked at the restaurant entryway and smiled. "That's my husband." She blew Gustav a kiss, then got out of Allen's car. She hesitated. "Gustav, how do you lock this thing? I don't see a key slot." Allen had left his Mastiff unlocked for his mother before she left.

"*You go on, dear lady. Go ahead and take the key. I'll lock up from the inside, then take off for the office. Allen should be available to unravel the mystery of the door's outer lock and I'll pass it on to you in the restaurant.*"

Rachel smiled broadly and then bounced towards Pavelli's. Gustav felt his heart warm as she bounded up the steps and planted a sizable smooch on Frank's lips. The man looked more than pleasantly surprised. "*My God, the man is crying.*" He could see Rachel open her purse and pull out a tissue. Well, she'd had plenty of practice doing that over the past week. The husband and wife walked into the restaurant, leaving Gustav to scratch his head. "*How the hell DO you lock this thing?*" He focused his energies and pressed a likely looking button. The hood popped open, startling a couple walking back to their car. He looked helplessly at the hood and then was fascinated as the thing closed and re-latched itself. How did it do that? His second attempt on a twist-switch started the windshield wipers and squirted the wash fluid. The windows darkened with the third try. This was silly. The car was an alien craft and was, therefore, female. He zipped back to the office, asked Ryan a question, asked Allen which button to push to lock from the inside and how to unlock from the outside, then zipped back and pushed a doodad on the back of the steering wheel column. Stupid cars. He then trotted into the restaurant and whispered something into Rachel's ear, not that it made all that much of a difference how loud he spoke, then left them alone.

Ryan had called ahead earlier to ensure the red carpet treatment, so Roscoe was alerted and ready. Rachel and Frank were met at the door and courteously escorted to a table with privacy. Without asking, Rachel was served Chablis, Frank a Guinness. Rachel wasn't surprised, though Frank was. She was handed a menu, but refused it. "Roscoe, surprise us. No allergies, and we both love everything." Roscoe smiled, winked and left them alone.

"Did your employer arrange this? He must be quite a guy. Rachel, I'm confused. The way you greeted me, the way our last conversations went...what's going on?"

Rachel smiled, feeling the love waxing in her heart once more, and more. She lifted her glass to him and he raised his own to hers in hopeful response. After a clink and a sip, she smiled and asked him a question. "Frank, why did God put you on this planet?"

Frank Gladstone scratched his head while Major McGuinness was looking at the first read-out. Nunzia had found the item before in her own research, but with so much else on her mind she didn't think to inform her Major of it. "My God! Those poor people. Those two *bastards*!" The picture of Vanessa Mary Blankenship showed a happy, youthful woman full of life and hopes, all cut short by (what else?) terrorists; triple-K variety. His military experiences had included seeing sights like that burnt out church, so the image of what it must have been like in person was even stronger for him than it had been for Allen. But, that woman had died in Selma. What was she doing here, for Heaven's sakes? The lady had been born in Florida and no reference was made of her being in Georgia, or any of her family for that matter. Something brought her here, but what? Or perhaps, who? What beef did she have with the ghost of Anita Edwards? Their lives were not concurrent. Florida, Alabama and Georgia were all considered part of the Confederacy. There weren't any descendants from either woman that might have tangled with each other. It was a dead end, so to speak. The report went into a folder, the one that had the double identifications of Vanessa Fitzgalen and Mary Safford on it.

  The Albany Heraldry Corporation had responded to the Governor's 'need to know' request on Major McGuinness's accessing the more personalized version of the Fitzgalen family tree (they didn't make a habit of releasing the seedier side of family histories except to proven blood relatives). It wasn't a high priority item for the company to protect, so only a little arm twisting and a promise that no one would be the wiser was sufficient, plus the usual 'use fee times three' for expediency. The multiple rows of squares and circles with identities under each appeared on his screen. He centered on the one with Ryan Fitzgalen's name in it and began to poke into his ancestral history. He scanned only the names at first and found not much of interest with the parents, the grand parents, but there was a military man in the great grandparent bar. Well, he couldn't pass that up, now could he? He clicked on the square and was startled to see a Civil War uniform adorning one Private Elijah Cooper. A double tap brought up a sidebar menu, including other pictures and whatever historical data was available. The man had died in action in the Civil War under the command of Major Benjamin Covington, part of the 'March to the Sea' campaign. "Hmmm, part of XX Corps." Where had he only recently heard that? Major McGuinness's eyes widened. It couldn't be! He pulled out the picture file from the Edwards video and shuffled through the entries. "There, that's the one." He pulled out the one with the ghost soldier. From his drawer, he pulled out an old fashioned magnifying glass. He studied the hat in the Estate records picture and then looked at the screen. "Rats." That image didn't have a hat on. He tapped on the menu bar again and pulled up alternate pictures. One showed the man wearing the hat of a Civil War Union Private that was identical to the one belonging to the Estate fiasco's ghost soldier. He checked the arm patch on the ghost picture. It was fuzzy, but, yes, the man was indeed a Union Private. The face on the ghost was not visible, but you could tell that there weren't any muttonchops or beard. A moustache was possible, or even a goatee. The genealogy pictures showed Cooper to be a clean-shaven man. Could it be? What were the odds? He looked at another folder, one he had received from the historical records from the Estate. Sixty-five faces looked back at him, two thirds of them didn't fit the description of the ghost-soldier at all. Half of the remainder was questionable, mostly from physical stature. That left nine probables and one of them was Cooper.

The military man ran his fingers through his hair. What other surprises might be hiding in this man's history? Things got pretty sketchy above this level, so he decided to go the other way. Once again he scanned names. Children? Nothing jumped up and barked. Grandchildren? Ditto. Greats? No. Wait. Carl Hawthorn? The last name was a definite bell ringer. Great, greats? NO WAY! A double tap brought up the second person that had perked his interest. "Allen Hawthorn? Holy Mother of God!" He backed up and rapidly scanned pictures of each male descendent of Ryan David Fitzgalen. No descendent closely resembled the old seaman. That would mean… "What in ding-dong blue blazes are we dealing with?" He had to get this information to D'Palermo.

Of all the Task Team members, it was the new person who had kept his head. Russ saw the downward spiral of excitement and emotions into a group state of mind that wasn't objective. And that was putting it nicely. That was when disaster typically struck.

"I said I am going to call in the Feds to take over if we can't calm down. Now, we have an excellent working group that can accomplish a lot if we don't lose our perspective." He had his SatCom in hand, thumb poised over the panic switch. That stopped the others and allowed a breath of sanity into the room. Even Nunzia felt embarrassed for having stepped beyond what was proven and believing things based only on speculation. Right or wrong, she still had to proceed by the book.

"Russ is right. I got caught up in the moment and owe this group an apology."

Paul took a breath. "We all were, partner. Look, you could still be on the right track that this may mark Biblical prophecy, but let's take it calmly and professionally. In my haste, I made a major mistake a few minutes ago. The four horsemen did not herald the anti-Christ and I am having serious difficulties believing that any modern day horseman who heralds the Son of God would bop about the Hudson Valley in a limousine." There was general laughter, still a bit nervous with adrenalin withdrawal.

Zachary was stroking his partner. "You know, I was wondering. My true passion has been to detect ghosts. Once I'd done that, the follow-up was left to others, usually either exorcists or tour guides. IF we prove beyond the shadow of a doubt that the Hawthorn group is hobnobbing with hobgoblins, what happens then? Do they get arrested, lab tested, or sentenced to talk shows for the rest of their natural lives? Dagmar, you and I make a living from exposing things that are of interest to the general public, so it makes sense for us to be here. What is the long term goal for our law enforcement contingent?"

Nunzia and Paul were taken aback and looked at each other. Their jobs had always been to accomplish a goal, not to question the aftermath. Paul said, "That isn't for us to decide. We have to do what we are ordered, and we've been told to discover the full nature of unexplainable circumstances that may or may not pose a hazard to the safety of J.Q. Public."

Zachary continued. "I can accept that, but what I am having trouble accepting is skulking and hiding from people we have come to call our 'targets'. Who made us the assassins? Is there any reason why we don't just call them up and schedule a meeting? They've been cooperative on all but one issue so far."

The brief peek into rampant fanaticism still haunting their minds made this bit of logic seem all the more compelling. Dagmar in particular agreed with changing how they interacted with the Hawthorn group members. That was when Nunzia's SatCom rang. She opened the connect, listening for a few minutes, nodding almost constantly, then snapped her fingers to have her PC opened and fired up. Her Guard issue SatCom had a line-of-sight download transmitter that passed along a significant amount of information to the PC. She closed the conversation with a "Thank you, Sir. I'll report in, tonight." Turning to the Task Team, she said, "Lady and gentlemen, it's a whole new battlefield."

X   CONFRONTATION

Ryan, Gustav, Allen, Melissa (taking a break from her school work), Marianne, Vanessa and Ralph were brainstorming ideas on using this newfound knowledge of belowground spirit entrapments. The office had paled for atmosphere, so they had hiked back over to Marianne's place. There had to be a better way than to have Vanessa and/or Gustav wander about hoping for a chance ankle grab. A spirit would have to be aware that someone was aboveground and looking for them, but there was no guarantee of that being true in every case. Annie's prisoners, including her own children, had displayed no such sense.

The idea of using Atlas was bandied about, but there was too much unknown about that group spying on them and it wasn't even known if Atlas could detect 'spirit a la subterranean'. Marianne's house phone rang, and she picked it up. Within seconds, Marianne held her hand up for silence. After another minute, she asked the person to wait for a moment and then thumbed the 'mute'.

"It's Sgt. Nunzia D'Palermo. She requests the pleasure of our company at a place of our choosing to 'discuss the events of the recent past and other items of mutual interest'. She also says that she hopes that it will be possible for Mr. FITZGALEN and his DESCENDENT to join them." Silence. "Well, what do I say?"

Ryan nibbled his thumbnail a couple of times, then sighed. "I believe it's time to lay some cards on the table. Accept the invitation. Might as well make it tonight. Tell Roscoe we'll need a table for eleven at eight. Marianne reconnected and informed the caller of the details, nodding to Ryan to indicate that the date had been accepted. She closed the connect and Ryan began to speak. "Ladies and Gentlemen, I am an old man. In these many years, I have learned many things. One of the most important bits of hard won wisdom is that the best way to destroy an enemy is to make him your friend. This group has unearthed some of what there is to know. We need to know how much they have discerned and what they plan to do about it. Ghost spying is out with that dratted mutt, so this is the only way I see for us to go."

Allen asked, "Does that Atlas Company make a fashionable muzzle that might be duct taped onto its poster-dog?"

Another call came in, but this time there was a smile when Marianne pushed the mute button. "Guess who's coming to meet the Family? Any objections to having Frank Gladstone pay us a visit?"

Ryan gave a resigned nod of the head. "What the hell, why not?"

Fifteen minutes later, two cars pulled up in the driveway. Frank was nervous at meeting his wife's family (?), for the first time (??). Things were so confused. Rachel grew up with her first family. She married Carl and had Allen; that was her second family. He, she, Allen, Jerry and Janet, well, he supposed that was family number three. Now this? How many families was one person allowed to have? The old Frank Gladstone would have put his British boot down on this nonsense not all that long ago. Yet, to keep what he had thought he had lost and now had miraculously found, Frank would have given up a lot of what he had come to value. Pride was first on the list, as it often was with warring couples who had seen the precipice up close and personal. "Do you think they'll like me?"

"They'll love you. Just be yourself, and don't be afraid. They can sense fear and that can trigger an attack." The look on his face told Rachel that Frank would need some humor lessons. Well, if those were available anywhere in bulk lots, it was here. "I'm pulling your leg, Dear, you'll do fine. Really."

Rachel reached to open the door, but Frank objected. "Shouldn't we knock or ring the bell or something?"

"Frank, Honey, I'm home here. There's no need to knock. We'll just have a nice, quiet, peaceful chat." She opened the door. They walked in.

"FOR HE'S A JOLLY GOOD FELLOW (repeat three times), WHICH NOBODY CAN DENY!" Frank was in shock. Rachel wasn't far behind. What happened to 'quiet and peaceful'? The lot of them converged with smiles and handshakes and welcoming words. Before much more could be said, the men had whisked away one overwhelmed Frank to the kitchen to pop some of Gustav's hidden stash of German Ale and to male-bond.

Rachel sat down on the love seat by the fireplace and the other ladies did likewise. "What just happened?"

Vanessa answered, *"It was a spontaneous guy thing. Dates back to cave man days, I think. Not to worry, Ryan has good instincts on things like this. Picking up after himself? That's another story. Now, give!"*

"Huh?"

Marianne leaned forward. "You heard the spook. Tell us the juicy stuff. Exaggerate where you can, but don't leave out anything. We have to discuss this. It's a cave girl thing, you know."

Melissa added, "Do you mind if I take notes? Allen tells me you are a good role model for me. Oh yes, sign me up for those cooking lessons." The older ladies shared a split second glance that spoke volumes.

The spirit was contagious. Rachel leaned forward and began with her nearly having an accident when surprised by Gustav in the car, relating each remembered detail and ending with how she accidentally mislead Frank as to the nature of his expected first meeting with the Family. In between those two endpoints, "Frank wants to be a good husband to me and sounds willing to take up Ryan on that offer of employment. That would keep Frank from his commuting and ironclad time commitments at his current job and give us a better chance to learn to work with each other. I was in the restaurant when Gustav re-issued that offer from Ryan. We'd be much better able to coordinate kid care and schedules if we're both on the team here. Worth a shot."

Marianne leaned back, chuckled and commented, "I can't believe you are the same Rachel that was falling apart about this whole thing just a short time ago. Did my Gustav really do all that for you?"

"And then some. Marianne, the man is a saint! No wonder you love him so. What a father figure. From what I've seen of how he cares for you, it must have truly broken his heart when his son died so early in life."

Marianne Cabrini knew more of that part of Gustav than Ryan did. "It did that. It was before I knew him, but I've come to know him pretty well. Better than Ryan, perhaps, in ways. Oh, and there's news! Those people who have been following us around? We're going to have dinner with them tonight. Oh dear! What do we do with Frank?"

"We take him with us."

Rachel was speechless, for two seconds. "Gustav! Are you nuts? What about keeping Ryan's secret? And how about wearing some ghostly chains so we can hear you sneaking up on us?"

Before she could go further, Marianne held up her hand. "It isn't much of a secret, anymore, or not as much as it used to be. The Guard Sergeant that called requested that 'Mr. Fitzgalen and his descendent' be there. Looks like someone's been doing their homework."

Vanessa added, *"Rachel, Honey, we don't know what this will mean, but I've learned to go with what comes. You can't keep fighting every thing that doesn't go according to the original battle plan. Most times the changes wind up being the best for everyone concerned. We'll just have to wait and see what unfolds."*

Allen had his hand on Frank's shoulder. "Frank, I want to thank you now, before witnesses, for all the trouble you've gone through on my behalf. I didn't always make it easy for you, and you kept an even temper no matter how many times I pushed your hot buttons. You're OK with me."

Ralph chimed in. "That's some lady you have there. She's been a real super trooper in my book. If Rachel thinks you're the man for her, and she does from my vantage point, then you're tops in my book, too."

Ryan added, "Frank, your lady has found out a lot about herself and that's good for both of you. She's stronger in some ways, now, and that's easy to take the wrong way. She hasn't rejected you; she's accepted herself and gained independence from it. She's with you because she loves you, not because she feels dependent on you. That's a real improvement, as you will come to see. Now, how would you like to give her the greatest present of all to celebrate your reunion?"

There was no argument there. The three of them moved to the front porch, just in case there would be an argument involved with Elizabeth Gladstone in the process; no sense on upsetting the ladies. Allen pulled out his SatCom and Frank used it to talk to his ex-wife regarding an unplanned extra sleepover for that night and to his two children about an unplanned career change. There was mistiness in his eyes when he finally thumbed the disconnect, but he was smiling. "Ryan, set it up. I'm your new employee! Uh, what exactly is it that I'll be doing?"

While Frank's head was spinning from the answers he got from his question, Roscoe was setting up the usual meeting room. It was sad that he wouldn't be seeing Gustav anymore, but pleased that the Hawthorn group, as they called themselves now, was still sticking together. Eleven people. No, Ryan had called to make it twelve. Odd bird, that Ryan. Always there with the group; he never said much. Yet, Roscoe knew that Ryan was the defacto head of the clan. You didn't make the income as a waiter that he did by not knowing your customer group dynamics. He and Ralph were cut of the same cloth. Twelve people coming to dinner, and a dog? That made thirteen, sort of. He was tempted to yank their chain by setting it up to look like the 'Last Supper', but decided against it. Something about the way Ryan spoke told him that this meeting was too important for that sort of joking around. Seven-thirty. They'd soon arrive. He hoped the mutt was house trained.

The Task Team was putting the last personal touches on for their meeting. Dagmar's hair and make-up was up to video production level, Atlas was thoroughly brushed, Russ's suit was de-linted, Nunzia's uniform was to spec's. Paul left his Sergeant's uniform in the closet, preferring this time to go two-piece. That kept his service weapon well hidden. You never knew.

Paul reviewed Nunzia's earlier presentation in his mind. He remembered talking to his Reverend about prophecies in the Bible. If prophecies were holy foretellings, then they had to come about by God's design. If Hitler had been the anti-Christ (many might think so), then would someone going back in time and trying to assassinate him and save millions of people from extinction be actually going against God? It was like that poor soul that was walking alongside of the Arc of the Covenant. One of the designated carriers had stumbled and the Arc was in danger of toppling. The man had braced it from falling, saving it and what was inside of it from damage and was rewarded for his efforts with death due to disobeying the Lord's command of 'no touchee'. Being a Christian was sometimes damn confusing. Why did he feel the need to pack his piece tonight? He didn't know, but he didn't leave it behind, either.

The five of them got into two rentals obtained at Johnson's Ford a few hundred yards down from their hotel. The directions were pretty clear and the infamous traffic circle was finally getting more decipherable. It wasn't too confusing, once you got the knack. Sure attracted its share of idiot drivers, though.

The Family got to Pavelli's a little early. Ryan wanted to be there first for psychological and political advantage. The Task Team had decided to do the same thing for the same reasons. The limo pulled up the same time as the two Ford rentals. Well, thought Ryan, might as well make it a level playing field. Vanessa and Gustav had stayed at Marianne's for the time being. Ryan felt certain that he could connect with Vanessa when and if the time was ripe and Gustav was now pretty good at homing in on the 'happy-joy' beacon the Family could produce. The two groups met in the lot, introduced each other, and then moved en masse to the front door of Pavelli's.

They opened the door and found Roscoe waiting, seeming ever so slightly non-plussed. Neither group would ever know that there was a betting pool going on as to which group of guests would arrive first. The new bartender-trainee had won out, being the only one ballsy enough to bet on a tie. The kid pulled in over two hundred dollars on that one and forever earned the tag on the end of his name of 'the Greek'. No one really knew where the term had come from, but the English language was like that.

The private meeting and dining room had a large round table, as per Ryan's instructions. Dagmar thought of the Paris Peace Talks she had read about, since much of that to-do initially was to determine the nature of the table the participants would sit at. Ralph was more the romantic and, along with half the others, was more reminded of King Arthur and his famous furniture. Frank wondered at first at the high chair, until he noticed the Chihuahua. The lady at his arm whispered into his ear. He looked at her, surprised. "THE Atlas?" She nodded. Frank wasn't informed of too much regarding the true nature of the Family. He was left with instructions from the apparent titular head that he was to keep his mouth shut, but ears, eyes, and mind open, and something about his hanging on to his grip on reality. Ryan had a flair for the dramatic, at times.

There was no head at a circular table, but there was soon little doubt of who the true heads were. Ryan had Ralph to his right, then Marianne, followed by Rachel and Frank. At that point, the Task Team began with Russ, Zachary/Atlas, Dagmar, Nunzia and Paul. To Ryan's left were Allen and Melissa. Dagmar looked sidelong at her youthfulness and wondered about her role in such a group, with just a twinge regarding Melissa's superior photogenic qualities. The Task Team had elected Dagmar as their primary spokesperson. Tea and coffee were poured, orders taken and the double doors shut by the headwaiter. Taking the lead, Dagmar aimed her first comment directly to Ryan. "Mr. Fitzgalen, I presume?" The chess game had begun. The Task Team knew that a piece, or pieces, was/were missing from the board, as spirit sensitive Atlas was sitting on his custom high chair, contentedly nibbling at a doggie nicety.

Ralph studied the board. The king was white, by virtue that it was he who had arranged the playing board a la Pavelli's and that constituted the first move. The black queen had made a bold opening gambit in response. Would the white king respond in kind?

"Dagmar Yaddow. I've seen you many times on CNN. You have always struck me as tops in your profession. Since you and your group have called this meeting, I think it would be politic for you to state your intentions and desires first." The white king feints with misdirection, neither confirming nor denying the queen's question, and then he sets the first rules of the playing field. Ralph looked at the other players. They were patiently waiting in reserve for their moves, if any, to come. How would the king and queen use their assets, he wondered?

Dagmar recognized the significance of the responses, for there were more than one. This king can move more than one space at a time. This chess game would have different rules than the traditional one. "As you may have guessed, we are a team that has been tasked with the responsibility to unravel the mysteries that revealed themselves at the Edwards Estate last Saturday. My companions represent various agencies and therefore have various reasons for being here. No crime has been committed, other than possibly a bizarre case of vandalism. I'm here because this is a newsworthy story. Zachary Lorriman's career involves the detection of ghosts, so he has been a logical team member. Sgt. Paul Wasserman and Sgt. Nunzia D'Palermo represent the police and National Guard, respectively, and add their investigative talents and information resources to the mix. Russ Anderson is an FBI Special Agent with forensics experience. These last three are mainly tasked with making sure that the general population is not endangered by forces such as the ones witnessed at the Edwards Estate."

The queen has shown herself capable of multiple moves as well. She has demystified the playing board by identifying her pieces. Interesting. Truth, or misdirection? Truth, Ralph thought. The queen wants an honest game, which fits her reputation. The FBI presence has discomfited the king mightily, he noticed. Now the glove has been laid down. Will the king respond in kind?

"Quite an impressive set of credentials. Allen Hawthorn, to my left, is the CEO of Hawthorn Enterprises. Until recently, our late Mr. Mendelssohn held that position as an interim post. Allen's father, Carl, was CEO until his untimely death in a vehicle accident when Allen was only four years old. To his left is his lady friend, Melissa Banks, who is also an RPI student along with Allen. To my right is Ralph Kithcart, my right hand man who has taken up some of the slack left by Gustav's departure. Marianne Cabrini was Gustav's office manager and still fills that position as we make alternative arrangements for legal representation of Hawthorn Enterprises. Next to her are Allen's mother, Rachel, and his step-father, Frank Gladstone." The king responds in kind, but goes no further. He leaves it up to the queen to further reveal her goals for the game.

"Mr. Fitzgalen, or may I call you Ryan?" The king nodded. "We have amassed evidence of some pretty startling things that you may be of help in shedding some light on."

"Dagmar?" The queen also nodded. "Fine. Dagmar, perhaps it would help matters if you outline what you have discovered so far and we will do what we can to fill in the blanks. You will hopefully accept that there may be some matters we deem important to keep from general knowledge for business security reasons." The queen requests cooperation, the king sets limits. Will either of the two use any of their pieces or were they just a show of force? If the queen responds to the king's request, that will show a lot of how the game will proceed.

"Very well. We believe you to be Ryan David Fitzgalen, USN, retired on medical discharge. You were at Pearl Harbor shortly after the Japanese attack." The conversation temporarily stopped as Frank Gladstone had something go down the wrong pipe. Dagmar looked at him. He hadn't been present at the Estate, as far as they knew. A new addition? Ill informed? Things began to settle down and no Heimlich seemed to be imminent. The queen continued, still confident, but just a little bit wary.

"Something happened to you, possibly due to the nature of the recently declassified experiments the Navy was conducting in the field of high level magnetics. Allen Hawthorn is your great, great grandson. You had a great grandfather who rode with the same company of Union soldiers that was involved in the tragedy of the Edwards Estate and we strongly suspect that his spirit was the one that was shown in the video of the conflict there Saturday. You assisted in the fight against the spirit of Mrs. Edwards that day, though we don't know the nature of the reasons for that conflict. Spearheading that fight was the spirit of Vanessa Mary Blankenship, who died in a KKK provoked church fire in Selma back in the 1930's. Somehow, she was involved with your marriage to a woman who had been declared brain dead in St. Louis about twenty years later. That woman's name was Mary Safford, but something happened and you married a woman whose name was Vanessa, but happened to be almost physically identical to Mrs. Safford. Mr. Mendelssohn, who died at the Estate, remains with your company in spirit form and ditto for the spirit of Vanessa Blankenship Fitzgalen. We believe that your group engineered many of the details of the Edwards Event for purposes only known to you, but those actions initiated that ghost battle that cost the life of your Mr. Mendelssohn. You have kept the presence of the two spirits you keep company with away from this meeting, as you didn't want our dog to detect them. Now, Ryan, would you be so kind as to illuminate us on where our 'theories' fall short of the mark?"

The queen doesn't NEED other pieces. The white team appears stunned. In fact, Rachel was patting her husband's cheeks. "Frank? FRANK? FRANK!" The black team was a little confused. Why did the husband of the mother of the CEO just faint and why did the rest of the Hawthorn group seem so happy about the fact…with high fives, no less? The white rook sitting next to the white king wondered if his sovereign purposefully kept the new chess piece in the dark for this very reaction.

FBI rook Russ leaned over to the correspondent queen and whispered, "Are you sure they aren't aliens?"

Dagmar was biting her right pinky fingernail, a habit she had so ingrained that. in her early days of broadcasting, she had once duct taped her hand under the news desk. "I'm, not sure."

Ryan turned to his opposition. It didn't seem wise to try to dispute what this obviously talented group had unearthed. He was more concerned now in finding how far this information had gotten to. There wasn't much choice, as far as he was concerned.

"My congratulations to your team. So far, you have been entirely accurate in your 'theories'. I might fill in some blanks, but you did well. So, now what do you propose?"

The king bows to the queen's firepower. He wishes to find out the queen's terms. Is this check, or checkmate? Probably check. Ryan doesn't give up easily and likes to change ball games. Is the queen overconfident and will that be her downfall? The black knight Guard spoke up. "Then, it's all true? You're in league with ghosts? Why? To what purpose?"

The queen looks in poorly concealed annoyance at the piece that broke ranks. The black team hasn't been tried under fire long enough, it would seem. Another weakness? The king nudges the player to his left; a gesture indicating similar equality among the ranks. How noble.

Allen answered by stating the purpose of the Fitzgalen Family. Almost all the cards were on the table. He went further to say that to allow this to become general knowledge would, most likely, destroy their mission due to public panic or religious fanaticism reaction. The white team each noticed that this last statement had struck a chord with the black pieces. Allen looked at Ryan, who nodded, and then continued. He filled in the gaps regarding the entire Union foraging party, the split personality of Annie Edwards, the tragedy of Annie's two children, the slaves who became twice liberated. He went further to describe what had happened at Gustav's interment with Bernhardt, their desires to continue their liberation mission for such trapped souls that might still exist in the dark earth and would any of them like to assist them in this effort?

Ralph almost had to laugh. The queen had thought she had control of the playing board. The king had used his young knight to blindside the entire opposition. The effect was so that the offer to merge forces wasn't even recognized. The entire black team had been stricken with a case of the 'duh's. Yet, the words of cooperation were there as a first exposure, like when a vacuum cleaner salesman would put the contract of sale on the table, but leave it there without further comment. A man could learn a lot from

Mr. Fitzgalen in the arts of verbal warfare. Ralph also knew that there was little for Ryan to lose, since his enemy had his camp so thoroughly scouted. If he knew his friend, Ryan would pull one more whammy, for effect. Ralph saw Ryan close his eyes and concentrate. Moments later, the patrons of Pavelli's heard, from behind the closed double doors of a private dining room, a frantic staccato of non-stop, high-pitched barking.

A thousand miles to the south, there was a bit of barking between a devotee of Tarot and a believer in pendulums. Normally, people of the non-mainstream prognostic professions observed professional acceptance of each other's ways of searching the mists for truth. Alcohol, in this case, amplified each practitioner's defensiveness of his art. Fingers were being pointed into each other's face and chest to emphasize points that the other person was far too dense to understand. The importance of the argument suffered a sudden loss of priority, as each protagonist found himself floating in the air, each suspended from a massive arm that was attached to a bearded, blue-eyed face. "Gentlemen, I don't understand much of what you two are jabbering about. I do understand that you are both drunken bozos that need a taxi to take them to their hotel rooms. Now, there just happens to be one outside this establishment with your names on it. Are there any questions? No? Good. The waitress that's had to put up with your noise is a nice lady. Her name is Susan. I like her a lot. You like her, too, don't you? She deserves a big tip, doesn't she?" Both men, still dangling, grappled for their wallets and tossed several denominations onto the table. "Good boys, I'm right proud of you. Now, let's go meet Mr. Cabbie."

Hammer deigned to lower the men enough so as to let their feet touch the ground every other step. It looked almost like they were walking on the moon. Barry Nicholson was behind the bar cleaning glasses and stacking them with absolute precision in their appropriate racks. This was fun and he couldn't wait to see what working in the hospital would be like. Just think of all that inventory!

Atlas's machinegun yapping had finally been brought under control. *"Is that all the ferocious beast is capable of?"*

"Give it a break, Herr Gustav. He had the element of surprise back then. Suppose you had a cock-roach suddenly appear on your nose?"

Zachary was doing his level best to put a lid on the scolding from Atlas. He had to resort to the thumb/index pinch again, but even then the dog kept growling and bristling. Atlas focused on the side of the room where the condiment table was, the Task Team's eyes gravitated to the same location, the Task Team's hair on the back of their necks doing a fair approximation of what could be seen on Atlas.

Ryan nodded slightly and smiled, then asked if he could borrow a couple of those dog dainties that Atlas seemed so fond of. Zachary didn't take his eyes off the area of suspicion, but nodded to the leather pouch next to his plate, which was passed over to Ryan. Ryan unzipped the pouch, extracted two yummies and held them about ear high, one in each hand. That diverted Atlas's attention and gave the room a welcome spate of silence. The Task Team saw Ryan let go of the biscuits with the dramatic flair of a stage magician, but they didn't fall. They just stayed in the air. Inarticulate expressions escaped the five visitors (and from one of the home team), while Atlas alternated his focus between each treat and their respective modes of transportation. One of the treats began to lower itself to within a few inches away from the dog, who sniffed it and, very carefully, took it. A minute later, the other treat met a similar fate. Atlas seemed at ease now, judging by the wagging tail.

Ryan had just won a final strategic advantage and even Ralph had missed the significance. The white king executed a gentle checkmate when he addressed Zachary, "I'm sure that your hound will still sound the alarm with strange entities, especially those that are not equipped with one of your doggie treats. You have witnessed an effort to manipulate solid objects on behalf of Gustav Mendelssohn and Vanessa Fitzgalen. Both are very friendly and helpful entities to those who do NOT interfere with our mission. Your early spirit alarm will likely no longer function, now that he is familiar with both of OUR entities. My team WILL be allowed to pursue their purpose without undue outside interference. Do I make my point clear?"

Ralph shook his head and smiled. The black team wasn't even in the same league. He had to speak up, though. It seemed right to do and Ryan usually allowed that as reason enough to jump in. "We're concerned about how many others have your awareness of us. Who else knows so many details of our group?" He had already eliminated Zachary as a likely problem; too solitary. The FBI, the Guard and the police? Those were more worrisome, especially the last two. Ryan may have been mostly worried about the FBI involvement, but Ralph realized that the Bureau was far too hidebound to go chasing after ghosts.

Nunzia was still wide eyed. "My...Commanding Officer, Major McGuinness. He's the one who had helped a lot with the research. I doubt he's told anyone, yet. Probably waiting on my report first to see what it was he could report on."

Dagmar was next. "The CNN Science Desk is doing some research for me, but not on you people; mostly on how to use animals to detect spirits and, well, ways to deal with them."

Melissa asked, "Deal with which, the animals or the spirits?"

Dagmar was nervous in answering that. "The, uh, spirits."

Marianne didn't like the sound of that. "Deal with them, as in how?"

This was looking like it might get ugly. Paul could sense his service pistol, but what did he honestly think he was going to do with it? Dagmar said, in a small voice, "Exorcism."

The Task Team held its collective breath. Saying the 'E' word where there were two bonafide dead people floating about seemed, at best, politically incorrect, or P.I. for short. Paul had a passing thought that, in his business, P.I. also stood for personal injury. He steeled himself for reaction to the upcoming action, whatever it would be. He could feel the energy begin to rise in his right arm and hand as he took a quick scan of the potential targets. Russ sensed more than saw Paul sizing up the situation and then automatically took his own assessment of options. Both came to the same conclusion that Nunzia had already reached all of two seconds ago...options were nil when it came to human defense against spiritual presence.

Six home team people (and two entities) reacted strongly indeed and took the Task Team by complete surprise. They laughed themselves silly. The Task Team collectively sighed, then decided that laughter was a good thing to join in on. Roscoe opened the door and stopped. People were out of their chairs. People were laughing, some nervously. What did he walk in on? Ryan waved him in and invited everyone to return to his or her chairs. Food was an excellent aid to the conversation, slowing words down to measured and bite sized bits that didn't have such indigestion potential. Vanessa had taken a liking to Atlas, as there weren't many animals that were able to actually see her. Those that did see or sense her never acted too friendly. She had always loved animals in the past and had no compunction now against robbing various plates of tasty treats to get in good with the 'sweet little doggie'. She even managed to pet him several times. Floating bits of entrees unnerved the Task Team. Russ asked, "Does it take a while to get used to this sort of thing?"

Frank had the occasional giggle at the unreality of it all; a protective reaction to help keep his sanity from complete free fall. He had to bite his lip when his wife answered the FBI forensic specialist. "Actually, it's not as bad as it used to be. We can all see them, Gustav and Vanessa, that is. Ryan figures that spirits radiate a type of energy that is not registered by most brains. Atlas is an exception to that rule. Ryan's perception broadened when that Navy experiment affected his atomic structure. The rest of us had similar mind expansion during the Edwards debacle. Frank is the only one without 'the sight', as it is called."

Dagmar was getting back into her interview mode as her natural fallback to a reality check. "Can you touch them? They can interact with matter, so can they...harm you?"

Marianne was about to say no, but remembered the shiner Vanessa had given Ryan at the Estate. "Very unlikely, though I've read about cases where a supposedly evil minded or insane entity was alleged to have pushed someone over a cliff. That has never been proven and we've had hundreds of experiences with entities. Annie Edwards was an exception to the rule, as she had a severely split personality. She had three fractured selves. One was crazy, powerful, but relatively harmless, one was raging, not as powerful, but able to deceive and aim the power of the one I just mentioned, and the last was the sweetest woman that ever floated the earth. Someone might get accidentally clobbered by a flying object launched by a poltergeist, but that's pure accident and never intentional, from our research. It's more like a mindless tantrum. Gustav once told me that Annie's mad self lacked the normal 'hold-backs' a sane mind would have, which helps explain the incredible and destructive power she wielded. Brain damaged people have been known to cause immense harm because they just don't have the programming to not commit all their force to an action."

Rachel was next and this part would be a major decision junction. Allen had already planted the seed earlier. "People, you guys are good, real good. We are astounded at how much you were able to find out about us. Our Family would like to ask whether you might like to assist us in our mission. Zachary, we're especially interested in you and Atlas. Can he sense only by sight?"

Zachary responded to the last question first, as the first question was too big to have registered its import yet. "I'm not always sure. He seems to use sight as his main method of detection. If there is a lot of emotion involved on the part of the ghost, he gets upset when we near such an area. There were some plantations of particularly vicious owners where Atlas just won't go near. I don't think that it was the presence of any spirits so much as echoes of their sorrow that was absorbed by inanimate objects. Other times...wait a minute. What did you say? You want us to join you? Did you say that?" Zachary's expression looked like a game show contestant's who had just been given the grand prize.

His Task Teammates were too busy listening to his response to have caught it either. They collectively looked at Rachel, then each other, then at the other Hawthorn group members to see if this was a collective offer or something one of these people popped off with on their own. They were met with searching eyes, waiting for their answers. Task Team forks went for morsels (unclaimed by Vanessa) just to buy time where nothing was expected to come out of their mouths (not polite to eat and talk, you know). The Family followed suit, encouraging the other team to take their time. Ryan said, "We don't expect an immediate answer. You all have lives that you've mapped out and we're asking you to make some changes. Oh, Frank? You don't have a choice in the matter, anymore. You're officially Family, now, ever since you passed our initiation requirement."

Frank weakly asked, "Wha... What did I do?"

Rachel kissed him on the cheek and smiled lovingly. "You fainted, Honey."

"Oh, that's nice, I guess. Huh?"

"Later, Love. We've got a lot of talking to do later. Marianne, if you don't mind, I'll skip your hospitality tonight. I'm going home."

The night wore on. True to his word, Ryan and his entourage never pressed the Task Team to make a decision. They encouraged questions, though, and asked many of their own, not all regarding the paranormal.

Melissa bent Dagmar's ear a lot, wanting to know more about how a woman had risen to become such an internationally known mass media persona. For her part, Dagmar found Melissa to be surprisingly quick on the uptake, deep on the insights, and became aware of her growing desire to take this bird under her own wing. "What potential," she sensed. This was more than just a pretty face, and the rest of her for that matter. "Oh, to be that age again."

Ralph had hit it off pretty well with Russ. Paul gravitated to that group, but tended to remain quiet and observant. Nunzia instantly targeted Marianne. Both were organizers, both were formidable in a fight and, wonder of wonders, both were of Sicilian descent. Neither were fluent in their grandparents' native tongue, though both could come up with some colorful phrases when the occasion demanded it. Nunzia had to hear more of what the two run-ons with Hammer had been like.

Rachel spent a lot of her time soothing Franks jangled nerves and Ryan had attracted the attention of Zachary, who, by this time, had managed to accept that bits of food did indeed float in air and land in Atlas's surprisingly big stomach for a dog his size. Gustav and Vanessa wandered here and there, when she wasn't lavishing attention on her new pet (she had clearly asked Zachary right to his face if she could have Atlas for her very own and he didn't say no, so…). The snippets of conversation were a good sign that there was communication at least, a growing mutual respect, obviously and, perhaps, inklings of new friendships. When he wanted to, Ryan could attract friends like Florida attracted retirees. Gustav and Vanessa strolled and took in the tones and words as they blended together.

"You mean you would really let me sit in on one of your broadcasts? REALLY?"

"So Vanessa wasn't able to get the entities to cross over, just because she was a ghost and a woman? That really bites. Is it hard to get ghosts to realize they're dead?"

"That's why your snap kick was caught by that bruiser? Your petticoats got in the way?"

"She sat on my plate? The sausage? Is *that* what you guys broke up about? Oh, gross!"

"Well, maybe there was a little danger, but it was worth it. We got all those soldiers to cross over, plus the two kids, plus returned the 'mad Private' to sanity and salvation, plus we got Annie put back together and got her over as well."

"I want you to go over that dream sequence with Mad Annie again, especially the part about the slave revolt."

"How on earth did you manage to get that horse path established with all the right of way and property rights hurdles?"

"She CLOBBERED you? A black eye?"

"And then, I started dressing for comfort and you wouldn't believe all the nice guys that came out of the wall acting like a herd of love sick puppies. You have GOT to meet Barbara. She's going to freak when she hears I was talking to you!"

"On HORSEBACK? Through a FURNITURE STORE?"

"The Bureau isn't quite what it used to be. We are now interdependent with the newsies on information gathering and it seems to be working out OK. Now the main rights the people we arrest want to hear about are the ones to publish their story."

"Vanessa traded places with Mary? Christ! Is that legal?"

"A lap full of coffee? That poor truck driver."

All were enjoying their social intercourse, but there was something about the head of the Family speaking that caused other conversations to gradually die down by unspoken consent, as they all tuned into what Ryan was saying to Zachary.

"There is no other feeling in the world like it. It is the finest service you can perform for any of God's creations; to remove the bondage that prevents him or her to seek the company of their creator and of all those loved ones that went on before. I've been doing it for a century and it never fails to bring up all the deepest emotions in my heart. Now that I can share it with others who have been blessed with the sight, the sharing magnifies the joy. The problem is, I am only one man, albeit a long lived one. This job is far too big for just me. The God's honest truth is that I'm overwhelmed by the shear magnitude. We need help, but we also need discretion. We need alternatives for detection of these entities in need. Atlas may or may not be the answer, but it's a possible start. Our resident spirits may or may not be able to sense underground like Annie did, but it's worth trying…" Ryan noticed then the lack of background conversation. He slowly turned and looked around behind him to find that he had an audience. Decades of discretion and avoiding attention made the scrutiny a little uncomfortable for him. He stopped talking due to awkwardness, but it was the best thing he could have done. There are times you have to shut up to make progress. Knowing when such times were wasn't Ryan's strongest point.

Zachary was the first to speak, stepping around Ryan to join the others. "I have been looking for this, without knowing it, for the past twenty years. I am very tired of doing half a job, when I can even get to that job. My business interests provide me with enough income to pursue my career, but it takes up so much of my time. Ryan, I will accept your offer to incorporate Atlas Petite Pet Supply, Inc. as a sister subsidiary to Hawthorn Enterprises, in return for a salaried part time directorship of what is now your affiliated company, plus a full time participation in your mission. I will have my lawyer call yours in the morning." The two men shook hands.

"I accept the terms, Director Lorriman. But unless your lawyer has access to a medium, he or she will deal with our paralegal, Marianne Cabrini."

Russ Anderson was next. "Ladies and gentlemen, this has been one of the three most memorable days of my life, my marriage and the birth of my son being the other two. I regret I cannot join you as a full time person, for my roots and my family are in Pennsylvania. But maybe it would not be to your advantage for me to leave the Bureau. I want to be part of this, with all of my heart, but I can best be of service if I can retain my connections and resources in the FBI. I will give you my personal SatCom connect number and my word that nothing said here will leave this room by me. I will have to make a report to the Director. For that matter, all of us except Zachary have to report to someone. I guess we need to decide on what it is that we're going to report."

Dagmar Yaddow took that as her cue. "Since I have the rights to break the results of this effort on the news, I will coordinate the report with everyone here, especially with you, Ryan. The public has a right to know the truth. I will not compromise that. Your work is too important, though, to be compromised. We'll strike a balance, somehow. I feel it can be done. Like Russ, you don't need me running around sniffing gravesites so much as you can use what I am able to gather from my sources, or to spread information across the globe. That will be my contribution to this effort. Now, correspondents have a limited professional lifetime, so I won't always have that capacity. Perhaps I can see if Melissa might be brought along as a protégé. Tell me, dear, is it too late to change your major to journalism?"

"Do you really mean it? HELL YES!" Melissa was bouncing up and down like Tigger, thought Vanessa. Good for her! The brat needed some direction in her life and this path could take her far.

Paul spoke up next. "Everyone, I am a policeman. My place is on a police force. I'm sure of that. You don't need a ready gun and the type of investigation you require isn't my strong point. I need to be where I can do the most good for the most people and that's back in Georgia. My work on the Force and with my church pretty well takes up what time I don't spend with my home and family. Put me on the Second String for emergencies. If there's something I can lend a hand with, you'll get my best effort. I'm sorry."

Nunzia saw the want in Paul's heart and sensed his realization that this tempting path wasn't the right one for him to take. She had seen that look before and it had made her heart ache for him then, as it did now. She went over to the man and embraced him. To anyone else, Paul Wasserman looked solid as a rock, but Nunzia could feel the trembling deep inside of him. What she didn't know was that not all of that reaction had to do with declining the Hawthorn offer. She whispered in his ear, "Walk your path, dear friend. Our ways keep meeting and I'm sure we will meet again. Go home to Betty and the kids. They need you there. I will always love you,

Paul."

Nunzia's last three sentences had pretty well summed up the cause for Paul's growing internal turmoil. She turned back to the gathering, missing the misting in the policeman's eyes. "As for your offer, Ryan, I too must decline full time participation. My life is the Guard. I've sworn my honor and service to my state and that's where I belong. I'll join my dear friend, Paul, on the Second String. You can call on me anytime for research. The Guard has resources that might surprise you and hopefully will help you."

Ryan sighed. It was not all he wanted, but was far better than the worst case. Such was life. These were good people and he had made friends of potential adversaries. Not bad, for a day's work. "So be it. The hour is getting late and our brains are fogged by emotional strain and rich linguini. I suggest we each consider what we feel would be the right thing to do at this juncture as far as reports to superiors go, but don't lose sleep over it. We'll do a working breakfast tomorrow. Since most of you are at the Holiday Inn, we'll score a conference room and have it catered. Eight thirty, people. Bring sharp pencils and hot PC's."

Late that night, Rachel awoke. She turned to see the face of her husband, awake. "Can't sleep, Honey?"

"Hmmm? I guess not…lot on the mind. Rachel, there is so much to think about, so many changes to take in. It seems so clear, yet so unreal, like I find myself in a waking dream I can't wake up from."

Rachel snuggled up to her husband, delighting in how it felt. "I understand, Frank. It was like that for me at first and it still feels that way sometimes. I really can't believe how little time has passed since Allen and I went to that first meeting with Ryan. I feel like a lifetime has come and gone. There's so much I want to share with you and that's a wonderful feeling. And Baby, I'm so very happy you have given me my family back after I turned my back on you. Please forgive me."

Frank recalled those days of uncertainty and anguish, alternating between feelings of outrage and depression. Yet, "You did what you had to do. The result was miraculous for all those spirits and for you, too. I can see what Ryan said was right. You are much stronger, more whole now. It seems a shame that growth has to be born so often of pain. You make a beautiful butterfly, Rachel." Frank sighed.

Rachel knew that sigh. She sat up. "There's more, Love. Something is troubling you. What is it?"

"I'm blind, Rachel. All of you have your sight, now. You all say I'm part of the Family, but am I? Do I even want to be? I'm not sure, Honey, but I am sure I want to be with you. It's so confusing."

The wife reached out and caressed the husband's face. "I was blind here at first, too, and I became a part of the whole before I gained my sight. There are many ways to see and many ways to serve. Give it time, as I did.

You will find your place here. It's the way it works in this Family." Rachel hugged her husband, feeling content. The feel of her next to him, loving him again, gave Frank's heart peace. There was much to do tomorrow, but that was tomorrow. He closed his eyes and felt the breath of his wife warm on his neck, like gentle ocean waves. With that peace, he fell asleep, content as well.

XI WEDNESDAY

The combined teams went to work in earnest. Major McGuinness had been told last night that things were winding down and to expect Sgt. D'Palermo back in Georgia by the next day at the latest. Milledgeville Chief of Police, Mark Hamm, relayed Sgt. Wasserman's report to Mayor Linda LaRoche that the Task Team had been successful and that the upcoming news report that evening or tomorrow morning should wrap things up. The FBI office in Pittsburgh was pleased to be getting the services of one of their top forensics specialists back within the next twenty-four hours. There was a backlog of things that needed Special Agent Anderson's legendary attention and skills. Melissa was absent, to the disappointment of the correspondent. She had to be back early to turn in all her missed work, to get back into her class routine, and to change her major.

Melissa had been buttonholed by Barbara Meissner, but declined to explain anything for the time being. Barbara would have to be satisfied with having to wait until Melissa had the time and mental focus to share her recent past with her friend. Part of her disclosure delay was to see just how much was going to be released to the general public by the Task Team and the Family.

If the distraction of young men had been annoying before, the convergence of what seemed half the student body was hysteria producing. She would just tell them to catch CNN for a special report. Later that afternoon, she found out that the report would come out that evening, given by Independent Correspondent Dagmar Yaddow. She was the one that broke the Edwards event in the first place, people said. Melissa made the mistake of telling someone besides Barbara that she had met Dagmar yesterday personally. From that point on, Melissa had to jog between classes, lock her dorm room door and turn off the phone. She opened her door long enough to tape a sign to it that read, 'GO AWAY'. Evening came and Melissa managed a meal with what was still in her fridge that wasn't growing legs. She did let Barbara sneak in and they patched CNN into Melissa's PC. At nine PM, precisely, the 'Special Investigative Report' logo flashed across the screen, with the appropriate and expected horn blaring announcement music. Many in other time zones were staying up past their bedtimes or waking up in the wee hours to catch it; many others would review their recording of it in the morning. Melissa smiled when Dagmar's face came on. Barbara asked, again, if she had really met her. Melissa responded with a finger to her lips and a 'Shhhh!'

"Good evening. I'm Independent Correspondent Dagmar Yaddow.

Four days ago, our country, our world, was stunned by the events that took place in a small city in Georgia, the city of Milledgeville." Still shot: the energy bolt explosion...two semi-transparent figures doing battle on the porch of the Edwards Homestead Estate Main House. "Our investigation indicates that the two entities seen are indeed the residual essences of Mrs. Anita Edwards (portrait of her with her husband), former plantation owner, and Vanessa Mary Blankenship (picture of the newspaper clipping), a young school teacher from Florida that died in Selma, Alabama, as a result of a Klan related church burning (split-image, same newspaper, obits on one side, burnt out church on the other).

"A group of people associated with the Hawthorn Enterprises Company, based in upstate New York, were caught up in this whirlwind of paranormal events." There was a still of the group on the porch, with the two women reaching to help Vanessa. "The specific identities of these people are not important, for it could have been anyone. Chance, according to the investigation that includes resources from the FBI, the Georgia National Guard, the Milledgeville Police Department, the famous ghost hunting team of Lorriman and Atlas, and myself, was what brought these innocent bystanders to the forefront of international attention. What made these people unique was their bravery under terrifying circumstances. They perceived that the entity to the right was about to be destroyed by a force they felt in their hearts to be malevolent and rushed in to lend their strength and support." Still shot, closer crop showing two women reaching out to support a falling female spirit, then back to a live shot of Dagmar. "Accounts by these people of what happened after their exposure to these violent and unknown forces become blank at this point. It is the opinion of three independent psychologists of mass stress induced event sublimation." No mention was made of these three professionals now enjoying a complimentary Caribbean cruise. "What that means to the layperson is a memory loss due to the extreme degree of stress they experienced. Post-traumatic shock. One of the people involved was apparently part of an identity protection program. The miracles of plastic surgery can produce amazing results. This man, who chooses to be known only by his first name, happens to resemble someone that had existed a long time ago." Still shot of Ryan as he appeared in naval uniform in Hawaii. "This person may have to be relocated again and his facial features changed to protect his life and livelihood, as well as that of his Family."

"Even more tragic was that the turmoil of this most strange event claimed the life of the Hawthorn Company's legal representative, Mr. Gustav Mendelssohn." Split screen, include still of Gustav from the video taken after the confrontation with Hammer. "Mr. Mendelssohn died of a heart attack brought on by the stress of his heroic efforts. I attended the man's funeral and found that he was a true Samaritan, a man with a great heart. I may never tell another lawyer joke out of respect for this man and the things he stood for.

"In all the years of ghost stories, both from professionals who have dedicated their lives to this venue (action footage, people in white lab coats doing things) and from people sitting around firesides looking to spice up the evening (live stock shot, scouts roasting weenies), no malevolent intent or danger of human safety has ever been proven to originate from the spirit world. What we saw last Saturday was no different from the injuries that have been reported from the curious paranormal phenomenon called 'poltergeists'. If someone receives a bump on the head, it was the luck of the draw of being in the wrong place at the wrong time. No malevolent intent was shown to harm any human in this event."

Still shot that included the ghost soldier. "The Union soldier we saw in the video just before the camera was destroyed, we feel, was the spirit of one of the members of XX Corps of the Union Army under the command of General William Tecumseh Sherman. It was the determination of our team that the energy expenditure of the battle between these two spirits animated this being into a separation from the resting place he had been consigned to for so many years." Back to Dagmar, with a still shot of Annie and Vanessa in the screen corner. Melissa smiled. Of all the statements that could be taken two or more ways in the report so far, this one was the cleverest misdirection of all. The average person would assume that the Civil War soldier experienced a separation from the grave. Only the insiders would know it referred to Private Cooper's backsides being freed from his saddle. The public had the right to know the truth. It looks like it was up to the public to look for the correct interpretation, if they felt so inclined.

"What the reason for this confrontation from beyond the grave was, we will never be able to report. Those entities are, as far as our thorough search has shown, gone for good from Georgia soil. They have passed on to wherever it is that spirits go, taking with them all evidence of their ever having visited us other than the video you have seen and some charred remains of roof tiles and broken glass, now on display at the repaired Main House at the Edwards Estate.

"Such mysteries are not unknown in our country and elsewhere. There are people who make a living studying such happenings and, it appears, they will have one more entry to add to their list of bizarre circumstances where our scientific capacity to investigate paranormal events falls short of the task. Even as we speak, ESPER, an international group of non-mainstream professionals seeking to find answers in ways unusual to the average layperson, has sent investigators to this same city. CNN anchorman Jim Dunnel is scheduled for an interview with the president of this world recognized and renowned organization and I'm sure that this will prove to be another colorful resource of opinion regarding this once in a lifetime event. This is Dagmar Yaddow, Independent Correspondent, reporting to you live from Kingston, NY. Good evening."

At the CNN main office, Jim Dunnel groaned. He was going to rip into that ESPER esoteric stuffed shirt tomorrow night and show the world the charlatan he really was. Now he would have to treat the fakir with respect appropriate to a professor of divinity. "Goddam correspondents."

Down the hall from the anchorman's desk, Janice Hardin breathed a sigh of relief. There were over a dozen backlogged folders sitting on her desk she could now pay attention to. The Science Desk wasn't meant for a one-subject focus, but that was the way it worked, sometimes.

"You really met her? She asked if you would change your major? You're going to sit in on a broadcast?" Barbara Meissner was floored. She was about to say that some women have all the luck and that most of them were blonds, but she remembered that scene at the Edwards porch. Would she have rushed to the aid of a battling banshee? Barbara kept her sharp tongue wisely in its sheath. "Do you think you might get me in to see her someday?"

"I already told her about you. Dagmar said she would be up for a visit in a week or two, depending on her assignment load. You'll see her, then."

Barbara looked at her friend and laughed. When Melissa asked what was so funny, Barbara took on a professional announcer tone. "For CNN, this is your roving correspondent, Biker Babe Barbie, signing off." That set off the pillow fight that eventually spread to the entire dorm hall.

"Why?" Major McGuinness scratched his chin while sitting at home with his wife, watching the news.

"Why what, Dear?" his wife asked.

"Hmm? Oh, sorry. I was just lost in thought. The report wasn't exactly what I had expected, that's all." To himself, he wondered what his Nunzia had done, and why. He'd find out tomorrow. The Major's insider information on what the Task Team had been researching, plus his many years of dealing with human nature (he could 'smell the bullshit before the tail went up') led him to the conclusion that the report he had just seen was all true, but filled with carefully worded double meanings. His eyes continued to rest, unseeing, on the screen that now featured a medley of commercials. "What happened up there?"

Mayor LaRoche (scotch on the rocks), Elroy McBean (rum and Coke) and Chief Hamm (Busch) were sitting in the Mayor's living room. "Not bad, your honor. That defuses a lot of the fear factor and amps up the interest in the ESPER group convention that's coming here. Chief tells me there's been only one drunken/disorderly situation so far, which, by the way, was elegantly handled by that big biker character, Hammer. Does he have a last name? Anyway, the manager of The Inn has thanked us for having him there, several times. Turns out that the fellow has become something of a local celebrity. The guy said that Hammer diplomatically hauled two rowdy ESPER's off their feet, shook a generous tip for the waitress out of them, then stuffed the two of them into a cab."

The Mayor winced. "That's *good* publicity for The Inn?"

"The patrons gave the guy a standing ovation and I hear his tip load for the night set a new record for The Inn."

The Mayor wondered what this world was coming to. "Back to business. Now, that Dunnel talk that's going over the air tomorrow, how do we capitalize on that?"

Elroy smiled. "I've already talked with the ESPER president, Mike Firanzo. For our kind treatment of his following so far, he's assured me of a glowing report of Southern hospitality all of them have found in this fair city in their upcoming membership newsletter and on the Dunnel interview. Also, I got a call from TimeLine Films. They want to do a documentary of that Sherman group passing through here. Pending your OK, that will hit the air in two weeks; short time frame, but you have to ride the interest wave. They'll be looking for locals for extras, by the way. TimeLine will give you room for ten extras with single lines and thirty walk by's to distribute as you wish for your personal PR pleasures. Now, I've drawn up a tentative list of people you might need favors from, someday..." So it went, into the night. Political lives are not as cushy as some people may think.

It was eleven PM at the Holiday Inn bar. Toasts were raised to old and new friendships. Melissa was called and everybody wished her well. Dagmar even said hello to Miss Barbara Meissner, who, after she returned the phone to Melissa, went screaming down the dorm hall about what had just transpired. Rachel and Ralph, on a signal from the fatiguing Task Team members, escorted Ryan to a seat. Clueless, the Family head acquiesced to superior numbers and allowed himself to be plopped down. Zachary handed Atlas over to Allen and joined the lineup of his teammates; Family fledglings standing before Ryan in review. Marianne was the senior mortal female Family member, second only to Ryan, and therefore drew the duty of master of ceremonies.

"Boss, it's time to close this chapter. Before we do, there is a little matter of 'Family Member Induction' that needs to be attended to. The envelope, please." Frank reached into his jacket pocket and pulled out a white, sealed envelope and handed it over to Marianne. "Thank you. Ryan, our Family just grew more than ever before. Before these fine new members go home, there remains one last thing that must be done so that their membership cards can be issued and validated." Marianne handed the envelope to Ryan. "Will you please, in a clear and audible voice, read the inscribed message."

Ryan had half expected some kind of flowery speech of values and welcome. He should have known that such was not necessary in this company, with these people. They had already proven their worth beyond such formalities by just being who they were in life. Ryan opened the paper inside the envelope and saw that there was only one word on it, hand written in beautiful calligraphy, which he later had framed and hung in his living room. "And cupids? Who's the artist?" Ryan looked at the assembled new members, knowing what was coming and delighting in the anticipation. He said, raising his eyebrows and smiling broadly, "BOO!" Right down to the last man and woman, the lineup of inductees fell, faux faint, dramatically to the floor with a collective moan.

Gustav was standing right behind Ryan. He leaned forward and asked, *"Have you considered a breath mint?"*

They two men had been watching, along with the rest of the patrons, the TV over the bar play a rerun of Dagmar's report. One of the two spoke, "So that's what it was all about? You know, I owe those ladies some serious sorry's. Think I can send them some flowers or something?"

"Can do, Hammer. UPS will ship overnight for $21.95 to each location, which I can find on any people-search. Arrangements run from $15.65 to $32.50, not including tax, which in Georgia is eight and one forth percent, and..."

"Barry, enough! Just arrange it, will you?"

"Sure, Hammer. Done deal."

XII THURSDAY

Rachel and Frank swung by Marianne's place in the early hours, before the sun was up, to say a temporary goodbye to everyone except Ryan. They had already shaken hands or hugged with him last night. For once, he had said, it was his intention to *really* sleep in.

Breakfast was waiting for them and those attending, including Allen, Frank, Rachel, Ralph, Marianne, and Zachary, who had dropped off the rented Ford that morning and thumbed a ride with Frank and Rachel. All had hauled themselves out of bed for the pre-dawn send-off to the newly re-united couple. Elizabeth Gladstone, Frank's ex, only lived twenty minutes further west from Marianne's home, which happened to be right on the way for Frank and Rachel from their home in Hurley. They had to pick up the kids at their mother's in Boiceville and get them back in time for their school day. Elizabeth had leant a hand by taking over the kids while Frank went off to save his second marriage. Frank was still reeling from the heaping helping of confusion and events. Adding to that turmoil was that his ex-wife seemed not only willing, but also apparently happy to help him resurrect his crumbling relationship with Rachel. It was one more confirmation to him that women will never be understandable to men.

Now was the time when Rachel needed to reconnect with Jerry and Janet, her husband's children by Elizabeth. Relations between Rachel and Elizabeth weren't gushing, but they weren't exactly cold, either. Women who might have become close friends felt the influence of old baggage that came when one marries the other's ex. Things got more complicated when the new guard didn't live up to what the 'ex' expected of a good role model for her own children. What resulted was an amorphous veil between the two that gently but firmly kept them from too much closeness. Her most recent activities, including running off to Georgia, had served to further darken Elizabeth's view of Rachel, considerably.

The Family could see Rachel's nervousness underlying her excitement at a new and fresh start with her husband and family. It was a path only she could walk, but that didn't stop everyone from being as supportive as Doric columns. Sipping his first cup, Ralph yawned and asked, "Jerry is sixteen and Janet is fourteen. Is that right, Rachel?"

"Yes. Both are a handful, especially Janet. At age fourteen, they know everything, nothing you tell them is correct, anything you ask them is an affront to their independence or right to privacy, and each day finds attempts to avoid a household chore. If I ever find the man who invented the hormone, I'll sic Atlas on him."

The aforementioned canine was happily munching on a strip of bacon that had been filched from the pan Marianne was working from. Another piece was floating in the wings. Zachary wasn't fully used to that kind of departure from normal reality, but it didn't have the startle factor it had the day before. He said, "I'm sorry, but Atlas farms that sort of thing out to his cousin Guido in the Bronx. Let me know and I'll instruct Guido to bite off that nasty person's knee caps."

Marianne giggled. "So Atlas has connections in the Chihuafia? What do they do, black market soup bones?"

Zachary was beginning to blossom. "That, and naughty doggie magazines. Did you see the triple foldout in this month's Dachshund of the Month? Hollywood's all abuzz!" Zachary was on a roll, but that stopped suddenly when the last bit of airborne bacon took a detour and got stuffed into his own mouth. Vanessa went back for another treat for 'her doggie'.

Rachel smiled and said, "You hadn't been informed, but Vanessa has claimed Atlas for her own. You are now just his manager and chief of pooper scooping. She has just laid down the law for you that no one is allowed to make politically incorrect jokes about little dogs."

Zachary finished munching the 'treat' under the baleful stare of what used to be his pet. Atlas had jumped up on Zachary's lap to emphasize his disapproval with full facial proximity. "Sorry, Vanessa. Won't happen again. Mind if I occasionally slam big dogs? Really, some of Atlas's best friends are Wolfhounds and Danes. All I ask is for him to play it safe and avoid bringing home an unwanted litter." That broke Vanessa's focus and the last bit of bacon fell mid-journey to the floor. Atlas sailed from Zachary's lap to nail the tidbit before it could get crushed underfoot. Said launching, though, left the launch pad a bit uncomfortable...small dogs have a surprising amount of mass. "Whoof! Atlas, be careful with those back paws!"

Allen chuckled at what Zachary couldn't see but could surmise. "Good one, Zach. Got her to drop the bacon. Shame you can't see or hear your handiwork." Allen thought for a moment. "Say, is that sort of thing possible? Ryan got his sight from heavy magnetism. We got ours from exposure to the Annie/Vannie battle." Allen ducked another bacon bit and Atlas became a ground-to-ground treat-seeking guided muscle. "Versatile little guy. Anyway, might there be some way to expand the sight safely for Frank and Zach?"

The two men just mentioned were learning to wait during sudden pauses in the conversation, for they weren't pauses to anyone except them. Both had their attention set on full. Allen interpreted after a moment. "Gustav said we should take this up with Ryan, but that it may be possible. There's no way to determine how much of a danger it might be and the method is beyond either of them for the moment. He also wishes you two good fortune on today's family reforging. Same answer from Vanessa."

After saying his thanks to the general direction Allen had been looking at, Frank asked Zachary, "So when are you going to take Atlas for a spin around the cemetery?"

Zachary answered, "Today. Hey, why not? I'm ready to get right into action. Allen and I talked about it just after we arrived. We might ask one of the earth angels to take a trip to the SPCA to see if we can find another critter with similar or even better sight and sense than Atlas has."

Marianne perked up her ears at that. "I want a kitten!"

Ralph spoke up next. "I saw this great oldie with Clint Eastwood driving around with an orangutan. Think the SPCA has any of those? Might be fun to drive around with a big monkey." Five seconds later, "You watch your mouth, Gustav." Frank and Zachary joined the chuckles on that one. Both could guess the sort of jab Gustav had just fired off. "For those who didn't just hear, Gustav had to take off on an errand. Now, let's talk a little more on the animal angle…"

Misfits, thought Frank. They're all a bunch of out-of-the-ordinary people that have gravitated together for purpose, support and fun. Not one person here could be considered one of the herd. That was part of the power of this group, he estimated. Each individual's uniqueness complemented the others. Zachary certainly seemed unique in his own ways. But, what about Frank Gladstone? He felt so damned ordinary. Perhaps he was the token Joe Average required to meet some Federal guideline. His wife said he had to feel his way through things earlier that morning. When he had replied that what she said sounded pretty good and bounced his eyebrows a couple of times, she bloody wonderfully attacked him. It wasn't going to be dull. That was for sure.

The time had come for departure. The sky was just seeing the blush of pre-dawn and birds were beginning to sing. The Gladstone's Dodge Foxglove, a conservative van-like arrangement, pulled out of the driveway and made its way west. Frank knew his wife was going to need some reassurance. "Honey, I told you that the kids were excited about you coming back home, really. You'd be surprised how much Janet groused that you were not at home."

"You've got to be joking. Janet? We argued almost every day about something or other. Jerry and I usually get along fairly well, but…are you sure about Janet?"

Now this was novel, thought Frank. A man explaining the mind of a teenage girl to a woman. "She has some issues of her own, Love. Some of them are with herself, some with her mother, a lot with boys, some with me being with you and some just with the world in general. Were you really all that much different at her age?" That was an interesting question. How would she know? The person with bad breath is usually the only one that isn't aware of it. The long delay Rachel gave without an answer was, in itself, an answer. "I thought not, or you would have said something right away. Hey, you tell me that I have to give it time and find my way with the Family, right?"

Rachel knew what was coming. "Well, yes, I guess so."

"How about we apply your own sage wisdom to yourself?"

"I thought men never listened. Trouble is, you're right on that one. Honey, you know what."

"What?"

"I don't think you're stuffy at all. I love you."

They drove on in warm, hand holding silence, seeing what scenery early winter had to offer along the way. To the left, paralleling Rt. 28, were the resurrected Catskill Mountain Railroad tracks. Both recalled that it had taken a core of dedicated choo-choo fanatics up until five years ago to get that section opened up for their train rides. There was quite a spread in the local papers on the event and it was a definite tourist draw. As they drove along, the westbound tourist train (a steam locomotive, five cars and a caboose) was slowly overtaken. Leaning out of the engine window looked to be an aging, gray haired woman dressed in traditional overalls and engineer's cap. Even from this distance, one could sense that this was a person who had found herself and was doing what she had always wanted to do. Rachel had met her before, having taken the rides with the kids as they were growing up. She had never felt that much of a kinship to the woman, until now. Frank and Rachel waved to the engineer and were greeted in return with a wave and a toot from the train whistle. A few minutes later, the train receded into the landscape of the past.

The trees racing by, bared of leaves, allowed the pessimistic something to feel depressed over. The same vision also gave the optimistic a greater opportunity to see a depth of landscape that the leaves hid in the warmer months. These thoughts were offered to Rachel by both Angel and Cat in a cooperative effort to calm her nerves. Those two entities in Rachel's mental Parliament were getting almost buddy-buddy lately. Yet, the closer they got to Elizabeth's, the more on edge Rachel felt. Frank sensed it, somehow, though there had been silence since they passed the train. Perhaps it was her occasional soft sighing, or just the prolonged silence itself. He gave her hand a gentle and long squeeze. "It'll be all right, I promise."

It was funny, she thought. He didn't seem so sensitive and empathetic before. Who had changed, she wondered? He, or she? Both? They passed Onteora High School, then made a right, a left and another right, and then pulled up into the driveway. Rachel pulled the door handle, praying as she did so.

Two teenagers bolted through the house door and ran to give Rachel a taste of Fitzgalen medicine served Gladstone style. The hugs and cheek kisses were completely unexpected by their recipient, who proceeded to return both and leak out of both eyes. Frank walked past the scene to the porch where Elizabeth stood, watching. "Well, Frank. Looks like the prodigal wife came back. Will it be for good, this time?"

"For better, Betts, I believe. My new job is still in the definition stages, but things look pretty exciting."

It was a nice try to accentuate the positive, but Elizabeth wasn't buying. "The children seem to have forgiven her for taking off." For many years, Frank Gladstone was peacemaker, fireman, diplomat and lion tamer when it came to keeping things to a reasonable level of civility. Speaking his own mind, honestly, would have only fed fuel to the fires. Times change, people grow.

"You gave them plenty of practice." He smiled. That felt good.

Elizabeth turned and looked at Frank. "Why, you stuffy Brit. That's the first time you've stood up to at me. God knows I've baited you long enough. Did you misplace your stiff upper lip somewhere?"

"Betts, I've seen a lot in a very short time. Rachel played a role in the changes in me, but the thought of losing her like I lost you forced me to look damn hard at myself, honestly for a change. I'm sorry you and I didn't make it. You're a good woman and I'm a good man. Both of us were too pig-headed to see that we were yelling about molehills of bad when we were standing on mountains of good. I won't let that happen to me again. What you do is up to you."

"Frank Gladstone, that's the most you've ever opened up to me!" She wanted to say more, but Rachel, Jerry and Janet were walking back to the porch. Rachel went up to Elizabeth, and surprised the heck out of her, and everyone else for that matter, by throwing her arms around the woman.

"Elizabeth, I'm so glad that Janet and Jerry have you for their mother. I'll do my best for them, but I'll never replace you. I just wanted you to know that. Come on, kids, you have school today. Now don't give me that 'let's play hooky' look. 'Pushover Rachel' got lost in the sauce. Meet Sgt. Rachel, now MARCH, two, three, four..." Off they went, with the children goose-stepping back to the car.

"Frank? Was that Rachel the Wimp?"

"Used to be. She downloaded a software upgrade."

"Damn. Get me the number of her 'puter-geek. Uh, Frank? Something I've been meaning to tell you." That stopped Frank mid-stride, as he had just begun his walk back to the Foxglove. The last time he had heard those words, she had told him that she was leaving him.

"Yes?"

"All those things I said about you in the divorce countersuit paper?"

Did he ever! "Yes?"

"I didn't mean half of them." With that, Elizabeth turned around and went back into her house. Frank's first thought, as he slowly resumed his walk to the Foxglove, was to wonder at how often miracles would be appearing in his new life. His second thought was to wonder which half of the counter-accusations in that document was it that Betts DID mean.

As they drove off, a shaken woman watched from the protection of

151

her window sheers. It was funny, sort of. The divorce had granted her the independence from Frank's stifling influence she had craved, seasoned with residual co-dependence of a sort. Frank still relied on her, from time to time, mainly for the shared custody duties. But there was more to it than that. Something nagged at her. Despite the divorce, he had continued to be the man she had left…a wimp. The wimp had found another wimp, and Elizabeth had once chuckled to think that birds of a feather would seek out their own kind. But, hadn't she and Frank also sought each other out? Did that make her, also, a wimp? Impossible. A wimp wouldn't have had the guts to realize the hopelessness of a doomed marriage and initiated the painful steps necessary to break it off before all the parties were completely cold to each other and the children were damaged beyond repair. Wasn't that bravery, of a kind? Didn't her decisiveness allow fresh starts for everyone while there was still time to make new lives for themselves?

So, why did his return volley of fire shake her so badly? Why was she so taken aback at his unaccustomed openness and honesty? Why was her successor's positive change in demeanor so disturbing to her? Why did her children's forgiveness and their caring so much for Rachel, the woman who had turned her back on them, eat at her? Why did she wait until so many years after she had left to give Frank any kind of apology for the awful things she had aimed at him back then? Why did Elizabeth Gladstone hide behind curtain sheers and continue to stare at her own empty driveway?

She turned away to a now quiet house, a now empty nest, with a now gently aching heart, saying a single, quietly whispered word. "Wimp."

Major Kenneth McGuinness drummed his fingers on the desk. Sgt. D'Palermo stood before him in a posture of a defiant child. No, he thought, not a child. Her actions seemed considered. Her denials were firm, though poorly plausible. She was the picture of feminine stubbornness, which was a redundant phrase if he had ever heard one. Well, he'd see about that. Major McGuinness touched a button that quietly told the Corporal outside his office that he was not to be disturbed until further notice.

"Sit down, Sergeant."

"Sir, if you don't mind…"

"I do mind. Sit DOWN, Sergeant." She did, reluctantly. Major McGuinness calmly took off his jacket and hung it up on the old-fashioned oak and brass pole near his desk. He then popped out the collar insignia of his office and put them in the drawer. Finally, he took his desk chair and wheeled it over right next to where Nunzia was sitting. The Guardswoman watched her Superior Officer, suspecting what was coming next.

"Nunzia, it's me, Ken. Screw protocol, for now. Anything you tell me starting now and ending when I put my trappings of office back on will remain in this room forever. I'm getting old, Nunzia and I've no doubt in my mind that you have witnessed a miracle or five. For some reason, you have seen fit to keep it from the world. That I could have let pass. Having it also be kept under wraps by an FBI agent and a news correspondent? That's too much for me to let go by the wayside. I trust your judgment as if you were my own daughter. More, actually. I haven't trusted either of my daughters' judgment since both of them married men they were far too good for. Talk to me, Nunzia."

She looked at the man, into his eyes and into his heart. It's funny, but a person can't do that unless they look into their own hearts at the same time. She'd looked there before and found nothing that contradicted how the man had lived his life. This was the guardian of her sovereign state, her mentor, her Commanding Officer and her trusted friend. Besides that, he already knew a good percentage of what she had promised to keep hidden. He waited, patiently, respectfully and would continue to do so all day, if he had to. The man was stubborn. Most of them were, but this man was their patron saint regarding that personality quirk. The silence continued as she remained on the fence, until interrupted by a tap on the window. There was nothing there except for the morning frost, for this was the north side of the building and the last to warm up in the morning sun. Guardswoman and Guardsman looked at the window, when it tapped again. The Major muttered, "What the hell?"

Nunzia's eyes were sharper than Ken's by a large margin, so she spotted it first and walked over to the window. "Ken, come here for a minute." The Major followed Nunzia to the window, his eyes following her gaze. There was something there in the thin frost. He took out his glasses (bifocals; he refused the simple surgery to correct his vision) and looked again. This wasn't possible! He turned to begin a sentence with either who, what, when or why, he hadn't decided which, only to see a Mona Lisa smile on the woman's face.

"Nunzia, would you please explain this to me, since you seem to know what's going on?"

"I've been given permission to speak to you."

He looked again. Scratched into the frost were two words, 'It's OK'. "Did you have someone do that? How?"

"Ken, we're on the third floor. You do the math. Now, let me tell you a story." The windows were government spec thermal quadri-panes, so the message stayed there during the whole narration. It was past eight when the warmth from the outside began to decrystallize the note on the window. Until that time, the Major kept looking back at it just to reassure himself that he wasn't listening to a fairy tale, or rather, a ghost story.

The debrief concluded. It was complete and thorough, as he had come to expect from his favorite Sergeant, including the likelihood that there may come a time when she would need to request an emergency leave for an indefinite period of time. Now the shoes had switched feet and it was Nunzia's turn to sit in silence, waiting for Ken to respond. He said nothing as Ken, but reached into his drawer and replaced his collar insignia, then walked to the rack and put on his uniform jacket. "Sergeant." Sgt. D'Palermo rose to attention. "What you have told me is to remain between us. That is an order. Do you understand?" Sgt. D'Palermo replied in the affirmative, then, for the first time between the two of them, broke military protocol, hugged her Commanding Officer and kissed him on the cheek. She saluted, about-faced after being dismissed, and left the office. Major McGuinness managed to hold his military facial demeanor until the door shut. Then he smiled and muttered to himself that the Guard could attract a lot more recruits if they could alter their inter-gender saluting procedure to follow D'Palermo's example. The more he thought about it, the more traditional views of service protocol began to crumble to the ridiculous. Just imagine, he thought, what a surprise bunk inspection might turn up. He looked at the couch, walked up to it and stood at attention. His Corporal had cracked open the door to see if his Commanding Officer was ready for his morning paperwork and saw the Major addressing an empty couch, saying, "At ease, soldiers. You, stop saluting anytime, now. And you, there. Safe that weapon."

Ryan was awake. Ralph wasn't there, so it was back to do-it-yourself. Gustav made an appearance during his second cup and the look on the lawyer's face prompted Ryan to ask, "So, whose Tweety-bird did you eat this morning, Sylvester? Things settled down south?"

"Ship shape, mein commandant. Say, have you heard about the new military protocols likely to be proposed by Georgia's National Guard? If passed, the South may yet rise again."

"What?"

The Green Machine was on the move. Ralph dropped off Allen and Marianne at the office where Ryan would later meet them for the 'reading of the will' scheduled for early that afternoon. In the meantime, Allen would begin training in how to run Hawthorn Enterprises. Gustav would assist them, then later have the rare privilege of sitting in on his own worldly assets disbursal, which was almost as weird as attending his own funeral. Vanessa and Zachary/Atlas (Allen nicknamed them 'Zatlas') went back across the river with Ralph to fish around the grave pond where they had landed Bernhardt. The Rhinebeck Cemetery wasn't that much older than some others around within driving distance, but it seemed a good place to start and the Beekman Arms was hosting a nice lunch buffet today. An army travels on its stomach, Ralph would say, if anyone asked.

It was a crisp Thursday, October 5th, 2047. There was no snow this year, so far, but the temperature was much colder than back in Georgia. Had Gustav wanted to write a message in window frost up here, he would have needed a chisel. The grass was covered with crystallized dew and the ground was hard and crunchy to walk on. Ralph parked his car off the cemetery road and they began to stroll around. Atlas was allowed to walk along and follow his own nose. No one was really sure as to which way to go, so they walked aimlessly, unless you counted the natural canine interest regarding scents left on grave markers by other dogs. Atlas showed no signs of leading because, so far, there was nothing he felt inclined to lead towards. Vanessa broke off for a while to a neighboring hillock to see if she could begin to imitate Annie's talent for searching the ground, but found nothing.

Ralph called out, "Hey Vanessa, try on that Frederick's outfit of Gustav's. Someone's bound to go for your ankle then!" There must have been a response, judging from Ralph's facial expression.

Zachary asked, "What did she say to you?"

Ralph replied, "I don't use that kind of language."

They mainly stuck to the older sections of the cemetery and got nothing for their efforts. It was getting near lunchtime and Ralph's southern blood was getting chilled. Atlas's nose and toes were even colder, despite frequent breaks when Atlas snuggled in Zachary's overcoat. When Ralph said that Zachary looked pregnant, Zachary peeked inside his jacket. "Man, was yo mama ugly." He let Atlas down for one more piddle break before they got back into the car. It seemed a little disrespectful to have one's canine companion marking territory on a rock that might be inscribed with 'Beloved Wife', but no one rose up to complain. That's when Atlas froze. His gaze seemed to be aimed at a section of the cemetery with very little weathering, a dell peninsula into the surrounding woods. Vanessa noticed that something was up and zipped over to where the men were standing and wondering.

"*Got a nibble?*"

Ralph was scanning the dell. "I think so, maybe."

Zachary shook his head at that. "What?"

"Zachary, you're going to have to get used to it, like I did. Vanessa asked me if Atlas had caught scent of something." The dog hadn't moved yet, but just then took a few steps forward, then stopped again. A low growl (for a Chihuahua) provided bass for the soprano and alto of the local birds. Two men and a ghost baby-stepped behind Atlas as he moved a few feet, stopped, moved again, growled and stopped again.

"Go on, Boy, I know what you're saying. It's OK, Buddy, I'm right behind you. Keep going, attaboy." Atlas began to make more regular progress with his partner's encouragements. Ralph and Vanessa cocked their heads as they witnessed the ghost hunting process, looked at each other and shrugged. Now they moved at a constant pace and were forty yards away from the road when the dog stopped at a gravesite, sat down and whined at Zachary. "Bingo."

Ralph was amazed. "He found someone? Son of a bitch! And from that distance! Vanessa, see if you can sense something." Now that she could focus her attention to a more circumscribed area, Vanessa closed her eyes and opened herself up to whatever might be down there. Neither man moved. Atlas was warming himself once again in Zachary's coat, but his head poked out through a section that was left with one button undone, watching his 'treat mistress' very carefully. The men looked at the stone, as they waited. The marker was a simple affair done in traditional gray granite, standing three feet high and three across. It read, 'Here lies Cassandra Petrocelli, faithful wife, beloved mother. Born August 4th, 2019, died September 10th, 2046. You are missed.'

Ralph began to relay what he was hearing from Vanessa. "She says that there is something down there, but it's hard for her to get a clear image. There are impressions that suggest fear and anger. There's worry, she says. The stone says the lady was twenty-seven when she died, last year. She couldn't have been buried alive, could she?" Some of the possibilities were beginning to occur to Zachary when he saw that something had straightened Ralph's back. Ralph looked at Zachary. "Vanessa thinks that whoever is down there may have been murdered."

The import of the 'M' word struck Zachary hard. On its heels was the implication of how the rest of the statement was worded. "What do you mean, 'whoever'?"

"She says that the impressions she is getting leads her to believe that whoever is down there is not female. Vanessa, we'd better wait until we can get the rest of the Family assembled here, or at least Boss Man and Gustav. Come on. Whoever it is, he, she or it has waited a year. A few more hours isn't going to hurt anyone."

At the Arms, the three traded thoughts as well as the language barriers would allow. Ralph felt as if he was working at the UN. He felt it was not a good idea to call in the troops just yet. The will reading would be taking place in a couple of hours and this sort of distraction might cause a problem. It could wait. Zachary had talked about a number of ghosts that were murdered, but they were all above ground and usually located at where the murder took place…but not always. Ralph asked him if anyone had ever seen spirits in mining caves or perhaps while scuba diving old wrecks. Zachary hadn't heard of any, but didn't know if anyone capable of that sort of sensitivity had ever really bothered to search such difficult to reach places. Ghost hunters were usually attracted to reports by local citizens, and most citizens (except for miners and certain construction crews) were above ground. The idea put Zachary into a thoughtful mood. How hard might it be, he thought, to score a ride on a submersible and visit the Titanic? He dismissed the thought, as he didn't know how a Chihuahua might physically react to that sort of environment, given the pressure changes and air mixtures. No, he'd leave that to the team entities. He was going to mention that line of thought to Ralph, but something stopped him. It was the memory of the 'Revelations fever' he and his group had experienced the day before. Would public awareness of 'the land AND the sea giving up their dead' start something that even the talents of the expanded Family couldn't hold back? He'd tell Ryan and let the Family head decide on where to go with that one.

Charlie Chase was a young lawyer Gustav had contacted a month ago, appointing him as his official legal representation, just in case. He had been prompted to do this because his medical doctor told him that he ought to slow down a bit if he wanted to stick around a while. There was too much to do regarding the Edwards debacle at that stage for him to slow down, but one could always plan for emergencies along the way. Charlie was a recent addition to Gosten and Pemmen, a local group to whom Gustav had farmed out some minor subcontract work. Gustav had taken a liking to Charlie. He had all the naiveté and idealism he had had when first coming off the legal production line. The reading was to take place in Gustav's office, as per the wishes of the deceased. Present were Charlie Chase, Allen Hawthorn, Marianne Cabrini, Reverend Hoppenfeld, Valerie Knudson Mendelssohn and Martha Scholldorf Mendelssohn.

Ryan had opted for the security and privacy of the viewing room. He'd had more than his share of public exposure recently and wanted to cling to what little isolation there was left to him. He was able to monitor the proceedings from the set-up that played a role on that first day he had met Allen and Rachel. Had it only been a week and a half since that afternoon? The monitors showed the attendees take their seats and Charlie beginning the reading with the usual introduction about being of sound mind and body, followed by the 'bequeaths'. Gustav stood behind Ryan, listening in as well. He wondered how ghosts could listen to such things, about how communication was so one-way between spirits and mortals. He had no real eardrums to speak of, so why was he able to hear what was coming over the speakers? It was one of the questions he would try to ask the Man Upstairs, if he was ever allowed to get there and if he was allowed to ask questions. Now wasn't that a thought? A lawyer in Heaven not being able to ask questions? It couldn't happen, he decided, for that would qualify at least for purgatory.

Ryan and Gustav heard the distribution of Gustav's worldly wealth fairly evenly between his semi-widows, with a 10% kickback to the Reformed Church. Knick-knacks and shares of stock in Hawthorn Enterprises were pretty much dumped on Allen and Marianne's laps, to be distributed or kept as they saw fit. On the viewing screen, Valerie seemed touched by the proceedings. Martha's face was one of stone.

"Martha wasn't always like that, Ryan. Before our son, Garrison, died, she was a bright spot on anyone's horizon. Death is mostly tragic to those left behind. It wasn't so much that she blamed me, or even herself. She blamed God. Ever since that time her heart became ice cold. Nothing I could say or do ever changed her hard feelings in the least. She refused to be counseled and, instead, put up walls to protect herself from the world, creating *an impregnable fortress."*

Ryan was about to magnify that face on the screen, but held back upon thinking of Gustav's feelings. "A prisoner who did nothing wrong, self-sentenced to life. I've seen it before and it's a hard nut to crack. I'm sorry, Gustav. That must be hard on you, too. You loved her, and still do, don't you?"

"I suppose. I loved what she was and still love the woman I feel is buried somewhere deep inside of her. I do not love what she evolved into, but rather pity her. Ryan, can love be ala Carte like that?"

Ryan laughed at that. "Gustav, old friend, love can be whatever it damn well pleases. Corinthians gives a great definition of aspects of love, like it not being possessive, or harboring a grudge, always forgiving, always giving and all that. Kahlil Gibran was another one of my favorites regarding that general subject. They have good rules of thumb, but an expert in obscure bits of information like yourself probably came across the Greek approach where there are five different names for love, for they felt it came in five basic flavors. I don't remember them all, but one was of parents, one for your country, one for an opposite sex. Let's see, probably one for a friend and one for God. They likely added one for self, since there was a god associated with it."

"Narcissus, I think. But that's the wrong kind of self-love. He's the guy who didn't just take a mirror along on a date; the mirror WAS his date. You know, Ryan, we must be getting to be old farts, the way we get off on tangents on subjects neither of us are qualified to teach on." Gustav looked at the screens, for he didn't have much heart for going in to see his first beloved, so desiccated of heart, up close and personal. What he wouldn't give to see that old smile on her face again. Charlie wound up his reading. There were no objections from any present. Charlie was pleased, being able to perform this last service to the highly experienced mentor that had taken him under his wing for a brief time. They don't make barristers like that anymore, he thought. More the pity.

Ryan's personal SatCom buzzed. He checked the ID screen and was pleasantly surprised. Ryan took the call, while Gustav watched the screen as the ending moments of the session drew to a final close. Ryan hit the disconnect and looked at Gustav. "You wrote in the window frost? Gustav, you are finding your dramatic self at last." Another call came in.

"Busy day, Boss." Gustav couldn't hear the phone conversation. He wondered if it was just because he believed he couldn't. After all, how could he walk on the ground, but walk through a door. How could he hear without eardrums, or have emotions and feelings. He was dead and his brain was six feet underground right now. Another thing that death couldn't erase in his psyche; going off on questioning binges. Ryan was doing little but just listening for the time being and Gustav could hear people shuffling out of his former office, but his mind stayed on the thought line. Someone who has lost a leg might have a foot pain because his or her brain was wired to believe

that a particular nerve went to that particular place. The loss of flesh often did not lose the awareness of that flesh. Why was he holding on to this? Was it something to do with Martha? She had lost a part of herself, their son. It shouldn't have been an event that permanently crippled, just one that was worth grieving over and eventually gaining acceptance. What had happened in her life before he had met her that made this tragic event far more debilitating than it had to be? How many times had he asked himself that over the decades?

His reverie was interrupted when Ryan thumbed the disconnect. "Son of a bitch! Gustav, arrange a meeting for the whole Family. Call Roscoe and make reservations, then call Kingston Limo. I'll want a conference call. We especially need our FBI recruit."

It must have been pretty intense, for Ryan to brain fart like this. This might be fun. Gustav held out his hand and asked to borrow Ryan's SatCom, since he had left his own back at the Edwards Estate. Ryan was leaning forward on his chair, his eyes darting about in high gear, his right hand waving his SatCom towards Gustav. It kept waving, until he became annoyed that Gustav wasn't taking it. Finally he looked to the right to see Gustav's hand outstretched and the SatCom device passing right through it. For a moment, Ryan had a confused look on his face, then, "Oh God, PLEASE tell me I'm not going senile. Gustav, I'm so sorry."

"Forget it, Boss, I'll shamelessly play on your guilt strings when it serves my purposes later. What the heck was it that got your mind so distracted? Who was that? Rachel? Ralph?"

"Ralph, and get this. Atlas came through, big time for a small mutt. What's really nuts is that the entity he dug up died last year, reads as a man in a woman's grave and Vanessa is getting an impression that the person was murdered." Allen knocked and peeked in.

"Guests are all gone, folks. Hey, what's going on…? Never mind. I'll just go get my 'whole new ballgame' glove."

Ryan was still in command mode and, since Gustav's ability to use communication devices was somewhat handicapped, Allen would have to do. "Allen, go back into the office and tell Marianne we'll be right there. I was going to set it up at Pavelli's, a meeting, that is, but we'll hold off on that for now. We'll just stay here. Ralph, Zachary and Vanessa are on their way here. See if you can get Russ Anderson on the horn, Sgt. Paul Wasserman, too. Hey, Janet and Jerry should have been shipped off to school by now. Where are Rachel and Frank?"

Allen shook his head and, just before he closed the door, said, "Ryan, someday I'm going to have to tell you about the facts of life. You know, birds and bees?"

The Boss turned red. The door shut. Gustav howled. Allen hit a speed connect to the circuit that would flash on his mother's receiver. It was a bell and whistle that basically said 'Call back when you finish whatever it is that you are doing.' He did it again for Melissa's, Paul's and Russ's units. Making an executive decision, he did the same for Dagmar and Nunzia. The Task Team came as a group and they worked well as a group. Why screw it up by inviting half of the group?

Ralph's Green Machine's shoulder belt had a clip for his SatCom. It was a jerry-rig that worked out better than the fancy set-ups. He could hear from it, talk into it, stop the car and easily unclip it and take it with him. Earplugs sometimes gave him headaches and he never got used to hearing different conversations in each ear. Car phone ambient speakers for callers didn't float his boat, either. The clipped unit gave a direction to the voice. They had crossed the bridge and were on their way to Gustav's office, with Zachary and Ralph in the front seat. Atlas had taken a liking to Vanessa that Zachary had never thought possible and was, even now, playing games with her in the back. Vanessa kept popping over to the opposite side of the back seat, with Atlas happily chasing her with more enjoyment than some canines got from Frisbees. Zachary supposed that everyone had his or her price. Peek-a-boo and bacon were Atlas's.

"Hey, Zachary, what's got your mini-mutt going?" Ralph turned for a moment and saw the alternating seat side game. Turning face forward again, he checked his rear view mirror by moving it down a bit. Now wasn't that interesting? The fact that ghosts don't reflect in mirrors for the 'sighted' wasn't included in the orientation lecture.

Allen and Marianne set up Gustav's desk screen and patched it into the office PC. The phone system was set on 'conference call' in anticipation of, hopefully, a full response. Vanessa showed up early, to Atlas's 'left behind' disappointment, and asked Marianne what sorts of munchies that Atlas might like were in the office. Marianne dug up some frozen Vienna sausage that Gustav wouldn't be using anymore. The coffee machine was activated and people began to arrive and settle in.

FBI Special Agent Anderson was on his lunch break when he got the call. The ID told him to wrap the other half of his sandwich and deposit it in the staff fridge, then get outside where his calls weren't as closely monitored. He thumbed his newest connect number.

Georgia National Guard Sgt. Nunzia D'Palermo was coming out of the shower after a good run earlier. She spotted her unit flashing and, with the towel around her, sat on her desk chair and responded.

Milledgeville City Police Sgt. Paul Wasserman was in his cruiser, showing the colors to those ESPER weirdoes. 'Friendly but firm presence' was his mantra. Things were much simpler before the town elected a mayor who was so tourist and convention oriented. However, he was the first to admit that the improvements in the school and fire department were worth at least some nuttiness he had to deal with. There were rumblings of a stadium in the not too distant future and his heart leaped at the thought of something local he could take his son to. Paul drove by the entrance to the Edwards Estate and saw a small group of people walking with divining rods, pendulums and other odd implements. "Toto, we're not in Kansas, anymore." His personal unit sitting on the charger next to his shotgun began to blink in a new pattern, one that didn't herald his wife with a home emergency. "Already?"

Independent Correspondent Dagmar Yaddow was wiping the make-up off her face. At least it wasn't as bad as it used to be. Pancake make-up was de rigueur, not all that long ago, in order for her to look human to the cameras and like a hooker doll in real light. The new stuff was just a light, water-soluble coating that was electronic-sense-friendly. Her skin tones were now applied by computer in a process not all that much removed from the way they used to 'colorize' the old black and white programs. Her make-up assistant came up and whispered to her that the signal she had asked her to watch for was blinking. The correspondent nodded, dabbed off the last of the face paste, then walked to her ready-room. As soon as she closed the door, Dagmar allowed the percolating excitement to show itself. "Yes!"

One by one, the 'Second String' reported in. None of them felt put down by their chosen nickname, for they had decided on it themselves. They were still members of one Hell of a varsity, playing one Heaven of a game. They were, however, surprised when it was Allen who addressed them when all were present. Did someone usurp the Boss's throne? Maybe Ryan was stuck on the john? He drank enough coffee.

Melissa had felt the buzz on her hip, but her lab proctor was not going to let her go for another fifteen minutes. Melissa had many good virtues, but patience was not one she owned in abundance. A few moments of stewing later, she smiled sweetly to her (male) lab partner and told him she had to go take care of something of a feminine nature. The professor (female) needed something more concrete. A whispered reference to the stress of the weekend having changed the migration timing of her personal monthly cardinal was sufficient to allow Melissa to slip out early. She fast-walked back to the dorms, punching the connect on her SatCom (a streamlined, feminine, personal model) as she went. The meeting was already in progress, much to her annoyance.

"OK folks, this is your friendly neighborhood CEO of Hawthorn Enterprises coming at you live from hysteric Kingston. With the exception of our youngest bombshell, Mumsy and Frank, we seem to all be present. For you with mortal wax buildup in your ears, we will interpret Vanessa and Gustav's comments for you. I decided to make it a full meeting, because we have been met with a task that is a little outside what Ryan and the other aging veterans are used to. OW! Hey, ease off, G-cubed. Anyway, we need the talents of the extended Family. Folks, it would appear that we have a murder on our hands."

"Allen, this is your mother. Sorry to just call in. Frank's here, too. I only caught that last sentence about there being a murder. Did we miss much else and who killed who?"

"ALLEN! I just got out of lab. Did I miss anything?"

Marianne couldn't resist. "If you blonds weren't so busy primping, you might get here on time once in a while."

Rachel responded, "Atlas, I'll give you a pound of bacon if you go pee on her pillow."

Melissa added, "And I know a nice lady Chihuahua, if you take a dump in her slippers."

Allen would have enjoyed letting things degenerate further, but there was work to be done and he didn't know how long he would have the full Second String on line. "Put a sock in it for a few minutes, people. Listen to the situation. We need whatever you can come up with for a battle plan." Allen went on to describe today's events at the Rhinebeck Cemetery. Those on SatComs thumbed their digital record modes rather than take the time and distraction of writing down what was to follow. "Ralph connected with the Rhinebeck Library and found the obit on Cassandra Goode Petrocelli, 2019-2046. She was married to a businessman from Rochester. There were three other local obits/burials that coincided with Cassandra's, but those were interred in other cemeteries and pickled in other funeral homes, so we haven't yet figured out how the male presence in a female's grave came to be. It doesn't seem likely that someone switched coffins, accidentally or otherwise."

Russ volunteered, "Check out missing persons for the month afterwards and see if there was anyone related to or allied with the deceased. Keep the whole list, because we don't know the questions to ask, yet. I'll check our own records from the Philadelphia office. Paul, got any friends up north?"

From Milledgeville, "Don't got squat as far as police connects. That's Yankee land, you know. Let me see what the Chief has and I'll get back to you. Allen, tell you what. How about the Second String doing the research end of it and you guys go grave robbing. Maybe you can get some more info from the ghost horse's mouth. Dead men DO tell tales, I hear."

Ryan laughed. "Tell me about it."

Nunzia felt left out. "Hey, fellows, what can a helpless innocent girl do?"

Dagmar had to take up that baton. "Nothing, because that phrase 'helpless innocent girl' does not apply to you. 'Helpless', my ass! Your Major puts you in a tank to *limit* the damage you do to an enemy. How's about you receive photo and other information regarding the deceased from the cowboys and hit the Mormon I.D. site and the genealogy angles. It may be important when we try to put things together, or seek out people to talk to. I'll see what my friends in the regional news group have on their files."

"WAIT a sec! What do I do?"

Rachel asked, "Who was that?"

Marianne said, "Ryan, I think. Useless old toad, if you ask me."

"NOW JUST A DAMNED MINUTE HERE!"

Vanessa focused energy and patted her husband on the head. *"Down, Fido, they're just yanking your chain. You should be proud of them, like they are of you."*

The Family patriarch allowed himself to be consoled. "All right, all right, I concede to the majority. Vanessa and I have already talked a bit about what happened at the cemetery today. The gravesite is a relatively new addition to the original cemetery. Most new graves are located in alternate sites within the Rhinebeck Township, as the original graveyard is nearly filled up. They still shoehorn some into the old site with sufficient money or if the family is old enough to retain reservations like the Mendelssohn clan. This grave is right next to the Astor Home for Children, a long standing effort to help troubled kids in a controlled school environment. Forgive me if I get too detailed because, at this point, I'm not sure at all what details are important. Once Atlas pointed out the spot, Vanessa was able to get ill defined but strong impressions, like music with heavy static. The reception wasn't good enough for conversation and she wisely refrained from pushing it without the full team there. The words 'fear, anger, worry, and murder' came to her mind and it 'felt male'. I'm opening up the floor for spontaneous inspiration."

Zachary volunteered, "Two people in one casket? Ground-sound equipment might be able to penetrate the coffin, if that's the case, depending on the material."

The Guard stepped in. "Squeezing two into a casket would be hard, unless one or both were cremated. But if so, why bury together unless there is some sentiment involved?" Nunzia had finished toweling herself off and was nearly dressed. "Perhaps there is another body buried with the casket, but not inside it. If so, whoever aced the victim might be the person who shoved the dirt in later when everyone else left. The grounds keeper?"

Gustav and Vanessa held back, as their voices would have to be reiterated for those on the phone connects. Rachel was next. "Getting too complicated, I think. I lean to a simple switch of bodies. But, why? And what about all of those emotions Vanessa talked about?"

Allen dovetailed with, "Are we sure there was one spirit there? Maybe it was one dominant overshadowing the passive. Ryan, you said things were ill defined."

Ryan responded. "Perhaps, but I don't feel that's right. There were a lot of soldiers in the ground back in Georgia. Both sane and Monkey Annies were able to detect them as discrete packets despite the crowding. I lean to a single entity with the haziness due to lack of practice on Vanessa's part. Dagmar, you're good at encapsulating. What have we got?"

"This is Dagmar Yaddow, independent tea leaf reader. We have a one-year-old grave, with a male-like entity within, I.D. unknown, from whom a sensitive ghost receives a variety of strong and upsetting emotions and impressions that might indicate a crime of murder. The inscription on the grave is of a woman with an Italian type name, who was a mother slash wife and died prematurely at the age of twenty-seven of causes yet to be determined. She is of a family that either has money slash influence or has historical roots in Rhinebeck."

Ryan nodded to Allen, who put closure on the meeting. "OK people, we have our assignments. I say we leave the site alone until we can meet again. How does 24 hours grab everyone?" No one objected, though Melissa said she was sorry that her work load prevented her from assisting, then, after taking a breath, told Dagmar that she had officially changed her major.

"Great, kid. Send me your transcript and course requirements. I want to see who's teaching what. You may want to consider that changing colleges is a possibility."

That brought silence from the Troy connection. Allen reached out with, "Hey, Baby, you and I will work things out, OK? There's nothing that the Family can't handle. We'll talk tonight, promise. All right, as CEO of Hawthorn Enterprises and, since Ryan gave me permission to pretend like I'm the Boss for a whole fifteen minutes, I officially call this meeting to a close. We'll do another lunch call tomorrow at noon, EST. Good luck, Family members." With that, the connect closed. Most of the Second String had to go back to their real jobs, or classes. First string members gravitated to their natural duties, which were whatever each person thought was a good idea for them to be doing. It was a fluid arrangement that worked well, most of the time.

Marianne and Ryan worked towards stealing Charlie Chase from his firm to do work on a regular though part time basis. Allen looked on, as he was going to be doing the brunt of CEO work soon to free up Ryan for more important matters. They weren't ready for a new full time lawyer, yet, but legal documents for the specialty condo business were now compounded with new paperwork from the 'wealthy dog owner supply company'. That's when Allen was suddenly struck with an idea.

"Hey Ryan, how come you get all the fun?"

Activity stopped, heads turned. Ryan said, "Excuse me?"

"I was thinking, G-cubed. You recruited people to take the load off your shoulders so you could ghost hunt with fewer restrictions, right? You have longevity, but the workload is more than you can comfortably handle. Right?"

Ryan looked at Vanessa, Gustav, Marianne, then back at Allen. "OK, that's a given. Why do I feel like someone is about to change the ballgame again, and without my permission?"

"Why were you the chosen one to chase spooks, anyway?"

Ryan answered cautiously. Allen was setting out rugs for his foot to step on. One of those rugs likely hid a tiger trap. "Because, Vanessa had trouble getting entities to listen and I was the only one who could see and, hear, spirits…oh…good Lord, I've been cloned!" Marianne dropped her jaw, as did Vanessa, Ralph and Gustav. Allen had just put the coup d'grace on Ryan's primacy in management of tardy entities.

Zachary established his talent with forward thinking, as if his dog supply empire wasn't enough of a hint, by giving out with a merry laugh, patting Atlas on the head and saying, "Well, little fellow, it looks like you might be having some company, soon."

Allen, thinking he had gotten the jump on everyone, turned to Zachary. "Excuse me?" Ryan smiled to think that the wonder boy was possibly about to find someone besting him at his own foresight game.

Zachary responded with, "Well, you have six people and two ghosts who have the gift of sight and hearing, on top of your other Family members who are willing to work but need some 'seeing eye assistance'. Tell you what, Ryan a.k.a. Methuselah; you open your school for entity travel agency representatives. I'll hit the kennels to see if we can find a few more ghost sensitive team bow-wows."

Marianne said, more firmly this time, "I WANT A KITTEN! DAMMIT!"

Marianne, Zachary and Vanessa took a short drive to Sawkill Road in Kingston, where the SPCA had been located since anyone could remember. Over the past decade, they had expanded in size and business savvy to the point where more than one area pet store had closed up shop. There were exotic birds, horses, reptiles, rodents, tropical fish, pot bellied pigs, skunks (de-stunk) and other unusual animals on top of the traditional dogs and cats. There were big city zoos with fewer paws and hoofs. Ulster and Dutchess Community Colleges and SUNY New Paltz all had either Veterinarian or Vet Assistants programs, Animal Husbandry majors, Animal Psychologist/Behaviorist majors, and advanced (and well funded) Animal Nutrition programs that used the SPCA as their satellite clinic. Pur-Diet was a merger of the old Purina Pet Foods and Science Diet that provided all manner of specific needs foods at no cost to the SPCA, other than their good will and endorsements of their products. The college programs offered the SPCA a tuition fee for using their site as a satellite education facility, plus provided significant skilled manpower, which even further reduced the SPCA's expenditures while they still raked in a significant income stream from those donation cans on business counters. On top of that, the Ulster County Corrections Facility was able to farm out some of their 'public service alternative sentencing' bodies there to unexpected advantage. Working with animals had been shown to be the platinum punishment where, statistically, prisoners showed the least criminal recidivism. That statistic had prompted establishing new studies to confirm what old studies had already proven; animals give unconditional love, which was something many inmates found to be a completely new eye and heart opening experience.

Atlas had to be left behind at the office on this trip. Fortunately, he had taken a shine to Ralph, who missed his goldfish, Mako. Mako had become the Milledgeville Cab Company's unofficial mascot and had been moved to the main office. So far, no one had informed their former employee that said fish had been given a last name addition: 'Kithcart'. That first and last name combination proved impossible to pronounce for people with sore throats or that were recovering from dental work. The former goldfish owner grudgingly admitted that Atlas had certain etiquette advantages over his old apartment companion. He didn't swim in his own piddle and he didn't try to orally recycle his own poop. That last bit had always given Ralph reason to wrinkle his nose and had once been the reason given for a prim and proper though promising date to be suddenly cut short.

The three Family members made their way into the main SPCA reception facility, where a lively and smiling female 'Pet Seeker's Counselor' greeted them. "My, but don't you two make a lovely and loving couple. Let me guess, you want to fill your home with a likewise loving and devoted pet. Please come this way with me and we will begin the compatibility screening procedures that will guarantee you will be matched with the best possible companion species and breed for your specific situation." Zachary and Marianne looked at each other. Were they at the SPCA or an adoption agency? "Oh, I know it seems like a lot of to-do, but we have found this the best way to reduce unsatisfactory couplings and traumatic pet returns." Man, did this gal ever have her lines down pat?

Zachary thought it even sounded logical, but the hot item they were looking for wasn't likely listed on their standard mutt-match questionnaire. "Ma'am, if you would be so kind to humor us, perhaps we can reach a happy medium. Your system sounds excellent and we will be happy to participate in it. Before making a possibly unnecessary investment of time, would you allow us a tour of your establishment?" Marianne wondered if Gustav was channeling his ponderous vocabulary through Zachary. "We place a lot of stock in intuition and natural selection. If we find a couple of candidates, then we'll take your surveys to see which of the ones we find would be the best one for us." Zachary did the 'Rachel nod'. "That's fair, isn't it?" He didn't wait for an answer. "Wonderful! Thank you so much for your kindness, now if you will just lead the way, we're all yours."

Marianne made a mental note not to buy a used car from this man. The 'Pet Seeker's Counselor' wondered what had just happened and at what point did she lose control. Vanessa was impressed.

They followed the young woman through the double doors to a long hallway. It must have been a hundred yards, minimum. Every twenty feet, each side had another set of double doors opposite each other, each with a tag on it identifying the genus and species that one might find down that hall. Zachary insisted on going down a dog hall first. Marianne felt obligated to humor the new kid in town, so through the doors they went.

Not all dogs are sensitive to spirits, but dogs are pack animals by instinctive nature. It took only a few to start the chain reaction. The crescendo of barks started with five, but the explosion of sympathy barking cued up so fast that no one got a fix on which dogs were the ones who first spotted and reacted to Vanessa. In a few more seconds, the noise level got to be painful enough where all four had to flee the hall. Vanessa's head was weaving from the unexpected emotional wave of frenzy of so many upset animals more than from the noise itself.

The Counselor looked at her two adoption candidates. "I'm so very sorry! Er, are either of you wearing a perfume or cologne of some kind? I've never seen them react like that!" Marianne and Zachary insisted they had no contact with anything smellier than shower soap and lavender shampoo from when they had showered that morning. Marianne suggested they just might take a stroll through the KITTEN (emphasized) department, after elbowing her companion discretely in the ribs. What could Zachary do but acquiesce, while thinking, "Sorry, Atlas, no lady friend on this go 'round. Maybe next time."

From inside, a hallway of felines witnessed a familiar face peer tentatively through a partial opening in the double doors. It seemed as quiet as a hall with one hundred and ninety-seven animals was going to get in the early afternoon. The Counselor looked around to see older cats snoozing and younger ones playing or feeding off of their moms. People were there, as always, monitoring cats, cleaning cages and petting the hopefully temporary residents. Future cat owner prospects were being towed by other counselors who were busy uttering pleasant platitudes regarding the advantages of owning cats over dogs. Those same counselors could, in a blink, switch positions on the superiority of owning a dog, or ferret, or cockatoo. There was such a peacefulness to it all, which made working here a calming and rewarding position. The SPCA even had a petting volunteer organization that was more than half made up of senior citizens. That endeavor was added when it was found out that the health advantages to human infants from physical loving contact also applied to animals and human elderly. The previous year, a cooperative effort by local nursing homes had purchased a special ordered van that made the rounds six days a week with furry packets of therapy that were eagerly anticipated by home residents, particularly those whose human relations were less than regular with their visit schedules. Some of those relations would be in for a nasty surprise when will-reading time came.

When the Counselor was sure that all was as it usually was, she asked Marianne to step inside first, which she did. Aside from a passing interest at a new face, the cats showed no adverse reaction. The workers and volunteers noticed the extra caution being taken and wondered what was going on. Zachary was next and the three of them stood in the entryway, almost holding their breath. The Counselor breathed a sigh of relief. Nothing was out of the ordinary and things were as they should be. She smiled, though still confused over what had happened in the dog hall, and beckoned her charges to step quietly as this was a naptime for their feline adoptee hopefuls. "There's a mountain range of untapped love potential in this room. All it takes is for someone to…" She froze. Zachary froze. Marianne looked behind and saw Vanessa's head and chest peering through the door, looking like some horror flick hunting room trophy. Scores of feral voices gave an eerie growling/whining sound that cats offer when they sense that something's not quite wrong, but not quite right, either. It wasn't loud and it didn't sound like things were going to go to the dogs, but it was most peculiar. Cats weren't pack hunters by trade, but tended more to the solitary, and their hunting techniques usually shied away from prolonged running while yapping one's head off. Therefore, a unified feral screech was put on hold until something more interesting came along.

The workers took a few steps back from the cages, first looking at the animals and then each other. The Counselor, not knowing what else to do, continued what she started out to do. Taking very quiet and slow steps, the three began to walk down the aisle. Her voice was a little shaky as she rattled off her memorized pro-adoption encouragements. The familiar voice soothed the fur of most of the felines, though not all. That was good. The ones that calmed down were probably just sounding off in sympathy, as happened with the dogs. That would leave the ones who were actually sensing a spiritual presence still bristling and vocalizing. Marianne, behind her back, gave an index finger wave for Vanessa to carefully follow. She asked for a brief pause as she adjusted a contact lens that she didn't actually wear (a trick she had learned from Rachel). Turning around, she had made the executive decision for Vanessa to walk before them, allowing her and Zachary a view of which cats actually followed her progress by visual tracking.

A fourth of the cats did just that, which brought up the problem of having too *much* of a choice. How to pick from among so many? Marianne whispered, "How do we decide from the ones that react?"

Zachary answered by returned whisper, "By how they react." Marianne watched carefully as the cats, with sight enough to focus on Vanessa's slow progress ahead of them, moved their heads in concert. Volunteers and workers began to take their breaks, whether it was time for them to or not. SPCA Counselors took their pet owner prospects to other halls, not wanting to upset them. That left three living and four visible (to some) visitors. All the reacting cats had varying degrees of bottle-brushed tails. The kittens were oblivious to it all. Perhaps their brains had to develop more before they would inherit the sensitivities necessary for feline/ghost awareness, or maybe they didn't know enough of the world to differentiate the usual from the unusual. There was, however, an exception to the rule. Halfway down the hallway, there was an enclosure where a nursing mother was sacked out while furry milk leeches purred and suckled, paws kneading and eyes closed contentedly. In that one enclosure, there was a jet-black long hair that was sitting at the cage door, fascinated. In contrast to the background of growling, the kitten's mew stood out like a SatCom panic-alert chirp at a Brahms concert. Vanessa had been devastated at all the cute and cuddlies that treated her like a pariah, when she would have given anything for one of them to be able to nestle into her lap and purr under affectionate stroking. Only Marianne could see Vanessa's look of wonder and surprised happiness. Zachary was about to suggest that they try to pick up the kitten, only to stop cold when he saw the mistiness in his partner's eyes. It didn't take much to figure out what was happening and he choked a little himself. The Counselor saw the kitten at the gate, looked at the moistening faces on the couple, and came to the correct conclusion that she had, once again, taken a role in giving a family some love in their home. That was the only thing she had figured correctly, not that it mattered.

Vanessa came up to the cage door, but the kitten's mother had other ideas. There was something she did not understand approaching her kit and that was enough to change her growl to a venomous hiss. Vanessa stopped and sadly remembered a cartoon, years ago, about another entity that had roamed the world in a frustrating search for a friend. Now, here she was, 'Vanessa the friendly ghost'. Marianne saw the development and her eyes met Vanessa's. She signaled for Vanessa to back away while she in turn walked slowly to the cage door. The kitten was fascinated with Vanessa, but enjoyed the attention from Marianne as well. "We'll take this one."

"Are you sure you don't want to look around some more (please say 'yes, this is the one')?"

Zachary knelt beside the cage door and looked into the brown and black doll eyes set into a ball of fur that seemed to absorb light like a black hole. "I think this one will do quite nicely. Boy or girl?"

"(Whew) That's Ebony. She's a little lady and one of the most even-tempered in this litter. Would you like to hold her?" The look on Marianne's face dictated who would be the first to cuddle the kitten. The guide opened the cage door, now that the mama cat was more sedate with Vanessa moved further away. Marianne took Ebony into her hands, she was so small, and brought her to her chest in a motherly, cuddling, sighing way. Ebony's mother had seen this sort of thing before and was both pleased and sad. That was the way of mother cats. She never looked away until her kit's new guardians were out of sight, followed by that troubling mist that had upset her earlier. Once they were gone, she laid her head back on the pillow. The mother cat had a different name for her little one than the one that the caretakers had given her. Not that it mattered, now.

Zachary went with the Counselor while Marianne sat in the waiting room with Ebony purring in her hands. Vanessa came up carefully and sat next to Marianne who shifted her arms to allow Vanessa to pet Ebony as well as she could, too. The two of them cooed and 'aw'ed' all the time Zachary was filling out papers. All this, for an ounce of fur? When he came out, Marianne and Vanessa rose up to leave, hardly taking notice that Zachary was completely loaded down with paraphernalia, including a litter box, 20 pounds of litter in a bag, a scooper, a brush, special shampoo for kittens, vitamins, special food for kittens (twenty-four cans in the starter kit), an ear de-mite kit, a different brush for flea removal, a doodad for tick removal, a collar with tags, a refillable catnip ball, a stock of catnip, special drops for immunization from everything from distemper to lyme's disease with a laminated schedule of dosages. That was the first load. There were still the two bowls and bowl holder, the litter box lid, a box of litter box liners, specially formulated 'accident' stain remover and deodorizer, a fabric covered apparatus for sharpening claws, and an instructional MiDi on everything regarding feline care from kitten to cat to saber tooth tiger. It was no wonder that the front doors to the SPCA were doubled and opened automatically. Zachary had decided to talk to Ryan and Allen about opening up an 'Ebony Line' of kitten products. The Atlas 'Puppy Primer Line' didn't hold a candle to this and this was just the starter kit! All this high profit margin stuff for something that would be just as content with scraps and laps? What a racket! By the time he had loaded everything into the trunk and rubbed his back for a minute, the ladies had long since piled themselves into the back seat, totally engrossed with the newest Family member. Zachary wondered how Atlas was going to take this sort of competition. Then he smiled. Ryan, Ralph and maybe Frank were in for some affection competition as well. In that respect, the kitten was the king or queen of feline beasts.

By the time they got back to Marianne's, Rachel and Frank had already arrived and were being updated on the progress and new ideas. Everyone was listening to Ryan recount every successful method by which the early Family was able to affect a successful transition of a spirit from earth to, wherever. Notes weren't encouraged, for though the methods were roughly similar, each case had to have a seat-of-the-pants tailoring on the spot. Every entity was different, so the rule of each encounter was: 'wing it'. The arrival of Ebony ended any semblance of academic order. The men of the house didn't even attempt to check out the new fur ball, as it was instantly surrounded by a feminine enclosure making cuddly sounds. Atlas was not pleased at all with the new addition, so Zachary consoled his friend. "Get used to it, Atlas m'boy."

Ralph snorted and told Zachary that Gustav said to inform their mascot that members of the opposite sex were all aliens. As Ralph refilled his lungs (that whole sequence was related on one breath), Ryan simply said, "Amen."

Zachary said his back was a little sore and asked whether Allen might pull a few meager items required by the SPCA for kitten care out of the trunk. Allen was happy to oblige. As soon as the young CEO was out the door, Zachary motioned for the men folk (the women were ignoring male contact for the time being, having moved en masse to the couch) to bear witness at the bay window. Frank, Ryan, Gustav, Zachary, Atlas and Ralph watched as Allen popped open the trunk and stood, transfixed. It didn't take much of a lip reader to recognize 'Crap on a cupcake!' from Allen's mouth. Half a minute of looking from various perspectives ('Maybe it won't look like as much if I lean this way?') later, Allen looked at the bay window and called out, "A little help here, please?"

Zachary laughed and sent Ralph out to lend a hand. Those still with him at the window asked what could be such a big deal, until they saw the two men loading up from the trunk. Zachary leaned over to Ryan, who was mesmerized at the unloading process, and said, "There's a real gold mine out there, Ryan. I've already got some of the preliminary work on your new income stream worked out in my head, including the future twin-sister company's name. How's this strike you: 'KITTEN KABOODLE'?"

The door opened and the two men huffed their piles into the house. Ralph called out "Marianne! Where do we put this stuff?"

Marianne looked up just long enough to indicate that he could put it wherever he pleased and kindly don't interrupt her again in the foreseeable future or she will tell him exactly where he *could* put it all. Ralph had heard about the new potential company and it's affect on the opposite sex, and then he looked at the ladies again. "Christ in Heaven, they're addicted already! Is this legal, Gustav?"

Ryan told Zachary and Frank that Gustav sadly admits to the genetic predisposition of the feminine gender to buying anything and everything for the cute hairball producers, including the expense of undergoing a somewhat pricey series of allergy desensitization procedures, if necessary. Zachary mentally added air purifiers to his growing list of products offered by the new company. Ryan saw the look of the newest human First Stringer's face. "Zachary, I thought you were divesting your time from Atlas's Petite Pet Supply Company to devote more time to ghost hunting." That brought Zachary up short. He was an astute entrepreneur and the excitement of the new outlet for those talents he had been blessed with had temporarily put his new career out of his mind. You couldn't serve too many masters, could you? Ryan laughed a little. "Not to worry, Zachary, we all wear more than one hat here. Let me show you something my father once clued me into."

Ryan went out and got some pebbles from the driveway and garden areas. He brought them into the house, got a small glass and put it on the kitchen counter. Gustav had seen this before, but Frank and Ralph were as curious as Zachary about what Ryan was getting at. They, too, were feeling the crunch of too many things coming down the pike. "Gather round, you masculine men who resist the wiles of cute kittenhood." He picked up a few rocks. "Here are some of your research projects." He put the rocks into the glass, one at a time. "Here are some of your personal time suckers; you may each label your own unique concerns upon the stones." More rocks went into the glass, more were picked up. "Now, here are the nuts and bolts of just day to day life, including (drop stone) meals, (drop stone) shopping, (drop stone) personal hygiene, (drop stone) home and auto repairs and maintenance, (drop stone) desires for personal entertainment and life enrichment and one more (drop stone) for miscellaneous." To all appearances, any more stones added would simply roll off the top of the rock pile. "Gentlemen, is this glass full?"

The obvious answer was 'yes'. All knew by now that nothing was obvious in this Family. No one dared to answer the obvious. Allen was the only one who ventured what they all were thinking. "The real answer is 'no' and none of us knows why. OK, guru, what's the meaning of life, here?"

Ryan was pleased with the answer. He pulled out a creamer pitcher from the cupboard and filled it with water. "Observe, grasshoppers. That glass is your lives, already seemingly jam-packed. This pitcher holds your duties to the Family. He poured the water in the pitcher into the glass, and the water went in with no problem at all. "Your lives have a lot of room for expansion that you aren't aware of. With time management, delegation and improved performance, you fellows haven't begun to reach your maximum potentials. Fear not, friends, for the Family is strong and growing."

Frank took that demonstration to heart. He needed to know that he would be able to do more than he had so far, not only with this new group and new mission, but also with his life with Rachel and his children. "Now that's cool," he said, showing his age. Allen leaned over to him and suggested that, if he wanted to communicate with Jerry and Janet better, he might consider switching 'cool' for 'smooth'. It would be a start, anyway.

Rachel and Frank had to take off to be home in time for the kids to arrive from school. They would swing by later that evening to introduce Jerry and Janet to the Family. Ryan wanted to take a personal gander at the graveyard site in question and to see if Ebony did more than just react to above-ground entities. Atlas came along to scout around other areas, should things get dull or stalemated. Between Allen's car and the Green Machine, Ryan agreed to no limo this time around. A limo could carry the same number of people, but Ryan sensed the need of 'action and control-oriented males' to get behind their wheels.

Still, if groups were going to get bigger, then old ways were going to have to change. Perhaps he could shop around for one of those small busses. The drive took twenty minutes, on the average. Gustav made sure to get into Allen's car along with Zachary. He watched very carefully to learn what buttons did what, and even pointed to a few, asking questions.

"Hey, Gustav, what's with the sudden interest in my car's technology?"

"Just curious, no real reason. My, what a lovely day."

"Right."

Vanessa and Marianne were the only two ladies in the foray this time and, of course, both were making sure that Ebony felt perfectly at home in the back of the Green Machine. Ralph chatted with Ryan. "So what are we talking about, breaking into roving teams? On top of the sighted living members, we've only got two spooks, plus two animals and two men who can't see but can certainly help, not including the second string. That's enough for either two fully armed divisions, or maybe three or four scouting units, especially if we can get the animal angle to work for us. And how about all those other entities above ground we don't want to forget about? Is there a list of places to hit?"

Ryan responded, "Actually, we were running a little thin on prospects a while back. Half of the better-known hauntings we've visited were bunk. The others we had handled already. I hired an article-clipping service that scans all magazines, papers, transcripts and even speeches for any kind of reference to ghosts, in any language. We got a lot of false hits on that one, early on. For instance, someone might write that a given politician or bill doesn't stand a *ghost* of a chance; there is more than one athletic team with the team name of 'Spirit', and FBI and CIA people sometimes are still referred to as 'spooks'. We were overwhelmed with all the references we got, so Marianne hooked up a 'human reader' service to winnow out the obvious coincidental references, which narrowed down what we looked at by almost 90%. But it still left us with a backlog of investigation possibilities that'll keep us entertained for a while. I expect the Edwards incident is going to spark a whole new surge in items regarding the spirit world, which is both good and bad. We're more likely to twig onto a larger number of candidates, but there will also be more public scrutiny of potential sites, and of us, should we arrive at one of those sites. I suppose that having working teams without my presence will help with that, but that idea is a little hard for me to take. I've been the one to see each entity off and that feeling of joy is my reward for the work that goes into it. I've got the most experience in this and it should be used."

Ralph had carried countless business people in his cab. He actually listened to what they had to say. "Ryan, ever hear the definition of the most effective executive?"

"Great, my own medicine. No, my good hack. Pray tell."

"It's a man or woman who reads a document written by a subordinate that doesn't measure up to what that executive could have done by himself or herself, who signs that paper and sends it off with little thought about it, because their talents are better focused on the bigger picture." Ralph's was the lead car. He pulled into the Rhinebeck Cemetery entrance and up the tenth of a mile to the spot where Atlas had first caught the whiff. Both cars pulled off the narrow road and everyone got out, with their leader still chewing on that last bit of offered wisdom.

Marianne said "Brrrrr. Ebony, you stay inside here." She undid the top two buttons of her coat and tucked the kitten in; similar to how Atlas rode with Zachary when he didn't have the sling available. Ralph suffered a pang of envy for the feline's privilege. Ryan wanted to let the kitten take a shot at it first, so they stopped walking about fifteen yards away from the gravesite Atlas had discovered. Marianne was against letting her kitty out in the cold, but Zachary had been prepared for that. He pulled out from his 'starter kit extra-options handy carryall' something that looked like a modified fuzzy glove (the patented 'Kitty Cardigan') and had Marianne wrap Ebony in it. Marianne held Ebony in her hands and used her as a directional indicator by following her eyes. It reminded Vanessa of an organic Star Trek tricorder. The reaction was surprising. As soon as Ebony was pointed in the direction of the last resting place, supposedly, of Mrs. Petrocelli, she made a surprisingly audible growl. Marianne instinctively brought Ebony closer to the protection of her bosom, but wondered why the different reaction by the kitten to the entity before them, compared to the more friendly mew that greeted Vanessa earlier. Might Ebony be partial to female entities?

Ryan stepped forward. "You can return Ebony to your warm protection; it looks like we have a bonafide 'karma kitty'. Now, let's go introduce ourselves, shall we?" Ryan stepped up to the gravesite, as did the others. "Vanessa, see if you can pick up the same feelings you noticed before." Vanessa walked up to the foot of the grave, closed her eyes once more and allowed her awareness to reach into the ground. Whatever it was down there, it didn't seem at all at peace. She could sense periods of frantic negativity, punctuated with brief intervals of relatively sane muttering and moaning.

"I wonder if he's sane. It doesn't feel normal, like what we've met before. I sense periods of incredible anger merging into feelings of great sorrow. Every so often, I sense the image or word of murder. Wait, the movement, it's stopped. I think he's aware of me. Everyone, be quiet. He's edging closer."

"GO AWAY!!!"

The whole Family jumped back, though Zachary was a little slower on the response. He mainly reacted to everyone else reacting and the fact that Atlas had an accident. Marianne screeched from both the force of the voice and Ebony finding purchase for all her claws. Even Gustav was thrown for a loop as he ducked for cover behind a handy monument. The Family backed off to regroup. Ryan called for the role.

Ralph started. "I heard two very loud words that sounded like 'go away'. Definitely masculine, sounded frantic, and I think he has an amplified public address system down there with him. I'm OK."

Marianne was next. "Ditto on the concert pitch reception. Ebony took up needlepoint on my boobs and, before you ask it, Ralph, I'll apply my own band aids, thank you."

"Rats."

Zachary was the least pleased looking of all and was still leaning forward after his backwards jump. "Atlas peed. He's never done that before. Jesus, Atlas, you must be half bladder."

Ralph handed Zachary the keys. "Green Machine's got a pair of overalls in the trunk I use for work, and there's spare warm jacket next to it. They're not the cleanest, but they're dry."

"In a moment. I have to give my report, don't I? I heard something. It wasn't as loud as you're describing and it was pretty vague; couldn't actually make out anything that made sense. You know, it's odd. There might be a biblical parallel here."

Ryan asked him to explain quickly and then to go change before he gets chilled. "Not much chance of that. You'd be surprised how much heat Atlas puts out. Anyway, that whole Revelations thing the Second String came up with earlier was too close to the last Bible chapter for anyone's comfort." Marianne agreed that it was startling, and pretty frightening, when she had heard it. "I had thought about going ghost hunting in sunken wrecks, but wondered what the world might think if anyone heard of the sea as well as the earth giving up its dead. Now that I'm over the shock of the flood, this entity response reminds me of that passage when Saul was confronted by God, who asked him why he was persecuting God's people. Saul's entourage had heard something, but wasn't able to make out anything intelligible; just thundering gibberish. That sort of thing is mentioned in other places as well. Now, I'm going to change in the G.M. Nobody peek."

Vanessa was still trying to make sense of what had just happened. *"I felt more than just the words. There was a force behind them that reminded me of Annie's power. It wasn't the same, though. It was less on finesse, more on turbulence and malevolence. Whatever it was, the force almost lifted me off my feet. Ryan, that's the first time we've ever had an entity reject a first approach with that sort of vehemence."*

Allen could only report that he had heard what the others did and that he was all right. Gustav took his turn. *"Did anyone else sense the fear in that voice that I did? Look, Vanessa is a female entity presence. The entity is a male presence in a female's grave. Maybe there's a hot button there. Ryan is mortal, and may not be able to connect as clearly as a same sexed entity like me. I'm going to take a shot at making contact."*

Ryan and the rest cautioned Gustav to be very careful. Stirring up a hornet's nest twice sometimes gets them four times as mad. *"Hey, I was a lawyer. Who knows better than we on how to be diplomatic?"* Gustav strode forward. The Family members looked at each other and then took a few giant steps backwards. Atlas and Zachary returned and Allen explained what was going on. He could see that Gustav had stopped at the base of the grave and was standing stock-still, eyes closed, hands and arms slightly forward.

"WHO THE HELL ARE YOU?!"

Gustav turned to the Family with a triumphant look on his face and said, "See? *A much more civilized response. It was a question rather than a command.*" Ralph asked Ryan if Gustav was off his nut. Ryan replied that he had suspected it from time to time. Allen took his turn as being Zachary's interpreter for ghost speech.

"*Good evening, sir. My name is Gustav Mendelssohn. And who might you be?*"

Allen told Zachary that the spirit had declined to identify himself and that he had opted for the 'F', 'M', 'S' and 'Z' words in the process.

"Z?"

"*I understand that you may feel nervous about meeting someone who can hear you. I represent a group of people who have a great amount of experience in assisting those such as yourself. Do you know where you are right now?*"

The response this time was still agitated, but not quite as much. "*If you're asking do I know that I'm dead, that's a no-brainer you nit-wit. Hey, how come you can hear me?*"

Gustav turned around to the assembled Family, who was gradually edging closer to support Gustav, now that it would seem that there was no landmine to step on. The lawyer smiled, gave a thumbs-up and went back to his first try at connecting with a spirit.

"*The truth of the matter is that I am dead as well.*"

"*Oh? Are you a new neighbor here?*"

"*No, not exactly. Well, I was recently buried not far from here. I'm kind of a free agent. You know, if you have to be dead, it's a lot more entertaining to be above ground than below. Would you like to come out of there and see the sun and sky again?*" There was silence. Gustav waited, wondering what Ryan would have done here. Keep waiting, or encourage the fellow some more? He knew enough not to hit on any really sensitive topics at this stage, such as how it came about that he was in a woman's grave. Another minute passed. "*Look, my name is Gustav. I'm kind of lonely and hope you don't mind me talking with you.*" Gustav's experience told him to stay passive and enforce continuity of conversation. "*You don't have to **talk to me** if you don't want to. It would make it more **pleasant** if you might tell me your own name. We could be **friends**, if you like.*"

Ryan was nodding in approval. Gustav was using the same psychology the man used when he was alive to get the confidence of the person he was representing, even if it was with someone he considered a bottom feeder. Whoever was down there, he was dealing with a pro up here. A response stopped Ryan's thought train.

"*Cute. You were either a used car salesman, a psychologist, or a lawyer, right?*"

"*Uh, well, yes, you're right. The third one, if you please.*"

"*I don't please. So, you're a dead lawyer that God didn't want in Heaven. That figures. He doesn't want me, either, and I don't want you. I don't want to see the sun, or the sky, or hear the birds, or see your ugly legal puss and you can tell that banshee bitch that poked around here earlier that she can…"*

Allen saw the reaction on Vanessa's face and Zachary saw the one on Allen's. "What did he say?"

Allen swallowed, and paraphrased. "He, would rather not be disturbed and described the two who have tried to do so in colorful terms. Wow, he has some vocabulary. We may want to see if he was a sailor." Ryan caught that, but was too busy listening to give a deserved rejoinder.

"…so you can just take your harpy hag and the two of you can go to h…can go somewhere else and just leave me alone. This conversation is ended. GO AWAY!" Gustav looked like he had let down the world, the way he walked back to the Family.

"I'm, sorry. I didn't do so well. Guess I'm not cut out for this kind of work."

It didn't take Zachary much effort to figure out what was going on by Ryan's reply. "Old friend, you did better than I could have done. Your approach was brilliant and proven successful in the past. Each entity is different. You've made progress here and we have gained some more information we can use, once we have time to review it and compare to what the Second String can dig up."

"I learned squat, Ryan, and just reinforced his antagonism. What did we get out of that?"

Ryan smiled. Allen, Marianne, and an insulted Vanessa perked up their ears. They were clueless on the benefits of this chat. Zachary was getting frustrated with half-conversations. "First off, our target has an excellent vocabulary on top of the adjectives and is astute in his perceptions of Gustav's occupational background. That hints at a good education and an intelligent mind. And, most of all," he purposefully put in a dramatic pause, which the others knew he had done but that didn't stop them from leaning forward to catch the punch line, "…the man is afraid of Hell. He either believes he is being punished and belongs right where he is, or he believes that he is better off where he is now than where he might go to if discovered. The fellow is lonely and really would like to talk to someone. He started off actually conversant, but his fears quickly got the better of him. Come on, gang, let's hit the Arms and mull this one over. You too, Farmer Brown."

Zachary looked down at his borrowed overalls peeking out from under his winter coat. Did the Arms have a dress code? With this group, did it matter? Marianne was concerned, and spoke as they walked back to the cars. "But Ryan, just because they allow Atlas doesn't mean they'll accept Ebony."

Ralph had opened the door for Marianne to get in the front seat, then realized his mistake and opened the back so that the ladies could do more kitten-cooing. Ryan would have answered Marianne, but Ralph sensed a delicious gotcha handy and jumped on it. "Honey, just keep Ebony tucked in right where she is. If anyone notices, we'll just tell them that it's an unstable implant." He thumbed the child safety door lock. Slam!

Even through the soundproofed car, the men could easily tell that the words issuing from the back seat weren't ones of comfort and solace. Ebony must have already developed a sympathetic sense for her living mistress, for she could be seen batting at the window and hissing. Gustav smiled again, drawing on his reserves of resilience both as a German and a lawyer. *"Next time, we'll have her talk to our mystery man. She'll blast him right out of there."*

Ralph's enjoyment of his 'gotcha' was suddenly cut short when he realized that Marianne was in the back of the car he was about to drive. The Green Machine didn't have one of those privacy windows, either. Ralph looked hopefully at Allen and held out his keys. "Want to drive?"

Payback time. "NO WAY, and stay downwind! Now you can ride your own 'Thunder'." On the short drive to the Beekman Arms, Allen explained to Zachary about the horrors of the flatulent filly he had been blessed with in Milledgeville. They were going to get to the Arms well before others. Ralph and Ryan were getting chilly while waiting for Marianne to release her hold on the Green Machine's door lock over-ride button.

While two men pleaded to be let into the warmth of the retired taxicab, the Gladstones were having a conversation. "Frank, the school bus will be here any minute. We need to come to an understanding on bringing the kids along on this visit, or put it off. If we put it off, they'll suspect that there's a problem and that will get them worried that our old arguments might be starting up again, right?"

"Hey, Bride, you're preaching to the choir. You've been with the 'Family' longer than me, but if the whole thing were left up to me, I'd say just trust the people. They've been interacting with the world despite the unusual nature of their business for a long time. I say we just go and not worry about it, other than not saying hello verbally to Gustav and Vanessa."

Trust, Rachel thought. She trusted them to be mellow when they greeted Frank for the first time and he got 'barbershop chorus meets Welcome Wagon'. Still, in hindsight, it was probably the best thing they could have done. Maybe she wasn't right all the time. That had been an argument point in the past on his side of the fence. They were trying to remove the fences and, though it grated a little, "You're right, Frank. I worry too much. Close your mouth, Frank, because if you are going to make fun of me for trying to change my attitudes… Frank… Not now! Later. The kids will be home any second! FRANK!"

Half a minute later, the door opened and two teenagers entered their home. The daughter called out, "We're ho-ome! Where's (two heads popped up from behind the couch), whoa! Sorry if we interrupted something. Rachel! Wait! Don't hurt him!"

"Hold fire, Janet. How much can she hurt Dad with couch pillows? Let's hit the fridge and get the homework done so we can go on the visit tonight."

Down south, the regular (ordinary) duties of the Second String were coming to a close and their extra-curricular assigned tasks were starting up. Paul, Nunzia, Dagmar and Russ (who had finally made it back to his home state) were on their way home to fire up the PC links to each other and connect so that what each was doing would be available to the other on a quadrant screen.

Also below the Mason-Dixon, Hammer and Barry were having their late afternoon munch at The Inn. They still weren't used to the night shift hours, but managed to get in a good snooze till noon. The owner, Franklin Pesko, had just arrived back from a business trip and had wanted to personally thank his celebrity bouncer. The new bartender was also on Franklin's 'Hello, I'm your boss and I appreciate you' list. Franklin made his way to the table. What he had taken to be a man of small stature turned out to be his own size. It was just that the perspective of seeing the two together had made him assume at first that the other fellow was shrimpy. The Hammer guy was pretty big. "Hey, boys. Mind if I join you?"

Hammer said, "Free country, Mr. Pesko. Thanks for the job."

Barry added, "Yes, Mr. Pesko. Thank you. The math isn't right."

Franklin Pesko hadn't expected that last comment. "Excuse me? You're Barry Nicholson, right?" The fellow shook his head 'yes'. "What do you mean, the math isn't right?"

Hammer didn't like this. Barry had no guile and spat things out like a child, though there were some ideas in his head that were definitely of an adult nature. He smiled to think of that recent day at the bus station in Savannah. This was the boss, though, and he didn't want to make any waves. There wasn't anything he could do about it, though. They hadn't expected to see the boss come in and Hammer never could educate his friend on the virtues of judicious withholding of the truth.

"Well, Mr. Pesko, sir, I was working the bar last night and they were nice and let me take the money and give change to people. The drawer had seven hundred eighty-three dollars even when we started. Do you want that in the denominations?" Franklin was unable to speak. What was this all about? He just shook his head, no. "OK, well, we sold ninety-one drafts, forty-three standard price mixed drinks, twenty-nine specialty second level cost drinks, seven top price drinks. That comes to fifteen hundred fifty-four dollars even, added to the cash drawer should have made it twenty-three hundred and thirty-seven dollars. I looked just before closing and saw that there was exactly five hundred dollars less in the drawer. It didn't add up, sir. Thought you might like to know. I don't know what the tips total was."

Franklin didn't like to hear that. No business owner did. He had trusted his long time employees like a father and it hurt him deeply to hear that his trust might be betrayed. Yet, these guys were cons, or one of them was, and both were members of a biker gang. They didn't look like they had a head for this sort of thing, though. "Barry, can you show me your calculations on this?"

"Barry can't do that, Mr. Pesko. You see, he does this sort of thing in his head, never puts it down on paper. But he's never wrong, sir. I'm an accountant and Barry here gives me a hand. I've double-checked him hundreds of times and, if there's a mistake, it's always mine. Barry's a savant, Mr. Pesko."

A savant! Franklin had heard of such people. This guy seemed pretty functional, though. Maybe that was the way they were? Barry struck him as just a little weird, but it was hard to put his finger on what kind of weird. "Barry, do you know what happened to the money? That was in the drawer?"

"Yes, sir. Chuck took it. I figured it was how you paid him, but I wasn't sure so figured you ought to know. Maybe you deduct it from his paycheck or something." Chuck was the primary bartender; the one that Hammer had flattened after that lady had launched him last weekend.

"OK, Barry, I'm glad you told me. Please, if you ever see something like this again, keep me informed. Barney, oh, excuse me. Hammer, you're good for business. People really like you and no riff raff have come in since you ejected those two troublemakers. Just be careful, son. Being a big boy might attract other big boys looking to make a point."

Here was yet another person trying to do something good for him. Hammer wasn't used to this. "Yes, Mr. Pesko, sir. I'll keep my eye peeled. Cops and me are getting along pretty good lately and they already said something like that. We'll keep things safe, sir."

"Well, thanks again, the both of you. I'll be talking with you later. By the way," Franklin pulled out four hundred dollar bills and divided it among the two of them. "That's for you, not for the community chest." Franklin stepped over to his office, closed the door and picked up the directory. There was a company he had heard about from a friend/competitor that would quietly put in a hidden camera. Pilfering was the one thing every bar and tavern owner agreed upon to fight as a group, besides drunk customer driving.

The Gladstone family arrived to meet the Fitzgalen Family. Marianne's house was a two-story combination of stone and wood that gave the feeling of solidity and hominess. There were two chimneys, one of them with a live fire burning inside. The circular drive had a bank of five parking places. The Fitzgalen Team had used this place in the past for a retreat from the world and Marianne loved to play the hostess for them. Now the job was a little bit bigger with the still growing Family and she welcomed the extra mother hen that Rachel represented. Who, by the way, was just coming through the door with her own brood in tow.

"Everyone, I would like to present my step-children, whom I am very proud of. This is Jerry, who is sixteen, and Janet, who's fourteen." The approach that manifested by instinct was not the dog pile that had been pulled on Frank. They had other weapons in their arsenal. Ladies first.

"Oooo, look at the beautiful kitten! Can I hold it, please?" Marianne and Rachel led Janet to the 'ladies kitty couch'. She was handed, very gently, one playful and affectionate piece of portable diplomacy.

Zachary then made his strategic appearance with his own four-legged smile maker. He had discussed things about Jerry with Rachel, which automatically selected Atlas for the male kid pleaser. "Holy Christmas, is that really Atlas? Oh, man, that dog is really smooth!" Zachary looked at Ryan, who looked at Ralph, who looked at Frank; 'smooth'?

Zachary mentally shrugged. Kid vocabulary evolved faster than flu viruses. "Smooth is a fact, Jerry. Come on over here to the wicker rockers. Atlas loves a lap by the fire. Would you mind?"

"Me? I get to hold *the Atlas*? Really? Mom, you GOTTA get a picture of this. OK, Rachel?"

Rachel had been pre-occupied with Janet, but her subconscious caught the 'M' word. That was something new. Allen caught her eye, gave her a wink to indicate his being pleased and that he would score a camera tout suite. His PC was on the kitchen table. It only took a flip of a recessed tab and an e-camera card popped out. Allen did a quick pass to his mother, who snapped a half dozen shots of Jerry, then another half dozen of Janet. Allen dropped the device back into the PC and tapped the button that downloaded the data to the printer, which spit out light balanced and enhanced paper prints that were destined to be enjoyed by classmates tomorrow. Rachel caught Frank's grin and returned with a sheepish one of her own. She walked over to her loving husband, gave him a peck on the cheek and whispered in his ear, "You were right. I'm learning to trust your judgment more, so please be patient with me if I slip back to my old ways. I'm trying my best because you deserve nothing less."

While Zachary told Jerry ghost stories by the fire, Ryan listened and took mental notes of details on the man's different approach to ghost hunting. There was a new story being told that Zachary hadn't mentioned before. The funny thing was, the phenomena turned out not to be either a ghost or a hoax. It was about 'The Christmas Angel', though this 'Angel' was nothing to put on your Christmas tree. It would show up around late December north of Climax, Colorado, always in the late afternoon or early evening. Some years, it wouldn't show up at all. The eyewitness reports of those who survived were that people driving up a sizable hill's secondary road would be suddenly blinded by a light from low in the east. It seemed to come from the next hill over. There were plenty of evil alien and Michael Jackson's ghost speculations on that one by the supermarket news.

Over the decades, enough cars had driven over the embankment, with more than a few fatalities to warrant heaviest duty guardrails along the whole stretch of road. That ended the cars driving off the cliff, but there were still some nasty head-ons. To show how superstitious people still were, it turns out that one of those who died when the Angel first started its grim reaping happened to be a man wanted for murder in three states. That's when the Angel angle was indelibly attached to the event. From that point on, anyone who was affected by the beacon was looked on with suspicion of being accursed by God. Zachary literally camped out on the side of that stretch of road during 'Angel Season' two years in a row before he, too, saw the light. He took pictures of the blinding beacon from several points along the road by jogging along and snapping shots until the light mysteriously disappeared. He then took the camera home, printed up the shots, used trigonometry to calculate the precise location of the beacon, and drove to that point the next day. Sure enough, it turned out that there was a house at the very location his calculations pointed to. Zachary thought that someone was playing a vicious and deadly prank, so he called in the gendarmes. That afternoon, three detectives and Zachary crept up a wooded embankment to catch the wicked trickster in the act. All they saw was an old woman open up a second story window to add birdseed to her feeder. The window was on old-fashioned kind; attached by two hinges on the top. That required the bottom of the window to swing outwards and be held in place with what looked to be two thirds of a yardstick. When the 'window of opportunity' had passed for the beacon to make its appearance, the four investigators slipped back to the squad car, disappointed. It was on the trip back to the station when another blinding light hit. "Son of a BITCH!" he quoted himself as saying, nearly causing yet another local accident. Zachary told the officers what he suspected and they made a beeline back to the house. Zachary took another couple of pictures and the skinny of it was that the window happened to catch the sun just right at that time of year. The changing angles of the sun only caused the reflection to strike at that awkward location about three or four days out of the year. It didn't show up every year because one, some years it was cloudy, and two, probably because some people who saw it and survived were too afraid to tell anyone that they had been warned by God's angel. The poor woman, when she found out that feeding her birds had caused over a score of deaths, had to be institutionalized. She recovered most of her sanity, but could never be allowed outside the institution. As soon as she heard a bird chirping, she nose-dived into a deep and suicidal depression.

    Rachel and Frank sat on the double rocker and enjoyed the fire's warmth, as well as the story, though truly it was a sad one. Allen and Ralph were each breaking out a beer and getting settled down into some reviews of the Edwards memories, out of hearing range of the two kids. Gustav and Vanessa surveyed the scene. Removed from the rest, there was yet another conversation brewing. It would be a fateful one.

"Oh, Gustav, I'm so happy with how things are turning out. The Family is growing, Rachel is reunited with Frank, Allen with Melissa, Marianne has found Ralph, the kids are accepting Rachel as a mother, and we've new firepower on several fronts."

"It's nice, Vanessa, really."

Vanessa looked at her ghost partner. She knew his speech patterns a lot more than he knew hers, though he was catching up fast. *"Gustav? What's wrong?"*

People have trouble hiding feelings from people. With spirits, it's almost impossible. Flesh is far less revealing, as the spirit can hide inside. "I still feel I blew it at the site and, I blew it with both my marriages. Actually, it's mainly Martha. I could never reach her, Vanessa, no matter how much I prayed and tried and cried. I mean, look at all this! Everyone else has new or healed love relationships. I once, no, twice gave it all I had. Seeing Martha again brought up a lot of old skeletons in my heart's closet."

Vanessa looked at her 'old' friend. There was something she had been considering for some time. Now seemed like a good time to bring it up. *"What time does Martha usually go to bed?"*

"Huh? Well, she was an 'early to bed early to rise' person. Ran in her family for generations to be that way. I seem to remember that nine-thirty was about the latest she would be able to keep her eyes open. I'd be surprised if she had changed much...wait a minute. You're plotting something scary."

Vanessa looked at the clock. It was getting on to seven. *"Do you want to give something a try? It might help Martha."*

Long years of Vanessa's plots made him think twice about responding. Then, he looked around him once more. "I'll try anything. What do you have in mind?" Vanessa told him. He asked, "Could we harm her?" Vanessa reassured him. Gustav looked at the floor for a moment, then, "Let me think about it for a little while, OK?"

The Second String meeting had begun. Each of four team members had their PC's in front of them, each screen divided into four equal parts, each part having a screen of what they were working on. This way, each could keep an eye on the accumulating knowledge of everyone, using it to augment their own research.

Russ's screen had a list he was continually updating of missing persons and murders for the past two years in the Hudson Valley region. Paul's had a sequence of names listing the police contacts in the area he had been working on, with periodic entries added as Paul concluded each conversation with those people. Dagmar's screen had a date on the lower right quadrant that kept going back one day at a time. When something in the news transcripts from sources in the Hudson Valley area tripped a key word, that date would appear in the column beginning in the upper left of the screen along with the word or phrase that had flagged it. Nunzia's corner simply had 'working', along with the logo for the Mormon site.

The night shift had begun for The Inn in Milledgeville. Chuck came in, punctual as ever. It paid to be punctual, he would say. No one could see him laughing on the inside, until now. Barry felt a little bad for the guy. Chuck had been nice to him, letting him take charge of all the stock and inventory, even the stuff in the cellar. He didn't want to get such a nice man into trouble, but honesty to the person who paid your way was the way to be for him. Barry never liked it when the gang had stiffed some poor merchant or hotel owner. Hammer assured him that he had later sent whomever it might be some money for their troubles. Barry knew that Hammer was true to his word, for Hammer had never lied to him. There was a lot of the child within Barry's make-up and children knew when those they loved were not being truthful.

Franklin was in his office; the business office door was closed. He was watching a video screen of another kind of child…self-centered, spoiled, and one for whom the previously unappreciated word 'consequence' would take on a whole new dimension.

It didn't take long to confirm Barry's allegations. Franklin Pesko was shown that the truths shared by the simple minded should never be ignored. In the hour that followed, he witnessed five slights of hand with the cash flow. It was like watching his own son steal from him and realizing that he had been doing it all along. He couldn't help but grind his teeth at all those years of trust and faith in Chuck, having him and whatever girlfriend he might have going at the time over for a barbeque, laughing over a drink. Now the decision was whether to simply turn the man over to the law, to just let him go or, perhaps, to exact a revenge of his own. Franklin drummed his fingers on the table. There! Chuck just palmed a ten and put in a one. He had to admit, the guy was good at it. Maybe The Inn could use a magician act?

Martha Scholldorf Mendelssohn got ready for her last night at the Holiday Inn in Kingston. It would be good to get out of this town. It was *his* town. It was *his* valley. He was now joined to the very soil of that valley next to *her* son and she wanted out of there. It was from him that her son had arisen. She had lost Garrison and now her ex-husband could be closer to her son than she could. If God did exist, which she doubted, then the two of them were speaking to each other even now in God's presence. That bothered her a lot. If God did not exist, then at least the two people who had once been her heart's love sources were now sharing the earth together. That thought made her heart feel even colder. Her jaw set tighter as she shook her head. That preacher thought he had known Gustav. She snorted. No one knows anyone and, if they thought they did, they were deluded fools.

It was time for bed now. It wasn't so much that she was tired, but that her life had become a ritual used to pass the time until she, too, would go the way of her beloved Garrison. The sooner the better, she thought.

Sitting in church today, she had sought some kind of kinship with that hussy, Valerie. That Teutonic twit had insulted her by not wanting to hear her put Gustav's less than optimal husbandship into proper perspective. Martha didn't understand why Valerie kept scooting away. It gave minor but definite heart's ease for her to harpoon Gustav's memory. Shouldn't it do that also for that young biddy? After all, she must be no more than sixty-five, if she's a day. Give her another decade and maybe she'd mature. Whether she did or not, it didn't matter anymore. Come tomorrow, Martha mused, she would go home richer, but poorer. That thought stopped her for a moment. It sounded, sort of, familiar. She shook her head, dismissing it as nonsense.

Nine-thirty. Washing up was done, tomorrow's clothes were on their hangers and assigned to the far left in the closet for easy finding and wearing. No wake up call was needed, for she could wake bang on the dot, as long as it was always the same dot. Martha said her night prayer that she had been saying since she was a child, same words, same inflections, and with the same lack of any inner meaning. Not that she thought anyone was listening. Her family had been big on traditions, very big. Things were done just so and consistency was the key to succeeding, or just surviving, in this harsh world. Gustav and Garrison were the first lights to illuminate her gray and ordered life. Gustav had been a loving light, but one that hadn't disrupted her sense of order. Garrison wouldn't be bound to any feeding schedule, diaper dirtying schedule, or sleep pattern. He had shattered her regimented life, then left her to glue the pieces together as well as she could. The trouble was, none of the pieces fit together very well any more. Nor had their fit improved with age. Gustav hadn't been much help, though she did have to admit that he tried. As she lay there, the day's activities caused her to again consider his efforts to minimize the damage. It made little difference to her about the truths that he did his level best to get her to see. When it concerned matters of deep emotion, facts simply do not matter; at least they didn't to her. Counseling the man wanted? There was nothing more she had wanted to tell Gustav, much less a total stranger who would only pick her apart under a microscope and tell her more facts which wouldn't matter. It would not only have been a waste of time and money, it would open bottomless pits of pain that she had barely managed to put a lid on. She had done well to keep that lid on during her waking hours. It was her dreams, though, that she still couldn't control.

She hated, yet, craved the dreams. It was the only place she could treasure her lost son, to talk with him, to touch him. Come the dawn, though, she would waken to realize that it was only a dream. Each day, she felt her self dry up and harden just a little more. She felt tired and desiccated, but that was just old age...wasn't it?

Frank and Rachel drove home with the kids in the back of the Foxglove, comparing their photo mementos. These would be mass reproduced for their friends for sharing, and not-friends for the 'nyah' factor. Both were sure of a 'Phab-Phriday' tomorrow. Alliterations must be de rigueur for kids lately. Overheard was that today had achieved the status of being a 'Thilly Thursday', which made up for the 'Weary Wednesday' yesterday. The adults drove in silence, holding hands, content. Tomorrow was going to be whatever tomorrow would be. That usually meant busy, weird, fun, tragic, and eye opening. Which, when you got down to it, was what anyone's life was. Theirs just had the intensity levels cranked up a notch or five. Rachel was not fully content, though. Something had been nagging her for the past two days and it had something to do with Vanessa and Ryan, with Ralph and Marianne, with herself and Frank, and something to do with the Edwards Estate experience.

Ryan took off for his abode with Zachary and Atlas. Ralph and Marianne had kissed goodnight. Ralph hit the couch, grumbling under his breath about strict Catholicism. Marianne had agreed to declutter the pile on top of the extra bed and making a floor path among all the extra things shoehorned in the spare bedroom for Allen. Ralph had bemoaned Allen's capacity to snuggle while mumbling things about Melissa that was just too much information. Rachel and Frank had the kids tucked in and were heading off to bed themselves. Melissa had another half hour of research to do herself and then it would be time for her single bed. The Second String had long since ended the evening's research and were winding up the information collating in preparation for the noon meeting tomorrow.

That left Gustav and Vanessa, once again, alone. Gustav looked at the stars in the sky from Marianne's front porch.

"You know, old girl, it just occurred to me. This house is haunted."
"You don't say, old man? Think it will affect the market value any?"
"Only if we come with the sale, so, no."
"Are you ready?"
"No."
"Then, it's time to go." Gustav looked at Vanessa for a moment, lowered his head and quietly nodded. Vanessa and Gustav then stood side by side and closed their eyes. Both pictured the Holiday Inn restaurant where, a short time ago, they had such a good time together. Both sets of eyes opened to the new location, but the place was darkened, closed for the night. Two spirits then walked to the front desk to find a room number. There was one person manning the fort, as was usual at this time of night, but she was reading the paper behind the privacy wall just behind the desk counter. The last time Vanessa had participated in looking up a number of any kind behind a desk was back in Oahu, and she had watched Ryan do it. That was a very long time ago, long before they had been married, back in the days of rotary phone dials and party lines. Gustav had never had even that much of a

chance and half expected to flip through a guest ledger of some kind (he saw that once in an old Bogie movie), which shouldn't be a problem. If Mad Annie could turn Bible pages, he could handle a register. Though he had checked into many hotels and motels, he'd never actually seen what went on behind those ubiquitous counters.

The Holiday Inn Corporation had tried to keep up with the times. They bought out Ramada and Best Western and kept those hotels with their established names. Each hotel group was then aimed at a specific financially-capable demographic, from the Holiday Inn which out priced the Marriott and Hilton chains, to the Ramada which was aimed more at Joe Average and family, to the Best Western for the lowest prices anywhere (some called them 'hooker havens', corroborated by the fact that they had the highest percentage of cash business). Top of the line meant just that. Guests 'signed in' with a thumbprint that was compared to the initial Debi-Cred card swipe. There was no signed register. Room doors were opened with either a thumbprint scan, or a recorded voice command, whichever was the customer's preference; both, if the customer was especially security conscious. The latter was usually preferred as it allowed a person to enter their room without having to put down whatever they might be carrying, be it baggage or a sleeping child.

Vanessa and Gustav stood befuddled at what was before them.

"Will you look at all those buttons? Gustav, which one do we push?"

Remembering his debacle with Allen's car, *"Maybe this wasn't such a good idea. We might push the wrong one and flush the pool. We have some time. Maybe we ought to just walk into each room till we find her."*

"Now, Gustav. Normal intelligent people designed this mess for reasonable use by normal intelligent people and we're just as smart as anyone else. It shouldn't be that difficult to figure it out. Besides, there are hundreds of rooms here and who knows what we might walk in on? I am NOT that kind of girl." Vanessa began to study the banks of displays and buttons. What stood out most of all to her was a bank of buttons that were in groups of three's, each set of three with a number next to it. The numbers ran from 001 to 354. Vanessa traced her finger along the button bank, trying to figure out a way to bring up a name to go along with the number. Gustav was searching out a part of the desk that had a liquid crystal thin-screen with buttons labeled with the alphabet under it. It looked promising. *"I think I found it!"*

Vanessa turned her head to Gustav, but the motion allowed the finger she had concentrated her attention on to brush against of the buttons. Button bank 202 lit gently up on all three button lights. The far left one was brighter than the others. *"Uh oh. I may have done something. Would you help me?"*

Gustav took a look and would have berated his partner for clumsiness had he not recalled Allen's car hood, windows and windshield wipers. *"Push the same button again, perhaps it will turn itself back off."* She did. This time the button light got brighter. *"OK, push the button next to it, maybe it will interrupt the circuit."* She did. The second button now lit up more brightly than the first. Where the first one was yellow, this one was red. There was a third button. Both decided that enough was enough, third time was the charm and, after half a minute of deliberation concerning the possibility of activating an alarm that would empty the hotel, Vanessa pushed it. All three lights on the bank went out.

They went over to where Gustav had been and saw the bank of lettered buttons. This time, Gustav took the helm and pushed the 'M' button. The screen came to life and showed a list of names that started with that letter. There were seven, and one of them was the one they sought. Each name had a number next to it. Gustav took note of the name next to '211'. The screen had a time delay programmed in and, since it had been twenty seconds out of use, the screen went blank. Gustav squared his shoulders and Vanessa made ready to stand at his side when the desk buzzer rang.

Evan Mathers was a top-rated salesperson for Mallinkrodt Pharmaceuticals; an old and respected firm originally based in St. Louis but recently moved to Topeka. He was here on a good will tour for his company's customers to reassure them that all was stable and growing. His particular field of specialization and therefore responsibility was with radiopharmaceuticals. These were biologically safe radioactive materials (how many times had he been asked if that was an oxymoron?), which were designed to be injected into any given vein of a patient. That substance was tagged by a variety of means in order to haul that radioactivity to a specific tissue type or organ. Specialized camera systems produced by half a dozen competing manufacturers would use that radiation to produce a map of how that target organ or tissue was functioning, as opposed to other diagnostic tools that mostly gave information about tissue structure. That meant that his primary targets of opportunity were hospitals and diagnostic centers. His domain included three states and the eleven hundred customer locations included in that area. Over the past three weeks, he had stayed at a different hotel every night. Luckily, the drug companies paid their rep directors well and took good care of them with the finest in accommodations. Even so, the pace had its price. The speaker next to Evan's bed announced that he should wake up and get moving. He opened his eyes and saw darkness, causing him to dismiss the call as a front desk fluke or a nightmare. Moments later, the second message that was programmed to get someone hard to waken to move came on. Same message, but more urgent and loud. From ingrained reflex that overrode fuzzy conscious thought, he flipped the covers off and put his feet on the floor and shuffled his way to the bathroom. That's when every light went on in the bedroom and bathroom, and the shower came on at just the right temperature. That meant he was late and had better shift to high gear. Evan hopped into the shower and was lathering his hair when the shower turned off and all the lights went out.

Gustav wondered if that buzz, at this hour, might have something to do with their earlier mistake on the buttons. The desk person came up from the back room and tapped the switch that beamed the signal to her headset. The two spirits could hear half the conversation.

"No, Mr. Mathers. I'm sorry, Mr. Mathers, I didn't activate the… Mr. Mathers, it wasn't… MR. MATHERS!"

"I think it's time we left, dear lady. It would seem that Mr. Mathers is in a lather. Of course it might be fun to…"

"Come on, naughty little boy. Time to stop procrastinating. Gustav, this is important."

"I know, Vanessa. I'm frightened, to tell you the truth. Very well, let's get this over with."

The two of them went from the lobby, past the fateful restaurant, and arrived at the elevators. Ghost movies to the contrary, Vanessa and Gustav didn't fly around. Walking through walls was one thing, ceilings and floors were quite another belief system. It took another focus of energy to hit the 'UP' button, then, after the doors opened, to push the '2nd' button. The musak had a Blink 182 number on it. Gustav looked up at the speaker. *"At least they play the classics."*

The door opened and they turned left down the hall that was indicated by a brush metal plaque with black lettering to lead to rooms '200-225'. No loud noises could be heard. Mr. Mathers must have gone back to bed. The hall was dead silent, other than the soft noise of the air filtration system. They stopped. There was '211'. Gustav and Vanessa walked through the door.

While the two entities got their bearings in the dim hotel room, Melissa felt her head drop for the forth time and knew it was time to call it a night. She looked at her clock. Eleven-thirty. She'd hit the sack and get up early to finish up, wanting to have all her work done early to free up the weekend. Melissa turned to boot Barbara off her bed and then stopped. Barbara was sitting on the side of the bed against the wall, her head leaning and her mouth open, full crashed position. Melissa walked over and cleared the bed of books, papers and electronic devices and got Barbara into a more comfortable lying position. She tucked a pillow under Barbara's head and tossed a cover over her. Then, after securing her PC, Melissa turned off the lights. Barbara's key was easily unhooked from her jeans belt loop. Barbara's bed was the same as her own and, without a second thought or removing an article of clothing, Melissa laid herself down and quickly fell asleep.

Daniel Speck, a sophomore majoring in Theatre Arts, had been waiting for this moment. The lights had gone out, finally. He could tell by looking over the edge of the eleven-story dorm-building roof at the ledge below *her* window. He had two accomplices with him that night; frat buddies. Tonight, they were men on a mission. The harness that Daniel had brought was 'borrowed' from the locker used by the skydiver's club. That made it an easy harness to attach a rope to and one that left his hands free to do their intended work. His two henchmen lowered Daniel down over the roof. He had put his full trust in these two brothers despite the cans of amber antifreeze they had taken on board. Speck kept both feet against the brick wall as he descended down to the second floor. To make sure he had the right window, he had sent a paint ball just above the window after the sun had set and when the coast was clear. There it was! The men on the roof watched carefully. Daniel Speck gave the signal with a penlight and the rope stopped lowering him. A second signal flashed and the men edged the rope the calculated two feet to Daniel's right, their left. He had lowered himself next to the window column so as not to prematurely arouse attention of the dorm residents. Once situated, he shifted the burden that was slung over his back and removed his gloves. Daniel had to be able to use his fingers for at least four minutes to accomplish his task, and Fall night-times were cold in Troy, NY. He took hold of the instrument, and began putting it to the use it was designed for.

Barbara Meissner may sack out quickly, but after the first fifteen minutes, she became a light sleeper. Her eyes opened to an unfamiliar room, dimly lit with a couple of LED's from the SatCom recharge unit. That tapping noise, what was it? It was coming from over there, from the window. How could that be? The shades were drawn. Barbara Meissner, Melissa's best friend, walked over and opened them. Her eyes went wide. "Oh my God," she whispered.

Daniel saw the shades part to dimly reveal a womanly figure. There was his goal. It was time, now or never. He took his guitar and began to play the love song he had himself composed just the other day. Surely this display would earn him the affections at best, the attention at worst, of the woman he couldn't help but think of every day and night. He saw the figure back up a few feet, surely in amazement at his daring audacity. Faint heart never won fair damsel, they say. His fingers were getting colder, but his heart beat hot as the culmination of days of planning was reaching fruition. The figure came back to the window. He was winning her heart! Surely, if he had failed, she would have raced out the door yelling for help (at which point, plan B would be initiated with another penlight signal...a: lower the rope and b: head for the hills). Success! He could see the outline of two slender arms as nimble hands worked the window latch and lowered the upper window. That was odd. Why not raise the lower window, the better to facilitate his entry to the boudoir? In the cold moonlight, he saw two things he hadn't counted on. First, that the person he had serenaded was possessed of dark hair, not the expected blond. A wig? A dye job? A logistics mistake on the room I.D.? Second, was that the hands that reached out from the upper window were possessed of a shiny long thing that resembled a knife and it was making headway for the rope that suspended him. Realizing his predicament, Daniel gave a frantic signal and pushed away from the building to keep the rope and knife from becoming too intimate. The two men saw, and began to rapidly lower the rope, but not rapidly enough. The knife had nicked the nylon cord, starting a process that would culminate shortly before he could reach the…

Barbara heard the snap, the cry of panic, and a combination of a thud and a very unmusical twang that blended with the sound of wood breaking. She closed the window and went back to bed. "What is it about men and blonds?"

An hour's drive to the south, another second story room had been invaded. Martha Scholldorf Mendelssohn slept deeply, as she always did. She took up the middle of a queen-sized bed. Gustav smiled to remember that Martha always took her half of the bed out of the middle. There was a time when that habit was an invitation to more pleasant things in his memories of her. He looked at Vanessa. *"What do we do now?"* He half expected Martha to start at the sound of his voice but, of course, she didn't. That was both a relief and a cause for sadness.

"I've only been able to connect strongly with Allen, for some reason. Maybe it's because we're related. Let me try first and see what I can do. Perhaps our efforts with Annie have made a difference with my abilities here as well." Vanessa stood by the bed and raised her arms above the sleeping body. She closed her eyes and pictured in her mind the face of Martha Mendelssohn, then brought that face closer and closer to her own until it passed through hers. Behind that mask was revealed a vista that seemed endless and bleak. Vanessa, despite the depressing clarity of her impressions, felt no inkling on which direction to go, so she backed away and put the face back into the distance, then opened her eyes. *"I can get in, but there's no feeling on how to proceed from there. You'll have to try yourself."* She went on to describe what she had seen in as much detail as she could.

"Vanessa, I didn't know you actually succeeded at first. You never left her side, as far as I could see." That surprised her. Since she had only tried this with Allen and there were no witnesses to those escapades, she figured that she simply went with her totality into Allen's body, or mind, or something. If she said anything more about it, though, Gustav would probably latch onto it as a learned lecture topic in order to delay their efforts. Later.

Vanessa just nodded and described the procedure she had developed with Allen. Gustav followed suit. He did his best, when his eyes were shut, to focus on Martha's present face, not the one he had once known. It took all his military fortitude to keep impassive as the aged image of the woman who once loved him passed through his own. He, too, saw the bleak landscape, but his eyes were able to see other things, too. In the distance, there was a house. Their house. They had lived on a horse farm once and loved to go riding in the morning with Jacques and Queen. He could now see the fence posts and wire that corralled those fine beasts, but no horses were to be seen. No living thing of any kind was visible. What was he to do? Go to the house? What harm might he do? Wasn't he forcing his will on her, like he once did in desperation to save their marriage?

There was more. There was the feeling of...what? Words came to mind, like desolation, hunger, sadness, and, parched. Yes, parched. Bled dry. There was no life here. Whether this was a dream or subconscious awareness, there should still be life. He felt none of that here. Why? And why did his feet feel so heavy?

Vanessa was watching. Sure enough, Gustav remained visible, but she could feel his tension. The feeling didn't change, which probably meant that he was stuck at a decision gate. She felt he hadn't had time yet to confront Martha. That vista was too vast. So, on the other side of the bed, she repeated her procedure and re-entered the mind of Martha Scholldorf Mendelssohn. Though she was on the opposite side of the bed, her entry put her side by side with Gustav. She thought, in passing, how odd that was. Now that she was there with him, she too could see the house. "What's that place, Gustav?"

There was something different about the way she spoke to him, or sounded. It sounded more...real. "Our home. We lived there for five years or so." He stopped for a moment. Gustav sounded different to himself, too. What was going on? "We owned two horses that we kept in those corrals. This was once a happy place." Gustav sighed and then stopped in surprise. He sighed again. What? "Vanessa, I sighed. I mean, really sighed. How could I do that?"

"Oh, sorry, should have told you. You are in a dream now, I suppose. The rules change when you do that. I don't know how it works, but somehow your awareness of things change here. Right now, I'm standing across the bed from you, but I came in next to you. I wonder." Vanessa extended her hand and took Gustav's in her own. He could feel it, like he could when he was alive. He could also feel that heaviness in his feet abate. "In Allen's dreams, I could feel him when I touched him. You and I are now playing under both our own rules and Martha's. Where do you think we should go?"

Gustav looked in all directions. The only structure in sight was the farmhouse. That seemed the logical choice, so he took the first step. When he did, things began to change perspective. The dull gray nothingness that carpeted the vista evolved to an off color brown of tall dead grass. They found themselves on the farmhouse drive. Gustav spoke of how the place used to look, how it was set up. The newly married couple had wanted room and privacy. She had some money in her family from an inheritance and he had landed a good job with a respected legal firm. Dad had helped him out a bit, too. Financing the place was still a bit dicey, but it was worth it. He looked at the bare fields and spoke of the orchards that used to be there. As he did, some of the mists began to part to reveal (or coalesce to form?) ranks of the withered trunks of apple and pear trees. Holding hands seemed to keep their feet lighter, so, hand in hand they reached the point where the corral paralleled the road. There were troughs for feed and water in their usual places and even a salt lick, cracked with age. Further down, they passed the stable. Through the entryway where one door had fallen to the ground and the other hung on one hinge, they could see moldy hay in the two stalls and the rusty shovels and pitchforks. Next to the doorway was a decaying stirrup besides a dried up manure pile. Gustav looked again. Did he see something move? He decided it was his overactive imagination, so on they walked towards the house.

"Gustav, it's so depressing here. I can feel the emptiness trying to suck out the life from me. Holding your hand keeps it away. Guess it's a good thing you and I are doing this together. It reminds me of when I joined with Ryan on that boat. The two of us gained a strength from each other."

Gustav found that talking lightened the mood as much as their handholding lightened their feet. "Interesting. That makes me think of the Edwards porch, where eight of us touched and connected with each other and gained strength as a unified whole." They continued to walk, for distances were misleading there. Things happened in dreams when they were ready to.

A song popped into Vanessa's mind, and she softly sang it. "'For whenever two or more of you, are gathered in His name, there is love.' It's a comforting thought, though maybe not too applicable here."

"Isn't it? I remember hearing that song once at a wedding. Martha and I had considered it for our own, but chose something else. What is 'His name' that two or more are 'gathered in'? Most people think of a prayer meeting or a wedding, maybe a funeral. Taking the 'name of the Lord in vain' never meant, to me, saying 'God damn it'. Think of all the souls in Hell sent there because they slammed their fingers in a car door or dropped their bowling balls on their feet. That doesn't seem right to me. When you take God's 'name', you take on an agreement to live according to a set of rules based on the belief in God's existence. Your reward is God's love, which includes a whole lot of forgiveness and more than a little protection against worldly assaults to your spirit. You and I are here, now, to try and heal one of His children. That is consistent with His rules, so we are here gathered within the confines of the 'name' we have taken to ourselves. As a result, here is where love can be found."

If that thought was what they had to bring out in order to reach their destination, then it worked. Their next few steps brought them to the porch stairs. Vanessa wondered what it was about ghosts and porches that attracted the Fitzgalen Family members. Looking at the stairs, they could see peeling paint shards that had given up trying to protect the weathered wood underneath. Rusted nail heads were ranked in uniformity, passing in review as they trod up the creaking stairs. Both walked up to the screen door, whose screen was brown, rotted from rust. Gustav reached for the knob and it turned in his hand under protest. Opening the door, the hinges cried out in untended, oil starved agony. There was no need to open the main door for, like the stable door, it had been pulled off by time and its heavy weight from the doorjamb and was leaning sadly against the wall.

They walked into a dust-covered living room. Gustav remembered everything. There was the settee, the tea table, and the video screen. Over there was the couch and love seat. On the other side of the entryway was the kitchenette and dining area. Everything was covered with dust, the lamps, the area rugs, the shelves, and the Grandmother clock. Vanessa thought of something. "How long has it been since you and Martha lived here?"

That was an interesting thought. "Over forty years. Why are we here, or rather, why is this here? It wasn't there when you peeked in, but it was when I did and it stayed there when you arrived a second time. Did I do this, or is this an abandoned shrine in Martha's mind that she's presenting to me? Vanessa, can you sense anything, or anyone?"

Vanessa closed her eyes and reached out, but nothing was felt. That was unusual and she told Gustav so. "At the cemetery, even if there was no spirit to touch, I could still at least feel the lack of something where I was searching. Here, I can sense nothing at all, like back when I was alive. There are different senses at work here; perhaps the ones we used to have when we were alive. Do you smell something?"

Gustav stopped, closed his eyes, and gently sampled the air. There were traces of so many things; it was hard to pinpoint them. "Dust and mold, but there are traces of other smells. I can barely sense lavender somewhere. That was Martha's favorite perfume. Does that mean she's here, or is it a residue of her? Whose dream is this, anyway?"

"Gustav, I smell something alive. The lavender I can detect, but there's something else, a flower of a different kind, I think. It seems to be coming from, that way, that open doorway."

Gustav froze. Vanessa saw him lock eyes into the mustiness behind that partly opened doorway. "Is that Garrison's room? Your son who died?" Gustav nodded, barely. His feet felt like lead again. Moving them was a weary effort, but he could do it, had to do it, couldn't do it. In walking around earlier, Vanessa and he had separated their hands.

He reached out to her. "Help." Vanessa took his hand and that did seem to lighten his step some. It still wasn't easy, but it was more do-able. They walked slowly to the door, stopped for a moment. Gustav pushed the door in the rest of the way and then they stepped into the scented gloom together. The darkness was almost physical, like a concentrated cold fog. They passed through it, feeling like their progress was aided by a flow or a current of some kind. Vanessa and Gustav then saw her by the candlelight.

A woman's back was turned to them. She stood before a bed, and on the stand next to the bed burnt a candle. Yet, there were no shadows and the flame from the candle never flickered. This room had no dust, no mold, but no air circulation, either. It was clean to the point of sterile. There were shelves where unused toys rested, waiting. It was quiet, deadly quiet. The one window was clean, but translucent. They could see a warm glow behind it, as if a sunshiny day waited on the other side. On the other side of the room was a door. It was closed. Gustav and Vanessa had no doubt as to whom the woman was.

"Martha, I'm home."

The woman's head did a quarter turn, but they could see that her eyes remained transfixed on the bed, the single bed. They couldn't see through Martha to what lay there. "Shhh, he's sleeping. He's very tired. Walk softly." Then she turned back again. Holding hands, Gustav and Vanessa walked to Martha's left and saw what she had been so carefully watching.

"Gustav, is that…"

"Garrison, my son."

"Gustav, he's breathing." He could see that. Vanessa may be his support here, but his were the eyes that could truly see beyond the surface. He could see what had happened.

He spoke in soft tones. "Vanessa, do you remember Mary Safford? Her spirit was held to her body because life was still there. It was the glue that kept her spirit earthbound. The only way to free that fly from the flypaper was to have another take her place. You did that for her. Her spirit was meant to move on, but was captured by her mindless but living body.

"You are looking at the true spirit of my son, being held here by the force of Martha's desire to keep him here. His body had released him, but he's still here. Martha has strength in her, like Annie did, to take another's spirit and bind it from crossing over. It would seem that women whose children are denied them become powerful forces in this realm. Martha isn't quite as strong, though. Garrison doesn't walk the earth and see the sun. This is his only world, now. He will stay here as long as Martha focuses her energies to make it so."

It sounded right to Vanessa, but it only led to more questions. "But why is everything here so clean and flowery smelling? How are Garrison and Martha alive here when all else is dead in her dreams?"

The truth continued to unveil itself to Gustav. Was it his own natural intelligence, or was there some remnant of Martha's spirit that could still reach out to him? "Remember when Annie geared up for a show of force, how she sucked the warmth from the area around her? Martha has drained all of the life potentials of her spirit and focused them here in this alcove of her soul. Everything else has been left to rot, just to maintain this prison that holds the two of them. You felt the drain yourself. She needs all that power just to maintain the dream and to keep Garrison captive. It's dried her up, leaving her bitter and alone. I had no idea that this was happening beneath the surface. No wonder I was unable to reach her after Garrison died."

Vanessa looked to her right at Gustav. "How do you know all of this?"

"I…I'm not sure. I just, know." He looked at his son, his only child. The house, the land, and now this. It was getting to be too much for him to bear. There was the brown sugar colored hair that he once tousled lovingly. Despite his work obligations, play time between him and Garrison was something sacred, rejuvenating. There were times when he heard, 'Daddy, I don't feel so good'. That was when a cuddle, taking a temperature, and sometimes administering a prescription or a homeopathic would take care of everything except what a hug would supply. Then came the time when those simple remedies didn't work anymore and the medical community was sought out. The news was bad, real bad. Then came the denials, the rage, the sorrow and acceptance, but Gustav had never lost hope. Every possible second he could spend at home, he was there. There were nights where Garrison sat on Gustav's lap, sleeping, while he worked at the computer terminal. The keyboard was a remote model, allowing him to quietly tap away and not disturb the pain diminishing motion from the rocking chair. Moments were precious, and moments, one by one, slipped away. Keeping his son in a hospital had been decided against in favor of the comfort that familiar surroundings had to offer. Gustav remembered one such night where he had fallen asleep on the chair, Garrison's arms around his neck. Gustav woke in middle of the night, though he didn't know what it was that disturbed his sleep. It was odd. He hadn't remembered this for many years. Shortly after he had awakened, Martha had called out in anguish from the bedroom, 'Nooooo. Come BACK!' He had thought it was perhaps a nightmare, and then he felt something missing, something wrong. Garrison wasn't breathing. CPR was briefly considered, but what was the use? His son was out of pain now. He had crossed his finish line. And so, Gustav just kept rocking, gently running his fingers through that brown sugar colored hair. It was the saddest, holiest moment in his life.

Now, recalling Martha's cry in the night, Gustav wondered. Did his son visit his mother in her dreams to say goodbye, then found himself her captive? Did his spirit see his own body in his father's lap and run to his mother for comfort? At this point, did it matter? The spirit of his son was held captive. That was what mattered.

There lay his last, lost chance to hand down the Mendelssohn lineage, breathing, alive, yet not alive. This was wrong. This was very wrong. It was up to him to right that wrong. He knew that, but what could he do? This was Martha's dream. If he did something that woke her up and he and Vanessa were caught up in this existence, might they both get stuck here?

Some alarm in his heart told him that this was a very real possibility. He looked at his son, whose eyes began to open. One more time, the father ran his fingers through the brown sugar colored hair of his son.

"Father? You've come home? Mother said you would some day. Can we go out to play, now? I have been feeling much better. I'm not so sick anymore, Father. Mother says I have to stay in bed, though. Do I have to?"

Annie's children had needed little convincing by Vanessa that they were dead. He could tell that this would not be so easy with Garrison. This ancient child seemed fully convinced that he was alive. This environment where flesh could seem to touch flesh denied Garrison the ability to demonstrate ghost-hood by walking through a wall. Martha had him convinced he is still a boy who needs to heal, but Garrison wasn't fully buying it. But for the whole real truth to be perceived by his son, surely it had to come from a unified front of Mother and Father. He turned to Martha.

"Martha, this is not right. You know it isn't. Let him go, please, for God's sake."

"Gustav, he is my son, he is all I have. How can I let him go? If I do, what is there left for me to live for?" Garrison watched, and listened.

"Martha, he is your son and mine, too. But he is not ours to own. Garrison belongs to God and you are keeping him from going to where he needs to be for happiness and healing." Martha almost turned to look at Gustav, but her energies had been sapped too long. She couldn't afford to turn her attention, her gaze, or her energies away from her son. Garrison looked at Vanessa, and she felt a familiar knock at her heart's door.

"Husband, Garrison was taken away from us wrongly. He came to me to say goodbye and was about to leave through that door. I stopped him. I locked that door, forever. I have saved him here. He is protected from death. Look at him. He has color in his cheeks. He can breathe without pain. Look, all the medicine bottles are gone. I have done this, Gustav. How can such a miracle be wrong?" Vanessa looked at the locked door and realized it not only locked Gustav's son from where he had to go, but barred Martha as well. She opened her heart to Garrison.

"Life must end, Martha, for a soul to continue its journey. You are old and it will soon end for you. When it does, you will lose your hold on Garrison and he will go on to God, as he should. What will you say to Him, when He asks you why you held back the spirit he loaned us for a short time? That you were lonely? He may be our child, but Garrison does not belong to you, or to me. Let him go home. This isn't your home, or his, anymore. Please. Martha, I love you." Gustav reached out to Martha's hand and touched it. The hand was hard and cold, like stone. He pulled back. Even here, he thought. It has begun to sap even her, even here. Garrison gently entered the heart's door left open by Vanessa, felt what there was to feel, understood, then just as gently left the way he came. It had taken Garrison far less time than Jason and Rebecca to find what they once looked for. Garrison had inherited his father's quick mind and instincts.

Martha had not heard a man say that he loved her since, since the last time Gustav had said those words on the day their divorce was finalized. She didn't know then whether it was one more attempt to extend his heart to her, or a parting shot of a martyr. Back then, that three word phrase confused her. Now, it confused her again as dusty thoughts within her soul collided. Her head did another quarter turn, which is all it was capable of anymore. Garrison now watched his parents speak, finally able to understand what was going on. "Do you, Gustav? I don't know that love. I do know Garrison's love for me and mine for him. You have been gone for a long time, husband." Vanessa watched Garrison furrow his brow in concentration, like he was trying to remember something on the tip of his tongue.

Martha's spirit was in danger. It was drying up, turning to stone. She had almost completely run out of the life force needed to maintain this room. Would she be able to cross over if that process was allowed to continue? Gustav realized that letting things take their time and having both Martha and Garrison cross over together might not be a valid option. He might move on, but she might not. 'Where two or more of you are gathered'. That was important. It came to mind here; it had to be a key. How to make it work here, though? He could only think of one simple thing to try. Vanessa's hand in his had given him strength and kept the energy drain from affecting her. The laying on of hands was a healing thing. Martha needed healing and fast, for they may have years, or moments, to act. Gustav took Vanessa's right hand and placed it into Martha's left. He let go of the two of them and walked to Martha's right. That hand, he took to himself. He could feel his own hand begin to grow colder, as could Vanessa. She looked frightened, but was determined to go through with this. She felt sure Gustav knew what he was doing, that he would be able to make his plan work, whatever it was.

His mind raced, as he felt the cold and stiffness begin to rise up his arm. He looked at his son. That is where most of the life energies from Martha (and now Vanessa's and his) were being funneled. Garrison was the recipient. He thought of the war of energies at Edwards Estate. It didn't match. Back then; they were fighting an offensive force with a defensive force. This was different and, unfortunately, it wasn't the opposite situation. If it was, he might have devised a plan of action that would somehow be the opposite of those taken at the Edwards Estate. Martha was draining them and funneling the life into Garrison, the receiver. Isn't it better to give than receive? Why did that pop into his head? He looked at his son, who looked intently at him. Garrison reached out his hand to his father and another to Vanessa. The father smiled to think 'and the children shall lead'.

Gustav looked at Vanessa and nodded his head toward Garrison. In one move, fast enough to keep Martha from realizing what might happen and try to stop it, or wake up, Vanessa and Gustav grasped Garrison's hands, completing the circle. In their midst, a light began to shine and grow brighter. Vanessa turned her head away at first, afraid of being blinded. Looking right again, she could see that Martha's mouth was open in a silent scream. This frightened her, so she turned her gaze to Gustav, who was intently watching to his right. She followed his gaze and found that Garrison was sitting up and drawing her hand over his bed towards Gustav's hand, which was coming to meet hers. Garrison joined the hands of his father and his woman spirit guide and said, "It is time for me to go, Father, Mother. I'm tired of being in my room. My friends are waiting for me to play with them. Good-bye. I love you!" With that, Garrison was gone. He no longer needed the door that his mother had locked. Gustav and Vanessa looked at Martha, whose face was still frozen. The hands that held Martha's began to hurt, badly, like razors were cutting into their flesh. Both pulled their own hands away and saw Martha's hands begin to dissolve into dust, lazily falling to the floor. Out of the cuffs of her dress came more dust as the reaction worked its way up her sleeves. Gustav screamed to Vanessa that they had to get out of there, grabbed her hand and headed for the mist at the door to the living room.

Gustav stopped and looked back. He let go of Vanessa and ran to the door that led outside. It was locked. "Damn it!" He desperately looked around. Martha was still standing there, slowly dissolving, layer by layer. There, on her dress belt. A key hung there. It had to be the right one. He quickly retrieved it, rammed it into the door lock and turned the key. He tried the door again, but it wouldn't open. Nor would it, for anyone but the owner. Gustav sensed that and knew that he had done all that he could do for her. He went back and grabbed Vanessa's hand.

Going back through the dark mist was far more difficult and seemed to take a day, though it was but a moment to anyone in the outside world. What was left of Martha was reaching out to pull in what little life was left to be had, desperate to retrieve what she had just lost.

Gustav and Vanessa raced through a house that was likewise crumbling to dust. The boards of the porch creaked and snapped under their feet, tripping Vanessa who fell down the stairs. Gustav stopped long enough to yank her back up to her feet and continued to flee with her in tow. The withered orchard trunks leaned towards them, reaching out with hoary knotted fingers, twisting like arthritic eels. Yet, these tools of capture were too withered themselves to intercept the invaders.

Down the road and by the stable they fled. Through the open stable door they could see, watching them pass, the bleached skulls of two horses poke out into the ruddy light. From their sockets, a red glow shone as Martha expended her dwindling power into those withered bones. They pawed the dusty earth and began to run towards them. One tripped on the stirrup, and fell to the dry earth as a pile of fragile and splintered bones. The other kept coming after them to the tune of hollow hoof beats. But when it blindly hit the fence, it exploded into shards of bone and gristle, and left a mist of molded, rotted, leather smell. On the two ran to their starting point. The road began to lose definition, reverting back to that murky mist that they had first seen on entering the dream. There was a glow up ahead.

Ryan was sleeping fitfully. Something was not right. He was standing in 'Annie's apron pocket', the graveyard near the Edwards Homestead where Mad Annie had stored the souls of the slaves, the Union soldiers and their mounts. It was different, somehow. He looked around to see that, instead of grave markers, there were withered fruit trees. Instead of grass, there was a misty, dusty coating on the ground that made his walking slow and labored. He tried to hear the crickets, but they were gone. He should leave this place, for his work here was done, but where was the exit? The road to the apron pocket should be, over there, where that slight glow was. He walked towards it, avoiding the hungry, gnarled, hand shaped roots coming out of the ground trying to grab his feet. The closer he got to the light, the more it took shape. It was a…what's with the burning rose? Was this supposed to be a bush and the order got mixed up? Florists did that sometimes, he thought. Why a rose? Maybe they burned better, for it made a pleasant light and the smell was pleasing. But it was funny, because the rose spoke to him; like that bush spoke to Moses. Was this God? But, the voice was a child's. Maybe God is a child? That would explain a few things he had long wondered about.

"You are the one that the lady with my Father is reaching for. She can't see you, so you have to reach out to her. Call out to her. She is lost and so is Father. Please call her so she can show Father the way out. I've got to go back and help Mother. Thank you, sir."

It isn't your average burning rose that can ask you to do it a favor. Still, he was confused. If it wasn't God who was talking to him, then it must be the Son. That means that the woman God is with (?) is reaching out to him (??). "I'm supposed to help God and the Virgin Mary? No, the rose said that his dad is with a lady, and that the rose had to go help his mother. That means that God is with another woman. I wonder if the Virgin Mary knows about this? You'd think that God would know what had more fury than Hell." Ryan looked at the glow around the rose, which seemed to hover above the ground almost at eye level. The rose began to fade, and an image of a woman and a man began to take form before him. They were struggling in a land that was gray and sad. They seemed, familiar. Oh, yes. That's Vanessa and Gustav. Well, that was a relief. Even in a dream, the thought of pulling off a rescue for the Creator and Lady Icon's competition was a bit much. The rose said he should call out to them. Well, one didn't disobey a rose, now did one?

Even though the dream was not real, his mind connect to his wife was. Into the mists revealed by the rose, he reached out with his mind and heart to his beloved wife and beloved friend. It would be nice to see them happy and with him. Maybe they could have tea and coffee.

The landscape was blurred. The dead trees had all fallen, crashing and crackling to the parched earth and raising a black and gray cloud that rose up from behind and rushed forward with an anguished, howling sound. It was Martha's last hope to ensnare enough life to make the attempt on retrieving Garrison. Gustav and Vanessa, hands held, fought the murk and muck and made for the glow ahead of them. It had been distant and no amount of running had seemed to make any difference. Yet, in a moment, the distance had been cut to only a few feet. How did that happen, thought Gustav? Vanessa knew. Through the glow, they could see…

Ryan looked through the glow. There were his friends, now. Maybe they'd better hurry, for that nasty looking dark thing was rushing up from behind them, so he waved to them to come to his side of the glow. They seemed to be having difficulty, so Ryan reached his hand through the portal and clasped hands with Vanessa. That was the connect that allowed Vanessa to cross the distance between two minds. Gustav looked behind them and then found himself pulled forward to alight side by side with Vanessa. Seconds passed and the glow faded. Before it went out, the cloud reached the portal and it bowed the barrier out, stretching, but it faded and disappeared. "Hello, friends, nice of you to pay a visit." Gustav was staring at the portal that had now dimmed into nothingness, then he turned around.

Before him, Vanessa was hugging Ryan and crying. She was actually crying. He could see tracks of tears and she was sniffing, sobbing. Ryan was actually holding her. This was amazing! What followed was even more mind-boggling. They were in the Homestead gravesite and the other two had begun to walk down the path that led to the main road by the Main House. Before he followed, Gustav took note of the fingerlike roots behind him. They looked, hungry? Where had they come from? Perhaps from that big oak tree in the center of the graveyard. Well, he'd better scoot to catch up with the happy couple. Gustav talked while Vanessa was content to stroll with her husband's arm around her waist, hers around his and her head leaning against his shoulder. "Boss, do you know what happened back there? How were you able to pull us out of that mess?"

"Isn't it nice here? No ghosts. Even you two." Ryan gave his wife a squeeze and she returned it, then he gave a brotherly punch to Gustav's shoulder. "I was standing back there and saw a glow at the apron entrance. When I got closer, there was a rose in the middle of it that looked like it was burning. It talked to me and asked me to help you two. It faded, and I could see a very unhappy place with two very upset friends in it running in the distance. So, I wished you with me, just like the rose said to do. I blinked and you were closer, but you still couldn't cross. Something told me to reach through and connect. Hey, here's the Main House! Let's go in. I'm thirsty."

Gustav was about to say something, but Vanessa looked up at him from Ryan's shoulder. "Gustav, please. We're guests here. For the moment, just go with it." He took the suggestion, seeing the depth of desire in Vanessa's eyes that he not disturb her ability to touch Ryan, and joined his companions in going onto yet another porch into yet another house. Inside, the Main House was different. It looked a lot more like Pavelli's, but with only a few tables. The three of them chose one and sat down. Roscoe came in and poured coffee, but set a steeping glass mini-carafe with a thermal grip next to Gustav, who took it and gave a sniff.

"Apple cinnamon. Thank you, Ryan." There was honey, of course, and after stirring the steaming cup he had poured and prepared, Gustav took a long missed sip of his favorite tea. He closed his eyes, as the memories of what the aroma and flavor recalled came to mind. When he opened his eyes, things had changed. They still sat at a table, but the place was now the inside of Dot's Jury Box Café. "Did I do that?"

"Changing programs on me? Or ballgames? Ah, well, so tell me. What were you doing in that nightmare of a place?" Gustav related the story of what they had tried to do and of finding the spirit of his son locked in his mother's heart. "That sounds too much like Mad Annie. Friends, we have met spirits on horses, entities hiding in graves, and now this. A kidnapped child entity, by his mother, no less? I suppose it's job security. Are they all right??

"I think Garrison has crossed over, or…wait. A burning *rose* spoke to you? Vanessa, that flower smell you noticed in the house and in Garrison's room. Can you recall it?"

Ryan was dreaming, so his acceptance of almost anything as run-of-the-mill was just short of amusing. It was like talking with a sober drunk. Vanessa and Gustav were only dream guests and they retained most of their conscious faculties for reality. "Rose. Yes, that was it. It smelled like roses. It was hard to tell, with all those other odors on the outside of his room and there had been too many distractions for me to pay much attention after we got into it. Does that mean something to you?"

This was getting too much again. Emotions were welling up inside the tough outside of a man who had been a fighter all of his life. The military, the courtroom and even the battles the Family fought didn't provide enough steel. Gustav's iron control over his visible emotions collapsed. Gustav cried, as his memories of his son began to pour back into his awareness. Suppressed memories arose with poignant clarity of Garrison's birth, first steps, first words, and a million other moments blitzkrieged his own crumbling defenses. His Rommel had finally been given free rein as his marching orders. Two sets of arms had embraced Gustav's head and shoulders as his tears fell without hindrance. It took a few moments, or was it hours, but he was able to put the lid back on once most of the storm had passed. Through the sniffs and sobs that still echoed his heart's ache, Gustav told them that Martha referred to the swelling in her abdomen, when she was pregnant with Garrison, as her rosebud. "When Garrison was born, she proudly announced that the rosebud had blossomed into a rose. She had a favorite lullaby, Martha did, and often sang it to Garrison even after he became ill. It was an old Bette Middler song. You'll recall it, I suspect. It was pretty popular during both your lifetimes. It was 'The Rose'."

After a few moments silence, Ryan said, "So, your son guided you to me and even alerted me to your coming. Quite a kid you have there, Mr. Mendelssohn. When I die, I insist you introduce me to him. Deal?" A nod, a hiccup. "Good. Now, isn't it about time you go somewhere? I love your company, but my bladder is full and I'm going to awaken soon. Maybe you shouldn't be here when I wake up because dreams do funny things in those moments." Ryan's mind was rising from the complete acceptance of anything stage to the level where people are aware that they are dreaming. But how to get them back? Where were their spirit bodies? Did they have to find another portal and go back THERE? To Martha? No, no way they could go back the way they came. So, "Not to worry, friends. Look."

Since Ryan knew he was dreaming, he could control the dream. Dot's doors opened of their own accord and, through the doorway, they could see the dimly lit hotel room with two entities standing on either side of it with arms outstretched, looking like some ancient ritual. Vanessa didn't want to leave Ryan's side, for she had ached for so many years to hold her husband. Yet, she knew the reality of things and, biting her lip (which actually hurt), she kissed Ryan and joined Gustav as the two of them left a brief, borrowed, life. Ryan watched them go and mentally shut the door behind them. The call for the bathroom was getting more pronounced. "Darn, forgot to tell Gustav about his son going back to help Martha." He turned around to see Dot standing by the table and started asking where the men's room was. Dot smiled, waving a small piece of paper in her hand. He had been left with the bill. "Put it on Gustav's tab, won't you."

Dot raised her eyes and shook her head, but it was followed by a smile. How strange. Dot didn't look like Dot. Still, she did look vaguely familiar, like someone he had seen in a photograph a long time ago. "That's just like Gustav. Very well, off with you before you wet the bed. Go on, now, and bless you." Ryan got up and went through the doorway pointed out to him by, Dot? Odd. Dot never spoke with a German accent before.

The room was silent. Vanessa opened her eyes the same moment as Gustav did. *"Gustav, are we...dead?"* He took a step to the side and reached out, watching as his arm passed through the wall, then quietly nodded. *"It was so real, and so long. But, look at the clock."* According to the time, the entire journey had taken all of four minutes. The possibility that she could nightly share wonderful physical experiences with her husband without having to go through what she did with Mary Safford occurred to her, but realized that the idea had too many dangers with it. They had almost not gotten back. Ryan had created the portal for their return and that was probably a closer call than she would like to think about. Suppose he had awakened earlier? Would they be stuck inside his body, or mind, or what? The experience with Martha next called itself to mind. What a nightmare! Did Ryan get nightmares? Might she BE a nightmare some night while dream-visiting him and cause him to lose love for her?

Gustav's mind and attention were elsewhere. Martha lay before him, breathing not at all. Her face had the same open mouth silent scream look that they saw before she began to crumble to dust. Vanessa looked down at the bed and stepped back. *"Oh, God, oh, Gustav, I'm sorry."*

"Don't be." Gustav looked at Vanessa, she looked at him, and both looked down at the body. Gustav didn't say that, for it was a woman's voice. Vanessa didn't either, for the accent was more like Gustav's. Turning to the foot of the bed, they were greeted with the vision of a softly glowing entity. *"Danke."* With that third word, a young woman dressed in a waitress smock smiled, stepped back, faded and was gone. The face was only vaguely familiar to Vanessa. Not so, for Gustav.

After a couple of tries of focusing their energies, they pulled the sheet over Martha's face and then made to leave the hotel room. Vanessa stood closer to Gustav and then looked at the bed. *"The maid is going to shit a brick."*

"Since you bring up that general subject, dear lady, shall we pay a visit to your hubby and see if he's out of the bathroom, yet? Hope he woke up and made it in time."

XIII   FRIDAY

Barney (Hammer) Jenkins was talking to Kurt Mangela (paramedic), who had just brought in a cardiac arrest patient. Things had looked iffy, but chances for survival were now gradually improving with every minute that the person stayed on the planet. "I like what you do, Kurt. You bring people to the hospital where they can get better again. Closest thing I've done to that was putting a few people IN the hospital."

"Hammer, you think you're alone with that? Before I went for my rescue training, I was in training for middleweight boxing. We had qualifying bouts for the Georgia State Golden Gloves tournament twelve years ago and I was in the quarterfinals. There was this Hispanic kid from Norcross who was an up and comer, real fast hands and good footwork. He had just about had me on the ropes when I got in a lucky shot. Yeah, real lucky. Floored the kid. He died from what I have since learned to be counter coup. That's where the strike comes to the head, but the brain damage is from where it bounces off the opposite side of the skull. That was the last time I put on gloves that weren't made of Nutex." Nutex was stronger than the old Latex, had none of the problems with skin allergies, and came with one way moisture permeability that allowed sweat to be bled away from the rescuer's hands while keeping contamination bad guys out. "Lost a lot of fights since then and Death was on the other side of the ring. But I'll tell you, it's a lot more satisfying to win one of those bouts."

Hammer looked at the man who was half a head shorter than he was. Why did he feel so much smaller than Kurt? "Hey, man, I got pretty good grades in accounting. Think I might be able to get into paramedic school?"

Kurt had heard it before. The sirens and flashing lights dazzled lots of people, but not many had the stones to take the bad stuff. It got to him, too, sometimes. Kurt looked into the big man's eyes, then the rest of him. On the other hand, muscle like that would come in handy at times. "Hammer, let me see what I can do. Maybe your celebrity status can be parlayed into cutting some red tape. We need more people, Hammer. Who knows, you might be the next recruiting poster child."

Later, at dinner (breakfast), Hammer told Barry that he might be able to go back to school. "Great, Hammer. I'll need the curriculum load, cost per credit, information on grants and loans. We'll need a PC for your school and to do work for the CPA firm to earn money to live on and keep our debt load down, and they're on sale over at MaxMart for $497.44 with tax..."

"Later, Barry. I'm bushed. Finish your eggs and let's hit the hay."

"Sure thing, Hammer. Hey, Hammer?"

"Yeah?"
"I'm proud of you."
"Thanks. Same to you, buddy."

Melissa woke to the sunlight and shook off the cobwebs. Even though the beds in the dorms were identical, it was still a strange place she had slept in. Then there was that weird noise that half-woke her up last night. She stood up, gave a good stretch and smiled. Allen loved to see her stretch. Half the time she did it in his presence, it was just to get him distracted. The clock was running and there were things to do to get ready for the day. Melissa opened Barbara's door and walked down the hallway. Stirrings of life could be heard in some of the rooms, snoring from others. She unlocked her own door. Barbara was sitting on the side of her bed, giving her the oddest look. "Barbara, what's with the face? Didn't sleep well last night? Did you hear that noise, too? Why is there a rope dangling outside my window?"

Barbara ignored all but the last question. "Someone wanted to drop you a line. I'm going to my room. Thanks for the bed." With that, she left a confused best friend. Melissa looked around her room, to see if anything else was offbeat, and there on her desk was a box with a message. She picked up the message and read 'Please, for my sanity and the safety of silly male types'. Huh? Melissa picked up the box, which had apparently been purchased in the wee hours at the 24-hour store under the Student Union building.

"Beautiful Brunette Hair Dye?"

Morning routines had begun for the Second String. Their ordinary lives were already more than full, so the extra work for the Family had to be a labor of love. That was the only way to shoehorn more into a day whose schedules had been sculpted by other people who had come to appreciate their values as professionals.

Of the four, Paul Wasserman was the one with nagging misgivings. Nunzia still held a lot of influence on him, though his wife would never know that. He never mentioned her name in the house, both for his wife's and his own peace of mind. It's not what you said, he had learned long ago, but how you said it. Professional interrogators had nothing on the opposite sex for catching innuendos and hidden meanings.

Paul's dreams were troubled with themes of satanic flavor and that shook him. His roots in his faith ran deep and his denomination took a strict view of the Gospels. Betty looked at her husband, concerned. "Are you all right, Paul? You've been mind wandering a lot since you got back from up north. Is there something you want to tell me?" She was used to him declining the offer and understood that his occupation required it. The poor man worked so hard and he was so dedicated. Added to that were his deacon responsibilities to their church and his insisting on being at games and plays Eddie was involved with, and he even helped change diapers on Amanda. It had to be wearing on him.

"Thanks, honey, maybe later. It's kind of confidential, but nothing to really worry about."

"I understand. Here's your travel cup. Come home safe, sweetheart."

"I'll be careful, Betty. Real careful."

Zachary awoke. Atlas had his usual position, snuggled between Zachary's right arm and body, head resting on his master's shoulder. Waking up in a strange location was not unusual for the ghost hunter duo. Not waking up in a hotel was. The fold out couch had been previously slept in by Ralph, so the human half of the team figured that there had to be some major domo duties he ought to do for room and board. Zachary made more than just a pretty good cup of coffee and, since Ryan seemed to use that stuff as a food group, he decided to get up and put on a pot of his special brew. That included a dash of salt and eggshells in the grounds, with just a sniff of vanilla extract and chicory. There was one other ingredient, handed down to him by his father. No one had ever found out the secret. Time to spoil the Boss, he thought, getting out of bed and into his robe and slippers. Atlas opted for a few more minutes snooze time while Zachary muddled around, looking for the equipment needed for his project. It didn't take much time, for the condo wasn't that big or complicated. The secret ingredients he kept in a safe place in his travel bag. While the pot was dripping, Zachary took the time to boot Atlas out of the sofa bed, put it back together, tidy up and take his Lordship out for a morning yard blessing. Atlas wasted no time, got right down to business, and the two of them came back in just as the coffee was finished perking. A quick can of Atlas Cuisine for smaller dogs, ages 2 to 5, with a special balance of vitamins, minerals, ash, co-enzymes, anti-oxidants and detoxificants, went into a dish, bringing to a close Zachary's morning duties to his friend and faithful partner. Next came the Boss.

Zachary prepared the cups for him and Ryan according to specifications he had made mental note of earlier (black) and knocked on Ryan's door. He heard a grumpy sounding "C'min", so he nudged the door open.

"Special brew, Boss. Whoa! Did you have a falling dream and forget to wake before you landed?" Zachary heard only one third of the tired laughter in response to his allegory. "Here, this is my prescription for superiors who look like road kill." Ryan took the cup and was pleasantly surprised.

"OK, five percent raise and a bonus. What did you do to this?"

"Trade secret, Boss, which keeps me invaluable and overpaid. What would happen to me if I gave away the trade secret of the aromatic lure secret ingredient found in most of my dog food cans?"

The Boss took another sip. "So, what's in the dog food, since you're selfishly hoarding the secret that really matters to me?"

"Macerated old bedroom slippers." Ryan managed to get his cup back to the bedside table without spilling anything. Ralph was a great domo, but Zachary was a treasure of a mood lifter. Why didn't he ever marry, Ryan wondered, not for the first time? Zachary was on a roll, so, "So really, why the long face, Mr. Ed?"

"Cripes, Zachary, you're going to give Vanessa a run for her money. She's already pissed that you can't hear her comebacks. It's one of the few times that the one way-ness of spirit/mortal hearing abilities has worked to her disadvantage. They're both here, by the way."

That ended Zachary's roll. "Oh?" Something happen last night? "Uh, excuse my manners. Hello, Gustav and Vanessa. Hope I've not interrupted something serious."

"Actually, you have. Put those shoulders back up, son. I don't want to go over this more than once, so it'll have to wait for the conference. A situation has resolved, but call ahead to Marianne's and tell her 'tissue alert'. Scramble transport for breakfast, while you're at it, then hit me with a refill. Got it?"

"Gone, Chief. Consider it history." Off went a man on a mission.

Gustav asked, *"He's a weird bird, old man. Is he married to the mini-mutt"?*

Ryan stared into his cup, trying to figure out by smell and taste what Zachary had done to it. "I wondered about that, myself. It's none of my business, or anyone else's. I can't expect my privacy respected if the favor isn't returned, you know?"

"Gustav meant no offense, Dear, and you know that. Honey, you're going to need some rest. You've been up with us half the night."

The Boss finally decided to screw the analysis and just drink it. "You needed it, my friends. You two are the Family's twenty-four-hour guardian angels. The least I can do is pull a half-nighter for you in return. Now, we're clear on the following. Neither of you played a role in the demise of Martha. She was on her way out and your actions may have salvaged her very soul. You also liberated the soul of Garrison Mendelssohn, who even now is probably hobnobbing with Natalie on some heavenly hill. There is no cause for guilt, regret, or recriminations. The both of you should be awarded the Medal of Honor for your actions and, if you ever pull a stunt like that again, I will not rest until I find a way to kick your asses all the way to Hell and back. Do I make myself clear?"

"Ja, mein Capitan!"

"You know you're sexy when you get on your soapbox?"

"Oh for Heaven's sake! Look, take a flight over and make sure things are rolling on the other end. I'm going to want a report from Marianne before the conference on the status of the business...no, make that a report from Allen and Marianne. Make sure both participate on that. Tell Ralph to steal the coffee recipe from Zachary at all costs. Last night, Zachary promised a full list of all the hauntings he's validated for our yet-to-be-assigned scouting teams. We can't spend all our time on one site just because it's of a high degree of interest or difficulty. Since we seem to have more manpower, let's learn to use it to best advantage. Now, scoot. I need a shower."

"*Good idea, Love. Get yourself smelling nice for the girl of your dreams.*"

Zachary had just hit the disconnect, when he heard a loud command of 'OUT!' come from Ryan's bedroom. Something brushed against his cheek, which stopped him cold. It wasn't the first time he had encountered a touch sensation from the other side, but this one seemed stronger, more clearly defined and, well, affectionate. He touched his cheek and naturally followed that motion with a look to his fingers in an ingrained anthropological male behavior pattern of checking for lipstick smudges. Ryan came out, looking grumpily for his refill and saw Zachary's motion as it happened. "Not you, too?"

It was daytime. He was never exactly sure how he knew it, but he was sure of it, never the less. He could sense those above ground, sometimes, and they almost always came in the daytime. It made sense, for graveyards were frightening places in the night. For him, whether it was day or night didn't really matter. A graveyard was a place of hiding, of refuge. Of punishment. The wood of the coffin held the woman he could not forget, or forgive, or stop loving. It held something else. Echoes of terror, screams, crying, pleading. It was the essence of the most horrible of deaths, if you discount the artistry of the professional torturer of physical bodies. It had been the most exquisite of vengeances and it had sealed his pact with the Devil, who, so far, had failed to find him. He wondered, though. What Satan could possibly do to him that was worse than this?

Gustav arrived at Marianne's and passed on the Big Boss's mandates. Marianne looked around. "Where's Vanessa? Still with Ryan?"

That surprised the barrister. "*I'm not sure. I thought she was coming here with me. Marianne, why is your gender is so unpredictable?*"

Marianne continued her preparation of Ebony's breakfast. "I'll be happy to tell you, dear man, if you will accept one small caveat."

"*GLADLY! Anything you ask! It's yours!*"

"Whatever I'll tell you will be the absolute truth which you must never divulge."

"*Granted, certainly.*"

"That's not the caveat, just the pre-requisite. Are your ready for the caveat?" Gustav leaned forward. Marianne whispered. "Half an hour after I tell you the secret, I'll change my mind on what the secret actually is." Gustav's shoulders dropped.

"This has something to do with why Eden's resident serpent approached the woman first, doesn't it?"

"Would you like an answer to that?"

"No, thanks, you'd only change it half an hour later."

Allen came up with the SatCom still in his hand, though the connect had been broken. He looked upset. "Hey, Marianne? Gustav? The Troopers called. They said they tried to get ahold of Charlie Chase, but he wasn't responding. My name was next on someone's list to notify. Gustav, I'm really sorry to tell you this. Your ex-wife, Martha, passed away last night." Everyone came up to Gustav to express their feelings on behalf of their friend. Marianne noticed that something wasn't adding up quite right.

"Gustav, did you already know about this?"

"I was there when it happened. So was Vanessa. I've been instructed to hold off of the explanation until the whole Family is together. Oh, I'm supposed to issue a tissue alert, in case Zachary flaked on relaying that command. It could have been a lot worse and it might be of interest to our Family mission. That's all I can say for the moment." The Family could tell that the subject was one that moved their lawyer deeply, but it would just have to wait.

Marianne went into preparation mode. Rachel and Frank were on their way. Melissa had finagled her way to half a day at RPI and would be there for the conference call with the Second Stringers. Marianne calculated from years of experience, almost like a meal recipe. Three women. Give the heart string factor a value of six out of ten, no, better make it a seven, just in case. That's three personal packs and one large community box. The men will share that one. Keep a second pack in reserve. Eight people divided by two equals four small waste receptacles, strategically located. Yes, that should do it nicely. "Ralph! Kitty box duty. Front and center, soldier!" No sense giving people's eyes anything more to sting about.

While Ralph scooped and muttered, Melissa was humming in her dorm room, finishing up her packing for the weekend. She should just make it in time for the meeting. On her way down the hall, she took a piece of duct tape (Allen had taught her that the stuff fixes anything) and affixed a note and a small box to Barbara's door, then jogged off to the parking lot. The Resident Advisor passed her down the hall and was curious as to what the note might say. She was paid, in part, to be nosy. The RA took out her glasses, put them on and read, 'If you can't beat'm'. That was cryptic, she thought. Duct tape obscured the side of the box exposed to the hall. She'd reapply the tape after one peek, so, after looking up and down the hall, she carefully lifted the tape below the box that was affixed to the door and looked at the product name; 'Beautiful Blonde Hair Dye'. She replaced the tape and continued her way to the showers. Undergrads. Go figure.

Dagmar Yaddow and Russ Anderson were early on their distance meeting preparations. Their schedules were the easiest to manipulate as they had the most autonomy over their priorities. Their PC's were fired up and their reports ready to give. Despite this being extra work, both looked forward to it as they might a vacation. It was fun, rewarding, exciting and, on top of that, relatively inexpensive.

Paul was at the Milledgeville Public Library in a private cubical. Nunzia came in to join him, as expected. The room was soundproofed and the two PC's made for a nicer video view of what was going to occur. Over the past few days, Paul had been in Nunzia's company more than he had been since his days with the Georgia National Guard had drawn to a conclusion. His Southern Baptist fundamentalism was telling him that this was getting to be a very bad habit.

Ryan and Zachary (and Atlas) arrived at Marianne's a few minutes before show time, followed shortly after by Melissa. Vanessa popped in. It turns out that she was taking a mental vacation on the Edwards Estate porch and at the playground in Selma where she had seen Natalie. Gustav sensed more than just that. His soul sister had been given a taste of life again, thanks to their dream visitation (and narrow escape) of the night before. He felt sure that Vanessa's heart was heavy from that brief respite from death's numbness, and that she had sought out the sites where those four entities that were closest to her heart were last seen: Annie, Natalie, Jason and Rebecca. Oh, yes. Let's not leave out Jed. He shook his head. A ghost seeking ghosts of ghosts. What was the world coming to? And how would he be feeling a century or so in the future? There was a lot of novelty in being a member of Club Dead. But after less than a week, some of that novelty was already beginning to wear thin. Something was on her mind. He could sense it, but she was keeping that part of her well guarded.

Frank and Rachel had been there an hour already and had early on staked a claim on the love seat. The furniture had been arranged so that the video screen of the entertainment center would be used for the conference call. It was placed just to the left of the fireplace, so the coziness would dovetail with a warm fire. Couples snuggled, cups were warmed, then the connect was made.

The screen came to life, divided into four quadrants, each with a Second String member's face in it. Vanessa whispered to Ryan that it reminded her of Hollywood Squares. All greeted everyone else with smiles and anticipation. Dagmar and Russ each had their PC's configured to show the Family on the top on wide angle, and the three others below, side by side. Nunzia and Paul had theirs with Paul's focused entirely on the Family, and hers with the three Second Stringers and one quadrant left over for information display.

Ryan began the meeting. "Welcome, everyone. Before we begin, there's been an event of a very unusual nature that occurred late last night at the Kingston Holiday Inn. Gustav's ex-wife, Martha Scholldorf

Mendelssohn, passed away due to a heart ailment." Second Stringers all sent their condolences to the spirit that they could not see, but also noticed that the rest of the Family already knew of the demise, judging from their lack of sudden reaction. That made sense, though. When Ryan announced that he was going to relate the nature of the event, they also noticed that the First String assumed postures of complete attention. This part would be news to them. Interesting, they all thought. Ryan held this part back until all could be present. That felt good, like they were just as important as the others.

Ryan proceeded to relate each step of the way that was taken by Gustav and Vanessa. Extra time had been squirreled away for today's meeting and it would be needed. The report was succinct, but the story took almost twenty minutes to fully unfold and not one heart was left untouched. "This represents yet another (choke, pause, sip of water, a breath) place to consider when looking for entrapped entities, though I haven't even the beginnings of a clue as to how to find such unfortunates. This will have to be explored and discussed as insights are revealed to us. That is all I have to say on the matter. Write down any questions you may have, because this is too rich a source for debate. Wait till we can all get together in person without a time constraint. I now leave the floor up to our beloved Second String."

Nunzia went first. As she spoke, Paul was looking at his display showing the Family. They looked and talked like normal people, he thought. His imagination had been far too active of late. That's when he noticed something new in the picture. He cocked his head a little and then took the controls of his PC display. Using the options available, he began to scan closer each member of the Family, slowly so as not to distract Sgt. D'Palermo. The image stopped scanning when he reached Marianne. There was something on her lap that she moved her hands about. Nunzia was focused on her own screen for the moment, so Paul quietly moved the focus closer. There, on Marianne's lap, he could see something that sent shivers up his spine. A jet-black cat.

"Ladies and gentlemen, allow me to introduce Cassandra Goode Petrocelli." A series of pictures from various sources, including an engagement announcement, began to unfold themselves before the audience. "Born August fourth, 2019..."

Paul heard Nunzia's presentation that pictured a hometown girl that had married a man from Rochester and settled in Rhinecliff, a hamlet of Rhinebeck...all bergs being in the Yankee Empire state. Her ancestry included the Goode family, as well as the names Cariltoni, Elem, and Carbanora. Those were the names that were most prevalent in the grands, great grands, and great, great grands. The families had their proper share of soldiers, laborers, technicians, professionals, and a bum or two. Nothing barked for attention as a clue to the mysteries of a premature death and an either usurped or shared grave. There were a biological child, now aged five, and two foster children, ages nine and twelve. The foster kids were orphans and their family histories were equally unremarkable. "In short, if there are clues in this presentation, we were not able to pick them out. Paul, your turn."

Sgt. Paul Wasserman had researched police records of the area, looking for any hint of foul play regarding the main family names that Nunzia had come up with. He was able to tie in with the NYS Police and Kingston City Police records with the assistance of his superior, Chief Hamm. States shared police information, but only through proper channels. "When Cassandra died, an autopsy was performed at Northern Dutchess Hospital. The results of that study are in my possession. Things don't look right, so I'm holding the report suspect. Her high school medical records were sent to me and things don't completely jive. Cassandra had a mild heart problem that she inherited called a ventricular septal defect. There was a hole in the heart between the two larger chambers. It wasn't large enough to warrant survival surgery, but I found a medical excuse to keep her out of high output gym activities. As far as I can tell, the defect was never repaired, though the procedure is now relatively safe. That should have caused the left lower chamber to get bigger in order to compensate for the compromised blood flow. Since a heart attack was the post-mortem diagnosis, the heart should have been well studied in the autopsy. The report that I have makes no mention of left ventricular chamber size or heart septal defect.

"The second thing that makes me suspicious is another item in her school records. When she was sixteen, she slipped on the ice and hit her head, causing a concussion and a hairline skull fracture. This happened on the school steps, so there was a thorough record of it, probably for liability purposes. That should have left fibrous tissue changes and a thickening of the skull that would have been noticed in a standard autopsy report. Nothing was mentioned. The report was electronically signed by a Dr. Jamsid Churdivera, which is not that unusual, but it could allow someone else who knows the tricks to forge the paper. Dr. Churdivera was on the verge of retiring at the time of this report. He actually did retire a year ago at the ripe old age of seventy-three, two days after Cassandra's autopsy was performed. He moved back to live out his life with family and friends in Pakistan, according to a level one bio-search. Nothing is proven, but it's suspicious to me. Dagmar?"

The Independent Correspondent went over her news resources, which paralleled Paul's research. She also had access to police records, but was able to make contact with news information gathering colleagues as well. Paul shifted some of what would have fallen into his arena to Dagmar just for fairness of workload. "Mr. Steve Petrocelli, Cassandra's husband, met her through a dating service, of all things. They corresponded for a year and a half and then finally met. He later sold his business in Rochester, NY, transferred to this area and the two were married. Steve was a commercial electrician and a fairly good one, from my sources. There was a life insurance policy, but not anything to make your heart race. It seemed mainly aimed at funding three educational accounts for the kids. The two foster children were sent back to the foster program when Cassandra died, but have been recently placed with Cassandra's parents. The biological child is now with her aunt in Fort Myers, Florida, which was agreed upon in the Petrocelli will. A week before the funeral, the father had been reported as missing. Nothing has been heard from him since. His business has gone into receivership and the contents have been auctioned off; mostly tools and gizmos that can be bought at any supply catalog that caters to that profession. That's all I was able to come up with. I wondered if her husband missing was what triggered off the heart attack. Russ?"

The forensics specialist took the baton. "The FBI records on missing persons didn't dig up much more than what Dagmar has said. Steve Petrocelli has not used his Debi-Cred card, any other purchase card, or even his social security number since he was listed as missing. I did a scan of electricians around the country, but the physical matching program didn't come up with anyone solid. Family interviews at the time were fairly thorough, since there were issues of insurance and child custody involved. No one knew anything about his whereabouts. So, the FBI comes up with bupkis. The only thing I've got left for 'show and tell' is a video of the guy giving a talk to the Rotary Club in Rhinebeck. They've met once a week at the Beekman Arms since God created dirt. I'm going to throw on a clip of it now." Russ dropped the disc in and tapped the play button. The Family watched as a fairly non-outstanding presence droned on about the future of the electronics industry in the Hudson Valley. While Russ commented on the snore factor of the presentation, Vanessa zeroed in on the video. She walked over to Gustav and whispered something to him. He, too, listened with a new interest.

Marianne felt a slight chill at being lectured to by someone who was either dead or in hiding possibly because of murder, so she got up and stoked the fireplace, then threw in a couple of logs. She liked doing it and Ralph had learned to relax his chivalry routine on this issue after she slightly embarrassed him in front of the Family by tossing him a log and saying 'Man, go hunt, make fire, spit, lift heavy things'. The logs began to catch, giving a wonderful warmth and light like something out of a Yule Log special. The Second String saw Ryan stand up to summarize, then stop. They could see that the First String was listening and watching carefully, shifting their gazes as if there were multiple speakers. Ryan spoke, but not the summary he was about to give. "Russ, play a piece of that video again." Russ did. Ten seconds later, "That's enough. Good one, Vanessa. Russ, you did well. All of you did, by the way. We can eliminate the husband as the entity in Cassandra's grave." Marianne's big screen showed two Second String faces move forward and cock to the side in confusion, and another two faces turn to look at each other. All of them looked like they had missed something and were wondering how. They had been working on the information together for hours yesterday. The Family patriarch chuckled at their expressions, then continued.

"Not your fault, kids. Vanessa just pointed out that the voice in the tape and the one that we heard from the grave are not the same in any respect. The one in the tape is friendly, monotone, and boring. His vocabulary is good, but limited more to his industry. The one in the grave was lively and a different voice quality all together, as much as mine differs from, say, Russ. We now open the floor to brainstorming. This is the time when anyone can say anything as the thought occurs to them."

Allen: "Can we find a way to exhume the grave? If there's an extra or wrong body down there, that would pretty well identify who the resident is."

Paul: "Not likely. Unless there is an inquest of some kind, getting an exhumation order is pretty tricky. Is there another way to check the ground?"

Melissa: "At the Edwards Estate, I read where researchers were using 'ground-sound' scanners to detect bodies in the apron pocket."

Dagmar: "I know the company that did that one. They've been used in the past for finding hidden bodies and archeology stuff. They've been in my broadcasts a couple of times. Look, I even know some specific people there. We did lunch. I'll give them a call and see if we can get a tech team up here on the hush-rush."

Russ: "If it's not the husband down there, then there's someone else with an interest in Mrs. Petrocelli. I suggest someone up there do some discrete snooping to see if there was someone in her present or past, maybe an ex-lover or someone on the side."

The energy of the session increased, as did the crackling of the fireplace. Paul was scratching his chin to see if there was something else he could add when his eyes were drawn again to the Family on his screen. Specifically, Ryan. Something was odd about his face, his body, the lighting. It flickered, like he was in the presence...of fire? He zoned out for a minute until Nunzia elbowed him in the ribs. "Huh? Sorry! Sorry, I was thinking of something, er, how about I see who were the detectives in charge for investigating Cassandra's death and Steve's disappearance? You guys check high school and college for romantic interests that might have an ax to grind."

Melissa shivered at that. Barbara had told her about the dangling minstrel who flattened that bush two stories under her window. Barbara had only meant to scare the fellow, but the knife was sharper and cut deeper than she had planned. Fortunately, the young man only suffered fractures of his Gibson...but...do people like that hold grudges? "I've got a thought. Voice analysis might be an approach. Paul, if anyone else turns up as a possible, see if you can get us anything like a voice print like the one Russ came up with for Vanessa and Gustav to pour over."

Paul: "Will do, li'l lady. Are you guys going to take another shot at Cassandra's bunk mate?"

Ryan: "I'm going to give it a try myself. I can't reach down with the psychic connection like Gustav and Vanessa, but I was able to talk to Bernhardt."

Ralph: "Wait a minute. That mole has some strength to him and he's grumpy. What would happen if we did the same thing we did at the Edwards Estate, you know, the double diamond thing? That might give us some firepower if that guy takes it into his head to fire off a Mad Annie patented fireball."

Silence on the Second String PC's for half a minute, then Ryan interpreted. "Vanessa says that she was able to use that power once, but doesn't know if it could be used again. She feels it is worth a try, but I don't know. The mystery man seemed more comfortable with men than women to chat with."

Rachel: "Then, we'll do the double diamond, but you can still do the talking, like you were in a tank or something."

Ryan: "Great, that ought to earn the man's respect. Macho me hiding behind four skirts."

Dagmar: "Wouldn't he have to stick his head above the ground to see you doing that? If he did, wouldn't we then have a physical description to work with? Maybe that should be your game plan. Look, I'm signing off for the moment. I'll see if I can get a team up there this afternoon, so hold off on confronting until we can at least get that information. We'll do more research on our end, but since you guys are local, it would make more sense for you to do the in person stuff."

The Family agreed to disband the meeting. Nunzia thumbed a disconnect on her PC, then looked to her right. Paul was still there, looking at the screen, nibbling his thumbnail in that way he did when he was worried about something. She couldn't hang around, though. She had an hour's drive to get back to base. They'd talk about it later. As she got her car onto the road, she tried to review all the findings of the meeting to make sure she had all her facts straight. That proved difficult. Of all the things about being in close quarters with her current friend and former lover, it was the sense of smell that had distracted her the most. Old Spice was a very old aftershave fragrance, but Paul liked it and used it, or nothing at all. His sparse application of the stuff got her goat all the more. It was like that old saw; when you want to get someone's attention, whisper. Sergeants rarely put that adage into practice during working hours. But sometimes, the stripes came off the woman's arm.

"So, what do we do now? It's almost two." Ralph was a cabbie and used to moving. Sitting around, unless there was a plate or a woman involved, wasn't what he was used to. "Now isn't that funny," he thought. "...don't we men call a pretty woman a dish?"

Marianne smiled at Ralph's eagerness. This was no couch potato. "Chill, Love. If you're really antsy for something to perk up your schedule, we could take an hour off and get married." The background of chat stopped as if someone pushed a button. "Just kidding, Love." She walked into the kitchen. "EBONY! Ralph, get in here. Your kitten had an accident on the kitchen floor."

Ralph was shaken by the one-two punch. "Do Sicilian women come with manuals?" he addressed to no one in particular. Gustav answered.

"*Yes, they do, updated and revised every half hour.*" Gustav watched as Ralph walked, gingerly, into the kitchen. "*Seriously, Ryan, perhaps we ought to do some pre-contact scouting if we're going to take a shot at the gravesite later. Nighttime would be best for the Petrocelli site, I think, so there's no hurry. Maybe the fellow will be less testy at night, like Annie was.*"

Allen and Zachary went to collate and plan their approach to the possible sites in Zachary's files and to compare them to the list that Ryan's clip service had come up with. There were many the man/dog combination had visited and many more that they hadn't gotten around to, yet.

"You know, Zach, you'd think that there would be a greater acceptance of the presence of entities, with all of these reports."

"Allen, m'boy, you'd be surprised at the human capacity to shut out evidence that conflicts with their version of reality. Do you think Copernicus was the first to think the sun was the center of the universe, or Columbus that the world was round? That was becoming common knowledge with the common folk. Any one with a university education could do the math on the days and months and see that the heliocentric theory of the solar system was the way to go. And anyone could see the mastheads coming in before the ship, which would be 'flatly' impossible if the world was flat.. It was institutional brain hardening that refused to acknowledge the obvious. Those two people are listed as great thinkers, and they were, but more important, they had the brass to stand up against the powers that be. Everywhere you look, things have finally made their way into our culture that caused their announcers of existence no end of bullshit. Read up on the Tucker car sometime."

Marianne took advantage of her already warm PC hookup to the big screen and started catching up on office work. Ralph and Rachel looked on. The former wanted to know more about this part of the machine. He also wanted to be closer to Marianne. Gustav assisted on the effort, using the occasional pause in activity to explain procedures of the Hawthorn business to Rachel. Frank was beginning to feel like a fifth wheel again, so he asked directions to the nearest ax and woodpile. He could do at least that. Traveling in a car was known for putting one in a thoughtful frame of mind. Chopping wood added a tendency towards action steps into the mixture. In the back, there was an old-fashioned stump and woodpile combination that stood defiant in the face of modern home heating technology. Frank took a likely looking piece from the seasoned woodpile, placed it on the stump, and took a good grip on the ax he had retrieved from the back door mini-closet.

Chop. There was a ghost in the wrong grave, afraid of coming out, not wanting anyone's help, with shifting desires between being wanting to be left alone or to have company.

Chop. What right did they have to interfere with the last request of a dead man to be left alone? Was it more than just idle curiosity? The 'murder' aspect made it worth looking closer at, though. Do murderers have legal rights after they're dead? But, it's not proven that the entity is (was?) a murderer.

Chop. What possible reason would a ghost, not the woman's husband, have in clinging to a dead woman's grave for a year? Might he eventually come out on his own?

Chop. It sounded as if the old boy was mega-guilty about something. And that autopsy report. What fishiness was that?

Chop. That falsified...possibly...death analysis from that old examiner who took off across the Atlantic soon after. The guy had an exemplary record of service. It just didn't feel right to hold the doctor suspect. For now, anyway.

Cho-rack! The ax was stopped halfway through the log by a knot, stuck fast. It didn't finish splitting the wood, he thought. What are you doing, stopping there before the process was finished?

Thud-rack! Frank struck the ax/wood combination on the stump, making a little progress. What did it all add up to? Well, what are the parts of the jig saw? Turn them face up and see if there were any that fit.

Thud-rack! Stubborn piece of wood. Guilt...

Thud-rack! Murder...

Thud-rack! Fear of coming out in the open. It wasn't working, so he tried to pull the ax out. The wood had too tight of a grip. Frank took the two ends, then, and began to pry them apart.

Missing husband who was probably deceased and likely murdered as well. Kids abandoned. Husband not in grave. Autopsy - SNAP! The wood separated, leaving Frank with a piece in each hand. He looked at the two pieces, and put them back together. It fit only one way. Frank looked into the house. He was the newcomer; he was the blind and deaf one. Well, then, the worst thing that could happen was that he'd be wrong. He gathered up the wood, bringing the two pieces that fit together only one way with him.

Melissa and Vanessa were on their way to high school. Ryan knew many people around the Valley (though mostly through Gustav), as did Marianne. They pulled a few strings and got Melissa the job interview at Rhinebeck

Central High School. The Vice Principal himself, Jeremy Waters, was there to greet her. The supply of high school education teachers had pendulumed over the past century or two and, currently, it had swung to a paucity of educators for his learning institution. PC's and aides were invaluable, but they needed teachers for a wide spectrum of topics. He told this future teacher prospect (so he believed) of the benefit package, the wonderful lifestyle in Rhinebeck, the shopping across the Hudson River (Kingston was about half mall) and locally (Rhinebeck was a specialty shop Mecca). After the general tour, Melissa mentioned that her mother had asked about a friend who had passed away a year ago, Cassandra Petrocelli, though her name would have been Goode when she was there at the school. Jeremy Waters had heard of her due mostly to the woman's passing away recently, but he was too new at the school to remember her actually attending classes. However…"There's a teacher nearing retirement that you might speak to. She's the Art Department supervisor, Penny Supina. If you like, we'll stop over there and you can pay your respects."

After a stroll down lockered hallways, Melissa and Vanessa found themselves in a sizable classroom that was festooned with paintings, books, clay projects, paints, and other items. The elderly teacher before them had taken all of ten seconds to warm up to her visitor. "Oh, yes, I remember Cassy. Sweet girl, kind of a pasty complexion with some sort of a heart problem. She was my main lady, I'll tell you. Talented, helpful, bit of a wallflower, though. It was so sad to hear of her passing away. I remember she stopped in to pay me a visit a few years back. Things seemed to be going pretty good for her, if I remember right. Teachers love it when old students come back and tell us they remember us. Teaching is no cushy job, I'm here to tell you, so get that out of your mind right now. You get a lot of grief from above by state bureaucrats, and those you teach at high school level rarely appreciate you. But, it's like raising kids. They come back later on, after they've grown up some. That alone is worth the effort."

Before the kind lady could go too much further down this tangent, "Mom told me that Cassandra had a couple of boyfriends and that one of them might have the copy of her Senior Patroon; your yearbook? She would have liked to have something from Cassandra to remember her by, maybe some copies of her pictures in it. Do you recall who she might have been dating back then?"

"Oh, Heavens no, child. I stayed away from that sort of thing with my students. Besides, who was going with who changed on a daily basis." Melissa's shoulders dropped, she had been making progress. "But I *can* help you with the yearbook. Cassy left it here last year when she last visited for me to get some retired teachers' signatures for her. I still keep in contact with some of the old guard." Penny got up, gently, and slowly walked to the shelves of books that covered an entire wall. There looked to be little or no system and papers and books were helter skelter to the casual observer.

Vanessa commented, "*I'll bet she has the original Mona Lisa in there, somewhere.*"

Penny found the general area she had been looking for and was fingering through forty years of yearbooks. She had always kept a copy for her memories and recalled that she had put Cassy's yearbook next to her own copy. "I probably have the original Mona Lisa in here somewhere," she groused, as old fingers searched for the proper year. Melissa and Vanessa's eyes snapped to each other.

"*Someday, I'm going to put this all in order.*" Vanessa waited.

"Here it is! It's not the best filing system, but I know where everything is. Since I'm going to retire next year, I'm going to have to put all this in order."

Vanessa whispered to Melissa's ear, "*She's at least a partial clairaudient and doesn't know it. We've seen that in people who gravitate to artistic careers, something about the dominance of the right side of the brain. Maybe Ryan should hear about this?*" Melissa couldn't answer, yet. She had at least learned that much.

Penny opened the yearbook, and immediately her two guests could see that it had been filled with handwritings that mostly looked feminine. As Penny flipped the pages to the senior section, the predominance of women's pictures with writing next to or over them far outweighed any male chicken scratches. "There she is. That's Cassy, the poor girl." The picture showed a plain but friendly face. Each entry for the graduating class had a name and a motto underneath the picture. Some were pretty cryptic and reflected more the teen culture of the time, probably quotes of popular music verses. Under 'Cassandra Barbara Goode' was her quote; '...who plants one rose on barren ground.'

"That's so pretty, Penny. Do you know what it means, other than being a nice thought?"

"I don't know the author, but it's a line from a poem that she had as a personal affirmation. Let me see, 'For man must live his life on earth, where hate and sin and wrong abound, and he has justified his life, who plants one rose on barren ground.' That's pretty close to the quote. I've always liked that thought. It sticks in your mind and says a lot about who Cassy was."

"This is wonderful, Penny. Could I copy some of the pages somewhere?"

The old woman looked at the book of memories, then at this young woman who still had more memories in front of her than behind. "No, child. I'd prefer you take the book to your mother. I'm getting pretty full of years and someone someday is going to just throw a lot of this treasure into the recycle bin, or the Smithsonian. They'll probably throw me in along with it."

Clairaudience...being able to hear spirits...Vanessa thought of something. "*Sometimes I hear voices of people I used to know that passed away.*"

"You know, I really must be getting senile. From time to time, I even hear voices from the past. This place must absorb some of a person's personality."

It was worth a shot. Melissa saw what was going on and did her part to keep an encouraging and friendly expression. *"I think I heard Cassy's voice once."*

That stopped Penny's chatting. She had a knotted brow, like something sad or unpleasant had come to mind. "You know, I'd forgotten it, but shortly after Cassy passed away, I could have sworn I heard her voice. It was sad, frightened. That was so unlike the Cassy I knew."

"I remember the exact day I heard her voice…"

"It was the day after she was buried. Isn't it odd that this would come to mind? I hope you'll forgive an old woman and her mental wanderings. Please pay another visit sometime, and bring your mother."

Melissa felt a little guilty at deceiving this nice lady so, and the vice principal as well. Such misgivings had never been part of her musings in the past. The morals of Allen and the Family must be rubbing off on her. Melissa picked up an application MiDi for employment, which included tuition assistance if she was willing to sign on ahead of time. The shortage was that bad. Melissa had a passing thought and asked Mr. Waters, "Do you have a program for your students in journalism?"

"One of the best, but we're losing that teacher in a few years as well. Retirement is really killing us, even though the teachers are staying on as long as they can until the supply can catch up with the demand."

Melissa tucked the application MiDi into her shirt pocket and the yearbook under her arm, thanked Mr. Waters, and then took her leave. Vanessa looked at her as they settled into her car. *"Are you thinking what I think you're thinking?"*

"It *would* look good on my resume," she said, and then drove down the high school entry road in her 'SNAAB'. At the end of the road, Melissa then turned right, but pulled off in a public playground's parking area. Vanessa looked at Melissa curiously, seeing a furrowed brow. "Vanessa? Didn't Penny say she heard Cassandra's voice the day *after* the funeral?"

"Oh, God."

Everyone was interested in the yearbook and voted Madam Melissa to be a first rank investigative reporter. They went over, page by page, the prize. The time discrepancy between the funeral and Penny's sense of Cassandra's voice carried some chilling implications. That became a speculation dead end street until they could get more information. Frank and Rachel had left to be home for the kids when school let out. Janet had a sleepover engineered at a girlfriend's house and Jerry would leave for a school ski weekend. The happy couple was expected over later that evening, before they all took off for the cemetery. Word had come that a 'ground-sound' tech team would meet them there around eight or eight-thirty, depending on traffic. Meanwhile, the

Family had gotten to Cassandra's portrait and quote. Underneath the quote, there was a blurb about plans for the future. In Cassandra's case, it was to continue her education at Dutchess Community College.

"Popular with girl's, but not so much with guys," Ralph commented. "Look at her face. It's loaded with trust and morality. That quote confirms the picture." Sure enough, the activities pages for the students showed that Cassandra had belonged to the Sierra Club and the Student Conservation League. "Tree hugger. Now wait a minute, I mean that in a good sense. Don't you throw that at me, Dear!" Marianne set down her coffee cup, for now. Ralph flipped through the pages and counted five student handwritings strongly suggestive of a male hand. Four of them were your basic 'you're a good kid' brush off, but one of them was different. Over his picture, whose motto had been 'Give like a tree', was written: 'For man must live his life on earth…'

Melissa repeated the quote that Penny had told her. Ryan leaned back in his chair, saying, "That qualifies for being an item in my book. They're both into environment saving, both know the same quote, only this guy has anything remotely mushy in her yearbook. 'Lincoln Marfan', huh? Look at the eyes, Ralph. You're the face man. What do you see?"

Ralph looked into the eyes of young Mr. Marfan. He mumbled that the fellow probably never blinked when he talked to you. There was passion there, purpose. Looking through the rest of the book, he noted that there were no sports type activities to get in his way of doing whatever he did with his spare time. Lincoln and Cassandra were in the same clubs and the blurb under his portrait also noted the community college route. Who followed whom, he wondered? Lincoln had that same expression of intensity, no matter which photo you looked at and he didn't smile in any of them. Ralph decided, then passed on the book for others to continue to peruse. "Zealot."

Ryan got on the horn and called Russ Anderson. "We need a quick check of Cassandra Petrocelli's background at Dutchess Community College. See if you can get a snap shot, would you? Check for a boyfriend named Lincoln Marfan logged into the same curriculum. Thanks." He thumbed the disconnect, turned to his companions and announced, "I'm hungry. Hillside Manor."

While the Family wound up discussing findings so far at the Hillside, including Allen and Zachary's schedule for checking out other sites, Sgt. Paul Wasserman excused himself from his home's dinner table. "It's just a quick visit to the Rev. I need to get his angle on some things."

As he drove his cruiser down the county route, Paul did his level best to keep perspective. There were so many coincidences, most of them silly by themselves. He had to laugh at his reaction to the black kitten and, in retrospect, he realized that the fiery image of Ryan he had seen on his PC had been due to his being near the fireplace. It did look pretty weird though, and suggestive. Even so, something nagged at him. If he was going to be a Family member along with Nunzia and the rest, he'd have to put this issue to bed. As he continued to order his thoughts, Paul missed the fact that he had mentioned only Nunzia by name. Like so many investigative types, his talents were mainly honed for external examination.

He pulled up into driveway of Reverend Daniel Pocolis, who had to be the Peach State's only full blood Greek Baptist minister. The man was of the earth, solid, like Paul. They spoke the same language, but carried a different arsenal. Paul had already weighed his word to the Family against his concerns over personal spiritual matters. He had evaluated his own capacity to make an informed decision and found his perspective lacking. Sgt. Paul Wasserman was a man of his word, but more important to him, he was a man of THE Word. "Hi, Rev. Thanks for taking me."

"Anytime for you, Paul. Please, come in, son." Reverend Pocolis was an aging, portly man whose deep booming voice in the pulpit commanded both attention and respect. Many had been blessed with such a voice, but in this man it was connected to a spirit completely dedicated to service. The Rev had his weaknesses, particularly a nice home cooked spread, to which he had ample opportunity thanks to his congregation. Ever since his wife, Jolene, passed away from a blood clot subsequent to a hip fracture three years ago, it seemed the goal of his congregation to make sure that their Rev would never feel lonely, or fit into his old clothes. His home décor was simple, colonial, and warm. His living room had a fire prepared, with coffee and cookies (made that day by Mrs. Henderson, who he thought must buy her ingredients from God) on the lamp table between the two rocker/recliners facing the fire.

Paul sat down and picked up a cookie. "Nice. Mrs. Henderson's?"

That was a lot of small talk for Paul, who usually got right to the nub of the matter. That caught Rev's attention at once. Daniel Pocolis had saved many a soul, but had also salvaged many a sanity. One of his greatest weapons in his arsenal was his ability to read between the lines. "What's on your mind, son?"

"Rev, I need from you a promise of absolute confidentiality, no matter what you hear from me. Agreed?"

That Paul would have felt the need to ask… This was no simple infidelity or financial distress matter. The men had known each other better than that. "Agreed. Please, unburden yourself."

"You remember that work I was doing up north?"

Marianne called out, "Ryan, it's Russ on the line."

"Put it on public. Hey, Russ! What did you come up with?"

"Hello, everyone. Cassandra Goode did attend D-tri-C from 2037 to 2039. She had started off on a four-year bachelor's curriculum in Forestry Management, but opted out for a two-year associate's degree in the same field. On the surface, most people thought the reason for the switch was that the lady had met her dream fella and got happily-ever-aftered. Did some more digging and found this Lincoln Marfan guy you mentioned. My sources weren't able to find too many people who liked the man. He also was in Forestry Management, but stuck it out for the full four years. Took a job with NY State working for the Catskill Forest Preserve. The people I talked to said that Mr. Marfan was an intense character. Never blinked when he talked to you, you know?"

Ryan turned to Ralph. "You're a witch."

"The term is 'warlock', Boss."

Russ heard the side conversation. "Hey, Ralph? We're recruiting in our Bureau crystal ball department. Double your salary?"

"Not unless you allow Sicilian women in as well."

From over the sound system, "Sorry, we have to draw the line somewhere."

Marianne had come in from the kitchen and caught that last exchange. "Russ, Honey, how would you like to be an object of interest of your missing person's department?"

"Rejoinder received and understood, ma'am. Will transfer to Lima, Peru, Office on completion of this conversation. Speaking of that department, the missing person's, that is, Mr. Marfan fits that glove as well. He evaporated right about the same time Cassandra and her hubby left us. A first level search didn't find a hair. I'd have to have some extra juice for a second level."

Ryan thought about it. "May not be necessary. We'll let you know tomorrow after our rendezvous tonight."

"Good luck with that, everyone, but wanted to mention one more thing. Cassandra was tight with one of the professors in the Plant Bio Department. The prof told me that she thought one of the reasons Cassandra opted out of a B.S. was not so much to get married, but to get away. Mr. Marfan had a tendency to suffocate people close to him. Those were her own words, so no gallows humor was intended. Gotta fly, friends. Good hunting."

Allen threw in, "Hope you can get up here, soon. I would love to hear more of your war stories."

"Ten Four, CEO. I'll do my best to comply. This is the FBI signing off and all your rooms have bugs in them, except Marianne's. For some reason, those keep melting."

"WHY YOU…"

"Click."

Ralph leaned over to the steaming Sicilian. "If the FBI thinks it, we might as well go ahead and make it for real and legal." Marianne looked over, open mouthed, but stunned silent. "And unlike you, I'm not just kidding."

Driving to Marianne's in the Gladstone family Foxglove, "Frank, I'm a little nervous on this one. I mean, a murder involved, maybe two. A mystery man underground. At least with Annie, you knew what you were up against, sort of."

"Honey, let's keep perspective. I seem to recall that Annie was involved with over a hundred murders and had Allen in her crosshairs. But, I'm not going to force you to do something you're not right with. Shall I turn around?"

Rachel thought about it for a second, but only for that. Her main concern was for Allen, who would also be involved with the double triangle should things get testy. But Allen would be there whether she was or not. "No. Besides, we're already here." Frank pulled off into the circular drive, parked the Foxglove, and they both got out. At the same time they were walking up to the door, Ralph had popped the question. Marianne's home was usually a hive of activity and conversation. That everyone was sitting or standing stock-still, absolutely quiet, was very unusual. That no one looked in their direction in welcome? Highly uncharacteristic. That Marianne said one word, softly? From what Rachel had heard from others and gathered on her own, unheard of. That's when the room exploded with cheering and hugging, and more than a little clapping and jumping.

Frank said in normal voice, as whispering was no longer audible, "I was going to say 'charades', but that doesn't seem quite right."

"Color me clueless, Love."

Ralph bounded for the door. Frank and Rachel parted the waters to make way for a locomotive making a beeline for the Green Machine. Fifteen seconds later, Ralph burst back in. He made his way to Marianne, who was involved in a group hug. Rachel and Frank both wondered the same thought at the same time and walked towards the revelers. Sure enough, Ralph had gone to retrieve a ring. Marianne's eyes glistened through the tears when she asked, "When did you get this?"

"Two days after I met you, Baby. That was the day after I knew in my heart that you were the one for me." Rachel added her own mistiness and smiles to the brew, and Frank patted Ralph on the back.

"Well, old man, looks like the lady is going to make an honest man out of the cabbie. Think you can hack it?"

The look on Rachel's face brought everyone else to silence. "Frank, you made a joke? Oh, my God, Frank. You actually did it! EVERYONE, FRANK MADE A JOKE!" Allen came up from behind, spun the hapless man around, gave him a bear hug and laughed out, "You did it, you did it, you did it!"

"NOW SEE HERE, I have always been quite capable of humor if the situation…" It was no good. Two miracles in one evening, and the night was still young. Surely, this was a portent from above. After a mass of handshakes and back pats, Ralph came up to the beleaguered man.

"Looks like you upstaged me, 'old man'."

"Very funny, very funny indeed. I know you are all having some laughter at my expense, and I want you to know that I am not going to take it personally. It's always funny to blow things out of proportion, so, let's leave it at that, shall we?"

Allen called out, "Hey, everyone! Got Jerry and Janet on the horn."

Frank turned around and saw the large video screen, divided in half. Each half had one of his beloved children. They were dancing up and down and both had peer members behind them involved in applause and cheers.

Janet was smiling ear-to-ear, "Daddy made a joke!? Thank you, everyone!"

Jerry added, "Hey, Dad, we're all very proud of you. Really!"

Frank did his level best to look perturbed, but the mood was infectious. The laughter in his heart steamrolled over his childhood upbringing and cemented his ties to the merry mob.

After a few more well-intentioned barbs and the disconnects from the screen presences had been made, Ryan saw fit to rescue Frank from the kettle. That left the attention to mainly focus on the first miracle, which is where it belonged. "Frank, my boy, you have been initiated fully into the Family, now. I hope you feel more at home. About those insights you came up with this morning, you were right on the money. Lover from the past does in the one who jilted him and his successor, then ends his own life. Tell me, what kind of reception are we going to look for in the future from this Marfan guy?"

That the Boss would seek out his opinion (and value it!) was confirmation that his wife's ability to forecast far outshone his own. Frank thought for half a minute, knowing that Ryan preferred accuracy to speed, and put a priority to succinctness from others despite his own tendency to wax pedantic. A single word came to mind. "Explosive."

The tech-van rolled up to meet the waiting short version limo (Ryan wouldn't give in entirely) and Green Machine (the Family was growing, and Ralph was stubborn). When the crunching of the van tires on the frosted ground ceased, the melancholy quiet resumed its reign. Cemeteries were stark places on cold nights. The moon was three quarters full. It had been a chilly October so far and tonight was no exception. The colors of the day had been replaced by the gray scales of night and the landscape of stone monuments announced themselves with lines of cold, pitch shadows that black-stabbed the ground.

At a signal from Ryan, Ralph walked up to the van. The two tech men opened their doors, got out and slipped on their coats and gloves. The sound of the shutting van doors seemed a slap in the face to the unblinking granite faces, earning the living a suspicion of the attention and possible enmity of the deceased. More sounds came and went, signifying the unloading and interconnecting of devices made by man designed to find secrets hidden in the ground. There was no sense in Family members getting out of their warm cars yet. Who knew how long this procedure would take, or how long this night would turn out to be?

Ralph was bundled extra thick. Marianne had seen to that, as his southern blood was not used to the northern climate, yet. Three figures moved out into the moonlight, heading towards a particular unresting place. Those in the car could see the pale figures fairly well, as the dell they headed towards was downhill. About forty yards they went, and then stopped to plant their briefcase-sized device with a long rod attached underneath. The pale green readouts allowed those who witnessed from a distance a splotch of color that contrasted with the surrounding grays and highlighted the breath mists from the three men. Even with the windows cracked, not much could be heard of conversation, though muffled sounds of speaking were heard frequently. Both cars had switched over to battery, the better to hear what might transpire. 'Thump'. Did something drop? 'Thump'. No, that must be the sound search device. Allen had looked into the history of the thing and recalled reading that the noise used to be far greater. The sound generator used to be a shotgun shell. 'Thump'. All eyes were on the three men as they toiled up the grade back towards the vehicles. The two from the van went back to same and Ralph came back to the limo while rubbing his hands rapidly together. "They got their initial readings and are going to go analyze them. Depending on the construction of the casket, which no one thought to tell us would be helpful information, they may already have all they need. I'm going back to suck up some heat." He made his way to his beloved Green Machine, Marianne, Allen and Melissa. Time passed, five, ten, fifteen minutes. The van door opened and the two men got out with coats and machinery. Ralph told the three, "Looks like we're in for act two. See you in a bit."

Allen had heard the suppressed tooth chatter noise when Ralph had gotten back to the car. "Forget it, Southern Boy. Let a Yankee take a turn. I'm used to this kind of weather and worse."

Ralph grasped his own wrist and gave it a quarter turn. "Ouch. OK, you win. You don't have to be so rough. Whimper." So, Allen stepped outside and accompanied the men from the van down to the grave, chuckling at Ralph's comedy.

Melissa asked, "Should I be worried?"

Marianne answered, "No more than I was with Ralph." That didn't reassure Melissa one tiny bit. The Family watched as, once more, temporarily living men went to pry secrets from the permanently dead.

"I've never heard a noise like that before. What's this all about? Oh no, is HE looking for me? I'll have to hide." Spirits can see, but not by light reflection so much as that everything has energy just from their mass and existence. The entity

could see as dirt and rocks passed him by, but he could also see past those substances as if they were a fog only partially blocking his vision. There was the casket, and inside rested the one he loved. Into the casket he passed his being and with the corpse he merged. To hide, he had to match each of his features to hers. Perhaps that was how he had been able to escape detection for so long. He remembered some vague reference to a Bible verse about people wanting the mountains to fall down upon them to hide them from God's wrath. He could identify with that. The feet were first and he worked himself up to the head. He usually saved the arms for last, for the position they were in bothered him. No longer in the chest-crossed position, they were bent more like a begging puppy's might be and the fingers had dug themselves into the fabric of the coffin lid.

'Djumb'. The sound was different than the one heard above via the air. Also, this time the sound had changed slightly. It had a penetrating quality to it. He WAS looking for him. Absolute still, absolute quiet; the entity would have held his breath, if he had any. 'Djumb'. It penetrated the coffin. The entity could almost feel it. Terror struck his heart. What could he do? Strike back? Only if that was the last option, for that's very likely what it would turn out to be.

"We're getting through. Luckily, newer coffin designs may be more watertight, but they're not as dense to sound waves. Makes for easier carrying, too." Allen was looking over the man's shoulder at the detector's 4x4 display. He had wanted to SatCom everything to the waiting cars, recalling that those behind couldn't hear what was going on. The techs nixed the idea, saying that SatCom transmissions had been known to interfere with their device's performance. "There, that's the outline of the coffin. The brighter objects are metal and rock, which we tune out with filtering. Now, another shot." 'Thump'. "Yeah, that's clearer." Allen could see a green coffin shaped figure on the screen. The information was being relayed to the van as a failsafe, should anything go awry with the equipment. What was on the detector screen was not stored beyond whatever the last read-out provided. "Now, we'll filter out the frequencies from the wood laminate and man-made materials underneath, focus the beam, and notch up the gain a little." 'Thump'. "There, whoa! That can't be right!" Allen stared at the green display and saw the begging puppy posture of the deceased, but there was something else there. "Looks like double occupancy, gentlemen. OK, let's adjust for distance, top figure first."

The first tech lifted up the sound device and the second tech split the pole into what was now a 'V' shape. This activated the twin transducer head and created the ability to have two sets of signals be utilized. This gave three dimensionality to their data and a greater ability to screen out unwanted items based now upon depth rather than composition. It also eliminated the fuzzy areas on the image of items directly underneath the screened out elements. A third leg telescoped down to make a stable tripod, now that the precise location of the area of interest had been triangulated.

'Thudump'. Now the image was much clearer. There was no doubt that the fingers were just below shoulder level in a feral claw position and the mouth was wide open. Three men decided at that moment that the weather had taken a sudden turn for the colder. Not all of that impression was psychological, especially as it applied to their feet. "Not pretty, kid. Now for the basement." 'Thudump'. "Wha…"

From the waiting cars, what looked like a bolt of reddish orange lightning erupted from the ground. A split second later, the sparks of electrical equipment meeting its doom pierced eyes that had become accustomed to the night. The sound device control box erupted in a geyser of white and blue colors, meeting its death with an electrical scream that recalled iron fingernails on a chalkboard. The three men leaped back once, looked at each other through eyes half blinded by the blowout, and then dove for shelter behind any stone that would hide them. One of the techs misjudged distances due to his visual impairment and earned a moderate shoulder bruise. Both limo and Green Machine car doors opened in haste and everyone except the limo driver made their way down the slope to where Allen and the technicians were cowering. The driver, a brave man in his own right, decided that it was time to call it a night. Graveyards, moonlight and screaming exploding equipment were just too much for him. Ryan heard the noise of tire flung gravel and turned in time to see the limo drive off. He couldn't really blame the guy, though, and decided right there that only Family members would drive on expeditions like this, especially when it was this chilly.

Despite the after images that hampered their vision, it was easy to locate the gravesite. There were still the embers of deceased electrical components that formed a beacon. Melissa couldn't keep quiet. "Allen, are you all right?"

"Crap on a cupcake!"

"He's all right. You two boys still in one piece?" Ryan asked.

"Ms. Yaddow said you guys were into some weird stuff. Christ! What WAS that?"

His partner said, "Leave the box here till morning. I'm not going near that thing. Let's take a look at what's in the van."

Ryan made an executive decision. "We're taking this show to Marianne's. Plans for a confrontation tonight are officially scrapped." The two techs looked at each other. 'Confrontation'?

The van had to take on Ryan and Allen as well as the two techs. The rest piled into the Green Machine. Fortunately, two of the travelers were able to pop over to Marianne's without the need of hitching a ride. That left Ralph, Frank, Rachel, Melissa, Marianne and Zachary in the retired taxi. Marianne took up her station in the car that she had when Gustav had first begun to play matchmaker. This time, there were no complaints from her about the close quarters. Now that she thought of it, her complaints from before were perfunctory. She realized how she had been maneuvered back then. "Honey, are you aware of how Gustav played cupid with us?"

"Yeah, Honey, I do. Believe me, if anyone knows the powers of Mr. Mendelssohn's plots, it's me. I was almost committed to the mental ward thanks to him, remember? Let me tell you, I was about to kick some serious butt when the lot of you closed ranks to protect him. That told me a lot. He may be unconventional, but you can't argue with the results." Marianne rested her head on his broad shoulders.

Rachel was consoling Melissa in the back. "He's my son, sweetie. I was worried there, too. I was a lot more worried back at the hospital and the suite. Let me tell you something. I fretted a lot about Carl when he went out on a rescue call. You wouldn't believe the things I imagined might happen, like gas tank explosions, or a teetering car falling on him. He came back each time, but that never stopped me from worrying. It's part of our nature, I guess, which is both a curse and a blessing; like pregnancy, but don't be in any hurry to find out about that one for yourself."

Rachel felt her right hand taken up by Frank. She had almost forgotten he was there. Then she realized she was reminiscing about Carl while sitting right next to Frank. Melissa saw the 'oh, no' look on her face. Rachel's Cat hid her face with her paws, but Angel insisted she turn to face her husband to apologize. To the surprise of all three, she saw his face smiling and sympathetic. Frank kissed her hand and told her, "Carl was a great man and he was fortunate to have an equally wonderful wife who gave him a top notch son. Don't be afraid to talk about Carl when I'm around. In fact, I'd like to learn more about him, if you like."

Rachel could only get moist and say, "Ohh."

Melissa was also touched, but added another idea that had not occurred to Rachel before. "So, that's where Allen gets his chivalry."

Melissa and Frank saw the wheels begin to spin in their center seat partner. Both knew from experience that Rachel was out of contact for anywhere between a few seconds to several minutes. Zachary turned around to say something, but saw two people give him the 'shush' sign.

Rachel thought, "Allen got his chivalry from Frank? Carl is his father, but Carl died when Allen was four. How much can a boy learn in that short time? There's the genetic pre-disposition factor and I can see elements of Carl in Allen, but Allen was his own man, but was he as much his own man as I thought? Carl gave nature; Frank had offered nurture. How many children had grown to find out that their parents were adoptive, and spent countless hours of effort to locate their biological parents? Some of them were rewarded with the fruits of their labor; others were very disappointed. Most of them still looked on their adoptive parents as Mom and Dad, because they were. Anyone can produce a baby, but it was Mom and Dad

230

who raised it regardless of who 'fired the shot' or 'dropped the bomb'. Frank was a Dad to Allen, even if Allen never used that term out of deference to Carl. He still treated Frank with the respect due a father." Rachel turned her head to look at Frank. "So, Frank and I were Mom and Dad to Allen. He wasn't a substitute Dad; he was a volunteer Dad. Carl was a volunteer, too." Rachel moved closer to her husband, whom she loved more than she had realized.

"Frank, I love you," was all that she could bring to mind, but it was sufficient.

Ralph glanced into his rear view, then leaned his head to Marianne and whispered, "They're fogging up my mirror."

Marianne whispered back, "If they are, then there's nothing in that mirror you should be watching." She reached up and diverted the rear view to reflect nothing but Green Machine ceiling.

"Good point."

Reverend Daniel Pocolis leaned his rocker/lounger back and tamped a fresh pinch of tobacco into his pipe. Jolene had allowed it as one of his two vices, telling him that she had better always be his other one. "Holy Mother of God," he thought. There was so much to this, but it was all confused and jumbled. This poor man must be torn apart. Paul was strong, a real bulwark for the church. He was very ordered in his thinking and sometimes had trouble keeping a wider perspective when it dealt with spiritual matters. Ran in his family, he recalled.

"First of all, Paul, there is no doubt in my mind that this man is not the anti-Christ. That person would not need a Navy experiment to produce longevity, but would have it naturally when his father, Satan, caused him to be born. Ryan's purpose to quietly assist spirits that still roam the earth is not a goal that Satan would choose. The Four Horsemen impression; I strongly think that was a fluke. But even if it wasn't, the Christ was NOT one of the four riders, and the Horsemen of the Apocalypse did not herald the Anti-Christ. If anything biblical is implied in this man, it may be that he is one of the Four Horsemen heralding the Second Coming. I have serious questions on that one, but I'm keeping an open mind. As for the cat and the fireplace shadows? C'mon Paul. We're adults here. Tell you what, though. Since your heart is troubled, I'm going to pray for a sign for you to guide your course by. You keep your eyes to see and your ears to hear. You hear, son?"

"Gotcha, Rev. Thanks. I'll be in touch. Say hi and thanks to Mrs. Henderson for me, will you?"

"Will do," he said, opening up his door and placing a fatherly hand on the man's shoulder, "…and say thanks for her dinner invite to Elizabeth. Tell her Saturday night would be best and I'll bring the dessert." He closed the door. Of course he'd bring the dessert. His cupboard had enough home made cookies in it for him to declare war on the entire junk food industry.

Reverend Pocolis locked the door, which took a little longer than usual. His hands were shaking a little. He looked at his hands and wondered if it was the late coffee, the chocolate chip cookies, or did Paul's stories have more to them than he thought?

Paul was quietly thoughtful on the trip back. He felt better about things and felt that he had time to be prudent and observant. It was good advice, as always, from the Rev. He pulled up into his driveway and his wife met him with a hug and a kiss. She made sure he knew he was loved, then broke off long enough to tell him that he had an 'important call to return' light blinking on his private line. Paul said he would take it in his den and then closed the door behind him. The PC was open and the light indicated a video and audio connect was requested. The return number was familiar to him, so he hit one of the speed connects.

"Paul here." He could see the same gathering as before on the top half of the screen, with all three of his compatriots on the lower half. "What's shaking up north?"

Ryan didn't stand up this time, but he still commanded attention. "OK, Paul completes the Second String arrivals. First of all, the good news. Marianne and Ralph are getting hitched in holy wedlock!" Paul may be slightly narrow sighted, but slow thinking was not part of that equation. 'Holy wedlock' in the Family? Thanks Rev. Quick work on the sign. Paul leaned back, smiled, and then prepared himself for the inevitable 'and now the bad news'.

"We made contact with the mystery ghost and he made contact right back at us." That got Paul sitting up straight. From what he could see of the other Second Stringers, Ryan hadn't gotten to this point, yet. "There is a second body below the casket that actually does have Cassandra in it. We have a double occupancy here, with the ditch-hiker underneath the coffin. The ground-sounders were on a second testing run when something came out of the area of interest and fried their equipment to slag. I'm going to show you a sequence of images that the techies had left us with. They're on their way back to West Virginia as we speak and they won't need coffee to keep them awake for the trip. Dagmar, see if you can unruffle their feathers tomorrow morning, won't you?"

"I'll try, Ryan, but you don't make things easy."

"Understood. Check out the first image." The Family group shot was replaced on the distance participant's screens by varying shades of green. The coffin was obvious, despite the interference from various objects of natural earthly origin. "The next one has the rocks and metallic doodads on the coffin screened out." Much clearer, though the green colors were spooky looking. "Number three has the wood and man made materials screened out and greater penetrating power on the signal. There were more technical words involved in creating the high quality of the images, but they were spoken in tech-speak gibberish." The collective intake of breath came with the image of a woman who died in terror, clawing at the casket that held her from life. There was a rumbling in the ranks of every variation of 'God, no!' imaginable. "As you can see, Mrs. Petrocelli was not deceased at the time of burial. The other occupant, though, was most likely dead when the coffin was laid in the grave. Here's the last picture. I'm going to give you the cropped version at first." The picture showed a head and upper chest image, or, images. The clearest one was open-eyed and open mouthed. At the bottom of the screen, you could see her fingertips. Less clear, but still readable, was a second image. It was male and, even at this stage of decay, bore a resemblance to Mr. Marfan. It was somewhat obscured, though, as pieces of the top of the skull and his forehead were scattered.

"The tech team had filtered out all of the rock and metal artifacts. We still had that data, and I had them reinsert a particular bit of metal that they were able to isolate and return into the picture." On the image they had before them appeared the unmistakable outline of a handgun, the barrel resting under the jaw of the male. If you squinted just right, you could see the second figure's grip on the weapon. "There was sufficient dirt between the man and the coffin for me to assume that he had gotten to the gravesite, covered himself up sufficiently not to be seen, took a breath, covered his face, then pulled the trigger. I suspect he wanted to spend eternity in the ground with his beloved, which makes Mr. Marfan my 'A Number One' suspect. I believe Mrs. Petrocelli had met with an untimely end at Mr. Marfan's initiative…if not by his hands, than at least by his design. But this may never be proven unless we can extract a posthumous confession. Now, if you will watch carefully, you will catch a glimpse of what fried the equipment." The view backed off to a full coffin vantage. There was something rising from the center of the bodies. It was vague, glowing and lightening shaped. "I'm opening the floor to suggestions."

Rachel was the first to dive in, for she had been thinking about this for a while. "Why should we do anything? If a murder has been done, then the murderer has been punished, both by his death and by being stuck underground for what likely may be for a very long time, indeed. The man loved nature above the ground and now may spend centuries under it. What punishment could be beyond that and, for that matter, who are we to decide on whether the man is punished or not?"

Zachary: "Yet, by taking an attitude of 'let the bastard rot in his own muddy bed', we ARE judging and punishing. You've told me that you move stuck spirits along their path and where they go from there is beyond our scope of practice. To paraphrase and modify a 70's right wing sentiment, boot'em all upstairs and let God sort'em out."

Melissa: "Why would God want to bother with such a bastard?"

Paul: "God has bothered with many such bastards throughout the Bible and in more modern times. I've seen my share of people who came out of jail. Those who found God while there came out as changed men and women. A much higher percentage of those who didn't usually found their way back to prison."

Russ: "Not to throw a possible damper on the nice, neat picture here, folks, but we don't know for sure that the other fellow in the grave, the body, that is, is Marfan. There was some rot and post-gunshot disfigurement. Might it also be the murdered remains of Mr. Petrocelli?"

Allen: "Good point, but unlikely if you compare the lateral size of the two heads; that's the ear to ear measurement for you non-forensic folk. Lincoln Marfan was a slender, smaller framed man. Steve Petrocelli was a lot more heavy set. That isn't absolute proof that the entity and the body there are one or both belonging to Mr. Marfan, but it does up the confidence level a bit. Sorry we didn't mention that earlier, Russ. Forgot how thorough and detail conscious you government spooks are."

Russ: "No hard feelings, CEO. Oh, we'll be auditing your empire sometime, say, tomorrow?"

Marianne: "What has me worried is that the entity is a loose cannon that might pop off at someone just out of spite or chance misunderstanding. That was quite a whollop he packed into that ground-sound device. What happens should someone dig another grave next door to him?"

Frank: "Has anyone considered asking the fellow his opinion? The entity, I mean." The silence that followed prompted clarification. "We are all proceeding on assumptions. Most of us have heard that silly joke about what happens when you assume, and no, I'm NOT going to repeat it, thank you! Perhaps, before we decide on a course of action, we ought to extend a choice to what may very well be a destitute, remorseful, frightened spirit. We've already heard that he fears Hell, fears being found. He probably now feels that he has been found and is unsure as to what to do now. You know, even a condemned man might at least get an opportunity to confer with a man of the cloth. Maybe none of us are the right ones to lay the cards on the cribbage table for him." Rachel beamed at her husband. The short time since she had left her home, so much had changed in both of them and she was absolutely tickled with all of it.

Dagmar: "Well, Ryan, do you have a Purgatory Padre somewhere handy? It would be a bit complicated sending out applications for this particular penance giving."

Paul: "Actually, it might not be all that difficult. People, I have a confession to make and beg all of you your forgiveness. After that, I have a very good possibility of someone who would give this a go, if you were willing to let him try. By the way, the man I have in mind was a criminal psychologist before changing vocations."

While Paul related his talk to his church leader, Franklin Pesko had dropped his own little bomb at The Inn. "You want us to run the show, Mr. Pesko? Me and Hammer? What happened to Chuck? Won't he be here anymore?

He let me do all the inventory."

"Did he now, Barry? Well, wasn't that nice of him? Well, if that is what you like, you can just go right on doing all the inventory for me." Franklin Pesko felt a little funny about giving out work as a reward, but the savant seemed so happy about it. Go figure. "Chuck and I had a nice long chat about things and we decided, together, that he would be far better off at an alternative career. There's a casino up in New Jersey that he's going to be working at. His job is to make sure that people do not steal from their employer. I'm sure he will do fine there." He didn't go further to mention that this particular casino had been known for creative employee management techniques for those who broke the house rules, like fractured knee caps, and that was just for a suspected first offense. He didn't want these two promising employees to think their boss was a vengeful man. Hammer hadn't said anything, but was looking at his boss and scratching his chin. Franklin Pesko caught the look. Well, thought The Inn's owner, at least Barry wouldn't have that illusion.

"Is HE gone, Sweetheart? I really gave it to him, didn't I? That makes up for that oaf of a football freak that gave me the nuggies at college. Are you happy with me, Cassie Love? Honey? Please answer me."

"Reverend Pocolis here, is that you, Paul? Did something happen? Hey, that's fantastic! I'm really happy for you. What? Uh, run that by me again, slowly. You want me to talk to a dead murderer...uh-huh...and convince him to stop hiding from judgment...and to see if there's something I can come up with by way of salvation after death? Is that all? Oh, you want me there tomorrow, Saturday, and I'll be back for services on Sunday. But my schedule is...oh, you called the deacons and they'll cover for me. That was very nice of you. But, my car is on the fritz, and I...transportation is arranged? Yes. The tickets will be waiting at Delta. Yes, I understand. Of course. I'll be met there at the gate? Fine. No, it's not a problem. Yes, I'm sure. Have a pleasant night. Good night, Paul."

This went beyond coffee, tobacco, and cookies put together. Reverend Pocolis went to a rarely used Low Boy and pulled out a rarely used drawer. From it, he withdrew a never used 20-year-old bottle of Jack Daniels and let it breath air for the first time in its long life. A tumbler was loaded with a generous helping of ice and then it was back to the chair by the fireplace.

"Save a murderer's soul after he has died? How in God's Name am I supposed to do that?" Praying for a departed soul, saying that they had lived a good life and that this was hopefully sufficient for passage into Heaven was the meat and potatoes of most of his funeral work regarding those whose lives were less than religious, more delicately worded, of course. What had Paul gotten him into? And it took place in a Yankee graveyard? Jolene must be turning in her southern grave on this one.

His formal education had stipulated that you had the time from when your heart started beating till the time it stopped to find the Lord and gain salvation. However, there were always those nagging exceptions that kept popping up as unanswerable questions, such as what happens to infants who die? You couldn't say that they didn't live long enough to sin, because the Bible says we were born IN sin. You couldn't go the route of the child returning to try again in another life, for any mention of multiple lives would get you into instant hot water from a dozen Christian organizations who had strong opinions regarding that arena. All you could say was that God didn't mean for an innocent life to be denied salvation and, that in His infinite grace and wisdom, He has made a path for such tiny feet to trod. It sounded nice, but for all he knew, it was a sham. He reached for the tumbler to find it only had ice cubes in it. Wasn't that glass full a moment ago? Must have forgotten to pour the drink. Getting too old for this sort of thing. Short-term memory loss. He (re)filled it and took a long, tender sip.

Perhaps the idea was not so much to save, as it was to convince the spirit that turning himself in would result in a less harsh judgment than they would receive if he (or was it a she…Paul didn't say) waited till Judgment Day. Clemency/amnesty for turning one's self in, sort of. But how could he propose that? He had no control of that sort of stuff. "How can I know such things? I'm just a human, for Christ's sake. Ooops. Sorry." How was he supposed to talk to spirits, anyway? He'd never done it before. Maybe these people Paul spoke about would interpret for him. He looked at the tumbler. Is there a hole in that blasted glass? He filled it again, finding both inner warmth and creative solutions arising with each sip.

Maybe they could call up the spirit of Billy Graham, then get a nice choir to sing in the background. That might lure the son of a bitch…oops, sorry…out. Hey, it could happen. These people could do it! Sure, he had nothing to worry about. Piece of cake, or better yet, chocolate kip chookie (yawn). There was a pad and pencil by the chair. Reverend Pocolis made a few attempts to arrange both in his hands for some proper note taking. Squinting a few times to get the paper into focus, "Better put shum ideash on paper, sho I…can…beeee…zzzzz."

Zachary came back from Marianne's front door. "Hey! Who ordered the flowers?" FedEx had delivered three large bundles of beautiful arrangements, each addressed to the ladies of the group. One for Marianne, one for Rachel, and one for Melissa. There was no note, or any indication of who sent them. The surprise had men and women chattering on who might have sent them, each man denying and regretting their lack of responsibility in the deed. Each bundle of flowers was tied with a red ribbon, and on each ribbon there was inked in the first name of the recipient and a small hand-drawn picture. With Melissa's, it was a winged foot. Marianne's had a military parachute image.

Both turned to Rachel, who was beginning to giggle to beat the band. They both asked Rachel what her picture was and she showed them a hand sketched ice cream cone. It wasn't very much of a mystery to any of the recipients, and Vanessa punctuated the correct guess by taking her fist and repeatedly struck her other open hand, pivoting at the elbow. Most shouted out in unison, "HAMMER!"

Frank and Zachary were standing together, since Rachel had opted for feminine company for flower comparisons. Frank asked, "Did you understand that bit of humor?"

"Not a bit of it, old bean. I'm sure someone will explain it for the handicapped if we are patient and look pathetic enough."

The evening wore on for another half hour and, other than a frantic call from Kingston Limo to apologize for their driver's abandonment of their premier clients in the middle of a graveyard, there was nothing else of note or amusement. People began to filter out and things got suddenly quiet. Too quiet. Ralph looked around and saw only Marianne, Ebony, and a lot of cups and plates stacked up in the sink. "Marianne, where did everyone go?"

Marianne came out of the bedroom and looked around at the uncharacteristic solitude. "Why, those little dears. Hey, handsome, leave the dishes for tomorrow."

"If you say so. I'll get the couch bed together."

Marianne looked at her fiancé. She liked the way that sounded. She looked at the ring on her finger, where once another ring had rested. She liked the way it felt. "I don't think so." Ralph stopped pulling the cushions off of the sofa bed and looked at Marianne, standing at her bedroom door, unbuttoning her shirt. "I'm not *that* Catholic."

Rachel lay next to her husband. She had been so proud of him today. To think that the man was worried that he wouldn't make a contribution to the Family. What a fine day it had been, other than her almost needing a new pair of panties at the cemetery out of fear for Allen's life. Some life! This one had acquired her son, her son's girlfriend, her husband, and herself, not to mention the half dozen others. She wondered if Jerry and Janet might also be sucked into the Fitzgalen army. Still, there were so many wonderful points to counter the fears.

Those three flower arrangements! They were big enough to put a whole beehive into ecstasy. She smiled a little to think of her ice cream slam-dunk on the poor man. Well, he deserved it at the time, but it would appear that 'Ol' Hammer' has made a bit of a come back to civilization. That was so nice of him.

Rachel could picture the three bouquets, each being held by three couples: her and Frank, Allen and Melissa, Ralph and Marianne (yawn). That image remained with her as she began to slip into a partial dream state, where the three dimensions of conscious musings began to change into the far deeper dimensions of dreaming. Rachel could now literally see the three flower arrangements, though the people they were sent to were no longer in the picture. In their place was a narrow but wide table. The table had a tablecloth, but it was wispy and shroud like. On the table were three vases. They were tall and crystalline, seemingly identical with only one exception. The one on the far left, the one that had been held by her and Frank, was cut in half in a line going from top to bottom. The two halves were held together with that red ribbon, the one that had at first held her flowers together. She walked up to the table and looked at the ribbon. The image of the ice cream cone was gone. Replacing it was a clock face. More upsetting than that was the ribbon itself. It was unraveling. A single thread was being pulled from it by something she couldn't see. The room she had thought she was standing in was no longer a room. It had turned into a valley. To the west, the sun was beginning to set, creating elongating shadows all about her. Dark shadows. The line of the thread extended off to the eastern horizon, which now showed hills opposite from the ones where the sun was setting. It got worse.

Something was wrong with one of the bouquets, the one on the far left, her bouquet. Half the flowers were wilting, losing their color, bending over, and crumbling. Why? Why was this happening? No! NO! "Noooooo…"

Rachel woke. Frank was gently shaking her and calling her name. "Honey, you were having a nightmare. Are you OK?"

It took her a headshake or two to get her bearings. "Yeah, I guess so. I had the weirdest dream." She told her husband of what she had seen, but neither of them could (or would) tell why it would have such a great fright factor. It was almost prophetic in its content flavor, but why would it be nightmarish?

She yawned, comforted now to be in Frank's reassuring arms. "I'll ask the Family about it tomorrow, maybe. Good night, Frank. I love you."

Frank returned the sentiment, but didn't go to sleep right away. Rachel was too close to the situation to see the true meaning in the dream, for despite the multiple images within her dream, there was only one meaning. He was newer to and less immersed in the Family than she was, so he could be more objective. He also knew his wife and had heard her dreams relayed to him in the past. Finally, he had already begun to wonder about the similarities of what Ryan went through in the Navy to what had happened at the Edwards Estate. He suspected consciously what his wife feared in that part of her mind that didn't speak in words, but rather in images. The sighted members of the Family would long outlive the Second String, Zachary, and himself.

XIV   SATURDAY

"Hey, Kurt. Long face, chum."

"Hey, Hammer. Yeah, bad run. Kid and his car argued with a tree. Nobody won. Buy me a soda, will you?"

"Sure. What kind?"

"Brown and fizzy, with some sugar and caffeine."

"A man with classic tastes. Be right there." Kurt was sitting in the room that all ER's have, where emergency personnel get to fill out their reports. At least now they didn't have the quadruplicate copies that used to be the norm. Reports were still all quadruplicated, but now they were simplified computer entries that were shunted to proper locations electronically. Hammer came back with a couple of cans, both opened. "What happened to the car's fail safes? Fail to function?"

"Nah, they did the best they could. Kid was pushing ninety and went into a spin. Impact was to the driver's door. Car was torn in half. Front and side bags deployed, but there's a limit to what they can forgive you for. It was one of those weird ones where the girlfriend was in the next seat over and didn't have hardly a scratch on her body." Kurt didn't have to go into the psychological damage she would have to deal with. "Records showed his folks are out in Macon and are Episcopalian. We got denominations on call for most sects and beliefs."

Hammer had never heard that. "Didn't know they did that. Pretty thoughtful of them."

"Kinda. Actually, there was a group of people who got together fifteen years ago and hit a dozen hospitals in a class action suit for emotional trauma on how they informed the next of kin. Read about it a long time ago and I couldn't blame those people. ER's have always been running the thin side of staffing since I can remember and people get pretty stretched out here, but to be called by some nurse who just blurts out point blank that your kid is in the morgue and you need to come and fill out the paperwork immediately; common decency there doesn't even enter into the equation. Hammer, you sure you want a piece of this? You ever see death?"

"Yeah. Couple times. Stupid shit, mostly. One jackass in our pack overdosed. Saw him do it, too. Most of us don't do that shit anymore and it ain't like he weren't warned. Another was a road hazard. Car ahead of the pack must have sprung a leak from the oil pan. I saw the fluid hit the road and was able to avoid it. Guy and his chick on the bike behind me hit the slick, slid and went ass over teakettle over the cliff, leaving his hog jammed under the guardrail. They were decent folks, married even. No kids, thank

God."

Kurt thought that he'd better let the big fellow see the whole picture. "Hammer, even with my training, there probably wouldn't be much that could be done for any of them. That's one thing you gotta know ahead of time. It's better than it used to be, but more often than not we're there to just go through the motions for the sake of the loved ones left behind and for ourselves. All of us have to know that we gave it our best shot, that we gave that person the best chance to come back, but it was just that person's time to go. There's a lot of politics in this job, which you do your level best to stay out of, plus a lot of paperwork and a truckload of heartaches. You have to be able to put all that behind you because each time you win, man, there's nothing like it you will ever experience in your life. We've given parents back their kids, and kids back their parents. Everyone we bring back is somebody's loved one. It's getting so's I can't buy my own diner meals anymore. Been at this so long that I've helped almost every local's family in one way or another."

Hammer thought about that. He'd been 'free' of a lot of things that dragged most people down by his former choice of lifestyle. That was fine, but it also freed you from some pretty good stuff Hammer had found himself wishing for. Seemed that every ten years or so, all of your priorities did a major shift. Being appreciated and respected for more than just a quick fist or how many ladies were on his dance card was a new thing wakening in his heart. "Kurt, I want this, for real. Tell me what I need to study and I'll get started today. I know it won't be easy, but, I'm going to do it." Hammer had an intensity in his eyes as he looked into Kurt's cloud gray ones. "I want what you got and I'll bust my ass to get it."

Kurt smiled and pulled a MiDi out of his shirt pocket. "Thought (hoped) you might say that. Let's see how much of what's in here you can stuff into that melon head of yours. It'll take you two days just to scan it, two weeks to give it a decent read and probably half a year before you can make it work on even the entry level emergency grunt. I'll help, but it has to be all you."

"Thanks, Kurt. Nice to know I got two friends, now. Gotta go. Sorry about the kid."

With that, the big man got up and went back to his duties. Kurt watched him leave, thinking about the things he had heard about Hammer recently. He felt good about being the big guy's friend. Sure beat being his enemy by a long shot. He figured Hammer was in for more moral support than he knew. Kurt had buddies who visited The Inn where Hammer was now the chief bartender and bouncer. That guy would NOT let you drink and drive. America, Kurt thought, was the only country where a biker gang leader could grow up almost overnight and become a role model, sort of. A crash and some screams broke Kurt out of his reverie. He raced out of the cubical to see something that made even his jaded blood chill.

"Code 12, Code 12, ER, Code 12, ER." Psychiatric emergency. It was a guy the police had dropped off just before he had gotten there. Mainly, the man had looked drunk and just had passed out, from what the charge nurse had told him earlier. He had been put on a bed and was kept an eye on, but not enough of an eye. The guy had two nurses and the ER doc against a corner just outside the reception half-walled staff cubical. The nut had gotten ahold of a pair of scissors in one hand and held a pillow in the other in some bizarre imitation of someone with a sword and shield. He was advancing, ranting about stolen clothes and needles in his arm. The blood on the pillow-shield showed where the IV had been ripped out. Kurt was about to make a sprint for the man when he saw Hammer ease his way into the ER kiosk at a low crouch. The man was absolutely silent, moved with a grace that was belied by his size, and he moved *fast*. Two seconds later, the would-be knight was dangling from Hammer's left hand that had grabbed onto his shirt. The idiot tried to whip his weapon hand around to jab the scissors at Hammer, only to have the wrist of that hand caught, deftly, by Hammer's right. A quick snap of the wrist and the scissors dropped to the floor.

"Where would you like me to put him, Doc?" The ER MD wasn't sure. At the end of Hammer's arm was a cursing flailing madman. Fortunately, security arrived a few moments later. It took a full four minutes to secure the arms and legs and for a light sedative to take effect. The two formerly threatened nurses then threw their arms around the big man and gave him kisses on his cheek. One of them was old enough to be his mother, but other one? Well, sure beat his reception with Blondie and Spic Chick. Hammer spent the rest of his shift with two lip prints on his cheeks, refusing to wash them off. The picture of him so adorned was installed in the staff break room, and someone had written on it: 'Our Hero, Raggedy Biker Andy'.

As Hammer wound down his shift, dawn was breaking on the Parsonage. Someone was knocking. That was not very nice of them, given the size of his head. Reverend Daniel Pocolis stood up, regretted it, then made his way to the front door. It could be a death, or a birth, or a…uniformed limo driver?

"Sir, we need to leave in fifteen minutes at the latest. Just throw some clothes in a bag. I've got fresh coffee in the car. Here, you'll find these work pretty good. They're homeopathic."

The good Reverend did as he was told, putting the suggested five tablets under his tongue, then trotted off quickly to washcloth himself and change his clothes. He threw an extra pair of briefs and socks into a bag, with another shirt. Wasn't he going north? He grabbed a sweater.

In the limo, moving east at a good clip, the Rev enjoyed his first sip of coffee. The head size had reduced quite a bit, surprisingly quickly. "Son, what was the name of that stuff you gave me just a few minutes ago?"

"It's a hangover relief, sir. It's called 'Pardon'." That wasn't a good

241

sign. He had found that days that began with twisted ironies remained unpredictable for the rest of the day. That would prove to be the greatest understatement of his life.

Ralph opened his eyes. Nestled on his shoulder and against his cheek was a warm perfusion of very dark hair. Arms and legs of two lovers were comfortably entangled and his heart was at peace. They had met each other only a week and a half ago. Yet, all that they had gone through had made it seem like a year. His heart had a thousand things he wanted to tell this woman. He wanted to tell her about his parents, his childhood, his successes and failures, his dreams and so much more. Ralph then noticed Marianne's eyes gently flutter open and heard the most interesting 'grrrrrr'. Well, maybe they'd talk later.

Rachel and Frank were up and about. Allen and Melissa were stretching and yawning in Allen's old room. They had gotten the call from Zachary, who had gone with Ryan to bunk on his couch, regarding the morning plans. Jerry and Janet were both at their respective sleepovers and would be hanging out there for the rest of the day. Vanessa was back at Marianne's, purportedly to keep Ebony from being a pest. Gustav had opted for some private time and was watching the dawn while standing in that dell at the Rhinebeck Cemetery. He could see the blackened ground-sound device still there, though the hissing and smoking had long since ceased.

They had learned so much about this Mr. Marfan, he thought, but knew so little. Was Marfan mind-fractured, like Annie was? Certainly he was possessed of considerable power he could unleash, like Annie. Marfan trashed electrical stuff, like she could, but in a different way. Her power was more vibratory and thermal, according to Russ's analysis on the damaged cameras from the Estate; his was more like lightening. He was hiding from God or Hell, take your pick, lying in the grave of his one time lover. That didn't sound sane. He blew his head off and consigned the one he loved to a most horrible death. That definitely wasn't sane. So, great unleashable power seemed to be the purview of mentally deranged spirits. Wasn't that a lovely thought? Annie had a good side as well as a dark side, throw in a crazy side for fun. Where were Mr. Marfan's other sides? Were there any? Could he find out something now? Worth a shot, as long as he kept his distance. "HEY!"

From over the hill to his left, he heard a distant, *"Yes?"* It was a feminine voice.

He thought, *"We missed one, I see."* Calling out loud, he shouted, "I was talking to my neighbor, here. I'll come and visit you, later!"

"All right. Hurry back."

From the site Gustav was interested in, then came, *"Well, don't you get around? Did you get her tombstone number?"*

Humor? *"I'll dig it up later."*

"A lawyer with a sense of humor. You surprise me. What did you specialize in?"

"Oh, started out with anything I could get, but got into small business."

"So, how'd you bite it? Angry client?"

Gustav had to smile at that. In a way it was true. The fractured part of Annie they were battling was indeed fit to be tied. He sensed loneliness in that voice. *"Not far from the truth, though the autopsy said heart failure."*

"Me, too, kind of, in a way. (Gustav walked a few feet closer) You married?"

"Twice, didn't work out either time. Had a son, but he died in childhood."

"That's too bad. Sorry to hear it. Hey, what season is it? Can you see?"

"I can see. It's early October. Leaves are pretty well gone, few hanger ons. Plenty of evergreens here."

Talking about trees stirred warm memories in Lincoln's heart. *"I remember there was a patch of Douglas fir nearby. Most of the rest was Maple, Elm, a couple of Dogwood, and a big mother Oak."*

"You know your trees, friend. Were you a botanist or ranger or something?"

"I was with the New York Department of Conservation. Did a lot of forestry work in the Catskills ('Bingo', thought Gustav, and he walked a few more paces closer). *Hey, did you have anything to do with land development?"*

Silently, "Uh oh, careful." Aloud, "Yeah, but you'd like it. Special interest condo's that were built along Sierra guidelines. For every tree that went down, two went up." That was actually true and good thing it was. Vanessa had warned Gustav about how spirits couldn't lie to spirits and get away with it. What a horrible fate for a lawyer.

"Heard there were a few of those around. Not damned enough, though. It still matters to me, you know? Hey, can you see the tree colors and everything? Can you feel anything being up there?"

"I can see fine, just like before I died. Better, actually. My astigmatism's gone. Can't smell anything, can't feel the wind or touch like I used to, but there are other sensations. You can pass your hand through a tree and feel the life force resist you. Leave your hand in a trunk and you can sense something like a tingle of life tickling you. It's subtle, but you can sense it if you try." Gustav was now standing close to where Allen and the techies had stood the night before. The ground-sound box still stood, no longer smoking.

"God, that sounds sweet. There's wisdom in a tree. I remember feeling that, sometimes."

Gustav had talked to felons and other types of criminals many times. He knew that even the vilest had soft spots in their hearts, somewhere. He recalled a mass murderess named Buley, now on death row. She had never been able to sleep without her teddy bear. Mr. Marfan, for that had just been proven, sounded sane. At least, this part of him was.

Lincoln Marfan took in all of what was said. The part of him that hungered for company, for interaction, now began to come up against a wall. That wall separated him from the part of him that had murdered his lady's husband, then caused unspeakable cruelty on that same woman and, in the process, denied himself from pursuing the things in life he had come to understand as important. That part of Lincoln Marfan now came to the forefront. Gustav felt the ground change mood and military instincts caused him to dive behind the same neighboring stone Allen had made for earlier. From the ground, a split second later, came, *"GET THE HELL OUT OF HERE!"*, coinciding with a flash of power that crackled the air.

When a few moments had passed, Gustav peeked around the stone to find that the ground-sound box was no longer there. *"Where did it go? Did he vaporize it?"* Seconds later, it landed not five feet next to him, sizzling.

"Another time, then." Gustav made sure he was a good thirty feet away before delivering that line. Now, since he was here, why not take a stroll over that hill and meet that nice lady. *"Hellooo? I've come to pay a visit, madam."*

While Gustav introduced himself, Ralph spoke into the phone held by his one free hand. "He wants pancakes? All right. WHERE? They'd better be damn good pancakes. Right, we'll meet you there; Marianne knows the way, right? OK. Bye. Marianne, Honey, hit the skids. Ryan has a pancake panic attack."

"That would mean Rock City (yawn). Nice little family place, homey, cozy."

"You mean it's little."

"You obviously would never make it in the real estate industry."

"C'mon, sweet lady, we gotta make tracks. Why don't you hit the shower first?"

"IF we have to save time, why not shower together? (Giggle)."

"Lady, will you please save a little something for the wedding night?"

"Honey, you haven't seen anything, yet." She left for the shower, leaving Ralph to decide whether to follow or not.

The sign said 'The Best Little Pancake House'. The décor inside was 1950's, as was the music. Half the menu was pancakes and it smelled like coming home. There had been a couple of remodelings and expansions, and a period of time where it had been out of business, but the ambience had been maintained and so had the portions. One end of the single room dining area had been cordoned off after an early morning phone call. It had forewarned them of soon to arrive guests that may not fill that area with bodies, but would make up for it on gratuities as they had done in the past. Four tables had been merged into a large square and eight people joined to break bread. Ryan sat with right hand man Ralph at his right. The waitress thought it odd that he insist on the two corner seats to his left remaining empty. She had been told to set for ten, but breakfast would be for eight, so she asked a fellow waitress if that wasn't something to do with Sabbath. Were they Jewish? Her co-worker shrugged.

Ryan looked to Ralph. Marianne was sitting to Ralph's right, chattering away with Rachel and Melissa. Ralph was uncharacteristically quiet. "Ralph, you OK? The waitress wants your order."

"Huh? Oh, yeah. You got any pancakes with vitamins in them? Uh, all right, I'll take the banana walnut with bacon, crisp. You're welcome. Ryan, you could have warned me."

Ryan made absolutely no effort to hide his smirk. "No idea what you're talking about, son. I'll have the strawberry Belgian waffle with the ham, double order. You're welcome. Has anyone seen Gustav?"

Vanessa said, *"He'll know where to find us. Didn't say where he was going, though. Just wanted some think time."*

On cue, Gustav showed up right after the coffee was poured and the last order taken, looking like the classic cat after the canary match. Frank was sitting next to Zachary and Rachel, and heard the length of silence, the new direction of gazes and the look on faces change. Frank leaned to Zachary and said, "If I remember right, this is where we alter our soccer matches. Yes?"

An earlier reference to the UN had given Allen the inspiration to try a different approach to the interpretation routine. Rather than distracting the entity who was speaking by repeating every word, or paraphrasing after a pause, Frank and Zachary had been issued each a 'read only' display card tuned into a very thin and portable transcription pad that Marianne was even now engaged in using. Her light taps on the pad were not distracting at all and the two hearing impaired Family members could now at least read it from the horse's mouth.

"While scouting about the Rhinebeck Cemetery, I stumbled across Mrs. Bernedette Lawson, who suffers from a chronic coffin condition." Ryan admonished Vanessa for giving Gustav humor lessons. Gustav 'harrumphed' at the interruption, then continued. *"The old gal is firmly convinced that she is in a deep cryofreeze, as was specifically stated in her will that she be so once it was determined that nothing that then current technology could offer would help her condition. Her condition, essentially, was that she was an aging socialite battle-ax. Her site is a short stroll from Mr. Marfan's."* That Gustav would use that name as a fact forewarned everyone that their target site had been pre-visited. Their expressions were easily read by the speaker. *"OK, maybe it wasn't too smart of me to try it solo, but I felt I had to make up for my poor showing the first time I talked with him. Mr. Marfan has similarities to Annie. He has, to some degree, a fractured personality, though they aren't time bound for appearance. The one is a true lover of nature and seems a fairly likeable fellow who is extremely lonely. The counterpart is very testy, untrusting and threw a bolt that launched the ground-sound equipment for a hang time of about eight seconds. Likable Lincoln would treasure a view of the trees and, I believe, is truly contrite over past actions. Mad Marfan, hope you don't mind my poetic license, limits his spoken intercourse to the coarse."*

Marianne was eyeing the speaker. "You didn't get up close to that cannon, did you?"

"*Madam, I would have been foolish to do so, now wouldn't I?*"

Vanessa knew Gustav's talent for misdirecting an answer, and nodded. "*Singed your butt hairs, did he?*"

"*Madam, they will grow back. Mad Marfan does not have any spirits held in thrall other than likable Lincoln, so if we are to liberate anyone it will be that we are freeing this soul from himself. Nor has he shown any propensity for long distance voodoo, which should give Allen a breath of relief. The blast I saw this morning was not preceded by a drop in local temperature that I could tell. Allen, did you feel any such caloric fall? You did? Perhaps the ground insulated that effect for me or I wasn't close enough to be in his energy-gathering field. Hmmm, since he's a member of the underground, perhaps he gathers from something other than the atmosphere. He doesn't have quite the aim accuracy for thunderbolts as Annie did, but then, he's six feet underground and can only aim by trying to mentally sense where his target is. The ground-sound was probably a no brainer for him, since the sound wave was highly funneled and directional. A voice, though, is a different matter altogether.*

"*We must still answer the question as to whether intervention is advisable here and I agree with Frank that laying out the cards on the line for the fellow is the only civilized thing to do. Paul's preacher, I take it, is on his way?*"

Marianne shook her hands a couple of times to get the cramps out, then looked at her time organizer card and tapped a few times on it. "He got on the plane about twenty minutes ago, direct flight, pickup, only carry-on baggage, drive time...we'll meet him at the house in an hour and forty-five minutes. Oooh, here's breakfast!"

Ralph could see why they liked the place for breakfast. "Good Lord, do they raise lumberjacks around here? This makes the truck stops look pantywaist. The cook must measure batter with his hat."

Ebony was back home, though Atlas had been brought along. Marianne had come to grips with the fact that having a kitten in tow at a restaurant was not a good idea. Maybe Atlas would give her some decorum lessons later. Atlas looked at the spread with wide eyes. There just *had* to be some doggie bags on this one.

Frank volunteered, "You know, the idea of just giving a shout may be a big time saver. That covers a lot of territory and seems to get a quick response. Might be best to have our entities in charge of that duty, as we mortals might earn some straight jackets for the effort."

Vanessa agreed, but said, "*I'd like to do more on learning Annie's way of mind reaching into the ground. I got the impression that the soldiers imprisoned in Annie's apron pocket were not able to be conversant. Suppose there are more like them being held against their wills? 'Shouting the battle cry of freedom' might not get an answer. We only found out about the slaves by luck.*"

Zachary looked at his translate card. "Vanessa? Oh, thank you, Marianne, for doing this. Don't let your stack get cold. This is almost like being able to talk directly to my entity friends. Anyway, without a master to teach the apprentice, how might you go about learning that skill?"

"*Nice to talk with you, too, Zachary. I made a lot of inroad on dirty talking with Mr. Marfan and Bernhardt. Annie had no one else to teach her. She must have figured things out for herself, so she didn't even have the head start I do. Then again, she had a century plus to perfect her art. Speaking of time to perfect arts, Melissa, did you tell anyone your intentions?"*

All eyes went to Melissa, giving Marianne a chance to grab her fork for a while. "At Rhinebeck Central, I found an opportunity to land a job right out of college by teaching the journalism classes. It will put me here for a while, at least, and get a good mark on my resume. I called Dagmar about it last night and she was not only all for it, she guaranteed me she would stop in twice a year as a guest lecturer. I scanned my app over to RCS, adding that offer from Dagmar, and got a call five minutes later from the Vice Principal. Half my tuition will be taken up by their teacher-prospecting fund. I'm already on their medical plan as of today and the current journalism teacher has sent me a 'Thank God For You' card."

After a round of applause, the conversation went from single speaker to multiple discussion groups, trying to find a path that made sense on what to do for Mr. Marfan. Previous experience with Annie helped in some ways, but hindered in others. The old answers didn't seem to apply here, but that didn't stop them from trying to apply them anyway. The preacher was a dark card and could be a joker or an ace. Rachel asked whether any Second Stringers might be up for today's attempt. Ryan smiled.

"Any of you remember Major Kenneth McGuinness? He's *enlisted* on our side, now, and used his pull to score military transport into the Guard base at Newburgh. The Major and Sgt. D'Palermo will be accompanied by three non-military Second String personnel and, if Marianne's estimate is correct, you will see them very soon." Two minutes later, a large camouflage painted vehicle that seemed inordinately wide and square pulled into the lot. Chairs were scooted over and more coffee was ordered. Friends joined hands or hugged, as the spirit or gender encouraged. Allen and Melissa decided they ought to get back and clean the litter box before the Reverend showed up. Atlas and Zachary decided to fill out their car capacity. Marianne passed out more read cards to the guests (Zachary passed on his to Paul when he left) and they all enjoyed the interchange immensely. The Major especially wanted to witness Vanessa's purported abilities to manipulate solid objects.

Marianne looked alarmed. "Vanessa, NO! You get it out of your head right now. That isn't Rachel; he's a major, for Heaven's sake. Please, something dull for a change? That's better. Major McGuinness, would you please hold out your pen?" He did. "Now, let go of it." He did. The pen stayed in the air, then slowly found it's way back to the Major's pocket.

"My God, it really is true. Who put that lettering in my window? Was that Vanessa?"

Ryan answered. "Sorry, Major, no. That was Gustav, the fellow whose body you found in the hedges at the Estate."

"My word. Say, would you please let me in on a secret. I would really like to know what was done that first night in your suite at the Marriott that got you all in such a case of the belly laughs?" Nunzia added her desires to that request and the rest chimed in as curious.

Ryan hadn't thought of that one for a while. His eyes shut and his shoulders began to bounce. Marianne was in close to the same condition. Ralph had the sobriety to begin the story. "Somewhere (snort) along the line, one of the ladies commented that Mr. Mendelssohn's legs had never seen the light of day. Our fearless leader also mentioned that the fellow would probably live and die in a three-piece suite. The good lawyer said then that he just might surprise everyone and, by God, that he did. Sergeant D'Palermo, what you and your entourage didn't see was…"

The waitresses were totting up the bill when they heard the lot of them screech and belly laugh. That was good. Happy patrons tipped more. They weren't disappointed.

Kingston Limo had breathed a sigh of relief at the new transportation order from the Hawthorn group. Even now, one of their best men was transporting a man of the cloth, at Mr. Hawthorn's request, from Stewart Airport. "So, how was your flight, Reverend Pocolis?"

"Well, not bad. First class is pretty nice, I must say. So's the fancy cab service. Who set all this up, if I might ask?"

"Sir, it's being funded by what's now known as Hawthorn Enterprises. Nice group of people, though a little eccentric. Made a lot of bucks I hear with special interest condos. They've been our best customers for years. Forgiving lot, too. Thought we'd lose them after one of our drivers took off and left a bunch of them in the middle of a graveyard last night after some piece of equipment blew up."

What was he getting himself into? "That's, interesting. Say, is there a place I can pick up an overcoat. I miscalculated the temperature up here. This sweater is just not going to make it if I'm going to be outside."

"Already taken care of, sir. Ms. Cabrini seems to think of everything when it comes to their guests. On the seat in the back you'll see a couple of boxes. Those are warm clothes, sir, and arctic grade. Someone in your parish was able to provide your size."

Maybe they *were* witches.

By the time the rest of the Family had arrived at Marianne's, Allen, Zachary and Melissa had finished up the cleaning from the night before. For some reason, clean up hadn't been gotten to by Marianne and Ralph that morning. First and Second String members were welcomed by a warm fire and classical music. Frank was especially pleased with the choice of Vivaldi's Four

Seasons. 'The Kids' liked working on making a home welcoming and the process had more than once found them catching each other's eyes and sharing warm fuzzies. Atlas was content to lie by the fire and make the big critters step around him as part of his personal empowerment program. Ebony was getting to be an attention fanatic. If she wasn't prospecting for laps, then she would be chasing wads of paper that someone would roll up and flick for her. This was the environment of congeniality and hospitality that Reverend Pocolis found when the door was opened for him by a smiling parishioner who, a day ago, wasn't so jolly.

"Thank you, Rev. We all really appreciate it. Nice coat, by the way." There was a gentle whirlwind of introductions, handshakes and insistences that he be made comfortable before the fire with food and drink. Rachel sat next to him on one of the lounge chairs and Paul on the other side on the same love seat. Reverend Pocolis noticed that Paul had scooped up the black kitten he had been formerly concerned about and was stroking it behind the ears. For a tiny fur ball, the kitten put out a motorboat purr.

"Well, Paul. This environment seems to agree with you. You're certainly more relaxed and your face shows some burden relief."

"Rev, the place is just a reflection of the people in it. I don't know if it's their purpose that's so infectious, or the people themselves. Maybe both. Everyone here will tell you that they've changed a lot in a short period of time."

Rachel was quick to join in and agree. "Reverend Pocolis, my marriage was about down the tubes and it was ninety-eight percent my husband's fault, as far as I was concerned. It took me a week here, but I realized that it was no one's fault, but it *was* one hundred percent my responsibility. You grow here and learn pretty quickly about what's petty and what's not. My husband, Frank, became involved a few days ago and even he's begun to change. Yesterday, he actually made a joke!"

From the kitchen came, "I heard that!" Reverend Pocolis smiled. It was nice to see a marriage mend. He had helped quite a few and, though getting on in years, he was still looking for new ways to help others. 'The day you stop learning is the day you start dying,' was a favorite saying of his.

Marianne came up from behind him and reintroduced herself. "You must be tired from your early flight. Here." And with that, she began to knead his shoulders and neck with experienced and caring hands. The Reverend's eyes went up to the ceiling and a long sigh escaped, tinged with a rapturous moan. It would appear that Paul's witch was actually an angel; it felt so good.

"Marianne, (just a little lower, yes, there, aahhh, bless you) I understand you are recently engaged. Congratulations! How long have you two known each other?"

"Couple of weeks, Rev." The man's eyes went wide open on that.. "I know, it sounds nuts. Time is funny, here. It's the work, I think, plus how people react with each other. The week we were involved with the Edwards Estate was the longest week of my life. Someone could easily write a book about it. Ralph came into our group during a crisis and it was, in large part, thanks to him that we kept our sanity. I have never met a man so gallant and strong since my Michael passed away."

Ryan kept back. Usually it was he who led things, but his Family was doing nicely without him. Chatting with his own beloved was more than sufficient for the time being. Melissa looked at the scene and thought something was missing on their welcome wagon. "Ah ha!" she thought.

In another minute, the Reverend now had his feet up on an Ottoman, his shoes off, and his toes wiggling happily in the fire's warmth. "I'll make a deal with you all," he said, "…once a month I will come up here for this kind of welcome, and in return, I'll bring all the extra home made cookies my flock makes for me. I'd need maybe one small U-Haul trailer."

Marianne announced the proposal to those out of earshot and the Family all chorused their acceptance of the offer. Major McGuinness came by and asked, "Say, has the good Rev been introduced to either of the spirits, here? No? Ms. Cabrini, where might they be standing right now? Oh. Very well, Reverend Daniel Pocolis, to the left of the fireplace is the spirit of Gustav Mendelssohn. Over there by the settee and talking to Ryan is the spirit of his wife, Vanessa."

Rachel was a pretty good hand at the keyboard, and Marianne's hands were right where they should be, so she took a turn. Allen gave Rev the read card. He looked at it, and on the display there was a 'G', followed by, "So glad to make your acquaintance, sir. I look forward to working with you today. Would you care for the perfunctory display of ghostly manifestation?"

Rachel spoke up. "He talks like that. For us po-talkin folk, dat means dat duz you wan him to do some spooky stuff?"

"He isn't going to shout 'boo', or something like that, is he?"

Marianne was about to say that the man was too stuffy for such things, but remembered what happened the last time she had challenged him about that issue. "Gustav is diplomatic, Rev. I'm sure he will exercise restraint, as he always has."

There was a general snicker. Rev looked around and saw Rachel motion to the card in front of him. He looked down and saw the response.

G: "Horse droppings! Very well, something dignified."

Rev followed where the others were looking, and their gaze shifted to where Paul was sitting, specifically, to the kitten on his lap, which began to float off Paul's lap, still purring, eyes still closed. The kitten moved through the air, and gently landed on Rev's lap, just as content as before (even more so, as this lap was much softer). Reverend Pocolis stared at the flying feline and noticed that the read card right next to Ebony began to display something.

G: "Will that suffice, Reverend Pocolis?"

"I would say so, Mr. Mendelssohn." Dagmar and Nunzia saw the levitation and likewise marveled. Rev noticed then that not all eyes had followed the spirit's progress at first. "Am I to understand that some of you can see the ghosts, should I call them that, and others can't?"

Dagmar brought the clergyman up to speed on what had occurred at the Edwards Homestead during the previous week, using her talents of encapsulation and descriptive language. The recounting brought the whole Family together to listen, for it was also the story of what had forged a new phase of what they were becoming. That fully convinced Rev, beyond doubt, that this group, this home, had nothing whatsoever to do with anything Satanic. He also understood a lot better on how two people could know each other for two weeks and have it be worth years of gradual 'getting to know you'. "If only I were a younger man," he sighed. "Even so, I still have my flock."

Russ had been leaning against the fireplace and felt it was his turn to speak. 'If it please the Family, might I make a proposal?" The rest knew what he had in mind and told Russ so with their eyes. "Seeing no disagreement," Rev and the Major both shook their heads; did they miss something? "...Reverend Daniel Pocolis, Major Kenneth McGuinness, as a member of the vaunted Second Stringers contingent of the Fitzgalen Family and behalf of all of us, I offer both of you official memberships into our group. Know ye that First Stringers devote far more of their time and energies to the mission that we. Our job is to support when called upon, occasionally come up here to visit, ride in limousines and eat a lot. Would you be willing to take on those tasks and responsibilities in return for the honor of serving the Man in a very important and unique service?"

Reverend Pocolis didn't have to think twice, especially after being seduced by the neck rub. "My children, I would be honored to be your Friar Tuck. I am an old man, but what time I have on earth that I can pull from my duties at home, you are welcome to. My home, in turn, is open to any of you, any time."

Paul added, "He means that, everyone. Rev is your spiritual convenience store, open twenty-four hours, seven days a week."

The Major looked at Nunzia, who came over and gave him a 'daughterly' hug. "My helmet's in the ring under one condition." Allen asked the Major to lay it on the line. "I will join this august group only if my fellow inductee will stop hogging the masseuse and give me a turn."

"No need, Sir." Nunzia escorted her Superior Officer to the second rocker/recliner next to the Reverend, sat him down, and surprised him with a talent his young soldier had never told him about.

Ryan looked at his watch after the Major had sufficient time to melt, then at how his Family was evolving, yet again. The Fitzgalen blob engulfs two more victims, film at eleven. It was time. "People, saddle up. This posse is about to ride. Everyone scratch kitty litter now if you have to. Facility availability at the cemetery is somewhat grave."

That did it. Ralph, Zachary and Allen had discussed what to do if another horrible pun made its way into the conversation, especially if it was the Boss who did it. Ralph was the biggest, so he blocked Ryan's effort to get out of his chair. Zachary and Allen trotted to the kitchen and grabbed two rolls of paper towels, then proceeded to hand them out to the Family, three wads to a customer. That being accomplished, Ryan was hoisted to his feet by Ralph and Zachary, and turned to face those who loved him. Ralph spoke to the Major. "Soldier, the prisoner has been warned too many times. Your first duty in this Army is to execute pun-ishment for the perpetrator."

Major McGuinness knew he was going to love being part of this Family. "Ready!" It reminded him a lot of when he was much younger, when he would give it all he had in both work and play. "Aim!"

The prisoner protested. "Wait! Don't I get a last wish?"

The Major was going to fit right in. "Soldier, wish for our bad aim. FIRE!" Ebony went ecstatically ballistic at all the new wads on the floor to chase.

Allen, Zachary, Atlas and Melissa took the lead with Melissa's 'SNAAB'. The newly dubbed 'Military Machine' carried Nunzia, the Major, Paul, Dagmar, Ryan and Russ. The Green Machine followed with Frank, Rachel, Ralph, the Rev and Marianne. Ebony stayed home, sleeping by the dying fire. Gustav and Vanessa were already at the cemetery, chatting with a very stubborn lady who insisted on immediately being awakened from cryo-sleep.

Ryan had to raise his voice a bit, though this model of military movement was nowhere near as noisy as some he had been in, long ago. "What do you call this thing, Major?"

"Just a HUMVEE, Ryan. They've undergone a few revisions over the past decades, but they're still the basic transportation for the military. That shouldn't surprise you. How long did the military stick with the Jeep? These things will go places where the old Willy's Jeeps would only dream of; they're incredibly stable. So, what kind of firepower does the enemy possess?" Ryan told about the ground-sound machine. "I had no idea ghosts packed that kind of ordinance. You sure you want to tackle this turkey? What's the point?"

Good question. "Tell you the truth, Major, none of us are sure on this one. The guy's mind fractured. Maybe all we can do for the entity is to play shrink, or confessor. We'll warm up with a neighboring entity first to get our feet wet."

"How do you find them? Put out an ad?"

Ryan told the Major (the rest knew already, but still liked to listen) about the ankle grab method and the sensitivities of kittens and Chihuahuas. He also passed on a lot of the previous encounters, mostly found on hearsay or by accident.

Major McGuinness asked, "Do you find many spirits on battlefields?" He had a personal interest in that one.

"A few, not many, given the number of possible prospects. I've visited enough of them. I suppose that soldiers support each other before and after death. Regular people do that, too. Let me tell you about a church fire in Selma…"

Zachary and Atlas were in the back. He looked at the two youthful heads in the front and smiled. He was that age, once. None of his few tries at romance lasted very long. His passion for business creation and ghost hunting seemed to crowd out the average lady friend. That gave him a mild empathy for the fellow they were going to try and contact. Maybe he might lend a few encouraging words, zealot to zealot. He saw Melissa rest her hand on Allen's lap and Allen place his hand upon hers. Zachary looked on his own lap to see two big brown eyes looking back and he thought, "Any way you can come back as a centerfold candidate?"

Rev, Frank, and Rachel were in the back. Rev looked with envy at Ralph, whose fiancé was now rubbing the back of his neck as he drove. That was one lucky Yankee. He looked to his side and saw another happy couple holding hands. There was something about groups with a positive and constructive mission. It helped bond the people within together, as well as couples within those groups. One of the problems with the individualist society was that, while it tried to promote people rising to meet their own talents, it didn't bind the people together. If only more in this country could find such purpose in their lives, his job wouldn't be nearly so difficult. He thought of his Jolene. Their work in the church was what had amplified the wondrous bond they had naturally shared, making their love doubly satisfying. In the end, his was the gentle hand holding escort for her as she left this earth. He was glad he was there to perform that last act of love and grateful that God had kept him on his feet long enough to do it. It had not been a quick death. After she left, he had collapsed from exhaustion and was kept in the hospital for another three days to recover. The hospital told him as he left that he could go but he would have to, first, pace himself, and second, leave at least half of the goodies brought him by parishioners behind as a tip.

The motorcade rolled through the Village of Rhinebeck, continued south past the Astor Home for Children, and took the first cemetery entrance on the right. The vehicles wove their way carefully along the same very narrow and very old access roads that had been used for Gustav's interment. The great oak was the landmark they used to locate the final target. They drove on for another thirty yards, and then squeezed into a pull-off. "Are they there?"

asked Russ, wondering if Gustav and Vanessa were already at the site.

Ryan nodded. "They're there, standing next to that grave marker. It's the tallest one with the angel on top; the one with the ornate iron grating on three sides of it."

Nunzia whistled. "The old girl must have been into some serious money."

Another nod from the Boss. "And I'm sure she'll work that into the conversation somehow. It's too cold for anyone to type for your read cards. Melissa will be using a transmitter similar to the one we used at Edwards on Saturday. In the Green Machine Ralph will give each of you an ear unit. Since we don't know how long we'll be, each unit will have a small wire to a battery/main receiver/amplifier unit that will pin to your coat collar. These are programmed with a burnout shut-off should there be an EMP (electromagnetic pulse) or other power surge that would cause a damaging sound to your ears. Stay together and you don't have to stay far away, just not right in front of us. Wherever you alight, stay put. We may need your services, or not, but we can't afford distractions. Everyone clear?"

There was a chorus of 'Yes, Sir's', even from the Major. That got a heart warming laugh before leaving the warmth of the military grade heaters that were engineered to fight even Siberian cold, if necessary. Doors opened and everyone converged around the Green Machine. Ear inserts and battery/amps were installed on Melissa and the unsighted, and then they began their walk towards someone's destiny.

"Go on, Gustav, I had the limelight with Annie. Let's see what you got."

"You're too kind. Very well. Welcome everyone. Here lies Mrs. Bernadette Lawson, a Hyde Park dowager who can trace her lineage to the Roosevelts. I have informed her ladyship that she will be receiving distinguished visitors to witness her arrival to the future. She understands that she has been in cryofreeze since 1996, when her diabetes associated nerve and vascular problems became too debilitating for the medical community to compensate for. Madam, I will introduce you now to Dr. Fitzgalen and his distinguished staff, who will now begin the process of bringing you out of your misery and waiting."

Out of the grave came a proud and matronly sounding voice that mixed pride, hope, gratitude and cluelessness. *"Doctor Fitzgalen and staff. Thank you for coming to my succor."* The obvious pun possibilities of that last word had half the assembled throng biting their fingers to maintain decorum. *"I've waited a long time for you and am now ready to take my place in a whole new society."*

Allen barely intoned, "You're not kidding!" That earned him elbows in the ribs from both sides. Ryan's look did a lot more to bring things more to a serious nature. They may be practicing a little deception, but the goal was nothing to laugh at. 'Dr. Fitzgalen' began to talk to the 'patient', asking her how she was feeling, what she remembered of her era and details of the cryofreezing process that she could recall.

Reverend Pocolis asked Paul about who had prepared this elaborate hoax, and had it worked in the past? "Rev, they're winging it. I don't think Ryan had any forewarning of what as on the playbill. It's kind of like improv. They rely on each other's instincts and how they've learned to mesh."

"Doctor Fitzgalen, would you please tell those rabble in the back to keep quiet for this solemn ceremony? Have they no idea of who I am?"

Melissa had a hard time keeping the tone of the request 'solemn' as she intoned it into the throat transmitter. Ryan tried to keep the image going. "Mrs. Lawson, what you hear are both media witnesses and colleagues who are excited at your coming to light. We also have an interpreter who is repeating your words for those who can't understand you. Please forebear. These next steps are important to gearing your body and mind for what is to come. Can you stand up?"

"I am standing up, you quack. Can't you see? Where did you get your diploma? I want a second opinion."

"Mrs. Lawson, the medium you have been stored in is not of a clear nature. It's as dense as mud, as a matter of fact. I am glad you are standing already, for that will make things possibly easier. Can you reach above your head as far as you can, please?"

"Oh. Very well. I am doing what you request, but it seems silly and undignified."

They could just see fingertips peeking through the grass. Not enough to do an ankle grab or to hold onto with their own ghost hands. Nuts, thought Ryan, and sent Ralph to his car to rustle up some implements. Ralph quickly relayed the goal to the Second Stringers, and Nunzia redirected and accompanied him to the HUMVEE. She opened up a side hatch and pulled out two entrenching tools. "It would appear that our paragon of Hyde Park society is a bit on the shrimpy side."

"Now, Nunzia (this is a shovel?), good things do come in small packages."

"So do grenades. Let's move." The two trotted back to the gravesite and were about to apply them to further expose the hands that were reaching up when…

"WHAT DO YOU PEOPLE THINK YOU'RE DOING?" All activity stopped as they turned to face a young man trotting up the incline towards them. Zachary thought the fastest and met the man when he got a few yards from them.

"SHHHH! This is a religious ceremony. Aren't you the grounds keeper?" The man nodded. "Weren't you notified?" Now he shook his head. "Well, for Holy Saint Bridget's sake! Bureaucrats! We're from the Hyde Park Historical Ceremony Recreation Society," he hoped he wouldn't be asked to repeat that, "…and we've been hired by the Roosevelt Estate Foundation to fulfill a half-centennial ceremonial obligation to Lady

Bernadette Lawson. Did you know that she was a direct descendent of President Roosevelt himself?"

The groundskeeper didn't have a clue as to what the man was talking about. "The Hyde Park Ceremonial History Society?"

"Close enough. We have flown in, all the way from Georgia, the (possible) descendent of the White House minister during the Roosevelt administration. Rev, we're on a schedule, we have to get this done on time. Please, continue."

"(Continue WHAT?) Uh, Our Father, who…" That bought them time, as the Family united in the Lord's Prayer. Zachary elbowed the groundskeeper in the ribs, prompting him to join in. If the guy's mouth was busy, it would slow down his thinking processes, hopefully.

"What's going on out there? Why are you people praying? Am I in church?"

Ryan caught Gustav's eye and motioned him to run interference.

"Mrs. Lawson, in this day and age, we traditionally begin a great undertaking with a ceremony to invoke the powers above on your behalf. We have found it very helpful."

"Oh. I see. Very well. And lead us not into temptation, but deliver us from evil…"

Zachary leaned over to the groundskeeper and said in a slightly loud stage whisper. "Here is where there are two *small* ceremonial holes dug, no more than say, six inches deep, and…"

"STOP THE CEREMONY!" Reverend Pocolis froze just after his 'Amen'. His face burned with shame in participating in a false front. "You can NOT dig any holes, anywhere, without the specific and written permission of the Rhinebeck Cemetery Commission!"

"Who is that awful sounding man?"

"Mrs. Lawson, he is a bureaucrat. They are constantly causing trouble in our new world. Please be patient. We will endeavor to maneuver the person elsewhere."

"(Sigh) We had a lot of them in my day, too. The scallywags!"

"Amateurs," thought Melissa, "…if you really want something done right, you always call a blonde." Melissa slapped on her best Barbie smile, unbuttoned the top three coat and top four shirt buttons, flounced up to the flustered groundskeeper and let him have it right between the eyes. "Why, how did a young and handsome man like yourself get to such a position of authority?" She took his hand and shook it. "Mah name is Jennifah Rose and this northern cold has chilled me to mah bones." She held his hand in both of hers, the Family members looked on in awe. "Might y'all have something warm in your office jes for li'l ol' me while ah explain our li'l ceremony here? Now everyone, y'all just wait right here until we get back, or better yet, go take a coffee break or something. Don't hurry on back now, heah? This might take a little while." She now had his entire arm wrapped in both of hers, making sure his elbow rested against something soft. 'Jennifah Rose' led the now submissive puppy back the way he came, with only a momentary pause when she passed by Marianne, who managed a quick retrieval of the voice transmitter. Marianne quickly installed it on herself.

The Major said to Allen, "My stars, she's a walking weapon. Isn't she the one that dropkicked the big man?"

Allen could not have managed a bigger smile if he tried. "None other, Major. Any of your HUMVEE's carry an arsenal like that?"

The Guardsman still had his head cocked in amazement. "Only when the motor pool guards aren't looking."

"Is the nasty bureaucrat gone, yet? Can I put my hands down? I feel like I'm in a bank hold-up."

"Not yet, Mrs. Lawson. The man is now gone and the ceremony will continue." Gustav motioned to Ralph, who gave Nunzia the high sign. They ran to the grave, and Ralph pointed to where Nunzia would dig and he started on the other side. All saw two holes quickly dispatched and half saw two hands now fully exposed. Ryan snapped his fingers and pointed, and Vanessa jogged over to the grave. The two spirits showed their readiness. Ryan began.

"Now that we have invoked His blessings on this procedure, Mrs. Lawson, I will ask you to focus all of your attention and physical power into your hands. You will, God willing, feel two hands grasp each of your own. Those people will lift and you must will your body to become free of the medium it has been encased in. Are you ready?"

"I...I, think so."

"Then, let us proceed." He wished he would have checked first to see if a grip could be made, but things just don't always work out to the ideal when you wing it. If no contact could be made, then they'd punt, as always. Ryan held his breath. Vanessa knelt down and clasped both her hands about Bernadette's right hand. They caught! Ryan let out half a breath. Gustav then knelt, grasped and passed through the reaching hand. Damn! Gustav held up a finger for a moment to regroup, took a non-existent breath, focused with all his strength, and grabbed. Got it! Everyone exhaled as Ryan commanded, "Now, everyone together, lift, UP!"

They didn't want to take the chance of a weak grip by the dowager who never knew farm tools like Bernhardt did. Her main hand efforts had always been aimed at how long she could hold a teacup aloft. Progress was immediate, albeit slow. It took fifteen seconds to get the elbows and the top of the head to show. Marianne was relaying the play by play for the Second String and the excitement in her voice got them almost as worked up as those that could see the action. Ryan thought of something and quickly said, "Mrs. Lawson, I don't want your eyes damaged before the process is complete, so keep your eyes closed until I tell you. This is very important!" It wouldn't do to have her concentration on her hands broken by her seeing something very different than what she was expecting to see.

"I hear you, Doctor, and I will cooperate. I am very sorry about calling you a quack."

"You aren't the first to call me one, but you are the first person big enough to apologize. I am honored. Keep up the effort. We're succeeding." The dowager's face was now visible. Marianne intoned softly of the wrinkled, proud features, the gray hair, the horribly gawdy diamond earrings (I thought you couldn't take it with you), the dress she must have been specially fitted for as final attire. Finally, the feet made the air and she was gently placed upon the ground. Ryan walked up to her, the other two still holding her hands, and spoke to the woman. "Mrs. Lawson, before you open your eyes, you must be told that you are not going to understand much of what you see. I will explain everything to you until you indicate to me that you understand and wish me to be silent. You will open your eyes, now."

XX REVELATIONS

I open my eyes, expecting to see a modern and futuristic hospital room filled with attendants, orderlies, nurses, people with social standing and, perhaps, a reporter or two. Never in my wildest dreams did I expect to see this. I am standing in the middle of a graveyard and before me stand people dressed up in winter coats. It must be cold, though I don't feel it, even though my dress exposes both of my arms to the elements. I can see the mists of their breath in the air. What incredible madness *is* this?

The man in front of me identifies himself as the doctor who has been speaking to me, but says that he is no doctor at all. His profession is to assist people like myself in any way he possibly can and that includes having to tell the occasional white lie. There is a woman to my right, holding my hand. She is a beautiful young woman and her dress seems very old fashioned. Her eyes and smile are reassuring and sympathetic. On my left, my hand is being held by a distinguished elderly man who bows and smiles to me. Neither of them is dressed for the cold and neither shows any mistiness of breath. From their hands, I can feel support and compassion, but I don't feel their touch. Am I numb from the cold? I don't understand.

The charlatan doctor is telling me that I died fifty-one years ago, when 'Life-Works' attempted to put me into cryogenic sleep. Something went wrong and I was buried below where I am standing? Preposterous! Yet, he asks for me to look behind at a very tall monument and, there is my name on it with the date I was supposed to go to sleep. No, I wasn't supposed to die! This cannot be! This has to be a hoax, but look how old the monument is. Could it be true? I cannot feel the obvious cold. Is it possible? The charlatan reaches forward and passes his hand through my body. Oh my God. It's true.

I look back at the stone that bears my name. How tall the monument is, yet, there is nothing here to say who I am or what I was. Is that all my wealth and influence has purchased for me? How dreadfully shallow. How shamefully meaningless.

I turn around and see that another woman has escorted an old and portly man to me. He has a clerical collar on. She tells me her name, and his, and that he cannot see or hear me. Is he deaf and blind? No, for the two of them are talking now. He turns to face me and tells me that he wishes to offer a prayer for my safe journey to God. Everyone is kneeling, for me? No, my two hand holders remain standing at my side. Are these my guardian angels? An unlikely couple of angels, if you ask me. But I sense their love through their hands, and that is about all I can sense, other than sight and sound. Why is that?

The pastor is saying that we are all children of one God and that he wishes all a safe journey to Him when our time on earth is finished. I suppose that includes me. I wonder. Does anyone remember me? Did I do anything worthwhile? I must have. Look at these people. No one has ever done something for me for nothing. I didn't hire these people, and yet, look at all the trouble they have gone through. Lord, if you can hear me and if the prayer of a foolish old dead woman is one you would give response to, bless these your children. Would but that I could reward them. But how can I? I've been dead for over fifty years. All my wealth and influence is long gone. I have nothing but myself.

The pastor is through and I have to ask them of what might happen now. The man, the leader I suppose, tells me to look around and choose my own direction according to my heart. To my right, there is more of a hill. Behind me, no, just woods and a few more stones beyond my own forsaken monument. In front of me, I see only another hill full of markers. That leaves, my, left. I fear to look, for if there is nothing there, then perhaps there is nowhere for me to go. If nothing is there, then God does not want me and I will never see all those I cared for. Yet, there is nothing else for me to do. Looking to my left...

"Charlie! Is that you? Husband, how I missed you! Yes, I'm coming. Just a moment." I turn to tell these wonderful saviors of what I have seen and promise to tell God all about what kind of angels are walking this ball of ocean and land he had sculpted in Genesis. I reach to touch the man and my hand passes through his. Of course, I am as silly and naive in death as I was in life, but he is not offended, or amused. He simply bows and all of his followers do the same. What can I do, but return the gesture? I cry out, 'God bless you all', but not all of them hear me. Perhaps those who did hear will tell the others. Charlie is calling out to me, he beckons me to come and I must go. I take one more look around at the world. It is a fine day to leave the earth and see my dear husband again. I walk to he who stretches his arms out to me. *"Oh, Charlie!"*

Marianne concluded her description of the fading glow where Mrs. Bernadette Lawson vanished. It was in the very direction that their next quarry lay and, for a moment, Marianne had feared that she might get close enough to allow Mad Marfan to cause a problem. Charlie, who had to be her husband, must have been either lucky or smart, or pre-informed. Her voice brought to the Second String all the details of what transpired and, if the former excitement explained the former faster heartbeats of all who listened, the more recent emotions explained the tissues and trembling lower lips of men and women alike. Ralph and Nunzia respectfully replaced their divots on Mrs. Lawson's grave, carefully, so that you could hardly tell there was any disturbance in the ground at all. They made for their cars to warm up for a few minutes...mostly their faces. The arctic grade winter wear the Georgia contingent was wearing was quite effective in this relatively moderate climate, despite the fact that Southern blood ran a little thin. Each man and woman was alone with their thoughts, as they embraced them before they went on to the next battle.

Reverend Pocolis: "My sweet Lord! Bless Paul for him having dragged me into this. Were I to die today, I would still call myself blessed. No wonder these people work so hard and live so fast. Thank you for letting me be present for a miracle like this before I pass on. Let me take this feeling in my heart and give it to as many people as I can. I wish Jolene had been here to see this."

Marianne Cabrini: "She went to her Charlie. The sweet little lady. Thank God that society life didn't spoil her completely."

Allen Hawthorn: "I wish Melissa had been here to share that with me. I love her so."

Major Ken McGuinness: "These people are soldiers, every one of them, and I wish I had an army of people like this. I'd protect the world from itself."

Sgt. Nunzia D'Palermo: "The Major understands now, and so do I. It's going to be harder to settle for Second String after this."

Dagmar Yaddow: "That had to be the finest and most touching event I never saw."

Ralph Kithcart: "I will not cry, I will not cry, I will...oh, bugger it."

Paul Wasserman: "Not bad, Rev, not bad. Shame it's like a hole in one on Sunday. Who are you going to tell about it?"

Frank Gladstone: (too busy crying, being held by his wife).

Rachel Gladstone: "My big strong teddy bear (sniff). I love you."

Ryan Fitzgalen: "One more, Lord, hot off the presses and long overdue. Give her our best when you see her, will you?"

Gustav Mendelssohn: *"I like this part of the job better than my old part."*

Vanessa Fitzgalen: *"I was so afraid that Lincoln would screw it all up. Thank GOD she left before she got there."*

Russ Anderson: "A man gets tired of chasing criminals. This is the work I need to recharge myself. Wonder what I have to do to make First String?"

Zachary Lorriman: "Did you see that, Atlas? Was that sweet, or what? I don't know about you, but I'm hooked! Here. Have a victory biscuit."

Though below ground, he could still sense that there was a commotion somewhere and feared the One who he had defeated last night had returned with greater numbers. There had been other gatherings sensed in the past, but this one was different, somehow. Different often meant bad. He reached out with his senses, once the disturbance had calmed down for a few minutes, in the general direction he thought things were occurring. Something, no, someone was coming, slowly. It didn't feel male. It felt, female. Could it be? After so long waiting, could it be, her? The female presence was getting stronger. It didn't feel mortal, but more like the signature left by that ditz female that was with the lawyer creep, but it didn't feel like the same person. Closer. It must be her! His her! Who else would come his way? Then, she went away? Vanished? Where did she go? He couldn't be wrong. He had never been wrong. She had mocked him once more by making him believe she was coming to him, only to build up his hopes so that she could abandon him, again. That left him with an ache inside, an ache that cried out for revenge.

"So you see, Jimmy dear, the Reverend and mahself were called up all the way from our home state of Georgia, have you ever been there? You really have to come pay us a li'l visit. Anyway, as Ah was sayin, we were to have the honor of presiding over the sanctification of Lady Lawson's last remains. Ah'm the Reverend's apprentice and assistant. You know, it's so important to have something you really believe in and..."

Jim Kalp had wondered about how one person could talk continuously for so long like this. She had been going non-stop for twenty minutes and he still didn't know really what this was all about. Fortunately, he didn't really care. The lady was so beautiful and friendly, and that southern accent was driving him to distraction. She would get closer to him in her animation and actually lay a hand on him to emphasize a point, then move tantalizingly away again, but giving a smile that kept him in rapt attention.

She knew that she could never have gotten away with this sort of thing with Allen for that long. He had a life.

Allen got on the SatCom and party-lined the three vehicles that had since backtracked and parked closer to site number two. "Day's not getting any younger, everyone, and neither are we. I vote we take the love we were just given in our 'apron pockets' and visit someone who probably could use some of it." He heard agreement from many voices and so doors began once again to open and shut. This time they moved en masse down the dell to the last resting place of Cassandra Petrocelli. The ground-sound device had been discovered and removed earlier by the mystified groundskeeper. But when they got there, Ralph picked up a piece that had blown off and held it up. The Major and Nunzia looked at it.

"It's a signal transducer, large one, but pretty disfigured," evaluated the Major. "It bears a striking resemblance to a Barbie Doll head of my big sister's I put in the microwave when I was four, for a grand total of three minutes. We had to junk the microwave, because everything cooked in it tasted like bar-b-qued plastic."

Nunzia also looked, and said, "That's different than the damage we saw at Edwards Estate. There's more mechanical twisting and greater burn damage. Is he more powerful than Annie?"

Ryan walked up to the two and the others began to follow. It was good to know what you were up against, should it come to that. Allen said, "Not sure, but I don't think so. The damage to equipment via Annie was a by-blow, not due to a direct attack like there was on this machine. Still, this is an entity I'm going to be very polite to."

Ryan asked Gustav where he had stood before he took that last step that nearly got him baked. Ryan then asked the rest of them to stay back and keep a protective stone to duck behind handy. Ryan turned back and stood before the grave of Cassandra Petrocelli, flanked by his wife and Family. "Mr. Lincoln Marfan, we would like to address you. You have nothing to fear from us. We only wish to know if what we have to offer might be of interest to you." They waited.

The mention of his name caused Mad Marfan to beeline it to the coffin and hide in Cassandra's body. But he was too upset and confused to stay in those rigid confines for long. He rocked back and forth, like a person with autism might. *"He knows my name. How did he find it out? What else does he know? Did he tell anybody? Did he tell Him?"*

Ryan laid it on the line. "Lincoln Marfan, you are hiding from God because you fear punishment for things you did while you were alive. We know that you caused the life of Cassandra Goode Petrocelli to end prematurely, faked her autopsy report somehow, took your own life while hiding yourself in the grave meant for her, and we believe that you very likely took the life of Cassandra's husband, Steve Petrocelli. We know where you went to high school, to college, what you did when you graduated. You were in love with Cassandra and were rejected by her in favor of the man she married. She also left the program you two shared because your suffocating dominance over her drove her to it.

"Yet, we have come to understand that there is good in you as well. You have a true love for nature and fiercely desire to protect it. You have love in your heart for Cassandra and regret to some degree what you have done. Like all of us, you are a mixture of good and bad. It is up to God to review these things with you. You and He cannot do this while you hide in Cassandra's grave. Eventually, He will find you. Delaying that process will only increase the likelihood that God will not want to bother to redeem your spirit. We recommend you go over now and present yourself, with a contrite heart, to your maker. We have a Reverend with us who will do his best on your behalf to hear your confession and to pray for your soul. We will not force you to do this, but leave it up to you. We await your answer."

The day was clear and there were birds still singing despite the nip. You could hear the cars on Rt. 9 and the voices of children in the distance over at the Astor Home's playground. It seemed peaceful. Gustav could feel nothing. Despite his many talents, it was only Vanessa who could probe into the ground near the grave, and she began to feel the outskirts of the lava dome. She turned around to the others and said, *"Everyone, I think something bad is about to happen. Quick, get ready on the double diamond, but stay well behind a stone or monu…"*

Atlas barked fiercely at the grave. Vanessa turned around and saw *him* slowly rising out of the ground. The now familiar face from the school yearbook, older looking, was searching out his targets. The first one he saw and felt was a woman. He needed to take his rage out on a woman, and so he did. Mad Marfan raised his arms and from them came not so much as a fireball as an evil, arcing, electrical looking power glowing a malignant orange-yellow. In a blink, it split the air with a hiss and a crackle, right at Vanessa. As before, the bracelet fended off the blow, held before Vanessa in protective posture. This first blow, unlike the one Mad Annie sent, did not stop, but continued to writhe, crackle and seek out.

Reverend Pocolis saw the protagonists from the energies that were being released. "Oh my God in Heaven, look!"

Ryan didn't have time to curse his inattentiveness. "Rachel, Marianne, positions! Melissa… WHERE THE HELL? SHIT! Dagmar! No, Nunzia! Position yourself and put your hands on the other women's shoulders." Vanessa's arms had gone stiff, like wood, only barely able to bend. What was going on? Ryan grabbed Nunzia's shoulders. "Ralph, Allen, positions, now! Gustav, NO! CRAP! Someone MALE, ANYONE, complete the double diamond!"

Zachary crammed Atlas into Dagmar's hands and sprinted to the back of the cannon. Vanessa frantically worked to balance out the new parts in the equation. She didn't have the grace of time as before. *"RYAN! My arms!!! They're frozen solid. I can't move them!"*

"REVEREND POCOLIS, you are a HOLY MAN!" Ryan prayed that the bastard Marfan would hear that. "CALL DOWN A CURSE ON THAT SON OF SATAN!"

Mad Marfan did indeed hear that. *"No, not a holy man! God can't find me, not now!"* He had to act quickly, but how? He was winning a blitzkrieg victory, but there was no choice on his next step to stay on the winning side, even if it meant staining his hands with yet another taken life.

Reverend Pocolis cried up to the heavens. "Lord Heavenly Father, look down upon this scene and send your angels to protect your children against the murderer of your innocents. This entity has caused your little ones to become orphans, has caused a loving innocent woman and wife to die of horrible torture, deprived of her husband, whom this sinner also murdered."

"NOOOOOOOO!!" The Major saw the attention of the entity shift to the elderly man of the cloth, who just happened to be in an exposed line of fire.

"Rev, DUCK!" He dove for the man and tackled him just as a bolt had left the main stream and sought out hungrily for a mortal victim. It missed, barely, but squarely hit the SAAB's driver's door. For the first split second, the door buckled inward. The rest of that second saw the door ripped from its hinges and fly crumpled through the passenger compartment, snapping off the gearshift lever, and striking the passenger's door. The force was sufficient to blow that one off its hinges as well. Melissa's emergency siren warning of unauthorized entry began to screech. The break, though, gave Vanessa heaven-sent moments to recoup and balance the double diamond. It helped immensely and her arms began to bend again. Annie's power was subtle and organized. This stuff; it was raw and volcanic.

The Major looked behind him. Just up the hill were two SAAB car doors, one of which was leaning against an old sepulcher, smoldering. His lower back area stung and he smelled something burning. "Holy SHIT! That mother's packing serious hardware. Ryan! What can we do?" He could feel his skin prickle, like when he was being bombarded with heavy alpha particles. Hopefully, whatever this energy was, it was equally benign.

Ryan yelled through the crackling and hissing, "Vanessa, what do we need?"

"Can we get another diamond? I can work with this, but he's unstable dynamite."

Ryan looked around. "Russ! Frank! Take up positions, NOWNOWNOW! Major, you have to connect them. Rev, don't stop! PREACH THAT BASTARD!"

Reverend Pocolis had never faced evil like this. He looked to the sky, to ask how to begin. To begin, you pray. How do you pray? It was taught on a mountainside, once. Where before he did it to distract a silly groundskeeper, now he aimed every holy word at the heart of the menace. "OUR FATHER, WHICH ART IN HEAVEN..."

"And, Jimmy..."

'WHADAM...creeee....creee...creeee....' Jimmy jumped up. "What the HELL was that?" Melissa heard the collision sound, and that siren sounded like...

"Oh no! NO!!!" Jim might be young and in fairly good shape, but he was left in the dust by this no-longer jacketed nymph who ran like some Greek goddess. It took her twenty seconds to clear the crest of the hill, dodging around monuments and leaping stones. She crested the hill and saw her car with the gaping holes in it first, and then through those holes she could see the surreal lightening bolts that far surpassed the battle at Edwards for malignancy. It had to be worse. Vanessa was fighting with a triple diamond and she still looked hard put. Time had slowed down for Melissa. She could form complete thoughts between sprinted steps. Clear thinking had to be there, or someone, maybe everyone, would have car door sized holes in them as well. The Rev was shouting a prayer and that seemed to be distracting…"My God, Marfan's out of the ground!" That's who it was. Marfan! He was the aggressor. What's he fighting? A defensive opponent. That worked with Annie. It's not working here. Marianne saw that opposites weren't the way to go with Gustav's bonding with the bathroom door. Fire with fire was the way then, and now, but how?

Melissa had reached the triple diamond. Lincoln had been too tied up with the enemy arrangement that stymied his power and the pesky preacher who was too cowardly to come out behind a stone long enough for a clear shot. He thought perhaps he could bank a shot at the man off one of the cars, but only wound up exploding the windows of the Green Machine. It took all of Ralph's concentration not to lose it when that happened.

The corona of force that had made visible the spirits before was still there this time, protecting the living, illuminating the dead. Melissa took refuge behind that shield. *"Melissa, I'm running out of ideas. Gustav is on my other side, but he can't form up."* One of the arcing bolts snaked its way around the shield. Frank cried out in pain as the clothing on his shoulder smoked, but he held on with gritted teeth.

Rachel called out to him, but he said he was all right. He would later require treatment for a third degree burn to his right shoulder. Vanessa broadened the shield, desperately dividing her attention between smoothing out the diamonds' disharmonies and brainstorming.

Melissa refocused. "Can Gustav meld with you?"

Vanessa looked in her mind at the schematic. No, it wouldn't work. *'No, wrong chemistry. It would only weaken what we have. I'm getting stronger, slowly, tuning the third diamond when I get a moment."*

Vanessa needed time. Melissa called out. "Gustav, you have to be a darting swallow, understand?" Had she been of more military mind, she would have said 'harrier unit'. Gustav understood what she meant, anyway.

"Got it!" He focused on the great oak and appeared behind it. He got his bearings, quickly, and jumped out from behind it long enough to say, "Hey! Tree Hugger! I lied! We put to the ax over seven hundred acres of virgin forest. Nyah, nyah-yow!" The time between Gustav getting back behind the tree and the time when the bolt struck couldn't be measured. Bits of bark blew off the old oak. The ancient cemetery resident shuddered and, in it's own botanical language, screamed. Groundskeeper Jim crested the hill, saw what was below him and froze to where he stood. He could feel curious prickles on his skin and assumed (wrongly) that it was a case of the willies.

"Jesus, the man is a howitzer!" Gustav peeked from around the other side. "Yoo-hoo, nice try. Do it again and join me in my tree killer club. Christ!" 'KERACK!!' Both sides of the tree were smoldering.

Lincoln saw that he was in a taunting crossfire, but that the taunts were harmless. He'd get those two later. He had listened once in college to what had happened to Hitler when he decided to fight on too many fronts.

Lincoln's power came from the earth, which he had become intimate with for the past year. That power was limitless, if managed correctly. Time to use it to cut down his enemies.

The glow and hiss and number of lightening bolt branches striking the defensive shield grew, and kept growing. Melissa knew it was a losing proposition. This guy didn't have any bottom of the well. Vanessa's shielding had expanded again to protect the diamonds, but there was a cost to the strength of the shield's defensive integrity. The center of her shield had begun to buckle inwards. Marfan saw this and began to laugh maniacally. Melissa took it all in and knew that her side had to go offensive or soon fail. "Vanessa, you have to blow this guy back."

"*I can't. I've been trying. He's a bastard, but I pity him. That's stopping me each time I try to change to offense.*"

"Then replace his face. Vanessa, he's the KKK son of the Devil that torched the church in Selma. Believe it, see it, and protect the church! Protect Natalie!" Vanessa's buckling shield flattened instantly and began to bulge forward. The color began to change from a gold/green to more of a violet color, but the process stopped. Still, it was enough to startle Mad Marfan to silence and buy Vanessa a little time as he evaluated and regrouped.

"*I can't bring it any further. There are no faces to put on his. I never saw either of those men. It can't be faceless; it has to be something else. Melissa, please, tell me what to image! You're on the right track, but I can't think and he's getting stronger again!*"

It's not fair, she thought. It can't be up to her. She was the youngest member of the Family. It wasn't her responsibility to take this burden off of others, was it? Wait! 'Burden off of others'? Yes. YES! "Vanessa, forget people. It will work with *things*. Before you is a flaming hunk of wood, a mindless killer that is crushing the life out of you and Natalie. Natalie is looking to you for salvation, the wood is crushing her chest, the fire searing her lungs, you can do it now! You have the power, we give you the power!"

Vanessa defocused Lincoln and replaced him in her mind with the wooden crossbeam that had broken the back and ribs of her precious Natalie. Melissa saw Vanessa's eyes grow wide, then narrow to something she hoped would never be aimed at herself. Vanessa's mouth opened and no Banshee cry ever came close to the ferocity and outrage. The fine perturbations in the harmony of the three diamonds that Vanessa was attempting to finesse into place were suddenly blasted into alignment. Individual thoughts by the diamond members were brutally suppressed from the fury that was now Vanessa.

The now fully dominant sympathy the triple diamond had over its members drew them into the battle cry that would have sent bag-pipers diving for cover. The 'Yankee Yell' temporarily unnerved Lincoln Marfan and that was unfortunate for him. The defensive corona now rocketed forward in angry reds and violets, striking the entity with unheard of force. He was picked up as if by a tornado and, in less than a quarter second, was slammed against the giant oak and pinned there. Any other entity would have passed through the magnificent oak. Not Marfan, and not here. The two energy blasts from Marfan had suffused the oak with an incredible psychic energy that, though painful, had been in part absorbed. The lifelong sympathy and identification that Lincoln had for every fir, elm, birch and oak he had ever met created a touch enabling sympathy as powerful as the Milledgeville Civil War soldiers had for their mounts. Lincoln Marfan was caught in a vice.

Gustav, though behind the tree, felt a small tree-filtered fraction of that force send him head over heels into the woods, passing through trees, and found himself lying face down on the Astor Home playground. The children there had stopped playing and joined the playground monitors in staring at the woods, wondering what all the racket and shimmering lights were all about.

All Vanessa could see was the burning beam being snuffed of its fire and forced back to the church roof. She truly believed that she was protecting the church and Cherub Choir members from the heat and smoke. That mind-set force was severing the already divided essence of Lincoln Marfan. The furiously mad part of him gave no thought other than to fight back, to kill and destroy his enemies. Two fiery sources sought only to destroy each other. The good that was in him had no such natural desire to oppose and so sought an end to the turmoil in his fractured soul. It was that part of him, the peaceful component, that discovered a back door out. He knew he would never be whole with himself and, as Annie once thought regarding her own imminent reuniting with her counterparts, didn't want to be. There was another option.

Gustav came stumbling back from the woods to see the oak he had hidden behind suffused with an angry crimson glow. What he couldn't see happening was what the energy from Vanessa was doing to the life essence of the tree. Her own force was also absorbed, mixing and combining with the life force of the oak and Marfan's energies, creating a miracle or a curse... depending on your point of view.

Gustav had to see what was occurring, fearing that once Vanessa had unleashed this demon power, it might turn to do harm to her as well. Running to the side and getting far up enough to see the front of the tree, he witnessed Mad Marfan in his fury and impotence. But he could see something else, as well. Likable Lincoln was separating from Mad Marfan, judging from their expressions and actions. Lincoln's essence appeared to be going *into* the oak tree. It took only a few moments and the separation/absorption was complete. The resistance of the remaining entity shard then took on a much-diminished mien. Marfan's arms and legs became splayed across the tree like some frog in a biology class anatomy lecture. Gustav raced to Vanessa's side. Her stance had changed from what it was at the Edwards Estate. Her right foot was forward, she was moderately crouched, and both of her arms were extended forward. From each arm came a spout of force that resembled the fire cone from an old time tank barrel. The faces of the triple diamond were a cross between zombies and avenging angels. He thought, *"It looks like a Goddamn comic book cover."* Gustav spoke with all the command he could recruit into his voice. *"VANESSA, he's defeated, you have to stop now!"*

Was it too late? The look on Vanessa's face was not of this world. She was somewhere else. He looked at Melissa, looking for guidance, for the triple diamond participants had similar mind locks going, judging from their eyes-rolled-up expressions. "Gustav, she's replaced Lincoln's image with the burning beam that crushed Natalie."

"God in Heaven! VANESSA, the fire is out, Natalie is safe. You did it! Stop what you're doing, or you'll bring down the church on everyone, including Natalie. Please, we're all depending on you to stop it. Damn it! I'm not getting through to her. We need help!" But there was no other help available to be seen. Rev was still crying out his prayers and sermons, but this German had no memorized soliloquies to wield. Raising his face to the sky, the spirit of Gustav Mendelssohn cried out with all his essence, *"GOD HELP US!"*

It was so curious. The beam was back where it belonged and she was holding it there. Some silly male voice was telling her to drop it. If she did that, it would fall again. That was one of the laws of physics she had taught all the little children she had just saved. But, someone was tugging at her skirts. She looked down and there was Natalie. She wasn't smiling. Why? Hadn't she saved her from the burning beam?

"Please, Missy Blankenship. You gotta listen to what Mr. Gustav says. I can't help you here. Please stop, Missy. You're hurting people if you keep goin. Reverend Pocolis and Mr. Gustav called us to help you."

Us? A hand was placed on her shoulder. Vanessa looked to her right, and there was Annie. *"Child, you have to stop, now. Your own soul is at stake. I want you to some day join me for tea and rocking chairs. You won't be able to do that if you continue. The job is done, now. Let go, Dear. I love you, best friend."*

Vanessa looked at the beam and it began to take on a face, an agonized face. It wasn't a mindless bit of wood. Nor was it the entity with whom she had done battle with today. Vanessa was still in another place. It was…*"Ooohhh, Daddy, forgive me!"* Vanessa's left arm dropped, coming to a rest on Natalie's head. The little girl took the hand and held it with both of her own. The force dropped by half.

"I didn't mean to disobey you, I just couldn't stand what you did to mother." Her other arm dropped, and her hand was clasped by both of Annie's. The oak-crucified Mad Marfan dropped to his knees.

"I wanted to show you that a woman could make a difference in the world on her own right." Mad Marfan shook his head, saw his enemy, and tried for a thunderbolt. He demonstrated little more than a half-inch spark.

"Mother, forgive me for leaving you in his hands without me to help protect you from him. I couldn't help you. I tried, you know I did. But you didn't want my help." Lincoln would not accept defeat. He knew he could still win, could still destroy her and the rest of them. Mad Marfan staggered to his feet.

"You believed him, that you were not worth anything without him. I left to prove you wrong, too, to save you, Mother, to save you from yourself." Though for him the spiritual images were gradually fading, Reverend Pocolis saw the former god-like entity attempt walking like a drunken baby. The creature looked with venom at his target, only ten yards away from him, now, but fell on his face in the grass.

"I wrote you, telling you of all the good things that were being done, but you never wrote back. Mother, Father, I left to become the person I knew was within me, so that I could give you the daughter you deserved. But, you didn't want what I had grown up to become. You wanted your crippled little girl who didn't know enough to see her own handicap, who worshipped you who held her in that prison of the spirit." Lincoln Marfan got up on one elbow and then looked curiously at his other hand. It was changing. A wind of some kind was blowing and his hand was being blown a way like little grains of sand in a dust storm. He jumped to his feet, but only wound up falling backwards and landing on his rump, his back against a tombstone. With a drunken nodding of his head, he turned around. It was *her* tombstone.

The triple diamond had long since fallen apart. Some were sitting on the ground, some leaning against grave markers. Rev kept watching, and listening. There was a different force emanating from Vanessa, one that provided him with limited sight of Gustav, Vanessa and Lincoln. That sight, though, was continuing to gradually fade, but he could hear her clearly. James Kalp sat up on the hilltop, too far away to make much sense of what was going on, too afraid to get closer, too fascinated to leave.

"It is not you who should forgive me, though I do ask for it humbly. It is I who should and do forgive you. You didn't know your own prisons and couldn't bear to know them. That would have shown your lives to be more hollow, shallow, and false than you had feared in your dreams. To have that truth shown to you by your own daughter was too much to ask. I understand that now and hope you rest with the Father in Heaven." Lincoln Marfan sat looking at his hands. They were small enough to be those of an infant's now, and continuing to dissolve into nothing. The process continued up his arms, and his feet also began to disappear. He looked at the oak that he had been pinned against. Then he looked inside of himself and understood the nature of the punishment.

"I must go now, Mother, Father. Annie, you said you would come back and help, if you could. Dear, you were true to your word. Thank you. Did I stop in time? I did? That's wonderful. I owe it all to you, and to you, too, Natalie. Let me hold you one more time for now. Yes, there will be another time. Yes, I'll always remember you, and love you." Vanessa was coming slowly back to the real world. Lincoln was slowly leaving it, and any other world he might have inherited. As his chest

began to collapse, he turned his eyes to the avenging angel whose flaming sword had driven him from his sad little Eden in the ground. He tried to tell her he was sorry, but there was little left in him for projecting such a thought. It was silly, but the last thing to occur to him was a few stanzas of very old music that seemed appropriate to the moment. 'Dust in the Wind'.

XXI   SUNDAY

"Thank you Jim. This is Dagmar Yaddow, Independent Correspondent, with my northeast news resource, Melissa Banks. Melissa, we've seen yet another highly unusual event that harkens back to the one at the Edwards Homestead."

From the remote projection site, the cameraman panned from left to right in order to focus on Melissa. "Yes, Dagmar. As you can see from the previously recorded video being shown on your screen, there was a force release of proportions that rivaled those of the previous week." Shot of a foreign make car with both doors blown off, followed by a shot of a large sedan with the windows blown out, followed by a huge oak tree with two seared blast marks on its sides and being cared for by experts who did that sort of thing. "Thankfully, the investigative team that had been set up by the authorities for the Edwards incident was present and involved in this one. Since you just happened to be one of those people, the ball is back in your court."

"Thank you, Melissa. It has been our conclusion that there are indeed ghosts that remain on the earth after their life as mortals have ended. Almost everyone goes on to whatever next step awaits us, though no one is exactly sure what that step is. There are centuries of information and observations that corroborate that some entities are stuck on earth for reasons they do not understand. Some people have banded together to assist those spirits to the other side, that their restless souls may find a home at last. Melissa, you conducted an interview with someone who has gained notoriety for his spiritual pursuits for the past decade. Let's roll that."

The scene changed to two people sitting on wicker chairs in front of a fireplace. "My name is Zachary Lorriman, and this, as you may know, is Atlas. We have been successfully identifying and differentiating earthbound spiritual entities from hoaxes and shams for many years. My partner and I have been quite successful, but we have never been able to do much for those entities whom we have cataloged. The two of us have made a wonderful connection with people who are able to work with those entities and get them to make the crossover to their next step of existence. The vast majority of these entities are peaceful, loving, but confused. In the past two weeks, there have been discovered two very unusual entities that have had the potential for violence. To protect the general public, these people the world has become recently acquainted with and I have united our efforts to discover and face these entities. We have been successful, though there have been casualties: some property, and one man's life. I have been elected as the spokesman for the group and will act as the go-between for those interested in the services these people might provide."

"Really, Mr. Lorriman. Are you actually a ghost pest control service? Would you clarify what it is that you are stating?"

"Gladly, Miss Banks. We need to spend our time helping, not hunting. We have two advance teams that can quickly identify a true spiritual event versus some more 'earthly' reason for events or phenomena. We have sites you may visit on your PC that will outline what it is that we are looking for by way of classifying potential entity evidence. If it falls into a higher likelihood category, one of us will be in contact with that inquirer."

"And what kind of fee might you charge for such an unusual service, Mr. Lorriman."

"If someone wants to show their appreciation for what we do, we welcome donations to defray our costs. Otherwise, what we do, we do because we love the work."

"Mr. Lorriman, might we look forward to more of these shocking encounters, and might we fear things that go bump in the night, beasties under the bed, monsters in the closet?"

"Heaven's no! Please, keep in mind that entities are trapped, themselves. For the most part, they wander around trying to figure things out. Half the time, you can probably just tell them 'You're dead, you can go on, now', and they'll take the hint and move on themselves. Ghosts are not to be feared any more than an accident victim who needs the attention of a professional, or perhaps just a good Samaritan."

"Thank you, Mr. Lorriman, and you, too, Atlas." Shot of Melissa with Atlas on her lap, petting a happy dog. "For the RPI Department of Journalism and with thanks to my mentor and teacher, Dagmar Yaddow, Independent Correspondent, this is Melissa Banks, signing off."

The CNN screen now had only Dagmar's upper body featured. "That was well done, Melissa. Thanks for the plug. Even correspondents appreciate a pat on the back from colleagues from time to time. If you have an experience with a potential entity phenomenon, you may contact this group via a sub-category listed on the main page for Hawthorn Enterprises. The CNN Public Information Department will also be able to point you to resources that are available for you. That concludes this report. Thank you for watching. This is Dagmar Yaddow. Have a pleasant Sunday evening."

It was Sunday night. Everyone else was in bed. Gustav and Vanessa stood next to the oak tree in the full moon light.

"*He loved trees, Vanessa, the good part of him did. He's in there, now, once again helping a tree in need. Look at the burn marks.*"

"*Why, they're healing, and at a very fast rate from the looks of it. Is he human, or tree?*"

"*There's a thought. You might term the fellow as a Greek nymph wanna-be.*"

Reach inside the tree. You'll see what I mean." She did, and smiled.

"Oh, my. My hand feels something inside there; different than anything else I've felt. They've merged, Gustav. Might they evolve a new sentient acorn producer?"

"Why not? Anything's possible. It would certainly be a new family tree."

EPILOGUE   5 DAYS LATER

Two men were well into the evening of supervising the serving of the vanguard of upcoming ESPER conventioneers. ESPER had been profitable to the town and its members seemed to have a reasonably good time. Those that had given up searching the Estate for spirits had left, leaving a core of workers who were evaluating the sites and requirements necessary for a successful weeklong convention event. Locals that had been turned off by 'wackos' were beginning to return to The Inn again, now that the ESPER numbers were of a more manageable level. Barry had everyone's name, type of drink, and a dozen details of each customer's life memorized. Regulars and even just second timers were greeted by name and an always correctly made favorite night starting drink. Mr. Pesko's business had nearly doubled.

Hammer also had been happily busy. Between the hospital work, The Inn work, his studies and the occasional hog ride, his life had been more full and rewarding than ever. There were even hints of a new romantic interest. Roots didn't hurt all that much, when you got down to it. He was at a table, loading the glasses and left over nachos into a tub when he looked up to see a familiar face. The glass in his hand was set back down on the table as Hammer spoke her name, or at least, his name for her. "Spic Chick?" The crowd watched as a mountain man took three steps backwards and walked into another person waiting behind him. He jumped forward a step and turned around. "Blondie!" Back and forth his head turned, seeing the vice being closed. The two women were slowly walking towards him. In a brief moment of recall, he brought both his knees together. "Now, ladies, no need to give ol' Hammer more of your medicine. He's learned his lesson. Be nice, now." Rachel got to him first and wrapped her arms around the belly, now trimming down a bit without the volume of beer to sustain it. He was still too big of a man for her to get her arms fully around, so Marianne completed the circle.

Marianne and Rachel both tiptoed to give Hammer cheek kisses, whispered thanks for the flowers, and could they now be friends? Gently, the big bear wrapped his paws around the two former adversaries, grinning like a Yogi Bear with two full picnic baskets. Barry was watching and smiling, happy that his number one friend was so pleased, when he felt someone tap his shoulder. He turned. "Hi, Melissa. Thought I sent you in orbit in the parking lot driveway."

"I re-entered. Thanks, Barry, for the ride. You really came through for me." Barry got his hug and his kiss. That's all he really wanted, for he had a girlfriend now. She worked in the hospital with Food Service.

The rest of the Family, every one of them, then piled into the main room to share a few days of just relaxing and seeing the sights. One of the regulars in the room picked up his SatCom.

The Mayor was happily receiving the numbers for the last week when she received the call. Elroy, her aide, saw her pick up the receiver, listen for a moment, and then raise her hand to her forehead. "Oh, God. Not them again."

Jim Kalp remained at the cemetery, though he was annoyed at the occasional hearing of voices. Was he going daft? That old oak tree was becoming particularly chatty over the past week.

Members of the Tale:

Special Agent Russ Anderson - FBI forensics specialist.
Melissa Banks - beloved of Allen Hawthorn, RPI student.
Dr. Marc Benoit - Milledgeville ER MD.
Marianne Cabrini - Paralegal/office manager for Hawthorn Enterprises.
Natalie Canard - Selma grade school student, member of Holy Path
    Community Evangelical Church, deceased.
Charlie Chase - lawyer hired by Gustav for the reading of his will.
Dr. Jamsid Churdivera - Coroner, Northern Dutchess Hospital, retired.
Sgt. Nunzia D'Palermo - Georgia National Guard, Task Team member.
Jim Dunnel - CNN anchorman, evening shift.
Anita Edwards - plantation owner, deceased.
Bernhardt Elmendorf - farmer, deceased.
Robert Fellatini - Marriott concierge in Milledgeville.
Mike Firanzo - current (acting) president of ESPER.
Ryan David Fitzgalen - patriarchal leader of the Family.
Vanessa Mary Blankenship Fitzgalen - wife to Ryan Fitzgalen, deceased.
Frank Gladstone (children Jerry and Janet) - stepfather to Allen Hawthorn.
Rachel Hawthorn Gladstone - Allen Hawthorn's mother, wife to Frank.
Jeannie Hafner - paramedic partner to Kurt Mangela.
Mark Hamm - Milledgeville Chief of Police.
Janice Hardin - CNN Science Desk Editor.
Allen Hawthorn - CEO for Hawthorn Enterprises.
Reverend Curtis Hoppenfeld - minister of the Hurley Reformed Church.
Barney Hammer Jenkins - biker, employed by The Inn and Milledgeville ER
as part of an alternative sentencing program.
James Kalp - grounds keeper for the Rhinebeck Cemetery.
Ralph Kithcart - Ryan's major domo, former cab driver.
Patricia Kupfner - Milledgeville Stables owner/operator.
Mayor Linda LaRoche - Milledgeville Mayor.
Bernadette Lawson - society figure from Hyde Park, NY, deceased.
Zachary Lorriman - paranormal investigation specialist with his dog, Atlas,
    Task Team member.
Kurt Mangela - paramedic, Milledgeville Rescue.
Lincoln Marfan - previous suitor to Cassandra Goode Petrocelli, deceased.
Elroy McBean - Aide to Mayor LaRoche.
Major Kenneth McGuinness - Georgia National Guard, Sgt. Nunzia
    D'Palermo's Commanding Officer.
Barbara Meissner - Melissa Bank's best friend, dorm mate.
Garrison Mendelssohn - son of Gustav and Martha Mendelssohn, deceased.
Gustav Mendelssohn (ex-wives Martha Scholldorf and Valerie Knudson) -
    lawyer, deceased.

Barry Nicholson - biker, savant.
Franklin Pesko - owner of 'The Inn', a tavern in Milledgeville.
Cassandra Goode Petrocelli - murder victim, deceased.
Reverend Daniel Pocolis - minister at Milledgeville Baptist Church.
Nicole Redman - Edwards Estate tour guide.
Daniel Speck - suitor hopeful to Melissa Banks.
Percival Stains - boom camera operator.
Peter Steinbaum - boom camera operator.
Penny Supina - director of the Art Department at Rhinebeck Central High School.
Sgt. Paul Wasserman - Milledgeville Police, married to Elizabeth, son: Edward, daughter: Amanda, Task Team member.
Jeremy Waters - Vice Principal at Rhinebeck Central High School.
Bill Williams - boyfriend to Barbara Meissner.
Dagmar Yaddow - Independent Correspondent, Task Team member.

Printed in the United States
705100005B